HIGH PRAISE
for
Novels by Fritz Galt

"Perfectly suited to reading on an airplane — entertaining, and an easy read...Fritz Galt's novels are so in tune with our world today."

—Amazon.com

"Tightly plotted...exotic locations...well researched...Highly recommended."

—Tales from a Small Planet

"Five Stars! Thrills around the globe."

—Barnes & Noble

"In the midst of the World Trade Center, Pentagon, and anthrax situation, your accuracy and details about all of this are really scary."

—Reader Review

"Fritz Galt's spy thrillers boom!"

—Westfield Leader

ALSO BY FRITZ GALT

THE ADVENTURES OF BUTTONS BURNSIDE

THE KARTA CONSPIRACY

THUNDER IN FORMOSA

THE GENEVA SEDUCTION

FATAL STING

THE TRAP

WATER TORTURE

CHINA GATE

an international thriller

FRITZ GALT

Ɛ SIGMA BOOKS

CHINA GATE
an international thriller

Copyright © 2005 by Fritz Galt
All rights reserved.

No part of this book may be reproduced, stored in a retrieval system, or transmitted by any means, electronic, mechanical, photocopying, recording, or otherwise, without written permission from the author.

All the characters in this book are fictitious, and any resemblance to actual persons, living or dead, is purely coincidental. The names, incidents, dialogue and opinions expressed are products of the author's imagination and are not to be construed as real. Nothing is intended or should be interpreted as expressing or representing the views of any U.S. government department or agency of any government body.

CHINA GATE

Prologue 7

The Snatch 11

The Manhunt 93

The Raid 171

The Interrogation 207

The Verdict 291

CHINA GATE

Prologue

Beijing

Raymond O. Flowers sat hunched over his office computer, his right index finger poised over the button of his mouse. He had entered the amount of $50,000,000.00 and placed the mouse pointer on a button labeled "Transmit." Should he transfer the money? It was a large amount that would be easy to spot by American law enforcement agencies.

He lifted his handsome, Cary Grant-like face and glanced out his high-rise window. The streets of Beijing were purged of buses, cars, and bicycles by the highly contagious and deadly SARS virus. Only the occasional pedestrian hurried past, features obscured by a surgical mask. A sweet breeze swayed trees with their buds and young blossoms, belying the dangerous germs that it bore.

Behind him, his department was eerily empty, cleared of his smoothly efficient Chinese and American staff. His young family waited in the lobby twelve floors below. Their bags were loaded in a taxi, which stood ready to bear them to the international airport.

He checked his pocket for his airplane tickets. By noon, he and his wife Carolyn and two small children could be out of the disease-ravaged country and on their way to San Francisco.

Everyone, from the President of the United States, to his company's head honchos, to his loving family, depended on him to make the final transfer into the President's bank account in the Cayman Islands.

But it was a decision he knew he would regret for the rest of his life.

He closed his eyes and pressed his index finger down. The mouse clicked, and fifty million dollars transferred instantly from China to a secret account halfway around the world. It was an illegal act that he prayed nobody would ever discover...

Eight months later, the following article appeared in the *Washington Post*, touching off both the Chinagate investigation and the search for Raymond O. Flowers.

Prosecutor Probes President in Chinagate Kickbacks
"Missing Person" Key Witness in Case

WASHINGTON (AP) Under mounting pressure from Congress, President Bernard White appointed attorney Stanley Polk as Special Prosecutor to investigate the brewing Chinagate controversy that may cost him his office.

The story first broke last autumn when reports surfaced of the President receiving a large sum of money in his offshore bank account. This coincided with a U.S. Trade Representative-brokered deal with China. In the deal, Washington voted in favor of granting China World Trade Organization (WTO) status, raising the possibility that the mysterious funds were a kickback to the President from the Chinese.

According to a member of Stanley Polk's team, a key witness, named Raymond O. Flowers, transferred funds from China into the President's personal offshore bank account.

"Unfortunately for the special prosecutor, Raymond O. Flowers is missing and unable to provide the testimony that is most crucial to the case," the source said. "We will be looking into cover-up attempts by the President, including efforts by the White House to prevent Raymond O. Flowers from testifying."

Flowers would have to be living on the moon not to be aware of the controversy swirling around him. Many seeking him at the present time might pose a serious threat to his life.

Which raises the question: Is Raymond O. Flowers still alive? And if so, does he know that he can single-handedly clear or sink the President?

By mid-winter, Raymond O. Flowers' family was deceased, his job was a distant memory, and he was vilified in the press by the White House. He was all alone, possibly abroad, and running scared, somewhere in the vast, unruly sea of humanity. Raymond O. Flowers had become the world's most wanted man.

CHINA GATE

The Snatch

Chapter 1

Hadi Ahmed crept through the bone-chilling cold over a pass in the Shakai Mountains in Pakistan's Southern Waziristan region.

He had memorized the footpath days before, and his feet, clad in grass boots, landed squarely with each step.

He kept an eye out for lit cigarette tips, flashes of polished metal reflecting in the starlight, movement in the shadows of the mountains.

He listened beyond the padding of his own boots on snow and loose stones. Was there someone else out there in the icy stillness? Someone waiting to kill him before he delivered his precious news?

The last half hour of his climb was straight up the side of a mountain. There was no longer a path, only familiar rocks to grip with bare hands and a crumbling hillside in which to dig his toes.

"May Allah be praised," he muttered under his breath. Osama was nearly impossible to reach, even if one knew where to find him. Allah had concealed him well.

And with divine wisdom bestowed upon him, Osama did not use modern communications technology. Which provided Hadi an opportunity to make a living, relaying messages by foot to the al-Qaeda camps thirty kilometers down the valley in Wana, the regional capital.

At last, before he ever saw or heard it, he felt the presence of Allah's mighty lion. The warmth from Osama's fire seeped into the night air through a small opening behind a shield of stone. Hadi edged around the rock wall and crouched low.

"I have returned, most venerable one," he whispered.

Someone stirred inside the cave. The muzzle of a gun nudged a sheepskin aside, revealing a small fire flickering within.

Already a short man, Hadi had to stoop low to step inside. The sheepskin fell into place behind him.

He found himself looking into a circle of faces. The man with the straight back, large round eyes, and scraggly beard that was streaked with gray drew his attention.

"Most worthy one," Hadi began, falling to his knees. "With Allah's guiding Hand, I have managed to spread your message to the myriad minions at your disposal. The word has reached the far corners of the earth that you are offering a bounty for whoever Allah blesses to find Raymond O. Flowers."

"And...?" the soft, baritone voice said patiently.

"And word has reached us sooner than expected. A Triad gang called Sun Yee On has located him at a beach resort in southern China."

The round eyes curved into crescents of joy.

Hadi went on. "Following your instructions, I have authorized them to make the snatch. They will have him captive within hours, *inshallah*, Allah be willing."

"Good work," Osama said. The tension in the air was released when he spoke, his voice warm with praise. "Now I want you to inform my cousin, who is skippering a boat in the South China Sea, to take possession of our gift to Allah."

"What should the bounty be?"

Osama looked uncomfortably at his associates seated cross-legged around him, men of learning and worldly experience, but cool calculations running through their minds.

"Pay as little as you can. Do not reveal our hand."

"As you wish, sir." Hadi's eyes fell on a jug warming by the fire. He could smell the aroma of rich coffee, called *kahwa*, that the Arabs drank.

"Leave at once," Osama thundered. "Allah does not abide by fools!"

Hadi prostrated himself, lowering his forehead to the cold cave floor, then quickly scrambled to his feet.

The guard nudged the sheepskin aside with his AK-47.

Hadi broke out into the night, circled the stone shield, and began to lower himself hand by hand down the sheer slope.

Osama's cousin would take possession of the unwashed Westerner from the Triad gang by the first light of morning. By the end of the day, the chief crusader against the Muslims, the infidel President of the United States, would be subject to the Will of Allah!

Carolyn Flowers knew that giving birth to her third child would be fraught with danger. But, what could she do about it? Isolated in a remote Chinese prison with her two young children, she had no maternity or neonatal options.

She would have to rely on the prison's well meaning, but doddering, doctor in a medical examination room that had no heat, heart monitoring equipment, or anesthetic, not to mention an incubator.

She felt her first labor pains shortly after dawn on a frigid winter day when the prison's cinderblock walls were unable to keep out the blunt cold of a north wind. She interrupted Jane and Sammy's entertainment for the day, folding and refolding a page from a Chinese newspaper, and sat them down on the cell's lone bed for a lecture.

They would have to remain in the cell by themselves, but Mommy would be right down the hall. If they heard her being loud, they would just have to cover their ears until she came back. When she came back, she would bring them a new baby.

She searched their puzzled eyes. "Do you understand?"

They nodded.

"And where do you put your hands?"

"Over our ears," Sammy, at five the younger of the two siblings, responded and demonstrated for her.

"That's right." She turned to her seven-year-old daughter. "And what will I bring back?"

"A baby sister," Jane said.

"No, a brother."

She let the argument proceed until it ran its course. She had no choice as the pains were coming more frequently and lasted longer.

Jane finally terminated the quarrel by turning to her with a seemingly unrelated question. "Does Daddy know if it's a boy or girl?"

Carolyn thought back to her sudden forced separation from Raymond O. Flowers at the Beijing International Airport that fateful day the previous spring. She shook her head. "No, Daddy probably doesn't even know that we're having a baby."

"But Daddy knows that we're here, doesn't he?" Sammy said, in need of reassurance.

What could she tell her children? For all their father knew, they had died of SARS as had thousands of others that spring in Beijing.

"And Daddy will come and save us, won't he?" Jane asked.

Another painful contraction gripped Carolyn's lower abdomen. The baby was definitely knocking at the door.

Through a grimace, she made a promise she was sure she would come to regret. "Of course Daddy will come to get us."

It gave them all a small measure of comfort as she fell to her knees on the cold cement floor and shook the metal cage. "Doctor! Doctor!" she screamed repeatedly.

Raymond O. Flowers sat bolt upright in a large, soft bed. Then instantly regretted the sudden movement. He clutched his head that swam and throbbed from too much alcohol the night before. But his instincts were alert. What had woken him up so suddenly?

He wiped the night's sleep from his eyes. Early dawn crept under his hotel curtains. The central air conditioning hummed as loudly as the buzz in his head. Then he remembered where he was. He was staying at the premier resort on China's tropical Hainan Island.

He felt across the bed sheets and found no one there.

Little by little, he reconstructed the events of the night before. The resort had thrown an elaborate bash in celebration of the upcoming Academy Awards. The party had consisted of free champagne, balloons, fireworks, an emcee, and a very loud band.

He had met up with the gorgeous, leggy Sandi DiMartino on a balcony overlooking the freeform pool. Her sleek, bare arms had grazed his sleeve as she leaned over the railing, sighed, and surveyed the milling crowd in the distance. They had run into each other with increasing frequency over the course of the week, and their casual acquaintance had developed into a cozy intimacy.

He moved his feet to explore the far reaches of the king-sized bed. The covers were still tightly tucked in. He had not slept with her, although it was a strong possibility, given their attraction and all the booze downed the night before.

So, if nobody else was in the bed, what had disrupted his sleep?

He pinched the bridge of his nose and tried to stop the room from spinning.

Another of his nightmares could have awoken him. In previous dreams, Secret Service agents from the White House had tracked him down. They had fired at him with pistols. His country had branded him a traitor.

But why should they hound him? It was the President who had profited, not him. Even the press knew that the money had gone into the President's personal bank account. So Raymond had transferred the money. His oil company had made him send the Chinese bribe to the Caymans, or his family would face the rest of the year in SARS-ridden China.

Still, the public wouldn't hear it from Raymond, not as long as the entire Administration pinned the Chinagate scandal on him.

He opened his eyes and took a brief accounting of his condition. His head felt as if a dull mallet was pounding on his skull, but he had not woken up in a sweat. He seldom did anymore. He had grown used to such nerve-wracking dreams. He knew how to recognize and dismiss them. A revolving cast of bad guys took turns chasing him—some were from the White House, others from a Congressional subcommittee, the corporate security office of his former employer, and from China's feared Public Security Bureau. In the end, though, he would outrun them all with his in-shape, middle-aged body, or elude them using his familiarity with the Chinese street.

Something more immediate and real had caused him to jump up in bed.

Then he made out a bright speck on the carpet by the hotel door. He reached for his glasses and drew the wire arms over his ears. He tried to focus on the object, but winced at the effort.

He pulled his covers off and stood up to investigate. That turned out to be a mistake. He reached for the desk to steady himself. Easy does it. He didn't want to toss his fortune cookies. Step by step, he lurched stiffly toward the note. What kind of champagne did that to a guy?

At last, he stood over the paper that shone in the morning light. It was a torn fragment of stationery. He didn't recognize it, so it hadn't fallen out of his pocket. Someone must have shoved it under the hotel door. Careful not to bend over, he crouched down and picked it up.

Rising, he flipped on the overhead light and squinted to read the words.

It read: "Your family lives."

What?

He closed his eyes in the brilliant light. Then he slowly reopened them. He read the note aloud to make sure he wasn't imagining it.

"Your family lives," he said, his throat dry and his voice thick.

How could the message be meant for him? His family had died over eight months earlier in a SARS ward in Beijing.

Who else might the message be meant for?

Summoning up his strength, he pulled open the door and stepped out into the hallway. It was empty, too early even for housekeeping to be making their rounds.

He looked down at his rumpled boxer shorts and tank top and then at the note in his hand. In the dim light of the hallway, the note still read the same, but this time it seemed to be speaking directly to him. In a strong, masculine handwriting it said, "Your family lives, *you dummy.*"

Suddenly, the clouds parted, and he knew without a doubt that the note was meant for him. A second later, he knew exactly what he had to do.

He hustled back into his room and bolted the door. Then, without bothering to shave or shower, he pulled on the first travel clothes he could find. He had to check out of the hotel, leave Hainan Island, and head back north in search of his family.

He grabbed the desk phone and rang the front desk. "I need a bellboy right away," he slurred. "I'm checking out."

He dumped his neatly hung wardrobe into his twin suitcases and threw his travel kit, trash novels, and travel brochures into his carry-on bag.

The doorbell rang. It was the bellboy. His clothes still askew, Raymond opened the door and slid out the travel bags.

"I'll be right down," he told the obliging bellhop. "And I'll need a taxi to the airport."

He closed the door, and leaned back against it, breathing hard. He needed a moment to catch his breath, to quiet the kettledrums banging in his head, stop the churning in his stomach, and collect his thoughts.

Normally a meticulous man, he wasn't used to rushing into decisions, packing hastily, and heading off without a plan.

He found himself clutching the scrap of paper tightly. He smoothed it out and studied the three words that had suddenly brought his family back to life. It was incredible!

Was it true?

Raymond swallowed hard. His mind was reeling. It wasn't a dream, was it? Wish fulfillment at its most devious? No, the wooziness in his being, and the weakness in his knees told him otherwise.

Was the message a trick? No, it would be too cruel if it were a hoax.

But how could his family, apparently dead for the past eight months, still be alive? It was true that he had never seen them after they had entered the ward in Beijing, and had only been handed three urns to bury. If they had survived the raging epidemic, where were they now? And how could he find them?

His options were limited. The U.S. Embassy was on the lookout for him. The Chinese government was most likely complicit in his family's abduction and on high alert. Somehow, he must avoid all of them, and make his way back to Beijing.

He had to return to the hospitals that cared for SARS patients, and pick up the trail from there. Surely his wife Carolyn with her light brown hair and Jane with her mother's emerald eyes and little Sammy with his shock of red hair would stand out in the Asian city.

He slipped out of the hotel room and carefully shut the door behind him. Even the loud click of the automatic lock seemed to bang like a gong in his brain. Then he shuffled like hell down the hallway.

As he raced for the distant lobby to check out, he felt his wallet swinging heavily in his chino trousers.

At least he had enough money to stay one step ahead of the White House and the Chinese authorities. His millions could buy him anonymity from both governments' covert attack dogs and allow him to survive with dignity for years behind China's bamboo curtain.

Maybe his money would even be necessary to obtain his family's release.

He rushed under the restaurant's lofty ribbed ceiling that resembled the interior of a wooden ship. He streaked past the white grand piano that sat above a waterfall. The cavernous space had the grandeur of an old Hollywood set. But he would gladly leave all that behind in order to see his beloved family once again.

He entered a breezeway and pushed aside a column of colorful balloons blown into his path by a gentle wind from the South China Sea. The fresh air felt good and helped clear the last vestiges of alcohol from his blood. He was on his way to Beijing!

He weaved past the Chinese cleaning crew dressed like Vietnamese in their cone-shaped hats and pajama pants. They were leaning over short-handled brooms, whisking away confetti and streamers that littered the marble floor. What a wild pre-Academy Awards party that had been, all of which suddenly seemed so trivial.

He slowed to a walk as he entered the lobby, and straightened his worsted wool sport coat. To one side of him, a television was broadcasting the Academy Awards live. He paused for a moment to scan the few guests who lingered around the television. They made up a wall of Oriental faces.

Who had left him the note?

He looked at the words once again, scrawled in a man's hand. It was so cryptic, so melodramatic, in fact. But he put that thought aside. The three words offered him more reason to live than anything else in the past eight depressing months.

A veteran actor named Tudman Grier was making some inane comments on stage in Hollywood. The gleam in his eye showed that he knew he had the whole world eating out of his hand.

Then a correspondent cut in from London to announce that parties around the world were reveling in the achievements of their respective movie stars.

"We're even seeing unofficial fireworks for a British actress," the commentator said, "despite the current climate of fear from terrorism."

"Afraid they might be afraid," Raymond muttered to himself. He had no sympathy for terrorists, and little more for the politicians and press who conveyed and amplified the terrorists' threats to the common man. This morning, he knew no fear. He turned to resume his mission to check out and head for the airport.

Then a comment on screen stopped him dead in his tracks.

"For the moment, the celebration in Hollywood drowns out other events that would normally be making headlines today, such as the American President's current political crisis, called Chinagate."

Raymond turned to watch the news carefully.

"Last month," the anchorman explained, "under an avalanche of public criticism, President Bernard White appointed a Special Prosecutor, Stanley Polk, to the Chinagate case."

The camera cut to his attractive co-anchor, who continued on cue. "The accusations could be summarized as such: Recently leaked bank documents show the transfer of a large sum of money from China to the President's personal bank account in the Cayman Islands."

Raymond marveled at how poorly the woman read the teleprompter, stressing the wrong words in each sentence. What had she been drinking?

The main anchor resumed. "This deposit coincided with the conclusion of a lucrative trade deal with China, whereby China gained access to the World Trade Organization."

The woman took over. "Stanley Polk's team is currently seeking a key witness named Raymond O. Flowers, who transferred funds from China into the President's personal bank account."

The sound of his name on television made the hairs stand up on the back of his neck.

Then the screen dissolved to a blurry shot of him taken by a video camera with a telephoto lens. He was kneeling in a black suit before three graves in a cemetery. It was taken the day he buried Carolyn, Jane, and Sammy.

Suddenly, he was more sober than he ever wanted to be.

The news story cut to a young spokesman for the special prosecutor, who announced, "Our investigation has been hampered because our key witness, Raymond O. Flowers, is missing, or, we fear, the victim of foul play."

The young man surveyed the group of reporters menacingly.

"We will be looking into cover-up attempts by the President, including possible efforts by the White House to silence Raymond O. Flowers or otherwise impede him from testifying."

The co-anchor straightened in her seat, presenting a new perspective on her plunging neckline. "The President has managed to dodge questions up to this point, but it will only be a matter of time before the independent prosecutor and the public will learn about this mysterious, and potentially illegal, transfer of funds."

She looked at her anchor to take over.

"Whether the culprit is President Bernard White or Raymond O. Flowers, or the two were complicit in a crime, the truth is bound to come out shortly. And Mr. Flowers, if you are out there listening, now is the time to make your voice heard."

"Perhaps this is just another tempest in a teapot?" his female co-anchor extemporized.

"Try a tempest in *my* teapot," Raymond murmured. No matter where he tried to hide, the Chinagate affair was hounding him.

A low-pitched female voice sounded behind him. "Are you talking to yourself again?"

He spun around. It was Sandi DiMartino, the refreshing young lawyer with whom he had flirted the evening away. Many glasses of champagne and a short night's sleep in her own room hadn't changed the beguiling smile on her full lips.

But the whole world had changed for him in the past hour. And he looked at her as if she were a character out of a novel he had long since put aside.

He tried to return her smile—to let her down gently. But as he began to speak, he felt himself falling into the cool depths of her large blue eyes. The previous evening's frivolity and the similarity of their professions had made him share some confidences that he suddenly regretted.

He gripped the note tighter. He was still a married man, goddamnit. Maybe he had even sensed that Carolyn was still alive whenever the ladies circled closer, and god, there were many such opportunities in China. The gaping wound caused by his family's death from SARS the previous spring had never truly healed. He had hoped that someday another woman might eventually fill the tremendous vacancy left in his heart. But given how awkwardly he had flirted with Sandi the previous evening, he was destined never to love another woman.

"Do you remember what I told you last night?" he asked, hoping that their conversation had been lost in the noise of firecrackers or forgotten with the passage of time.

"You bet I remember," she came back. "And you've thought about my offer for legal services?"

It had been convenient to meet a lawyer at that critical point in his life. And the offer was tempting. He watched the President's ruddy face on the television screen. He looked so paternal, so knowing. What a crock. With one word to Sandi, he could identify himself as Raymond O. Flowers and sink the bastard.

But he was already impatient with the whole Chinagate scandal. He wasn't the least bit guilty, and that was all that mattered to him. Let the others chase each other around the lawyers' tables.

He knew that he could testify convincingly against the President, and it might make him feel good. But he had lives to save. His family.

Sandi's lean figure, soft and flowing blonde hair, healthy complexion, and row of gleaming white teeth were trying to beckon him to his doom.

"It must have been the champagne talking last night. I was getting a little carried away," he said. How much had he told her? Now he couldn't remember. "I'm sorry. I slept on it and I think I'll stick with the *status quo*."

She gave him a crooked smile that looked partially disappointed and partially understanding. "It's your decision."

She was damned right it was his decision.

He eased away from her. He should never have talked so frankly with her. What had he been thinking? If he had divulged his identity, that might open the door for the Chinagate bloodhounds.

"Leaving so soon?" she asked, looking disappointed.

He tossed her a lame, apologetic smile and headed for the reception desk. Love 'em and leave 'em. That was his motto.

Heading home. That fit even better.

He checked that the bellhop had lined up his twin Louis Vuitton suitcases and matching shoulder bag at the taxi queue. He would be in Beijing by noon. There, he would hit the hospitals at once, tackling each one in turn until he found someone who remembered his wife and children and could point him in their direction.

"Checking out, sir?" the efficient Chinese staff woman purred.

"Yeah. I'm in a hurry."

He handed over his plastic room key and drummed his fingertips on the counter while she brought up his account. Just charge him ten grand and let him get on his way to Beijing! A printer spilled out two weeks' worth of charges: room, minibar, gift shop, restaurant bills, and tabs from the pool and beach bars.

He didn't bother to read it.

"How would you like to pay today, sir?"

He already had his wallet open. He pulled out his VISA card and slapped it on the counter. He had placed Sandi's business card behind the VISA. He looked around for a wastepaper basket in which to toss it.

"Sir, your credit card isn't working today."

"Huh? Try it again."

The receptionist swiped it through the machine once more and waited. She shook her head.

"Is there a hold on it?" he asked.

"They won't give me the reason for declining it."

Holy shit! He felt the blood drain from his face. The interconnected world of the Internet and financial institutions had finally caught up with him. The Chinese and the White House might have been following every move he made, tracking down every place he traveled, recording every drink he ordered.

If they were onto him, he'd never see his family again. And if they got to his money, he'd have no way to get to Beijing.

23

He'd have to call the bank and clear up the misunderstanding. But what if it was worse than a hold on his account? They might have wiped out his entire fortune, the money he intended to live on for the rest of his life!

It was supposed to be a hidden bank account, untraceable, his exclusive means of accessing his nest egg in the Caymans. But clearly, the Cayman Islands' vaunted reputation for secrecy and discretion was bunk. How many other unfortunate sops had lost their fortune because of that illusory cloak of anonymity offered by the Cayman Islands? This was not supposed to happen!

"The VISA office doesn't open for half an hour," the receptionist said, handing him back his card. "You may use our telephone at that time if you'd like."

"Okay, sure," he said, easing away from the counter. "I'll come back."

But he had no clue what to do next. No local VISA office would know about his secret bank account.

He turned toward the lobby's open panorama. He faced the grounds studded with palm trees and surf that broke just beyond. The serene scene didn't bring him the slightest relief.

His head pounded, but his heart beat even harder against the wall of his chest. He felt an urgent need to get on the road immediately. But how could he, without a penny to his name?

He took another look at the three words written so forcefully on the scrap of paper. "Your family lives."

The power of the words gave him his only comfort and strength.

He tucked the message safely in his shirt pocket. In that note, he could hear his family calling out for help. He didn't want to imagine what conditions they might be living under. He wouldn't let them down. He had to find them. But how?

His thoughts seemingly frozen, he let his feet carry him out of the lobby, away from civilization, down the steps and out toward the sparkling sea.

Hiram Klug was determined to make his upcoming escape from his butcher's shop to the tropics exceptional. It would be like no other vacation he and his wife had ever experienced. But he was running late.

He slipped his blood-smeared apron off his wide girth and checked the Timex his wife had given him as an engagement present twenty years before. It was five-thirty and he had fifteen minutes to get to the Garden State Mall in Paramus to pick her up and leave for the airport.

He slid the row of pork chop packages onto a cart and wheeled them off to his freezer locker for long-term storage.

Customers waited patiently with snow melting off their overshoes and numbered tickets in hand. The ticket machine had been a lifesaver for Hiram. It kept a civil tone in his tiny New Jersey butcher shop among patrons who could be some of the most demanding in the world.

Ham smoked over hickory chips. Free range goose liver. You name it, they demanded it. So he jacked up the prices, sold the finer cuts of beef and everybody was happy.

Except when business took over his life and he let his marital duties lapse.

But this trip would change all that.

"Yer doin' ga good job, Busta. Keep it up."

Buster Klug, his nephew and protégé, nodded, but couldn't respond verbally as he was deeply engaged in counting out change for a hundred.

"I gots to go now. You take care o' ya."

Buster looked up. "You-a gonna miss da Oscah's, Hiram."

Hiram snorted. He hadn't been to a movie theater in years. Not that his sweetie didn't deserve it. In fact, she deserved far better than an evening sitting in some public theater seat that had been occupied by a different person every two hours non-stop for the past ten years. No, he was thinking bigger, like season's tickets to the Paper Mill Playhouse. If he could only get Buster to take over the business and give him some free time.

Yeah, he wasn't going to sit all evening in front of his television set watching some young turk he didn't recognize claim a trophy for some movie he would never see.

He had far bigger plans.

"You-a plane's waiting der," Buster reminded him, shooing him out the door. "Now go."

He took one last proprietary look around his shop, gave a wistful twist to his large lips, and lumbered out into the blizzard that had laid a white blanket of snow on his shop's parking lot.

He was tempted to grab a snow shovel to scrape it off, but sanity quickly restored itself.

"Oh, screw it."

He'd be gone a mere three weeks. The place wouldn't fall apart in that short span of time.

His boots crunched in the soft powder as he plodded through the dark evening toward his Ford Escort. The bucket seat was as hard as a block of ice. And the engine protested after having been left out in the cold for over twelve hours.

Chug, chug, wheeze.

"C'mon, baby," he urged, his thick fingers delicately twisting the key in the ignition. "Don't fail me now."

Wheeze, wheeze, wheeze.

He turned it over a final time, using the last ounce of juice in the battery.

Wheeze, chug, kaboom!

The good Lord was on his side.

The tiny Escort roared to life. He felt like he was controlling a mighty chariot as he pulled forward into traffic on the slick road.

He didn't have time to say goodbye to his shop, as he had to make an immediate left at the light.

He slid sideways through the intersection and aimed straight for the mall.

California Governor Hunter Bradley, who also served as the co-chair of his political Party's national committee, was called away from a raucous gathering of boozing millionaires to take a phone call. As he walked across the spacious, crowded hall, his eyes caught the large-screen television where a woman in a particularly revealing gown was handing out an Oscar statuette followed by a sensual kiss.

The roomful of men erupted with approval.

Hunter hadn't planned to attend Hollywood's biggest bash, the Academy Awards. However, he did intend to watch every second on television from his home, the Governor's Mansion in Sacramento.

There wasn't a movie star or producer in the state that he didn't want supporting his man in the upcoming Presidential race.

He had invited many of the Party's biggest contributors to his special soirée, in which they could place a friendly, tax-deductible bet on the awards results and thereby donate money and hobnob with the Party elite while sipping cold duck and watching the glitzy event unfold on TV.

His personal assistant, Lawrence, handed him the phone in the gubernatorial office. "It's Captain Brett Fulham," the young man whispered. "The head of security at the Academy Awards."

Hunter nodded curtly. He knew who Captain Brett Fulham was. As Governor, Hunter provided the annual Hollywood event with the best security that money could buy: state troopers, counter-terrorism experts, Los Angeles helicopter and SWAT teams, and security guards from the state payroll.

"Yeah, Brett?" he said, recognizing the heavy breathing of the state's main security honcho, a man he had personally selected to head the Security detail at the Academy Awards for the past three years.

"I'm standing here looking at a press truck belonging to al-Jazeera TV," Brett said. "Am I supposed to give it access to the premises?"

"Do the reporters have press credentials?"

"Yeah, their badges and passes check out."

"Then why are you calling me?"

"Jesus, this is al-Jazeera we're talking about," Brett said, sounding incredulous. "They're the ones who interviewed bin Laden, who filmed the Taliban and the Iraqis. Are you sure we even want them on American soil?"

"Sure we do. And, we have already given them prior clearance to document and telecast the ceremony from a journalistic standpoint. You know, interview people, use the live feed."

"Isn't that a bit risky? This is being broadcast live."

"Risky? Hell no," the Governor said. "The world should see democracy in action. Here we even vote for the films and actors we like." Not to mention betting on them.

"I'm just confused, sir. Who gave them the security clearances?"

"The Governor's office."

"*Your* office," Brett reiterated for clarity.

"That's right."

"Okay then," Captain Brett Fulham said reluctantly. "We'll let them enter."

Hunter hung up the phone, took a deep breath, then picked it up and punched in the number of his mansion's operator. "Get me the White House."

A minute later he was speaking with his colleague, William Ford, the Party chairman who was engaging in a Party fundraising event of his own.

"I'm just calling to say that the bird has flown into the cage," Hunter said. "Are your televisions turned on?"

"As they are across the nation. Thanks for your good work. How soon before we can expect the bird to lay an egg?"

"Within the hour."

The White House phone clicked off.

Chapter 2

The resort's lawn ended abruptly at a wide beach that stretched a mile in each direction. Raymond O. Flowers couldn't afford to let his business shoes fill with sand or saturate his pants in the sea. He wasn't ready to abandon all decorum and take to his heels.

In order to get to his family, he needed to solve his financial crisis. And he needed to do that fast, before the authorities swooped in and plucked him off the street.

He scanned the beach chairs set up under thatched umbrellas for any early sun seekers. Someone might have left a handbag or wallet unprotected. He wasn't beyond petty larceny.

There were few people in sight that early in the morning. Maybe there were some early risers further down the beach.

He leaned over and removed his shoes and socks and rolled his trousers halfway up his sinuous calves. Then, he stuffed his socks into his shoes, collected a shoe in each hand, and began to walk down the beach.

With each stride, his toes explored the cold, silky sand. He tried to fight off the feeling that he was resorting to criminal behavior.

What was he thinking? He was escaping the criminals. He was an innocent man without a penny to his name and he needed the Feds off his back.

But his concern about losing his nest egg or the White House dumping him in some lockup for life paled in comparison with his anxiety about never seeing his family again. He was sure they were alive, and they needed him. He picked up his pace. He would find a way out of his straits and get to Beijing.

The resort's daily beach walk had yet to assemble that early in the morning. Spent firecrackers littered the shore, brutal remnants of the previous night's party. Seashells clanked as they rolled ashore and poisonous jellyfish lay like innocuous plastic bags half-buried in the wet sand. He was vaguely aware of the purr of a motorboat in the distance.

There was no easy money lying around to steal. This wasn't going to be easy.

C'mon, he was a financial officer. He could figure out what had happened to his money. Maybe the account was simply on hold. If that were the case, he only needed to call the VISA office and confirm his sudden increase in expenditures. His feet skimmed quickly over the sand.

But what if it was more than the credit card company simply double-checking on a red flag sent up by its computers? What if a hidden hand had intervened? If so, he would have to move quickly and transfer the money to another bank account. Could he remember the routing numbers of other secret accounts? Damnit, he had destroyed all that information.

Then a handsome, tanned face came to mind. That diplomat from the State Department who had provided him with his current account. Raymond could depend on—what was his name, oh, yes, Merle Stevens—to access the money.

He reduced his blistering pace. First, he would call the VISA office, clear up the misunderstanding, and reactivate his account. Then he would settle the bill with the hotel. When the U.S. Consulate opened in Shanghai, he would contact Merle Stevens and ask him to transfer his funds to a different, more secure account. Then he could get on the road to Beijing.

He hated to lose time. And there were many steps to get back on the road to financial health. Fortunately, he was a methodical man, not prone to rash decisions.

After all, he wouldn't want his children to see him in such straits. Not only was the government threatening him, the potential financial disaster was deeply humiliating to a man who had spent his entire adult life keeping track of money.

If all went well, he'd check out of the hotel by mid-morning and still be on a flight to Beijing by noon.

He tried to settle his nerves by slowing down to a stroll and thinking about his family. He could visualize their faces. Carolyn could paralyze him with her playful green eyes and put him at ease with her ironic smile. Jane's cascade of dark hair never obscured the flat, open planes of her eager young face. And Sammy, God bless him, what a bundle of energy, could knock him flat on his back with his chubby, fiery red-haired, five-year-old determination to beat his dad.

He passed a swarthy fisherman with a cell phone hooked to his rope belt. Boy, he missed his own kind. What was his family up to? Under what conditions were they living? He hoped to hell Carolyn hadn't fallen in love with some other guy...

The motorboat continued to buzz in his ear like an irritating fly as it cruised parallel to him across the wide, curving Yalong Bay.

Two colorful figures appeared on the sandy horizon. They developed into a pair of mature young beauties walking toward him in what looked suspiciously like thong bikinis. He reddened as they checked him out.

He wandered past them in his tailored sport coat, long trousers, and bare feet. In the past year, he had lost some of the handsome glow of his features, what with his receding hairline, flaccid cheeks, and permanent hangdog expression. But his skin tanned evenly, his six-foot stature made up for his bad posture, and his determined look behind his wire-rimmed glasses convinced even him at times that he was up to the task, whatever that task might be.

As of that morning, he was a married man again. Hell, after burying his family in Maryland, he should not have felt so damned inhibited. But on a normal day since that funeral, he wouldn't turn toward the innocent scent of youth that wafted past him, and check if those really were thongs. If his heart hadn't hurt so bad, if he hadn't worshiped every aspect of his wife Carolyn, if he hadn't invested his entire soul and every breath in the happiness of Jane and Sammy...what kind of trouble would he have gotten himself into?

He gazed at the widening wake of the motorboat. Had somebody planted that pair of tall, busty brunettes in the sand to test his libido?

No, he wouldn't look around. Instead, he conjured up his wife walking toward him, a smile working its way around her face, drawing his attention away from her trim form. But she was wearing something very naughty, too.

He continued down the beach, passing a Hmong minority family out for a stroll before the heat of the day. They wore long pants and long-sleeved shirts as if they had dressed up for the occasion. Perhaps for the mountain people, the beach was something other than a place to let their hair down and relax.

He stepped across the wet grooves left by several high-sterned fishing boats. Fishermen had recently hauled them up the beach and were already drying their nets.

Suddenly his heel slipped and he nearly lost his balance. He swung his arms to remain upright, wrenching a few vertebrae in the process. He looked back. Like a plastic bag, a large jellyfish quivered in the sand. His right heel felt a sting, then his back began to tingle. Had the jellyfish injected him with some sort of toxin? Or had he merely pinched a nerve?

He looked up just in time to catch a gang of pale, majority Han Chinese approaching him. It was a loose band of men, not a tightly knit family like the previous group. Chilled by their expressionless eyes as they passed, Raymond picked up his pace.

Suddenly, a burlap bag flew over his head from behind.

What the—? He tossed his shoes onto dry sand and reached for the fabric around his throat. God, were they trying to strangle him?

"What's going on?" he tried to yell, but the coarse fabric muffled his voice.

He heard water slapping against the hull of the motorboat as it approached.

He tried to sink to his knees, create as much dead weight as he could. He had to get to Beijing, to save his family.

"Help! Help!" Could the Hmong family hear him? Maybe there were policemen on the boat. Perhaps the fisherman could help.

He looked around desperately, but could see precious little through the tiny holes in his hood. Every gasp for air that he took filled his lungs with the oily fumes.

Who were these thugs? Was it Beijing or the White House that had hired these goons to execute him?

Strong hands pinned his arms behind him, and he had to let go of the tiny gap that prevented him from choking. Then, working as an efficient team, the group wordlessly hustled him into the water toward the boat. His pants were saturated by the first wave.

Damn. This was going to cost someone. But whom?

For an instant, the coarse fabric lifted above his eyes. A brief glimpse revealed the fisherman holding up his cell phone and waving at someone in the trees. Was he calling for help? Then the bag slammed down over his face again. As he stumbled into the water, it became clear that the fisherman wasn't appealing for help at all. He was calling something off, or giving an "all clear."

Events were not going his way, and nobody seemed the least bit concerned.

Before he was even waist-deep in the water, he knew what he had to do: forget the money for a moment and try to escape. He had to find some way to free himself from the long arm of the authorities before they took him out of the game.

His obstacles to finding his family were mounting exponentially.

So who were these thugs? It seemed incredible that Washington could have dispatched hit men to that remote beach in China. It had to be the Chinese with some gripe against him. Or were the two working hand in hand?

He felt a twisting yank against his neck. He coughed and tried to unclog his crushed windpipe. Air wasn't getting through. With each faltering step he slogged through the water, he could feel the effects of depleted oxygen.

Okay, the first step was to stay alive.

What did they intend to do? Drag his corpse through the streets? The whole thing really sucked. But at the moment, he would trade everything for a single breath of air.

Then he felt several pairs of powerful arms lift him, and he landed hard on his tailbone in the back of the motorboat. While he was being transferred aboard, the bag slipped loose around his neck once more. He coughed until his windpipe cleared. Then a gush of air filled his lungs. He was euphoric to simply breath again.

The small craft rocked wildly as the men clambered aboard. Then someone opened the throttle, and Raymond fell back against the gunwale as they spun around and headed out to sea.

"Who are you?" he managed to croak. "Where are you taking me?"

In addition to the cold of his wet clothes pressing against him, a new thought sent a chill down his spine. What did he know about the island beyond the resort? Hainan Island had been his home for two weeks. But he didn't have a clue about what lay beyond the resort's walls, much less on the nearby mainland or at sea.

The men remained mute and unresponsive.

Oh this was great.

"You've got the wrong man!" he shouted at them above the deafening roar of the outboard motor as they accelerated.

Their silence was unnerving.

He couldn't reason with them, negotiate with the limited capital that he had to offer, even get to know who they were.

It felt like he was falling into a black hole.

Tiffany Klug was waiting curbside at Macy's, their favorite rendezvous point.

Hiram pulled up to the curb, but kept one eye on the security guard by the door, half expecting to be shooed away.

But the guard seemed reluctant to step out into the falling snow, and besides that Tiffany had her gloved hand on the door handle just seconds after he came to a stop.

"What took you so long?" she whined, throwing herself into the bucket seat beside him and letting several shopping bags land in her lap.

He caught the name on one bag, "Victoria's Secret."

That was uncharacteristic of her. He wanted to ask what she had bought, but clammed up. Was he still inhibited after all those years?

He fishtailed through the huge parking lot and guided them onto the Garden State Parkway heading home. Only when they reached the tollbooth, did he manage to glance up to his wife's face.

In the pinkish halogen glow, she looked lovely.

"Been to da hair dresser?" he asked, noticing the new frizz in her otherwise droopy red hair.

"You noticed," she said, not displeased.

"Yeah," he said, speeding up to merge with the fast-paced traffic. "You got dat certain look I remembered from our days in Florida."

The words sounded odd because he was exaggerating. In fact, they had only spent two separate weeklong vacations over the past twenty years in Florida. But considering the spirit of the occasion, he would allow himself a bit of drama.

"I don't know if they've got hairdressers in Purang," she said. "I asked my girl, but she didn't know."

"I didn't see any mention in da guidebook," he said.

Suddenly, the tiny Pacific nation sounded a bit alien to him. He hated to admit that his only source of knowledge about the place was a travel agent's brochure and a guidebook that he had checked out of the library. And that was already ten years out of date.

Which reminded him.

"You got every ting packed already?"

"Don't worry. Everything's fine. Kitty's got our luggage ready for the limo."

Bam. There it was again, another daunting concept. Hiram was not a limousine kind of guy. He preferred the trips where an entire family piled into the car to see off a grandmother at the airport. But, he sighed, he had to join the Twenty-First Century. People took limos from Jersey to Kennedy every day.

"So what you got in der?" he asked, nodding at the bags that sat so slim and elegant in her lap. "What is dat, a Victoria's Secret?"

He changed lanes to let her get over any embarrassment in fielding the question.

"Oh, I was looking for a bathing suit."

He let out a short laugh. "Sweets, I don't tink dey're called 'bathing suits' any longer. At least not at Victoria's Secret."

She gave him a funny look. "What do you know about Victoria's Secret?"

Now it was his turn to feel uncomfortable. "I switched over from dat Fredericks a while back," he quipped.

She gave his shoulder a teasing shove. It didn't move his bulk one inch.

He eased down the slick parkway exit ramp. Soon he was following a slushy back street through a small forest toward their home.

At last, their two-story house was in view. Sure enough, not only was Kitty waiting for them, but she was already standing by the curb with the limo driver. Hiram and Tiffany's two suitcases were already in the trunk.

Frost floated on his daughter's breath as she greeted them cheerily.

"Well I certainly do envy you," she said a tad too effusively. "You're off to the tropics."

"What?" he said. "Are ya telling me ya want us ta leave ya?" He looked over at the limo chauffeur, as studly a man as any that might find Kitty attractive.

"No, Daddy," she said, throwing her arms around him. "I just want you to be happy on your Twentieth Anniversary."

"I'll miss ya, Kit," he said, returning her hug. It was the first trip he and Tiffany were taking without their daughter. Now that she was a freshman at the junior college, she could certainly spend two weeks alone. But it did feel like he was breaking up the family.

❖ ❖ ❖

The al-Jazeera TV truck rolled cautiously through the maze of trucks and vans with their crews already hard at work.

Covering the Academy Awards was a strange, last-minute assignment for Abdul, who wasn't even well versed in American cinema. On the contrary, his journalistic instincts made him want to track down the stories that were shaping the lives of other young Arab men and women just as his life had been shaped.

Hollywood barely factored in.

Nothing about American culture threatened the Arab youth of his day. Fast food, music, fashion, and the mass media were all a natural result of economic development. Who he was was not determined by American cultural hegemony. In fact, he embraced American culture as a normal part of life.

He glanced around at the cables that snaked from cameras inside the building out to the trucks. "Watch out," he said, directing his driver to avoid disrupting a live broadcasts by one of his colleagues.

What did shape his life most profoundly, however, was the harsh treatment of Palestinians, a battered and long-suffering people. Abdul wasn't Palestinian, nor did he even grow up with Palestinians. He hadn't even dwelled particularly on their quest for independence and statehood as he perfected his English language skills at Cairo University.

But the Palestinian cause affected everyone's lives in Egypt, if not the entire Middle East. Abdul suffered under military law imposed by a figure propped up by the American government simply because he was useful in putting down the Palestinians. Abdul's entire country was dominated, from restrictions in the press and political freedom to the books sold on the street, by one man, Washington's man who sat in the Presidential Palace in Cairo.

After all, how would the Americans feel if their President was a puppet of some foreign power?

They rolled up to an impressive angle on the Kodak Theater. Spotlights reflected off the curved façade with a glittery sparkle.

"Stop right here," he ordered.

The driver braked and turned off the truck's engine.

Abdul checked over his camera crew, hunkered down in the back of the truck. "Let's set up a live feed from this spot," he called through the back window of the cab.

The crew set to work at once, and Abdul began to compose his thoughts. What could he say to the Arab world about the stars of Hollywood?

Since it was too early in the waking Arab world for anyone to turn on his or her television set, whatever he announced would reach few ears. Nevertheless, he was determined to do the event justice.

While his crew established a satellite link and rolled out electrical cords for lighting and the television camera, he thought he would stroll inside the building and take a look at the ceremony that was already in progress.

Chapter 3

Raymond grew increasingly woozy as he inhaled the vapors of the oily burlap sack. How much longer could he endure the smell before he collapsed on deck unconscious? And if that didn't knock him out, surely the nauseating rollercoaster ride in the motorboat would get to him. Even while two strong pairs of hands pinned him to his seat, the acid in his stomach rose up his throat with every swell.

The bag still blocked his view, and all he could do was listen to the slap of the prow against the surface and the drone of the motor. The men weren't talking. They were either professionals, or sullen types.

They had better be professionals. If they were going to kill him, at least they should do so quickly and efficiently. After all, the Chinese certainly were experienced at executions.

What was he thinking? Who would save is family then?

He would have to get to know his captors better. How strange that they needed to conceal their identities. Not only had they blindfolded him, but they were as quiet as mice. Maybe they were just going to rough him up and intimidate him so he wouldn't testify in the Chinagate trial. But he had given no indication to anybody that he intended to testify. This had to be some mistake.

He cleared his throat. He was ready to offer his silence to the President, even perjure himself. What did it matter to him if he let the scoundrel walk? He would get his family back in return.

But what did he know of his captors. Maybe they weren't from the White House after all, but from the special prosecutor who wanted the

President thrown in jail. Maybe they *wanted* him to testify! In that case, he would sing like a bird.

Until he knew who these thugs were, he'd just have to keep his trap shut. He wouldn't play his cards until he found out who these guys were and why they were holding him captive. In the end it didn't matter to him who had hired these smelly thugs that manhandled him so roughly. The sooner he cooperated with them, the sooner he could track down his family.

And with that decision to comply, his muscles began to relax. He would take his lumps in stride. He had already done his company's bidding, he had transferred the kickback funds to the President's personal bank account, he had watched his family being carted off to a SARS ward, sacrificed in order for him to do it. What more could he do for a President that he hadn't even voted for? Now he would either have to lie or die for the President, and he was *not* going to give the crook his life. That's where he would make his stand. Call him a liar, at least he would be alive to save his family.

The boat droned on. The clank of loading cranes tinkled in his ears. Perhaps they were nearing a port, possibly the capital city, Haikou.

That was no real capital city. Now Beijing. That was a real capital.

He allowed his thoughts to wander for a moment. Perhaps if he searched deep enough into his past, he could find who had written the note that his family was alive. Who was pulling the strings in his life? Who had triggered his breathtakingly quick descent from a well paid family provider to a widower, then from a solitary and honored figure in the press as he stood alone at his family's freshly dug grave in Maryland to becoming a haggard wreck trying to fight off a hit squad, barefoot on a remote Chinese island.

The whole tragic story had all begun in quiet, peaceful Beijing as the city eagerly anticipated the first green buds of spring.

Every industrialist and his head honchos were there in China's capital, including all the oil companies against whom his firm, Core Petroleum, was competing.

His mind replayed images of the easy life among other expatriates, professionally manicured yards in summer, dining in the glittering city at night. Cocktails with clients, beer and nuts at the wood-paneled bars with coworkers. Soccer games with Jane and Sammy at the International School. Hikes with Carolyn along overgrown stretches of the Great Wall.

If only Carolyn and their kids knew what a mess he was in.

Funny that the people he felt closest to during a time of crisis, the only ones he could confide in any longer, were his family.

His memories of Beijing changed abruptly, and surgical masks appeared on every face. Traffic was reduced to nil, with wide, tree-lined boulevards and sidewalks stretching empty in all directions. Anxious residents would tiptoe furtively in and out of grocery stores with their near-bare shelves, trying to avoid the deadly form of corona virus that caused Severe Acute Respiratory Syndrome. Schools across the city had shut their doors and he and his family were held hostage in their three-story villa on the outskirts of town. Rumors circulated of local villages and entire city blocks that had been quarantined due to outbreaks of SARS. Everyone knew someone who knew someone who had already died from the disease.

If he hadn't had a job to finish, they would have caught the first flight out of the epidemic-ravaged country. But his company wouldn't let him go until he had completed all the financial transactions necessary to cement what would become known as the "Chinagate" deal. Money he sent to the President's bank account assured China's status in the World Trade Organization. And because of that request to remain and line the President's pockets, his family had paid the ultimate price.

They had almost escaped the horror scene. Finally, with a go-ahead from Core Petroleum, he and his family had hustled with well-packed bags to the nearby airport. Checking each other anxiously for dry coughs and elevated temperatures, they had to make it past the medical examination station set up at the entrance to the terminal.

He had tried to suppress the tickle in his throat, a constant presence throughout the dry winter and spring months in Beijing. The cottonwood trees had released their seeds, and the city was adrift in a blizzard of white puffs.

Airline employees and airport workers had watched nervously through windows as passengers lined up to enter the terminal.

Then it was their turn at the nurse's station. He heard a murmuring of airport security officials behind the nurse as she took Carolyn's temperature, holding a thermometer to her forehead. The nurse cast a worried look at the rest of the family.

She signaled for them to step behind a white curtain that partitioned off part of the sidewalk. Inside, a man in a lab coat and stethoscope listened to their breathing.

With the cold metal instrument pressed against his chest, the tickle rose in his throat. And Raymond had coughed.

He shot a smile at the well-built doctor, hoping to elicit a knowing wink in return. Everyone in Beijing had some sort of respiratory irritation from the desert-like conditions and heavy presence of pollutants and dust in the air.

But the doctor only frowned deeper.

Thermometers in the ears. Beeps. The doctor didn't tell them the results.

Then, from the deserted vehicle lanes, Raymond had heard a truck or van approach, its brakes squealing as it pulled up to the curb.

Several pairs of hands drew the curtain back and daylight broke through to their family. Three medics rushed in and took Carolyn by the elbow toward what Raymond identified as an ambulance. Then they went back for Jane.

Raymond had tried to resist, but the doctor had pinned his hands behind his back. And when they grabbed Sammy, the robust little kid held onto him with all his might. At last his fingers were torn free from Raymond's pant legs and he went kicking and screaming into the back of the ambulance.

He had looked on in horror and disbelief, physically restrained from rushing to their assistance. The vehicle's flashing red light illuminated fear in the eyes of the rest of the travelers waiting in line. Several turned around and hurried back to their cars and away from the aggressive authorities.

Raymond had cried out for the medics to stop. He would call upon personal medical insurance, international evacuation services, and VIP hospital wards, anything but a public SARS ward, a death sentence for anyone who entered one. The disease was so contagious, that if one walked into a hospital healthy, he would surely catch it there. Nurses and doctors were dying by the thousands all across the city.

Then the doctor tried to strong-arm him into the back of the ambulance, which suddenly took on the menacing aspect of a paddy wagon.

He broke free and sprinted around to the front of the vehicle, trying to throw his body in its path. The driver gunned the engine.

"Carolyn!"

He couldn't see his family inside. They were locked in.

The ambulance advanced on him, and he backed up. It picked up speed and he had to step away, scratching at the windows and trying in vain to bring it to a halt. He found a door handle.

The ambulance dragged him several yards. The pavement scuffed up his shoes.

It wasn't a vehicle to restore health. His family was being taken away in a hearse. The driver veered, and Raymond lost his grip on the handle.

He fell to the pavement. "Stop!"

His cry was futile.

He had coughed once, and his family had ended up in the SARS ward. This time another set of equally implacable goons was taking him away. Should he resist any more than his helpless family was able to do? Should he be allowed by the gods who governed one's fate to survive merely because he was able to fight back, wrest himself from their clutches, negotiate with his troves of cash?

The sudden unfairness of it all hit him hard. He had no more right to live than his family. If he had to, he would sacrifice his life to get theirs back.

The bouncing motorboat brought him back to reality. Cold water washed around his feet. His captors couldn't see the angry tears welling up in his eyes. Like his family, he was learning how it felt to be kidnapped and taken away.

There was a man at the airport who had stopped to help him.

He was a tanned, young Westerner.

"I'm Merle Stevens, from the American Embassy. May I assist you?" he had offered kindly, helping Raymond to his feet long after the ambulance had disappeared down the highway.

The following two weeks had been sheer torture. He was so distraught that he couldn't even breathe. Like all other SARS victims, his family had been put into isolation from the start.

He wasn't even allowed to enter the hospital.

Some days he could only rely on statistics published in the newspaper. And the number of casualties was rising dramatically. One day, three hundred were reported dead. The next day three hundred and forty more died. There was no mention of what hospitals were reporting the deaths, not even which areas of the city.

He had wandered down the lonely streets of the Jianguomenwai diplomatic area to the Embassy for news. Merle Stevens, the tanned young diplomat, made calls for him.

His family was moved to another hospital. But he didn't know which one. There were twenty SARS wards in the city.

His wife didn't even have access to a telephone! Perhaps Carolyn had been separated from Jane and Sammy. Perhaps his little first- and second-graders couldn't remember where they lived!

Patients were being shifted by taxi and ambulance from one hospital to another in a macabre game of hide the bodies from the World Health Organization, there to get a handle on the extent of the epidemic.

Every time a taxi zipped past on the deserted road, Raymond tried to catch a glimpse of the passengers inside. One might be carrying his family.

"They're not sick," he had told himself and Merle Stevens at the Embassy over and over again.

One morning, sitting in the dull brownstone chancery building of the Embassy beside a dusty radiator, the words suddenly rang hollow. If they weren't sick when they left the airport, surely his wife, daughter, and son had caught the virus in the SARS ward. And two weeks was ample time to polish off any victim.

Raymond felt movement on the boat. Men were shifting their weight, perhaps preparing to cast a line ashore.

He heard cars in the distance, the noisy engines of Chinese-made vehicles with grinding gears and worn brake pads.

He had stared into Merle's face at the Embassy, and the young man's sad expression had told him everything. There was no cheating the SARS virus. He had better prepare to ship the bodies home, if he could even get a hold of the remains.

Raymond had wept openly in the man's office. He had never felt warm tears wash down his hands and forearms before. He had so much grief within him. The situation was hopeless, and he was powerless to do anything about it.

The only reassuring aspect to the entire ordeal, from ambulance to urns of ashes, was that the U.S. Government had assigned a single, familiar face to deal with him during his time of distress. Through intense investigation, Merle had been able to report on his wife and children's declining health, from "Suspected" to "Probable" cases of SARS. Then they were listed as "Confirmed" cases, and finally he had reported their deaths. He had been there to hand him their remains in three neat little urns to carry home. Without Merle, he would have been unable to step on the plane for his family's final trip home.

A final R&R for all of us, with emphasis on the word "rest," he had told himself as he sat stiffly in his First Class seat on the long flight to Chicago, then home to Baltimore-Washington International Airport. His only comfort was in knowing that the ordeal was over for his family at last. He was left alone to bear the pain.

And on that flight to Baltimore, he began to reflect on how his firm had ordered him to remain in China until he had made the President rich…and his grief had turned to anger.

Piedmont Personnel was a small security personnel firm, a government contractor, located in downtown Atlanta, Georgia. Its doors never opened for passing salesmen. Its biometric access control system only unlocked the door for its top executive Harry Black and his assistant Lou Marvelle.

It was seven p.m. and an icy evening drizzle rinsed the streets of Atlanta. Lou was holding the door open for Harry as he entered along with the biting north wind.

Harry removed his wet overcoat, stepped into the conference room, and took a seat before the television console.

Lou turned on the satellite communication equipment and the image of a dark-haired woman and four despondent young men appeared, their eyes shielded by wraparound sunglasses. Behind them, a curtain wafted out onto a sunny balcony. The studied informality of the furniture in the background spelled "hotel room" to Harry.

Running a security personnel firm was child's play for the former Navy SEAL. And the men Harry had lured out of the best-trained and most clandestine units of the military were happy with the higher pay and cosmopolitan lifestyle. America's move to privatize various aspects of government such as military and intelligence operations went down well with them. Tracing an American crook that spent his time cavorting in Asian resorts sure beat planting underwater explosive devices on North Korean subs.

"What happened to Raymond?" Harry wanted to know right off the bat. He had read the emailed report. His team had missed a golden opportunity to snatch Raymond O. Flowers off the beach at Hainan Island, someone else had beaten them to it, and he wanted to know who.

"We think he gave us the slip," one operative replied. "We even had Boris posing as a fisherman on the beach blocking that particular escape route from the hotel. Boris called us over with his cell phone, but we got there too late. Someone had helped Flowers slip through our fingers."

"How could we anticipate that he would do a one-eighty and check out of the hotel first thing in the morning? We were planning to snatch him later at the pool."

Harry cursed. "I don't think the problem was him. I think the problem was you. You must have been hung-over from the party. He was on his toes."

"Sir, if we drank, we only did so for cover. Hell, if we hadn't shifted the money out of his account and put a hold on his credit card, he would have left the hotel before we had a chance to nab him."

Harry studied the image of Badger McGlade, his computer genius, and then sank his head in his hands. "How were you planning to snatch him from the pool?"

"Well, we had men stationed at the pool and Carmen at the massage table. She was prepared to escort him to her room."

Harry shot the only woman a look. The American Filipina was an expert with her hands, from massage to martial arts.

"Don't look at me," she said. "I can't force a man to get a massage."

"So clearly, they didn't go up to your room. What was your fallback?"

"We planned to have men stationed at the restroom by the pool."

"What, holding their dicks all day until he needed to take a leak?"

The men had that sheepish look already. He didn't need to rub it in.

"So what makes you think someone helped him escape?"

"They took him away in a motorboat."

"Did he leave willingly?"

Badger shook his head. "I don't think he had this planned. When he learned that his account was empty he panicked. He didn't have time to set this up."

Boris Vukic, the tall, dark-haired intellectual in the group, seemed to agree. "I'm afraid this could be a Department of Justice job. It was too professional. They hired locals to nab him and whisk him away by boat. Who other than the FBI would have the means to locate him and spirit him away in China?"

"How about his company?" Harry asked the group at large. "He left their employ with a truckload of cash, not to mention blackmail material."

"That's a possibility," Boris conceded.

"Or how about the Chinese? Maybe they wanted some blackmail evidence to use as leverage against the President."

"That's also a possibility."

"So don't you see how damned important it is to get this guy?" Harry shouted, slamming his thick fist on the table. The impact sent Lou's grande lapping over. He looked at the once-dedicated machines of war that had been turned soft by money and life in the burbs. Their country needed soldiers with their talents. But he needed them even more. He had a company's reputation to uphold, damn it.

In the end, though, he fell back on an old theme that motivated them all. "Remember this: if we screw up again, we will lose our government contracts. And if that happens, you will lose your big, fat paychecks."

His videoconference counterparts stirred uncomfortably.

"So sit straight men...and Carmen."

They stiffened on camera.

"Gather up your equipment. I want you ready to check out of there. Reserve tickets to major Asian cities. I want you ready to fly to Tokyo, Shanghai, Hong Kong, or Singapore at a moment's notice. I'll work my contacts at Justice and also run Badger's tracker program. You can be sure I'll locate Raymond O. Flowers, and once I do, I want you ready to react and grab him. Remember, American needs that menace to society yanked off the streets and muzzled."

Chapter 4

After two long hours smothered in the scratchy burlap sack and buffeted by waves, Raymond sensed the motorboat slowing down. It cruised along with a reduced wake before finally cutting its engine.

But they were still nowhere near the sounds of the port. Without returning to land, he would never get to Beijing. Things were definitely moving in the wrong direction.

A man grunted and heaved him to his feet. He reached out and someone guided his hands to a metal ladder. As he felt his way up the rusty rungs, a broad rolling continued underfoot. He was still rocking on the water. Prodded forward, he took a tentative step over the top.

The toot of a working tug echoed across the dull roar of lapping waves. And beyond that drifted the distinct honking of street traffic.

His bare feet touched a level surface. He was onboard a ship.

But his exposed soles were not sliding across the varnished deck planks of a yacht, nor was he walking on the well-painted promenade deck of a cruise ship. He stubbed his toe on a row of rusty rivets. From the thick smell of rotting fish, he guessed she was some sort of fishing trawler or factory ship.

The clandestine nature of the meeting was beginning to annoy him. Who wanted him so badly that they would set up such an elaborate plot to whisk him away from the resort and sequester him onboard an anonymous ship in some backwater port? Didn't these guys have a life?

Then he tuned into voices, a sound he hadn't heard all morning. Men on deck were babbling in a foreign language that he couldn't identify, much less understand. It didn't sound like any Mandarin he'd ever heard. Yet it was singsong, perhaps Cantonese or Taiwanese. What did he know? He was a financial officer. The only language he spoke was money.

But he did know a word or two of Russian. After all, he had grown up during the Cold War, when Russian was taught in high school. In fact, he had used it to his advantage to eavesdrop on conversations among the many Russians at the beach resort. Maybe he could confound the kidnappers by appearing unable to communicate with them. If he wasn't what they wanted, they might let him go.

A rough hand guided him out of the sun into an echo chamber of sorts. He was thrust back against a wall and pushed downward. He landed hard on a metal bench.

"So," a voice grunted in strongly accented English. "What is your name?"

They didn't even know who he was? It was time to be difficult. "*Kartoshka?*" he asked. Potato?

Undeterred, the man repeated his question. "Who are you?"

"*Sabaka.*" You dog.

The man seemed to accept this and went on with his next question.

Raymond remembered some pot-bellied Russian men staggering down the beach in their underwear. He let his otherwise washboard stomach protrude.

"Do you know how to sail?" the man asked gruffly.

That one caught him off guard. "*Da,*" he lied. He had never even taken a cruise before, and he didn't know a jib from a mainsail.

"Good. What else can you do?"

Raymond decided not to treat it as a question. Instead, he launched into a conversational stream he had overheard among some topless Russian dolls lying under beach umbrellas. I have a boyfriend in Irkutsk. He's nuts about me. But his penis is too short. I can't stand the way he smells either.

The man grunted with dissatisfaction and left the room.

Raymond had had real conversations with real people at the resort as well.

He remembered how interested Sandi DiMartino had been in his long sob story. One afternoon lounging around the pool with daiquiris in hand, they had talked in lofty terms about his business. She knew oil, and enjoyed his anecdotes. Gazing down the length of her long, beautifully tapered legs splayed out on the lounge chair, she remarked how his stories reminded her of her own corporation.

Then he had launched into a diatribe against the morals of his superiors. "Asshole hustlers," he had called his bosses. "All of them."

Thinking back, the daiquiris had really loosened his tongue.

Feeling their personal space shrinking, he had moved his lounge chair up against hers to reveal some corporate secrets that he had hoped would make her skin crawl.

He remembered her lifting her heart-shaped face up to him. She had such a delicate nose and a wonderful structure to her chin.

"Yeah, the assholes go way beyond the company," he had declared. "All the way up to the White House."

"No kidding," she had concurred. "I've been following the Chinagate scandal."

At that point, alarm bells had gone off in his head. He had examined the light that played in her pale blue eyes more closely. He supposed it was natural that she would be interested in the independent prosecutor's investigation. After all, she had introduced herself as a lawyer.

"Do you believe the President's guilty of taking kickbacks?" she had asked innocently.

He nearly spewed out the drink he was sipping. "Guilty? He'd make Saddam Hussein blush. Oh yeah, the President took a bribe all right. I should know, that was the petroleum company I worked for."

She had seemed to make a mental note of his working for the company at the center of the Chinagate scandal, but said no more at the time. Instead, they had swum circles around the pool bar, with her playfully chasing him.

He had let her tickle his toes a few times.

Jerking back to the present, Raymond drew his toes away from the cold metal deck and flexed his numb, bare feet. Heavy boots approached in the open doorway.

"*Budut vamy?*" a man shot out. Just his luck. There was a native Russian-speaker onboard, and Raymond had no clue what he was saying.

He turned his head away, feigning arrogance. That might work for a minute. Not longer.

"*Vi ne govorite russkogo,*" the man shot out accusingly. Something about him not speaking Russian.

Raymond slumped his shoulders and hung his head, hoping it was an appropriate response.

"*Vrushko!*"

Raymond knew that term. Fake.

"Okay, so you're onto me," Raymond said in English. "What do you want with me?"

Even in his darkness, he could tell that he had stymied the two men for a moment. Then the Russian speaker stomped out of the room.

That left Raymond with the grunter, who said, "So what is your name?"

Raymond felt his wallet in his pocket. The slob could surely have determined his identity from the passport and credit card they would have found when they checked his wallet on the motorboat.

But maybe the guy couldn't read.

What kind of meeting was this anyway? How could he be of any value to these idiots if they didn't even know who he was? He felt like storming off the ship.

The man approached and towered over him.

"Okay, enough already," Raymond said. "I'm Casper the Friendly Ghost."

There was a grunt.

"What do you want me for? You've emptied my bank account. You've got all the money I have."

"We didn't rob any bank account," the man growled. "And you don't have a penny on you."

Some professionals these were. They didn't even know his identity, much less have the wherewithal to swipe the money from his offshore account.

If that was the case, then who was tampering with his bank account? Nothing seemed very cut-and-dried that day. And they had picked the wrong day to tangle with him. He felt his patience reaching a breaking point.

A weary President Bernard White looked up as his shiny-faced Chief of Staff walked across the plush blue carpet of the Oval Office with a buoyant stride. By evening, the seventy-year old President was usually exhausted from visitors and meetings at which he was supposed to be decisive and in command. He needed the energetic Chuck Romer to boost his energy and help him chart his way through the shark-infested waters of national politics.

Preparing for that night's Academy Award thank-you bash for Party donors held in the East Room, he needed to display as strong an image as he could muster. He could not let them smell blood.

As he had quickly learned on the job, half of a President's life involved deciding important matters of state, and the other half was spent trying to keep his political Party afloat. And the two parts were virtually one and the same. Every decision he made had a political dimension. So whenever he funded a charity, he needed to appease the fiscal conservatives with language about it helping the economy in the long run. He couldn't even throw out an opening pitch in Kansas City without assuring the Cardinals fans that he was on their side, too, not to mention a fan of the East and West Coast teams, as well as an advocate of both the player's union and the owners. And that wasn't to imply he wasn't an NFL and NBA fan as well. If only he knew how to play ice hockey...

What Chuck gave him was a rudder with which to steer, a political basis on which to proceed with the national agenda.

Sure, it was a cop-out as Chief Executive to let his Party's interests determine the government's agenda, but he believed in the fundamentals of his Party like he believed in the Bible. They were the bedrock of his existence.

Chuck slapped the early edition of the *Washington Post* on Bernard's desk. "The latest USA Today/CNN/Gallup poll shows your approval rating sinking below forty percent."

Bernard considered the news for a moment. If forty percent of Chico bought the Chevys he used to sell, he'd be a happy man. But Chuck wasn't exactly exuding happiness.

"Is that bad?"

"Yeah, anything below forty-five percent is in the danger zone."

"Okay, so how do we boost it?"

Chuck dropped into the chair opposite the executive desk. "I'm afraid that's not the question. The question is how do we keep from sliding further."

"It's that Chinagate fuss," Bernard said, jumping to his feet and circling the desk. "Why did the Chinese have to transfer the money directly to my account? It's so crass! Anyone knows you have a whole bevy of legal options. You can donate it to a 501(c) group or 527 committee or PAC or special interest group or get it to me through soft money contributors. You don't put money from a foreign government directly into my pocket. It feels so...dirty! And the whole affair's sticking to me like dog poop."

"It'll wash off," Chuck tried to reassure him. "They can't make it stick."

Bernard examined his shoes, and then twisted to check out the back of his pants. "Without a case against me, it will eventually blow over, right?"

"It has to dry first before it blows over, and we don't have the luxury of time before the general election."

"How about if I use a stick and pry it off," Bernard said, leaning over to pick up a sword given him by some head of state from the Middle East.

"Then it's on your stick."

Bernard examined the sword with distaste and leaned over to set it back on the bookshelf. While he was bent over, he looked around for anything else to be done while he was down there. Had John F. Kennedy, Jr. lost a Lego block? Had President Nixon left a bug?

"No!" Chuck cried, rising. "We need to stick it in someone else, and bury him in it." He grasped the sword from the shelf, twirled and lunged for the President's derriere that remained unprotected as he tightened a shoelace.

Just then, Gertrude, the Presidential secretary walked in, deftly dodging the sword to deliver a message to the President's desk.

The two men watched her come and go.

"But we don't want to stab me in the back," Bernard said straightening when the door clicked shut.

"No, who would want to do that? We've pinned this Chinagate affair on someone else."

"Stanley Polk's witness?"

"That's right, sir. He's a fugitive from the law. As long as Polk's main witness is on the run and looking guilty as hell, he can't make his case."

Bernard took the sword from his Chief of Staff and studied the keen edge that jutted from the elaborately carved hilt. "Exactly where is this witness, this Raymond O. Flowers?"

"We set him up with funds in Shanghai to abscond. He took the bait and is on the lam."

Bernard nodded with approval and began to put the sword away. "Whose money did he steal?"

"That's why it's so perfect. It's your money, sir."

"*My* money? I want it back," he turned and growled, leveling the sword at his young Chief of Staff. "I don't want my money swimming around out there where Polk can find it."

"Don't worry. You've already got it back."

That was a relief. Bernard gently returned the sword to the shelf and took his seat behind his enormous desk. He spread his hands out on the burnished surface. One thing still bothered him. It wasn't a loose end to his defense, rather a concern for a fellow human being. "Doesn't the witness, er, doesn't Raymond O. Flowers have a wife and kids?"

"We took care of them, too." A sinister note crept into Romer's voice.

"Don't tell me any more," he said, turning away. "I just don't want that man to surface again."

"Don't worry about him. But what's our strategy, sir?"

"For what?"

"You know. Boosting your approval rating."

Bernard sank further into his seat and swiveled completely away from his Chief of Staff. Hadn't they just been through all that? With luck, Chuck's efforts to shut Flowers up would reverse his skid in the polls.

Snow was falling through the darkness. That reminded him of his entertainment for that evening, the Academy Awards party he was throwing.

"Can't we just forget about politics for a few hours?"

He sighed contentedly and began to relax, an indulgence he had rarely allowed himself for the past three, grueling years. He would spend an evening among friends.

The limo ride into Kennedy was smooth. Salt trucks prevented the bridges from icing over, and soon Hiram and Tiffany Klug were past Staten Island and zeroing in on Kennedy.

Hiram tried to follow the highway signs as their chauffeur sped them through the night, but entombed as he was in the cavernous back seat of the limousine, he found it hard to see out the front window.

Tiffany dug her fingers into his biceps.

"Take it easy, Rammy," she told her husband. "Let him do the driving."

"Old habits die hard," he said.

"Well, this trip should break us of a few bad habits," she said.

The limo driver couldn't wait long dropping them off at the departure terminal. A policeman was whistling at the poor guy as Hiram tried to factor a healthy tip into the total payment.

"Will ya wait a minute? I'm payin' da guy!"

The young man took the money with a smile of accomplishment.

Just don't go back and bang my daughter, Hiram wanted to say.

The policeman was whistling at *him*, now. He had to move his luggage off the sidewalk.

"Geez, what are sidewalks for, anyway?" Hiram shot at the cop as he dragged the pair of suitcases along the wet surface.

"Hey, I don't make the rules," the cop shot back.

"Yeah, yeah, yeah."

"Come on, Rammy."

He plucked both pieces of luggage off the sidewalk and marched them in through the sliding glass doors.

He didn't set them down until they figured out which line to get in. He didn't want to "break any rules" by setting his luggage on the floor.

He was in for even more aggravation. Before he could take his place at the back of the long, snaking line, a young woman who was stuffed into a one-size-fits-all airport uniform began peppering him with questions.

Apparently, the little plastic nametag on her lapel gave her the right to pose the nosiest questions about what he had packed in his luggage. She demanded to know if he had packed it himself. Was he carrying any wrapped gifts from someone else? Was he transporting any items for another party?

All he could think of was…the mysterious bag from Victoria's Secret. He wiped the back of his wide neck with its permanent sweaty ringlets of black hair. Then he rubbed the perpetual stubble on his cheeks and glanced at his wife.

"Uh, none of dose tings, miss," he told the security agent.

She seemed to buy it. She slapped an orange sticker on both his bags and let him join the long line of those checking in.

"And dis isn't even an international flight," he remarked to Tiffany.

"That'll come soon enough," she replied in her knowledgeable way.

After finally extracting their boarding passes from the ticket agent, they found themselves in yet another security check. Hiram looked around. Okay, it was a busy place. People were flying in from all sorts of countries. He wasn't sure whom to trust. Should he watch out for the woman in a headscarf? How about the swami in bare feet? And was that group of Koreans from the North?

Tiffany seemed to be reading his mind. "Certainly is a hodgepodge of people."

"Your passports, please," the security agent asked.

"Dis is a domestic flight," Hiram protested.

"Your ticket reads through to Purang. I need to see your passport."

Tiffany had both passports in her handbag.

They looked so new and unused, Hiram was overcome by embarrassment. He hoped the Purang INS would manhandle his booklet, drop it on the floor, and stomp on it by accident. Give his passport enough wear and tear that someone might look at it and ask, "How many times have you been around the world?" And he would proudly open it up and point out the Purang visa. After all, that was halfway around the world.

"Will you take your shoes and belt off, please?"

"Huh?"

"Your shoes and belt?"

"We're blasting off in under half an hour, and you want me to take off my clothes?"

As soon as he said it, he realized that he couldn't force the man to skip any of the steps he was hired to perform. Hiram sighed.

"Just stay patient," Tiffany said, reading him like the tax code she knew by heart for her CPA job. "We'll be leaving all this far behind."

At the glamorous art deco Kodak Theater in Los Angeles, veteran actor Tudman Grier was as well known as any star in Hollywood. He had augmented his major Hollywood roles in romantic comedies with frequent guest appearances on television game and talk shows. He was neither too glib, nor too stupid. Just the kind of guy anyone would want to watch bantering all evening with Jay and David.

But this night his star was shining most brightly.

At last, all his hard work sucking up to distant, stuffy celebrities had paid off. All his best-buddy lunches with producers and talent agents had landed him the Mother of all Roles. He had to be smart, he had to be honest, he had to supplicate, he had to rule. He was hosting the Academy Awards.

The evening was rushing by much faster than he had anticipated it would after endless dry runs. Following several tedious weeks spent talking to numbered seats, handing out Styrofoam statuettes to stand-ins, and reworking his lines with a team of professional writers, he felt the actual event washing over him like an uncontrollable tidal wave. Sometimes he barely kept his head above water, other times he was going under and desperate to come up for air.

In the frenzy, he had called the Iranian filmmaker by his last name first. He had tried to converse with a lighting director who only spoke Polish. His mind kept racing backward and forward through his lines, and he could hardly remember where he was in the script. His producer had assured him that any blunders had gone "off to Pluto." In any event, he didn't have time to worry about his mistakes.

But he did worry about how he was coming across. He didn't want to play the bumbling fool. He was supposed to be the thirty-something teen idol with no ego. Okay, he was already fifty, but makeup and a rigorous workout routine in the gym took care of that.

But teen idols didn't lose their lines when confronted by Jennifer's bosoms. And if he really had no ego, certainly he could take a joke at his own expense. The least he could strive for was to look on the ball.

It didn't help that Mr. Martin was feeding him adlibs a mile a minute over his earpiece.

The low point so far had come when the documentary producer collected his Oscar for a film on wife-burning in India, and Steve quipped over his earpiece, "His pants are on fire," and he cracked up before a television viewership of well over a billion.

But Tudman Grier was a professional, and the show had to go on.

Chapter 5

While Raymond languished under the suffocating hood, his abductors stood outside the room arguing over what to do with him. Someone had tampered with his bank account, but certainly not these fools. What these guys had in mind, even they didn't seem to know.

Maybe while he had a chance, he could sneak a glance around. He leaned forward and rubbed a shoulder against the sack that covered his head. Without much effort, he could tilt it back and take in the room.

It appeared to be a storage compartment. Fishnets lay heaped along the side walls. Ropes with buoys snaked across the floor. It was probably a driftnet operation. Illegal, no doubt.

Incredibly—several knives lay on a table. They were meant for scaling and gutting fish, but he could use one to break free! He could bust through his bonds and get on the road to Beijing.

He stood and took a few steps toward the table near the door. The bag still tilted away from his face, he charted out the rest of the path. He couldn't afford to knock something over on his way.

As he shuffled toward the table, the drone of another boat reached his ears. As it grew louder, it seemed to be getting closer. Its engine chugged efficiently like a sort of pilot boat or launch.

He turned his back to the table and reached for the nearest knife. Its wooden handle was still wet from recent use. He turned the blade inward and began to saw at the rope.

Sailors from the newly arrived craft arrived on deck. They spoke briskly with strong accents using educated vocabulary.

He worked quietly and vigorously while trying to make out their conversation.

"We'll give you one thousand. Top offer," one of the newcomers said.

"He speaks English," the grunter said. "Like a native. Five thousand."

"Don't be ridiculous. I can get English speakers from anywhere."

Raymond sawed away with short, fast strokes.

"He's educated in the West."

"That only means he's corrupted."

Flexing his shoulders, he pulled the rope taut as he cut. One strand snapped in two.

"He's rich. We picked him up at a five star tourist resort."

"Does he have cash on him?"

He wasn't getting through the rest of the rope very quickly, and his bonds remained strong.

"You can have his credit card."

"What kind? I don't take Diner's Club."

Raymond couldn't believe his ears. They were haggling over him like slave owners at an auction. What did they expect him to do once he was bought? Another strand broke.

"It's a VISA."

"Okay, that will give you another five hundred. What about a family?"

"We didn't see a family, but he has a wedding band."

"Okay, that's good for another thousand, tops."

A few more sawing motions and he would be through.

"He's strong like a bull. You should see his shoulders."

"Can he do manual labor?"

The grunter hesitated. "Maybe only in a gym."

With an angry tug, he snapped the rest of the rope, and his hands broke free. For the first time in hours, he could flex his shoulder muscles and shake the kinks out.

"Okay," the brisk voice said. "Al-Qaeda will authorize two thousand five hundred dollars maximum. That's my final offer."

Whoa. Al-Qaeda, the terrorist organization, wanted him? What for, a suicide mission?

Then he heard their voices getting louder, closer. He gathered up the fragments of rope and tossed them out of sight.

He held the knife up in front of him. He would run them through.

A hand fell on the door latch.

God, he couldn't kill anyone. He'd better hide the weapon and bide his time. He slipped the knife under his belt and hurried away from the table to the middle of the room, remembering to clasp his hands together behind his back.

The burlap bag! The door popped open, and he shrugged the bag quickly back over his face.

"Sit down," the grunter ordered.

Raymond decided to push back at them and see where that got him. "What's going on here? What are you planning to do with me?" He flipped back his head to toss off the bag.

A hand caught the bag and pushed it roughly back in place. But that brief glimpse gave him enough time to take stock of his adversaries. The grunter had a broad, nasty face, pinched eyes, and brawny arms. He would be difficult to overpower. But not the other guy. The newcomer was a hollow-chested skipper with a starched white uniform and a trim black beard. He stood between Raymond and the door.

So that's what a terrorist looked like. The type who would behead him on an al-Qaeda website.

The terrorist skipper took a moment to examine him. The guy lifted the burlap hood off of his head and looked him in the eyes.

Now here was a man he could bargain with. Intelligent eyes, good complexion, well groomed.

Maybe he could even sell the President down the river to these guys. After all, he would be a bonanza of blackmail material in any terrorist's hands. Certainly worth more than $2,500. Maybe he could even get al-Qaeda to find his wife and kids!

But think where that left America. Suddenly he felt the weight of the world on his shoulders. Did he want to be the fulcrum on which freedom and tyranny teetered, with America on one side and the terrorists weighing down heavily on the other?

The price was more than the President losing his office. Raymond would be selling out America. The President would surely cave in and submit to the terrorists' demands rather than commit political suicide. The strings that al-Qaeda could pull in the White House would be enormous, influencing military and economic decisions, bringing the free world to its knees.

He regarded the skipper with skepticism. Could the handsome stranger with seemingly so much going for him, be one of al-Qaeda's brainwashed legions? Was he the kind who could hijack civilian airliners, bomb embassies to smithereens, slaughter schoolchildren, and blow up commuters on their way to work? Probably.

He would rather be caught by the Chinese or the White House and silenced in some menacing way, or nabbed by the special prosecutor and have his ass hauled back to Washington than to hold the free world hostage.

But in the end, what he really wanted was his family back. And he didn't have time to negotiate.

Instinctively, he grabbed the knife from under his belt and lurched forward. Seeing the knife brandished before him, the skipper stepped aside, clearing a path to the door.

But, not to lose his sale, the grunter lunged forward to slow him down. He caught Raymond with a fist to the side of the torso. That sent Raymond reeling sideways into the doorframe, but he held onto the knife. His forward momentum carried toward the open door. Doubled over from the sharp pain under his arm, he stumbled outside. Sunlight momentarily blinded him.

Where was he?

He was on the deck of some commercial fishing vessel, with the second boat, a large, powerful launch, tied up far below.

Smartly dressed crewmembers from the launch, who were lounging around, jumped forward from the railings.

They blocked his way to the ladder that he had used to climb aboard. That avenue of escape blocked, he checked in the other direction. Barefoot deckhands spread out across the deck.

Raymond's brief hesitation cost him a critical few seconds as the grunter caught up with him, a clenched fist landing heavily on his back.

Damn this guy! His survival instincts took over. Raymond fell to a crouch, spun around on the balls of his feet and jabbed the knife upward as he sprang upright.

The contact made a popping puncture sound, and he felt the tip slide easily into flesh and internal organs, followed by the flow of warm blood and mucus over his fist. The blade had penetrated one of the man's lungs and perhaps a major artery. But that didn't stop the guy. His heavy arms crashed down on Raymond's shoulders, causing the embedded knife to twist partially from his grip.

Raymond couldn't hold up the muscular beast, especially with the blood-lubricated knife tugging his wrist. He sank to his knees, a scarlet smear across one lapel of his sport coat.

The deckhands closed in nervously while the swarthy grunter's head slumped heavily on Raymond's shoulder. Then the man's body went limp and threatened to drag him completely to the deck.

He withdrew the knife and the grunter remained immobile. He had killed the guy.

Raymond heaved the man off his shoulders and rose to his feet.

The clean-cut officers from the launch also fanned out, not about to lose the prize Westerner they had just purchased.

The only escape route was behind him. And that required running fifteen yards across open deck. He wasn't so sure he could make it to the railing with what felt like a broken rib.

He chose a nearer spot, and ran toward it, angling away from the launch's officers.

He reached the railing before the others could react. He would show them an American in action! As he swung a leg over the railing, he could see the deep blue water far below. He would crack open like an eggshell when he hit the water.

Standing on the far side of the railing, his feet together and his back to the water, he waved the bloody knife at the sailors.

"You get any closer, and I'll use this again," he said, his voice cold and clear.

Nobody moved.

Now what? Suddenly an image came to his mind of platform divers in the Olympics. How did they break the fall? For one thing, they didn't wear glasses. With one hand, he carefully unhooked his spectacles from behind his ears, folded them, and slid them into his pants pocket.

He looked around behind him. The skipper's white boarding launch was some distance away. He had to jump clear of her.

With both parties edging in nervously, he tossed the knife onto the deck, released his grip on the railing, and leaned back. He wasn't about to attempt a swan dive. Anything would do.

Air whistled past his ears as he spun in the air and plummeted like a rock. His loose sport coat flew up over his eyes, and he couldn't see a thing. The flat soles of his feet hit the water first, shattering his back with a jolt of pain. He raised his arms over is head to avoid another bashing, and the next thing he knew, water was shooting up both nostrils like a fire hose. Fighting the blinding pain from all corners of his body, he opened his eyes only to see murky sea green.

He shrugged his shoulders out of his waterlogged sport coat and let it float free. Then he planed horizontally and took a few strokes away from the freighter. Fortunately, he had taken a gulp of air before hitting the water, but it didn't seem to last very long. His lungs were threatening to burst.

But his buoyancy pulled him upward.

In the darkness, it was difficult to judge how far he was from the surface. He willed his mouth closed, adding some frantic kicks to speed his way.

Suddenly the crown of his head struck something solid. He was directly under the launch.

Rubbing the sore spot on his scalp with one hand, he stroked desperately with the other, kicking his bare feet to make the far side of the boat. At last, he emerged with a splutter. Coughing water, he tried to take in a dry lungful of air.

A dizzy, throbbing mess, he was finally away from his captors, alone in the water. He fit his glasses back on the bridge of his nose and glanced around. Piers jutted into the harbor some fifty yards away. Nothing but stagnant water and oil slicks lay between him and escape. He could handle that. He had to.

His head hurt like hell, but somewhere in the future, he could dimly see his family cheering him on. He removed his glasses and dipped back below the surface. He propelled himself with even strokes despite his sore back and the body blow to his side. He had to reach the nearest pier before the terrorists climbed back down to their launch, gunned the boat to life, and plowed across the harbor after him.

An ice storm rattled the windows of Harry Black's downtown Atlanta office. But he couldn't worry about the weather just then. He had to act quickly to track down Raymond O. Flowers, the man that the Central Intelligence Agency wanted so desperately to hush up.

Who had gotten to Raymond first and nabbed him? Several potential culprits came to mind.

Special independent prosecutors Stanley Polk, the Chinagate prosecutor, certainly wanted Raymond as a witness. But such prosecutors operated outside the normal circles in Washington. In fact, Polk had set up his own office in a building separate from the Department of Justice, and had hired attorneys from the private sector.

Polk wouldn't have had the resources to track down and capture their star witness. But he could have sought the cooperation of the Attorney General to aid in the investigation, and that meant the FBI.

So maybe the FBI had nabbed Raymond O. Flowers for Polk before Harry's men could get their mitts on him. But Harry's job was to defend the President and keep Flowers out of Stanley Polk's hot little hands. Would the FBI turn the witness over to Stanley Polk? Or, like Harry, would they try to bury the guy?

The only way to know for certain who had Flowers was to call up the Attorney General, who led the entire Department of Justice that included the Federal Bureau of Investigation.

Harry wasn't on a first-name basis with Attorney General Caleb Perkins. In fact, he had never met the man, an aloof politician.

So how could he get Caleb Perkins to tell him if he had Flowers? As he was a member of the Cabinet, Perkins would be tightly connected with Chuck Romer, the White House Chief of Staff. He reached for his phone to call Perkins, ready to invoke Romer's name. Perhaps a white lie would get the busy Attorney General's attention.

He caught Perkins by cell phone, being chauffeured from his home in Arlington, Virginia, to the Academy Award Ball held at the White House by his Party's national committee.

"This is Harry Black speaking for Chuck Romer at the White House."

"Who are you?" Perkins said above the sound of slushy tires and the hum of his car.

"Harry Black of Piedmont Personnel. We're an Agency contractor."

"Make it snappy. I've got a party to attend," Perkins said, seemingly in good humor over the upcoming bash.

"Chuck needs information on Raymond O. Flowers. Do you know his whereabouts? Word has it that your men made a snatch off a beach in China."

"I'm not aware of that."

Was Attorney General Caleb Perkins stonewalling him?

"C'mon, Caleb," Harry said. "If you don't give us Raymond first, the independent prosecutor will fry us all. We won't have any political Party left come Election Day this November."

"I am profoundly aware of that fact."

Harry sighed with relief. They were on the same team after all. "Well, I'm just calling to say that I'm here when the time comes and you're ready to hand him over. I assure you, Piedmont Personnel can handle this affair with all due discretion."

"Thank you for your call, Mr. Black. We will be in touch."

Harry hung up the phone both reassured and disappointed. The Attorney General would cooperate with him if he had any information on Flowers. But it certainly didn't sound like Caleb Perkins had captured Flowers. Had the FBI even sent a team to China?

So how was he going to find Flowers?

His only other option was to run Badger's computer check on financial transactions, from airline tickets sold to credit card activity. Perhaps Raymond would try to access his VISA account once again.

Ten minutes later, he had his answer.

"Bingo!" The power of the computer to access any tidbit of information from around the world seemed miraculous to him.

The line on the screen read "Haikou, PRC, 2:34 a.m., GMT Account Display Failure, Cause: Hold."

Harry glanced at the row of clocks hanging across the office wall. The time was 3 a.m. Greenwich Mean Time. The transaction must have taken place within the past half hour. Either Raymond was free and trying to access money, or someone had taken his card and was doing it in his place. Either way, the credit card was in Haikou.

He checked his detailed Asian atlas. Haikou was a capital city that lay on the northern tip of the island of Hainan in the South China Sea. Raymond had made it from the southern shore of the island to the northern shore in less than three hours.

Could he get his men up there in time?

He reached once more for his phone and placed a call to his operatives on the southern tip of Hainan Island. Their beach party was over.

Hiram and Tiffany had to transfer to a connecting flight at Los Angeles International Airport.

It was the first time that Hiram had ever flown internationally, and it surprised him that in transferring between flights, he didn't need to pass through Immigration.

"Americans must not mind if terrorists leave da country," he mused aloud.

Tiffany gave an empathetic grunt.

Hiram looked around him at LAX. Every other person was Asian.

They were walking through the gateway to the Orient. The air traffic control tower seemed inspired by the Jetsons.

"Wasn't der some attack planned on dis airport?" he asked.

"During the Millennium crisis," she said. "They caught the guy entering the country from Canada."

"Yeah. I remember now." He had some vague recollection of the incident.

The thought that one terrorist could carry enough explosives to blow up the entire terminal made him shudder.

They walked across the squeaky floor under the watchful eye of security guards, not too subtly scanning the hordes that streamed past.

It seemed like they were looking for a needle in a haystack.

His chills passed quickly when they reached the gate for their Purang flight.

The gate attendants had already poured guava juice into paper cups for the waiting passengers. Island music floated softly over the intercom.

And the warm Southern California climate, along with the jovial tourists milling around in their Hawaiian shirts, set Hiram instantly at ease. Suddenly, all he could think of was palm trees on a tropical beach with a soft breeze in his hair and a cold drink in his hand.

"Rumba!" he said, turning to Tiffany with a grin.

She returned his enthusiasm with a sloppy smile of her own.

He knew at once: they had made the right decision.

Heading toward the restricted backstage area at the Academy Awards ceremony, Captain Brett Fulham allowed himself a moment of contentment for a job well done.

He flashed his security badge at the watchful armed guard, who threw a salute and let him pass.

Extensive security preparations for the past month were paying off, and thus far the event had gone without a hitch.

It was his third year managing security for the enormously popular televised event, and they had passed the critical phases. The electrical system hadn't blown, the audience hadn't died from gas poisoning, the Kodak Theater hadn't burnt to the ground, no heart attacks had occurred so far, and if any sniper was going to take a potshot at a celebrity, he would have done so by then, But, he reminded himself, just when he felt he was letting down his guard, he had to be most alert.

He worked his way through makeup and wardrobe with purpose. He took his job seriously, just as he managed the team at Governor Hunter Bradley's mansion.

If anything, he took the Academy Awards even more seriously. Should anything happen at the show, not only would the California economy go down the toilet, so too would his career.

He felt like the little Dutch boy with a finger in every leak. One unplugged hole in the defenses, and the entire dam would give way. The enemy, whoever they might be, would not get lucky on his watch.

He fought off a perverse curiosity as he walked past starlets stuffing themselves into bras, and perspiring stage managers reading off lists of names. The same hysteria took over the set each year, and it always surprised him what barely contained chaos it all was. He certainly couldn't operate that way.

He walked past world-renowned stars with their Academy of Motion Picture Arts and Sciences handlers, who did need identification badges. Those about to perform an act were having their wardrobe and makeup adjusted in small cubicles while they waited nervously for their number to come up.

Many celebrities who were taking part in the introductions also had to be seated in the audience during certain times since they were also nominees for awards. The whole process of nominating, awarding, and receiving seemed incestuous to him. And it was logistical hell for a floor manager.

But for the head of security, the place was a snake pit of potential disasters of a magnitude far greater than any single actress' career.

And then his phone beeped.

He picked it up. "Fulham," he said.

There was a long pause on the other end, with miles of static separating him from his caller.

"Speak up," he barked. "I can't hear you."

"This is Osama. We have men positioned to destroy your Academy Awards."

"Who is this?" Brett double-checked, unsure he had heard correctly. He stepped back against a wall in a darkened corner of the dressing area.

"This is Osama bin Laden," the soft, heavily accented voice said. "I want you to release top al-Qaeda leaders in captivity and also release Saddam Hussein or the Oscars will evaporate in a cloud of radioactivity."

"Is this a threat? Because if it is, mister, you are subject to federal prosecution."

"I already have three outstanding warrants for my arrest," the caller responded calmly. "Now don't give out another award until you have released my men from Guantánamo and released Saddam from captivity, or your show will evaporate in the blink of an eye."

The phone line went dead.

Brett cursed. He speed-dialed his office on the premises. "I want you to trace that call. Did you record it?"

"We're tracing it right now," his lieutenant said. "And we have it on tape."

Brett stepped out of the shadows. The lurid backstage lights revealed popular movie stars with ugly expressions. It was a show onto itself. But he couldn't dwell on that. The surreal comedy backstage and polished production on stage were destined to become a nuclear bomb busting drama the likes of which had never before been broadcast to the American home.

He dialed his strategic consultant on the police task force and told him the story.

"What should we do, Matt?" he asked.

Without much deliberation, Matt replied, "Don't let anything stop the show. If we give in to these guys, they win."

"I'll get back to you." He called his Hispanic operational commander who was in direct contact with all the units and explained bin Laden's threat.

"I need time to scout out what elements he has in place," Hernandez said. "All evidence to the contrary, we should proceed with the show."

"Well, I want every badge checked, every suspicious object examined, and every locked door opened. And I want it yesterday."

Brett took a deep breath and dialed the Governor's Mansion in Sacramento.

The assistant told him to wait.

While he stood hunched over with the cell phone squashed against one ear and a finger plugging his other ear, Brett heard the beep of call waiting.

He switched over to his other line. It was his office communications team.

"We traced the call, sir. It appears to have come from western

Pakistan."

"My God. Can you get the FBI to verify the voice print?"

"They're already on their way over here. But we're pretty sure that's where the call originated."

"Good work. Thank you."

Damn. He spent the next two minutes frantically running out of the building and through the cool night air to his operations center before a calm voice came over the line, "This is Governor Hunter Bradley."

"This is Fulham. I'm shitting bricks right now. I just got a terrorist threat. My office traced it to western Pakistan. He said he was Osama bin Laden."

"My, aren't you playing with the big boys," the Governor said from his mansion.

"I'd rather not. I couldn't tell if it was him or not. The FBI is verifying that. But in the meantime, we have to assume that the call was real."

"I agree. And what was the specific threat?"

"Something about releasing al-Qaeda prisoners from Guantánamo and Saddam from captivity, otherwise he'll blow up the awards ceremony with a nuclear bomb."

He could hear the Governor sucking in his breath.

"There's more, sir. He told us not to give out another award until the prisoners were released."

"Damn him. He's holding our ceremony hostage."

"Not to mention several thousand guests, among them Hollywood's elite. What should I do, sir?"

The Governor was decisive. "Inform the Academy that we have to suspend the ceremony for unspecified reasons until further notice."

"Will they buy that?"

"Are they willing to suffer the consequences? On the other hand, if this prolongs the show, just think of all the ad time this will give them."

Brett shook his head.

"About the prisoners," the Governor went on. "I'll call the White House at once."

Brett let his phone hand drop momentarily as the Governor hung up. His phone dangling by his side, he looked up at the illuminated edifice to the glory of American cinema. Where was the bomb planted? Above…outside…inside?

His arm throbbed as he gripped the phone. Every muscle in his body was tense.

At last he studied his phone and speed-dialed the Academy's president.

"This is Captain Brett Fulham at Security. I have bad news for you...."

Chapter 6

Raymond dragged his weary body out of the fetid harbor in Haikou, just moments before the launch rammed into the pier behind him. Raymond was already hoofing it down the street when the skipper managed to jump ashore.

He had to find somewhere in the sprawling capital city to disappear. Then he'd be on his way to Beijing.

Pounding in his bare feet and dripping clothes across a four-lane, Raymond found himself weaving in and out of shoppers along a palm-lined boulevard fronted by shabbily maintained office buildings and stores. The skipper's shoes slapped on the sidewalk just half a block behind him.

Raymond found a side street and turned down it, his heart pumping, and his legs stretching out for speed. He streaked past hair salons bathed in pink lighting. Fruit vendors beckoned to him with mangos, sugar cane stalks, and green coconuts.

He zigzagged down several lanes, squeezed between the ever-tightening walls of Portuguese-style buildings. He dodged between palms. Maybe he could hide from view. But the skipper managed to keep up, perhaps following the shocked onlookers that Raymond left in his wake.

He needed more cover. He was too exposed on the city streets, and the shops were far too small to melt into.

Then he saw a familiar sight, a wooden gateway standing squarely over the entrance of a public garden. He veered into its quiet confines, apparently designed around a tomb. Several arched bridges later, he found himself behind the artificial cliff of a rock garden created to resemble a canyon.

The sound of footsteps had stopped. He heard only the faint voices of couples strolling through the shaded park. Perhaps the skipper was waiting for him to reemerge from the park. Raymond checked out his options. Aside from ponds, bridges, tree trunks and shrubs, the garden offered little in the way of long-term cover.

He glanced down the rockery, with the razor-sharp edges on every rock face. If he were careful, he might be able to climb the thing and boost himself over the garden wall.

If only he had shoes...

His feet were already burning from the run along the pavement. He had nearly stumbled and fallen over sharp pebbles. Now he had to rest his weight on a couple of toes that gripped spiky rocks.

Either he endured the pain, or he would give himself up to al-Qaeda. It was his choice.

He left behind droplets of blood as he scaled the cliff, bracing his feet against the faces of the opposing sides. It was a daunting fifteen-foot climb, and each toehold magnified the pain of the preceding step. He had to lean on his hands to distribute his weight. His palms took on the indentations of the uneven surface.

A small boy looked up from ten feet below.

"Go on, kid. Scoot."

The little guy watched his upward progress without comment. Then he kicked off is sandals and prepared to follow.

"Shoo," Raymond said with a vigorous gesture. "Go away."

The boy's small nose crinkled up. Then he broke into tears, turned, and ran away.

"Sorry, kid."

At last he reached the crest, a flat surface that was flush with the top of the garden wall. He scrambled to look over the edge.

An alleyway followed the outer contour of the park. An open kitchen faced him, a woman stirring dumplings in a steaming vat on the back step of her apartment. The alley was barely wide enough for two people to stand abreast, no more. The woman was alone and preoccupied.

He lowered himself from the top of the wall, his hands slipping on the rounded tile surface.

He could hold on no longer and aimed his feet to land squarely in the center of the alley. The moment he struck the paved surface, he bent to a squat, trying to absorb the impact with his knees.

His soles exploded with white-hot pain.

He squeezed his eyes shut for ten seconds and tried to will the pain to transform into the opposite sensation, pure pleasure. For a moment it worked. It felt like his feet were gliding down an icy glacier, leaving steam in their trail.

He opened his eyes and straightened up. Only the woman noticed him. She didn't seem startled to see him suddenly materialize, as she poured cold water over her steaming broth.

It was time to blend in. He brushed off his sleeves and chose a direction in which to head. A sunny street lay one way, and the garden wall curved off in the other.

He chose the street.

Sunlight was filtering through the traffic of a commercial district. As people bumped against him on the sidewalk, he noticed that his clothes were no longer wet.

The old town behind him, he was among businessmen ambling off to their favorite lunch places.

Then he saw a hotel with a massive marble façade and a honeycomb pattern of windows. Taxis pulled in and out, ferrying fashionably dressed men and women.

He could blend in there. He hobbled to the entrance, careful for his feet not to leave a trail of blood on the marble.

Inside, he saw a cloud of blue cigarette smoke. The more, the better. He merged into the smokescreen.

The reception desk appeared by the staircase. Could he bluff his way into checking into a room? He could leave the next day without paying his bill.

Just then, a matronly woman in a pink silk jacket with tooth-shaped buttons approached him. She was stout, with a round white face that seemed primed for conversation.

"Are you looking for a girl?"

Just then he caught sight of the skipper in his distinctive white uniform drawing up short on the sidewalk.

"Yes, a girl would be fine."

"Please take a seat," the woman said, escorting him to the lobby's bustling coffee shop. He joined the groups of men in business suits with loosened collars slurping down bowls of soup. Too bad he had ditched his sport coat in the harbor. He no longer fit in with the swank crowd.

The matron offered him a plush chair. It was so sooty, he didn't want to touch it.

Young women had been circulating through the coffee shop. They now gravitated toward him.

The matron lined them up in a row of seven beauties, their individual expressions calculated to appeal to different tastes in companionship.

The front door opened behind him, and he heard the familiar slap of shoes on the hard floor.

He had to make a quick decision. He pointed to the one with the shy smile.

"Nine hundred *yuan*," the matron said.

It was not the time to bargain, but nine hundred yuan was outrageous and demanded a counter offer.

"If I like her, I will pay you three hundred."

The woman considered for a moment.

"Two hours for five hundred."

Raymond forced a smile. "*Hou le*," he said. Very well.

The women giggled at his Chinese and dispersed, all except the shy one.

"I'll swipe your credit card," the matron said, her palm outstretched.

The skipper was checking with the reception desk, probably asking if a foreigner had passed by or checked in. The ladies behind the counter seemed too busy counting money to deal with him.

Dissatisfied, he turned back to the room.

"Okay, here," Raymond said, sliding the wet billfold from his rear pocket. God, his fingers were scratched and sore. He handed the credit card over. "But I want that back."

"Okay, mister," the matron said in a worn, threadbare way.

Raymond watched her leave with the card. How long would it take for the hotel to realize that the VISA card was worthless? With luck, they would merely copy the card and bill him later.

The girl was trying to talk to him. "My name is Li Wei," she said.

He forced a smile and turned her by the shoulders to block the skipper's view of him.

"Where are you from?" he asked.

"I arrived here three weeks ago from Yunnan," she said. "Do you want a tittie massage?"

He considered various responses. If he offended her, he could lose his cover.

The skipper was rapidly approaching the coffee shop.

On the other hand, how could he impose himself on the poor girl? She couldn't be a day over eighteen, if such legalities counted for much in the world of prostitution.

In the end, he couldn't afford to create a scene. He gave her a smile. "Sure, Li Wei. A massage would be fine."

"Psst."

Tudman Grier straightened his bow tie as the professional comedian's voice whispered over his earpiece.

"This is Steve."

Standing just off camera onstage at the Academy Awards, Tudman frowned. Steve didn't need to either whisper or introduce himself, and he was interfering with his train of thought. He was just about to formally congratulate the singers that were reaching the climax of their number.

"You've got to stall for time," Steve said. "Don't introduce the next celebrity to hand out an award."

Tudman checked the cue cards. He was supposed to introduce a neophyte starlet next.

"I repeat, don't introduce the next celebrity."

Tudman glanced around, confused. Then who should he introduce?

The cue card man was giving him the cut sign, whatever that was supposed to mean. Still just off camera, Tudman gestured to the man who was prompting him. "What?"

The man pointed to the teleprompter at the podium.

Tudman stepped forward and forced an appreciative smile at the campy rendition of an old favorite that had been given new life by a new generation of musicians.

The teleprompter read, "Cut to commercial."

Okay, he could handle that.

"Thank you. Thank you very much," Tudman told the audience, bowing in his best imitation of Goofy. "And now for a word from our sponsors."

A crescendo of blockbuster music rose in the auditorium and the stage went black for the commercial.

Tudman held his index cards up to the light that emanated from the wings. There wasn't supposed to be a commercial. There had just been a commercial.

He waited for Steve to come over the earpiece and explain.

Before anyone got their act together to inform him what was happening next, the spotlight turned on again. Tudman was live, onstage, without a script.

The spotlight burned down on him as he stood behind the podium, and a red light illuminated above a close-up camera. The music died away and left the stage in silence.

Tudman looked around, held his earpiece and stared at the camera. In his best Southern drawl, he quoted Ross Perot's running mate. "Who am I and what am I doing here?"

It got some laughs. But he was dating himself. He needed to come up with something the teens could relate to.

"But must we always talk about sex."

A louder chorus of laughs—strained, nervous laughs.

"That reminds me of a joke my grandmother used to tell…"

He was dying out there. How long was he supposed to keep this up?

Then Steve's voice whispered in his ear. "Forget the grandmother. Tell them about the awards so far."

Tudman switched tactics and swung around to the right to face the audience from a different angle. He pointed to those seated to the far corner of the auditorium. "So, how do you like the show so far?"

The audience in that area cheered.

He frowned, and that brought out a laugh.

"And how about you people in the center? How do you like the show so far?"

A louder cheer.

This was so juvenile.

Steve whispered in his ear. "Keep this up for another half hour."

"What's wrong with that fool?" President Bernard White asked as he entered the long, high-ceilinged East Room of the White House. The donors party was already well underway with bigwigs mingling, champagne flowing, and a large-screen television dominating the room.

The emcee at the Academy Awards was sweating profusely as he stumbled through a string of stale jokes.

"Ah," the President's Party chief William Ford said, intervening between Bernard and the glowing screen. "It appears that a hostage situation is brewing at the Academy Awards."

Bernard looked up at him. "Tell me you're kidding."

"I'm serious," Ford said, a smile threatening to take over his expression.

"If this is some sort of joke," Bernard said, "It's not funny."

"No. It's entirely real. We just received a phone call from Osama bin Laden. The FBI is verifying his voice, but they think it's real. It came all the way from western Pakistan."

Bernard felt himself bristling at the sound of the name. Of the world's most influential men, Osama's name came before his own. He ground the toe of his shoe into the carpet.

"Well, what did he say?"

"He wants top al-Qaeda leaders released from Guantánamo and Saddam handed over," Ford informed him with a straight face.

"That's ridiculous."

"—or the Academy Awards go up in a nuclear explosion. Those are his very words."

Bernard stared at the idiot faltering on stage in Hollywood. "Then tell me why you're smiling."

"Because, this is your big break, sir," Ford said. "You've built your reputation on standing up to terrorists."

"Yeah, so tell me how I'm going to stand up to these terrorists. What are they going to do, drop a bomb, what?'

"They didn't say, sir, but our men are on the offensive. Don't you worry, sir. The Homeland is secure."

Spinning around to look at the massive hulk of the Kodak Theater, Brett Fulham was thinking fast. He considered his plan of action. It was not enough to simply hunt down evidence. He had to eliminate every possible source of the bomb. He would expand the air space restrictions, expand the perimeter. But did bin Laden say it was a bomb? He referred to radioactivity. Brett would have to stop the water supply, turn off the air conditioning units…

What else could he do?

Walking briskly from the dark parking lot, he suddenly came upon a team of Arabs fixing tripods in front of the lighted façade of the Kodak Theater.

He pulled back around the corner just as a young Arab in shirt-sleeves came jogging down the front steps—much like Marlon and Humphrey and Marilyn in bygone days.

He had to dispose of every potential threat. The al-Jazeera crew would have to go.

He turned and rushed back to his operations center. Hernandez looked up from his organizational chart.

"Stop everything," Brett yelled. "I think it's the al-Jazeera television crew. I don't think they're legit."

"Well, you can't just kick out journalists," Hernandez said. "We need a smoking gun."

"A smoking gun would be too late," Brett said, finding he was echoing the words of the Secretary of Defense. "We need a preemptive strike."

Hernandez looked at him dubiously.

"Okay," Brett relented. "Check them out first."

Hernandez shot out the door, picking up his two-way radio to assemble his men.

"Use the bomb-sniffers," Brett called after him.

The California state troopers had brought along a couple of bomb-sniffing beagles. They could detect explosives, from gunpowder to dynamite to plastique, through a sealed van. But could they pick out radioactive material?

He was sure his men needed to eliminate the threat before al-Jazeera launched its attack.

Automatic submachine guns were lined up behind Hernandez' empty desk.

Dogs began barking outside.

That was it. They had discovered explosives.

He grabbed two 9mm guns, thumbed the safeties off, and sprinted out into the parking lot.

Hernandez had swiveled two spotlights off the building and onto the crime scene.

Both beagles were barking like crazy and jumping up at the al-Jazeera truck. The Arabs were standing back nervously.

Hernandez had just thrown open the back doors of the truck when a violent explosion rocked the scene. Brilliant light flashed from the truck, and a concussion of air mowed down security guards and terrorists alike.

One Arab, the one in the shirt sleeves dodged for the cover of darkness.

Brett fell to one knee and opened fire, just over the heads of his security guards as they lay on the pavement.

The Arab reached a corner of the building unscathed.

"Damn it." Brett zigzagged his way forward, stepping over the bodies of fallen, bleeding men and approached the blast furnace of the burning truck.

The fur coats of both dogs lay scattered in bloody pulp over a space of several square yards. The stench of burning rubber and exploded dynamite filled the air.

Kneeling beside a television truck operated by a different production crew, he picked out the Arab hiding against the building. He dropped one submachine gun, shouldered the other, took aim and pierced the Arab's throat with a stream of hot metal.

The man fell to his knees, unable to scream, then flopped forward on his face, dead.

Just then, an ember from the burning truck fell into a pool of liquid. Flames licked across the pavement toward him. Only then did he notice the source of the leak, a punctured fuel tank in the truck beside him. He jumped clear of the flames just as they reached the loaded submachine gun that he had just set down.

Consumed by the flames, the lightweight gun came to life, firing off its full load of cartridges. The bullets discharged from the chamber and exploded through the clip like a series of firecrackers. Brett felt them penetrate his clothing and enter his body. Twenty or more of them bored into his being.

As he fell to the ground trying to shield his body from the possessed weapon, he saw a figure rising from among the dead. It was Hernandez.

Hitting the pavement like a porcupine wounded by its own defenses, Brett called hoarsely to Hernandez. "Radio the Academy." He rolled over in the wet, sticky substance that was oozing from his stomach. "Tell them that the show can go on."

At that point he lost consciousness, a sensation of triumph making a feeble, final surge through his mind just as the truck beside him exploded into a million fragments.

Onstage, Tudman put a hand to his earpiece.

"Hi, Tudman, this is Steve again," the earpiece whispered.

Tudman nodded to the live camera. Perhaps Steve would recognize his secret nod and go on.

"Can you hear me?"

Tudman nodded again. This time more obviously. "I'm testing out my donkey impression," he explained out loud to hold off the hostile crowd.

"Okay then. The show can go on," Steve whispered. "Introduce your next celebrity."

Tudman offered a little prayer of gratitude to whoever might be listening. "And now, without further ado…"

The crowd went wild.

He smiled and held up his hands.

"Thank you, thank you."

Then he felt a sheer lace, drop-shoulder sleeve brush against him.

In a black, strapless Ralph Lauren beaded original, Penelope had cruised up beside him at the podium. With a broad smile, she announced, "Our next category is Special Effects…"

Tudman gripped the podium tightly to keep his balance. His knees suddenly felt weak and he realized that his throat had gone dry.

But he had survived.

Attorney General Caleb Perkins arrived at the portico of the White House half an hour before midnight and let his driver take care of his overnight bag. He would be sleeping over in the Lincoln bedroom, and other guest rooms would be similarly filled like so many rooms in a frat house.

Trying to enjoy an evening with the President, his political rival, would not be easy, but he appreciated the opportunity to soak up the residence that soon would be his.

It was not easy to attend a party hosted by the very person he was preparing to defeat in an election campaign. But he had to occasionally honor the office, and show his appreciation to the President who had tapped him to be Attorney General.

He had to admit with envy that Bernard White looked Presidential. In addition to the white hair of an elder statesman and a beneficent smile, Bernard made one feel like the only person that mattered in the world. On the other hand, Caleb thought, referring to his campaign staff's war room papers on Bernard, the old guy was weak on social issues, overextended and vulnerable on his anti-terrorist program, and bogged down by a sluggish economy.

For his part, Caleb might be bald and portly, but he was a social and monetary conservative had a long and distinguished career as a state prosecutor, and was open to dealing with the Palestinians, the key, he believed to solving the terrorist problem.

He flashed Bernard his trademark ear-to-ear grin.

Flying in from some dark corner, Party chairman William Ford descended on them both. The moneyman, the man he needed to woo, rested an arm comfortably on the shoulder of Bernard White, the man he wanted to slay. Getting the Party chairman solidly behind the Caleb Perkins candidacy was a primary objective of the evening.

This was going to be tricky. Before he swung into action, he'd need a little champagne to lubricate the gears of his mind.

As if reading his thoughts, William Ford leaned toward him. "Let me get you a drink," he offered, "and let you two enjoy the Awards."

Caleb nodded and turned his attention to the television screen where he expected to see the nation's celluloid glitterati toasting each other with music, dancing, film clips, awards, speeches, and magnanimous applause.

Instead, the television cameras showed a bedraggled master of ceremonies, sweat pouring down his face, as he leaned against the podium and watched a breathless actress stuffed into a black Flamenco dress make a rushed introduction on a poorly lit stage.

Chapter 7

Raymond stood stock still in the cramped hotel room. He was facing out an open window into a quiet clothing market that sprawled along the back alley.

Three women squatted on steps behind their tables. As they rearranged their shirts, undergarments, and other merchandise, they gabbed among themselves. At a nearby table, a man bent over his sewing machine, his fingers working nimbly at his trade.

Direct sunlight didn't reach the little market scene, but all the colorful surfaces and varied textures were well illuminated by reflected light.

He listened to the shower running in his room's private bath. Li Wei was going about her preparations in a business-like way, not unlike a vendor selling her wares.

She had laid a plastic sheet over the single bed and dribbled warm water over it and asked him to position himself on it before putting herself through the shower.

He had no more interest in having her naked body slide over his than he had in buying the items on sale below.

He wasn't in the buying mood.

The truth was, he was scared. His heart was pounding. For the first time, he came to the absolute realization that he was alone. Nobody else would find and rescue his family. But he was so far from civilization as he knew it, that his chances of survival, and by extension their chances of freedom, were virtually non-existent.

He needed help.

"Mister, are you ready?" Li Wei called from the shower.

He hadn't stripped down. He hadn't splayed his limbs out on the plastic sheet. He stared at the small droplets of water that collected in the wrinkles of the plastic. It was as far from lovemaking as one could get.

Carolyn preferred percale sheets in summer and flannel in winter. They had found cozy repose under a down comforter each night for ten years. Sometimes naked, sometimes not. Sometimes frisky, sometimes just happy to be in each other's arms.

Steam was billowing from the partially open bathroom door. Inside was a foggy mirror.

He was with a hooker, and a minor no less. The police could barge in the door at any moment. He could be thrown into a Chinese prison! How would that help him find his family?

Okay, so he was not cut out to be a fugitive, to assume other identities, to make every moment part of a living lie. He wasn't like that. He was a forthright guy who wanted to do the right thing. And this certainly wasn't the path he wanted to take.

Li Wei's small black purse lay on the desk. He couldn't take her money. But that's what he needed. Cash.

He pulled away from the window and padded across the tile floor to the desk. From there he could see through the crack in the bathroom door clear through to the shower, revealing Li Wei's form as she soaped down behind the shower curtain. For a young woman, she was exceptionally well endowed.

He unfastened the snap to her purse.

"I'm thinking about making love to you," she called.

He cleared his throat. "Right."

He slipped a hand into the opening in the purse and found a wad of cash. He pulled out the money, which was held together by a rubber band.

"Are you feeling sexy?" she called. She leaned over and her hands spread the soap bubbles down to her toes.

He sighed. "Sure."

But this wasn't for him. He could envision the police breaking down the door at any moment.

"I have no hair," she said. "We come from a special people, and we have no hair."

"Oh."

Okay, how could he let her down gracefully and not let his manhood get in his way?

He put the purse back in its former position and stepped away from the bathroom. He slipped off the rubber band and did a rough estimate of the money. There were two five-hundred RMB bills. Impressive! Several fifties, some twenties, and a five.

There must be real money in this business.

He shoved the wad in his pants pocket. God, his member was getting aroused by the whole scene.

But his thoughts were cold and calculated.

"Bye, honey," he whispered, stepping past the bathroom door. She was just turning off the shower and stepping out onto the bathroom floor.

"Mister?"

He shot her a smile but kept on walking.

Her wet feet pursued him. "I'm all clean now," she said. "I'm ready for you—"

He swung the room door open and stepped into the corridor.

"What are you doing, mister?"

Geez, she was following him into the hallway.

He turned and headed down the staircase.

"Wait a minute!"

He turned at the first landing and saw her leaning over the banister with a look of bewilderment on her pretty face, her towel wrapped around her hair. It was probably a major blow to her timid ego.

"Take the money and run," he muttered.

His feet carried him down to the next landing.

He didn't hear her calling any longer, but footsteps were padding down the staircase above him.

He calculated fast. The two five-hundreds could get him a one-way plane ticket to Beijing. He was feeling pretty good about himself.

The matron in the pink silk jacket approached him.

"Is there any problem, sir?"

"No. None whatsoever."

Several people standing in line to check out turned to look past him.

"Mister!" Li Wei screeched from the last landing. "Where are you going?"

He looked over his shoulder and saw her leaning over, her white breasts with their cherry nipples swinging free, her ivory legs spread out defiantly. "You come back here."

He glanced around the crowded lobby for the white uniform. The skipper wasn't there to observe the scene.

He needed a cab, and fast, before the young woman streaked out onto the street.

"You pay this girl," the matron nagged him from behind.

Customers were laughing in the crowded reception area.

"Mister!"

He needed a cab to the airport. He hurried through the sliding glass doors and out into the gushing sound of traffic. He blinked in the brilliant sunlight.

"This way, sir," a low, male voice directed him. "Will you step this way, please?"

His first thought was that it belonged to his guardian angel, the American diplomat who had come to save him at the airport in Beijing. But no. He detected a Chinese accent.

He turned to see who the speaker was. It was the hotel doorman, shoving him into a waiting cab.

"Thank you."

He hopped into the tiny red car and closed the door. And there sat the bearded skipper.

"What the—?"

Then he felt the point of a knife in his side and looked down. The skipper's fist held a silver stiletto designed to easily penetrate a human body.

He had been snatched back.

His hopes of getting to Beijing that day were rapidly diminishing.

The taxi took off, and he felt himself pressed involuntarily back against the cold tip of the knife.

He sucked in his breath. He felt like a pinball ricocheting from captor to captor, occasionally glimpsing his own freedom, only to be shot back up the board for the lowlifes of the world to play around with.

The cabbie sped through the streets like he was trying to avoid a bomb he had just planted. Raymond gripped the armrest on the door to steady himself and keep the knife's point from penetrating his skin. Then he saw them passing by the loading cranes of the port.

"Are you *the* Raymond O. Flowers?" the bearded man asked at last.

Raymond turned to him. The guy had a big grin on his face. This wasn't supposed to happen.

"I have no idea who you're talking about."

The skipper held up the VISA card he had left with the hotel receptionist. "It sure looks right to me."

Raymond hesitated, gritting his teeth. Would acknowledging his identity, particularly because of his situation as a political time bomb for the Administration, to an enemy of the United States constitute an act of treason?

If the terrorists didn't kill him, the Feds would.

The stiletto's point began probing his skin, leaving behind a burning sensation.

With the sharp tip less than an inch from his kidneys in the back of a veering tin can, he didn't have much time to reason this out. The thought of bleeding to death on the floor of a taxicab in the People's Republic of China was bad enough.

But he gave it one last effort. "I don't know who you're talking about. That's not my name."

The skipper's bearded face wrinkled with humor and he emitted a laugh. Then he reached for his cell phone and placed a call. It took mere seconds for the connection to go through. Then the skipper let a torrent of Arabic loose. The only term Raymond could identify was the name Dr. Ayman al-Zawahiri. Wasn't he al-Qaeda's Number Two?

He collapsed in exhaustion, but the knife relaxed with him. He was under no threat of being knifed in the back seat of a cab. Suddenly, it became all too apparent. He was more than a terrorist's pawn, a Westerner to behead, a passport for the skipper to climb the terrorist ladder of success. He was the mother of all hostages! He was the Chinagate witness. They wouldn't harm him for anything.

It was the Feds who wanted him dead. And they might even put treason on the long laundry list of his existing charges.

Once Raymond got his family back, where would they live? In a cave in Tora Bora? Maybe his family didn't need him so bad. Unless they wanted to visit him in jail once a month.

The bearded skipper clicked off his phone and looked at him.

"I am now your new best friend," he said, his thick lips fixed in a smile.

"You're not going to use me against the President."

"At this point, why rely on your President? He would have you rubbed out if he could."

It might be true, but he hated it. "You know, I am trying to resist your coercion, and I'm not a willing accomplice."

"Oh, no. I can see that."

"Just for the record..."

"Of course not. I understand," the man said with a clever grin.

Raymond had nothing left to assuage his battered pride, other than, "At least stealing and cheating for the President is nothing compared with what you've probably got in mind."

"And what is that?"

Raymond gestured to the cell phone. "What you just discussed with al-Zawahiri."

"We discussed nothing. We'll just have to wait. Communication is very tricky, you know," he confided.

Raymond looked out the window as they left the outskirts of the city and headed up a verdant mountainside. Should he tell this man about his family? That he was on the cusp of finding them alive? A play for the man's sympathy could only help.

"You know, I have a family," Raymond said.

"I have a family, too," the skipper responded without feeling.

"I haven't seen them since spring."

"I haven't seen mine since last year," the skipper said. There was no sympathy to be found there.

"Someone has kidnapped them," Raymond said. "I was just trying to get to Beijing to find them."

The skipper furrowed his brow in thought. He had a high, smooth forehead that seemed capable of thoughts beyond wicked schemes.

"I have a proposition," the man said at last. "You work with me, and I'll help you find your family."

Raymond tried to weigh the options. Resist the terrorists, get brutally beaten up, and hope that Uncle Sam forgives him once he is finally rescued by an undercover commando raid?

Or play along with the terrorists until they slipped up and he could escape.

"You wouldn't help me find my family."

"You don't know the powerful resources at our disposal," the skipper replied cryptically. "After all, we found *you*."

Raymond had to concede that point. He looked out the window. They were still heading away from the port where he had swum ashore. He didn't know where the hell they were. He was entirely at their mercy

"Okay, I'll help you if you help me," he said at last.

He tried to look at the situation from the skipper's perspective.

Theoretically, blackmailing the President of the United States was a no-brainer. In practice, however, working out the logistics would not be so easy. The skipper needed to establish secure lines of communication directly to the White House. Beyond that, they had to establish their credibility. Most likely that would involve sending some photographic proof of his captivity.

He closed his eyes. How could he think like a terrorist?

There was a time when he did wish great harm on somebody. When he would have derived pleasure from someone else's fear. If he could get his hands on Core Petroleum's chief executives, he would wring their necks as they cried out for mercy.

Oh yes, he was capable of blinding anger. His thoughts traveled back to the return plane flight to Baltimore-Washington where his rage had first surfaced.

He dwelled for a minute on his acrimonious fallout with his company that wouldn't authorize him and his family to flee the SARS epidemic until he closed the Chinagate deal. It was a sweet deal for everybody involved and mostly above board. The U.S. Trade Representative had granted China various World Trade Organization concessions, thereby winning numerous huge contracts for American oil companies in China. That was all aboveboard. The kickback that his company had made him facilitate between the Chinese and the President's personal offshore bank account was the illegal part.

He had been operating outside the law the moment he closed the Chinese deal with the President. But, had he not done so, his family would have risked languishing forever in SARS-ridden Beijing. His company had forced his hand.

But that had turned him into a walking time bomb for the Administration...and a potential bonanza for someone like the bearded young man. This guy could milk the President for money, concessions, and an easing on the war on terrorism for years to come. He had no interest in helping Raymond find his family.

Once again his thoughts turned to escape. He still had those five-hundred yuan notes in his pocket.

He eyed his door handle and fingered the latch. But the knife instantly broke through his damp shirt and penetrated his skin. He froze, his muscles tense.

So much for the terrorist being his best friend.

"How about we find my family first?"

The skipper didn't seem in a negotiating mood. In fact, he seemed downright unfriendly.

"Or later. Whatever."

The taxi was rocketing around slow-moving trucks that delivered goods from the mainland to the mountainous interior of the island. Where in the world were they going?

Attorney General Caleb Perkins glanced past the President around the East Room of the White House. The large, rectangular room was lined with movie posters of American idols, a departure from the room's traditional use as a venue for formal parties, receptions, and dances. Behind an arrangement of tropical ferns, a Marine quintet was softly blowing on their horns. The warm, subdued lighting put Caleb at ease and made him feel at home.

By that time next year, it would be *his* home, damn it.

To Caleb's surprise, President White singled him out and drew him to a quiet corner. "I'm not in much of a party mood," the President confided, his voice conveying anxiety.

"Why's that?" Caleb asked. "It's party time. You've successfully navigated the shoals of three years as Chief Executive. It's about time you enjoyed the job."

Was there no end to his duplicity, he wondered about himself. Like a caravan wandering blindly in a sandstorm, surviving in Washington meant treading with agility on the shifting sands of loyalty. Should the President falter, Caleb would be the first to trample over his corpse and announce his candidacy. In the meantime, he would play the Party stalwart and buck up the President, who, incidentally, was acting peculiar, even vulnerable, that evening.

"I doubt I'll be around next year," Bernard admitted, eyeing the group as if a spy might be lurking in their midst. He lowered his voice. "Is Stanley Polk making much progress against me?"

"I wouldn't know. They haven't requested any of our resources. I don't know if a single agent is looking for Flowers."

"But if one did find Flowers..."

"I'm afraid my men would have to turn him over to the special prosecutor's office."

Bernard nodded, looking sick.

"However, I am aware of an Agency-contracted operation beating the bushes on your behalf," Caleb said, remembering his phone call from Harry Black. "And I am in touch with them."

"Have they found Flowers?"

Caleb looked around the room to make sure nobody was eavesdropping.

"Slipped through their fingers," he said.

Bernard looked like he was going to be physically sick.

At that moment, William Ford, the oily Party chairman, returned with a glass of champagne for Caleb. He made no attempt to hide a broad grin on his face.

"What's new?" Caleb asked.

"Not much," Ford said smugly. "The President just foiled another terrorist plot. Cheers."

"Where?" Caleb shot out.

"Oh, at the Academy Awards. It appears that some Arab journalists smuggled in a bomb to disrupt the ceremony. But our boys took care of that," he said, smacking Bernard across the shoulders. "We won't be hearing from that band of terrorists again."

"Oh, really?" Caleb said. "And which band was that?"

"Apparently some arm of al-Qaeda operating here in the United States. They say Osama bin Laden was on the phone with the ransom demand. Said he wanted prisoners released from Guantánamo Bay and Saddam released." Ford laughed, and the President laughed weakly with him.

The breezy tone in which Ford was imparting this earth shattering news made Caleb's head spin.

"But Bernard stepped up to the plate," Ford continued in a loud voice, "and hammered the ball out of the park."

Mechanically, Caleb clinked champagne flutes with Ford. He took a very deep drink. It was another coup for the President's war on terrorism. The President was a hero once more.

He walked off in a daze. Surely the President's popularity would rise after foiling al-Qaeda once again. Worse, the press might begin to point fingers at him and the FBI for letting the terrorists infiltrate so far. He shook his head at his rapidly diminishing prospects for higher office.

His mind turned to darker alternatives, and ultimately to his phone conversation with Harry Black. His only hope lay in the Chinagate investigation succeeding. But how could he help Stanley Polk prosecute the President? Should he volunteer to assist the special prosecutor by deploying agents to find Flowers?

Trading in his glass at the beverage table, he stared hard at the

President who had turned away. Was he capable of stabbing the President in the back?

"What can I get you, Mr. Attorney General?" the bartender asked.

"A rattlesnake," he said.

Here he was searching for ways to bring down the President as the guy was successfully foiling al-Qaeda plots to secure the nation. Caleb had thought of himself as aggressive, but never disloyal.

Nevertheless, he was beginning to feel aggrieved by fate.

His eye caught an intern easing her way in a slinky cocktail dress between party guests.

"Hey, Lori," he called out.

She winked at him. What a floozy.

Offering to help the special prosecutor would lose him his job. There had to be a more underhanded way of bringing down the President.

"Here's your whiskey, sir."

Caleb took a swig of the cold drink.

Lori was making her way toward him, a smile on her lips.

Aw, hell. He felt a physical rush of pleasure flooding his groin. If she needed him, he would relent.

She could bring any man to his knees.

Then, just over her shoulder he caught a glimpse of the President turning his statesmanlike profile to follow her swaying tush.

"Any man to his knees," Caleb breathed.

Lori stopped before him, the look of a vixen on her face.

But his thoughts were elsewhere.

"What's wrong?" she asked.

He could envision the President caught screwing a luscious young intern. The headlines would sink him faster than the Titanic.

What kind of soldier stabbed his own general in the back during a military campaign?

"Why the frown?" Lori asked, reaching toward him and gently massaging his temples with the tips of her fingers.

The President was still looking at them, his eyes narrow with jealousy and lust.

Suddenly Caleb had an intoxicating idea beyond that of defeating Bernard White. Stronger than winning the Presidency. It was screwing the President's girl on Lincoln's bed.

Then a shiny object caught his eye. He pried her long fingers away from him and examined her ring finger. She was wearing the most enormous diamond he'd ever seen.

"Where did you get that?" he asked, his voice cracking.

At that moment the President approached her from behind. Unannounced, he leaned his bushy white head of hair over her shoulder and whispered in her ear.

She giggled and turned toward him. The President's arms fell naturally around her waist.

"Haven't you heard?" she said, tossing Caleb a wholesome smile. "We're engaged."

CHINA GATE

The Manhunt

Chapter 8

Hadi Ahmed was nearly out of breath, having hustled the entire way up the mountain pass. Mortar shells launched by the Pakistani Army were landing on the far slopes of the neighboring valley. They were nowhere close to Osama's lair, but striking near enough to Hadi's home village to cause alarm.

He hadn't seen his family for over a week, and he was worried sick; but this mission was far too important to cut short. His earnings would keep his wife and three daughters fed for a year and allow him to install electricity in his humble home. His son could have those teeth pulled that were causing so much pain...

He tried to take his mind off his personal problems. He was engaged in a great *jihad* against the American Crusaders.

Daylight was just seeping out of the cloud-laden sky across the valley as he mounted the last few handholds up to Osama's headquarters, the tiny cave that held so much promise for Muslims around the world.

"I have news for the venerable one," he said between gasps for air.

Once again, the barrel of the assault rifle drew back the dusty sheepskin.

Hadi removed his Pathan hat and bent his compact frame even lower to enter. As before, a fire warmed the cave, but Hadi was already sweating from his run.

He glanced around the room and was surprised to see that there were twice as many associates seated around Allah's right hand than before. He fell to his knees before Osama and rocked forward until his forehead touched the cave floor. The surface smelled rancid from old meat and was coated with dust. What these people needed was a woman's touch around the place.

"I have great news for you, Allah be praised," he began.

He looked up and saw that he had the assembly's full attention.

"Raymond O. Flowers is ours!"

Osama clasped his hands together and offered a short, personal prayer to Allah. When he opened his eyes, his fervor had turned to practical matters. "Does my cousin have him?"

"Yes. According to his last transmission to your deputy, he is taking the heathen sacrifice to his ship."

A chorus of cheers arose from the entire group. They had clearly been primed for that moment. Their attention turned immediately to their leader, the great lion of the desert.

Hadi rested back on the seat of his pants and tried to keep his eyes from straying to the kabobs they had stacked beside the fire.

The conversation immediately lapsed into Arabic, a language with which he was unfamiliar. Perhaps they were trying to keep him from overhearing their deliberations. Yet, none of them was Afghan or Pakistani. He was in a den of foreigners, men with far greater knowledge of the world.

In the end, Osama turned directly to him, and he put aside all his wandering thoughts.

"It is Allah's wish that my cousin leave the area immediately. He should take the sacrifice to the open sea and proceed in the direction of where he will conduct his raid. Once at sea, he will contact the lair of all evil, the White House, and demand a ransom of US$20 million. My deputy will work out the details."

Money? So this was all about money?

"I beg to ask you, most honorable leader of Allah's *jihad*," he said, unable to stop himself. "But is all this effort just for money?"

Osama did not have to answer the question. He could have cut out Hadi's tongue for asking it. But he didn't. Hadi watched with awe as the great man paused to set him straight.

"Young guide," Osama said, using the translation of Hadi's name in English. "Money is just the beginning. Once the great heathen takes the bait, he will be ours."

"Ours for what?"

The room looked away in silent rebuke of his insolence.

"Ours to release our martyrs in prison. Ours to flood the world with fresh *jihad*. Ours to tear down the secular Muslim governments of the world one by one."

That sounded more like it. It was all for *jihad*.

"Thank you, my master," Hadi said, newly inspired.

The group seemed jolted by the power of the message as well. Hadi touched his forehead to the ground once more, then quickly rose and slipped out of the cave.

A final ray of sunlight penetrated between two clouds. It was a sign of good fortune for Hadi, his family, and the coming of Islam.

Carolyn Flowers' labor contractions were hitting hard and fast. She couldn't remember for the life of her what the breathing patterns should be. Raymond had stood by her side, holding her hand and stroking her hair during the birth of her first two children. They had practiced the patterns beforehand and his steady voice had calmed her as she breathed through her contractions five and seven years ago.

But she hadn't heard from her husband for over eight months, and for all she knew, he had been forced into a different SARS ward and perhaps succumbed there. She didn't want to think those thoughts. She wanted Raymond to see their baby that was on its way.

She clenched her fists as a new pain wracked her body. She clutched the rusty bed frame beneath the thin pad that passed for a mattress in the medical examination room.

This whole childbirth scene was going to be fairly primitive. Mercifully, her lower abdomen relaxed, so she could let go of the bed frame and rub her sore arms.

Paint had peeled from the cement walls, and a malignant rust stain had spread across the entire metal ceiling. There were no midwives present to guide her through the process. She let out a short laugh; at least the hospital bills would be minimal this time around.

The old Chinese doctor looked back over his shoulder at her, concern magnified in his eyes by his thick glasses. He was the entire maternity shift. And he probably hadn't delivered a baby in fifty years. Besides, she sighed, natural childbirth was rarely practiced in China any longer. She was surprised that, months before, the old guy hadn't suggested a caesarian and picked out an auspicious date for the operation.

Her muscles began to clench from the bottom up, at last gripping her chest, arms, and shoulders. It's for you, baby, she thought. I'm doing this for you, she told the unborn child.

"God, Raymond, where are you?" she cried, her fingers gripping the bed frame like a vise.

The delirium passed after a couple of minutes, and she found herself panting like a dog. Her hospital gown was saturated with sweat despite the icy room.

She frowned at the blue gown spread over her like a tablecloth. Don't let the editors at *Vogue* see her like that. They would be horrified. But she would gladly give up her fashion design career if she could only deliver this one baby safely, this one more affirmation of life.

Then, as the doctor rummaged through his medicine cabinet for painkillers, she began to wonder. Maybe the baby wasn't just an extension of Raymond's love and being. Maybe he had died of SARS, and the baby was just his replacement.

All of a sudden, she regarded her expanded abdomen with horror. She didn't want the baby. She only wanted Raymond.

The final paroxysms of labor were striking now, taking over her body every sixty seconds.

The room spun around, and she lost track of the details. Her only focus was on the corner of the ceiling, the furthest horizon line she had seen in nearly a year. Except for that horrible SARS ward, with the coughing patients sleeping beside her children, the nurses being taken away with fevers, the nerve-wracking races across town wrapped like mummies in the backs of ambulances, the new wards, new doctors with fear in their eyes, the endless IV drips, the frantic search for the right cure.

She and her kids had entered the first respiratory ward healthy, but developed coughs almost immediately. Then came the fevers that they couldn't bring down.

She knew what was coming next. Jane and Sammy had contracted SARS. Then she had caught it, too.

Was Raymond in the next bed over? A different hospital? The statistics in the newspaper had shown that men his age were particularly vulnerable to dying of the disease.

The pains hit her once again. She lost control of her breathing. She should be grunting or something, helping the child along the birth canal. Instead, she found herself fighting it. Pushing back.

"Raymond!" she shouted between gasps. "Are you coming?"

The doctor turned away from the medicine cabinet. In one hand he held several long, thin needles. This was no time for acupuncture! What good was the old fart?

God she needed this to be over, no matter what the outcome. She didn't care. How could she still care about anything?

The doctor twirled a needle between his thumb and forefinger and bent closer. Carolyn clenched her eyes shut and felt the needle puncture the skin of her belly. God damn it. She was going to pop.

All her hope was rapidly vanishing.

She felt warm droplets rolling down her cheeks. She blinked several times in the ocean of tears. Her horizon had become blurred. She was losing consciousness.

The airplane swept Hiram and Tiffany and their merry band of travelers high over the City of Angels. The Airbus 340-300 felt agile in the air. Banking to the north, it afforded the passengers a stunning view of the famous HOLLYWOOD sign.

Just beyond the clearly visible, but dilapidated letters, a handful of searchlights raked the sky. The lights seemed to originate from a large, well-illuminated building.

"Dat's da Academy Awards," Hiram said, and turned excitedly to his wife.

Tiffany stared out the window. "What's that big ball of fire right next to it?"

Hiram shrugged. "Probably just some special effects."

Slight air turbulence lifted him momentarily off his seat. It gave him a jaunty feeling, just like the buzz he had gotten from the first free mimosa of the flight.

"Yee-haw!" he said, abandoning himself to the rollercoaster-like thrill of the flight. "Ain't dis gonna be some vacation."

Or was he being too reckless? Was he about to throw away his entire life's savings on a mere three weeks?

No, he reminded himself. The plan was calibrated to fit their budget. It was limited to a round-trip fare and three-week hotel stay. He wasn't paying for eternity in paradise.

The difference between what he could and couldn't afford bummed him for a minute. He couldn't buy eternal bliss. Sooner or later he would have to return to the snowy, traffic-choked streets of Jersey.

"Hey, cheer up," Tiffany said, her voice tinkling like the sound of her wedding ring against her champagne flute.

He let the dreaded thought of returning home pass. As they turned out to sea, it felt wonderful leaving the world behind. In fact, wasn't it okay to live for the moment? Wasn't that what vacations were all about? An escape from reality?

The ride was turning into more of an emotional than a physical rollercoaster for him.

A tiny overhead television flickered on, and the in-flight entertainment began. The featured movie was an attempt at a period piece, but looked more like a bunch of rollerbladers hanging out in historical costumes.

And the same people were handing out awards to themselves in Tinseltown that night.

But Tiffany seemed caught up in the movie, and wasn't about to take off her headset for a conversation.

He turned his reading light on, and pulled the Purang guidebook from her carryon bag. First, he glanced inside the back cover. The yellowed library sticker showed that it had only been checked out once. It gave him a thrill to imagine that he was about to venture into uncharted waters. Squirming contentedly in his seat, he began to read.

The history and geography of the island nation were fascinating, but only so, perhaps, for someone heading there.

A former British territory, apparently the British had misfiled it, and forgotten about it, so the island declared itself independent in 1957. It wasn't until 1986 that the United Nations got around to recognizing it as a sovereign state.

The language spoken there was English, and there was no official bird, flower, or anthem.

Built on an eroded volcanic outcropping five miles in diameter, the single island nation rose less than ten feet above sea level at its highest point. Its chief product was bamboo souvenirs. And the tourist industry was the nation's primary source of income.

Hiram yawned. It sounded just perfect to him.

The government was a moderate Muslim state, with many of the island's early inhabitants being native Polynesians and Bangladeshis who had worked on the British sugar plantation.

It was not easy to get his broad body comfortable in the narrow seat. How did tour groups fly all the way to Australia?

He turned sideways and leaned his head against Tiffany's, and drifted off to sleep, a satisfied smile on his lips.

❖ ❖ ❖

The sun resembled a glowing mango as it slid behind the fronds of coconut palms. The trees lined a small one temple, one mosque port on the western rim of Hainan Island.

A motorized fishing boat was waiting at a concrete pier.

"All aboard," the skipper ordered.

The skipper no longer held the knife to his back. But then, there was nowhere for Raymond to run in the sleepy village. He looked down at the clear water. It was carried on a strong current from Vietnam. Jumping in would get him nowhere.

He was forced to heed the skipper's command.

A dark-skinned seaman scrambled to release the bow and stern lines while the skipper pushed Raymond into the stern. The residue of squid and octopus catches squished underfoot. The skipper tucked his stiletto into a tooled leather sheath and stood guard beside his quarry. His eyes didn't attempt to intimidate Raymond into submission. Instead, they seemed to empathize with his plight.

Then the three men set out across the choppy water. From his position behind the wheelhouse, Raymond could see an empty horizon.

The trip took fifteen minutes as they followed the curve of the shore.

Just as the sun dipped into the water, they churned to a halt before the dark prow of a rusty freighter.

The ship was a disgrace. Old paint flaked off her hull.

"Is this your ship?" Raymond asked, unable to keep the disdain from his voice.

The skipper nodded, unfazed. He motioned for Raymond to scale the steps of the metal accommodation ladder.

He complied, but with each rusty rung he climbed, it felt like he was entering a floating crypt. The ship should have been overhauled years ago. From the creak of her hull to the filthy smell emanating from below deck, he knew that she was living on borrowed time. She should have been sold for scrap years before. How could inspectors continue to grant licenses to such ships?

The fishing boat pulled away, leaving Raymond on deck with the skipper and a handful of standoffish men, a mosaic of nationalities, and assumed identities, he was sure.

A white-uniformed man greeted the skipper as soon as he set foot on deck. "A fax just arrived from headquarters, sir."

"Wait here," the skipper told Raymond. "And don't try jumping overboard again. It would be a very long swim."

He disappeared in the cadaverous ship's superstructure, and Raymond turned to watch the final sliver of the sun slip into the sea.

He could remember only one moment quieter than the moment at hand. On a still evening in late May, he had watched grave diggers in Maryland lower Carolyn, Jane, and Sammy's ashes into the rich, black soil.

Standing along a distant cemetery drive, the local and national press had kept their distance. Raymond's family represented a rare case of SARS deaths among Americans, while the disease continued to rage unchecked in China. He could still hear their shutters snapping.

Clad in a black suit, he had cut a solitary figure before the gravesite, his oil firm knowing better than to extend its sympathies at that time. Representatives of the White House were also notably absent. Nobody wanted to be associated with their deaths. And, having been raised an orphan and having raised his kids overseas, he didn't expect anyone to show up and commemorate their lives.

The clank of footsteps approached him from behind.

"You're one of us now," the skipper said softly. "Stateless and free. Here is your new passport."

Raymond flipped open the blue American passport. His photo had been carefully removed from his own passport and pasted into the new one. Beside his face read a new name, "Robert Block."

"How would you like to join our movement, Mr. Block, and work your way up?" the skipper offered. "You've got potential. With your American accent, you could go a long way."

Raymond had never considered listing his accent on his résumé. But he did appreciate the attempt to make him feel at home.

"Think it over," the skipper said, turning to leave. "Fire up the engines."

Suddenly, Raymond became aware that he was not completely alone. The silent pirates on deck created a chill in the air. "Uh, where are you going?"

"I have to send a fax to the White House," the skipper said over his shoulder.

"Oh," Raymond said. As darkness fell, the men wouldn't dare to harm the goose that laid the golden egg. He was al-Qaeda's new, number one bargaining chip.

The decrepit ship shuddered to life under his bare feet, and he saw black smoke begin to puff out of her twin funnels.

And, as the anchor chain clanked back into the bowels of the ship, they steamed southward, destination unknown, the fading twilight glowing purple against the Chinese rooftops behind them. And with the receding shoreline, his hopes of finding his family diminished by the second.

"Don't worry," he whispered to Carolyn, to Jane, and to Sammy. "I'll come back for you guys."

When his gaze returned to the ship, he saw that several deckhands were edging closer to him.

Of course they'd have to be friendly and treat him well. But then, gang rape hadn't crossed his mind.

Attorney General Caleb Perkins woke up in a foul mood.

He had spent a listless night alone in the Lincoln Bedroom. The actual experience of sleeping on Lincoln's bed wasn't anywhere near as satisfying as he had dreamed it would be, especially since he had fallen asleep knowing that Lori was buried in the President's arms just down the hall.

He rose before dawn that Saturday morning, and immediately shaved and showered in the room's private bath. He dug out a fresh pair of briefs and a starched shirt from his travel bag and quickly climbed back into his business attire.

He rushed out into the hallway just as a White House steward was passing by.

The man wheeled about in surprise, and then quickly recovered himself. "Would you care for an eye opener?"

"No, I'm fine," Caleb replied. It was too early for a drink, even for him. And besides, he didn't have the time.

He needed to get to a secure phone in the West Wing before the weekend staffers arrived. It was payback time, time to play hardball with the President, time to take matters into his own hands.

No matter how hard he tried to rationalize it, he had changed his mind. He would assign some field agents to find Flowers for the special prosecutor. He was going to dig up the key witness and sink the President once and for all in the Chinagate affair.

It was a long walk from wing to wing in the executive mansion, for a long time the largest residence in America. So when he finally reached the Oval Office, he was out of breath.

To his surprise, some lights were already turned on. Gertrude, the President's elderly secretary, had driven to the office from her Montgomery County home to finish up work that had piled up during the week. At the moment Caleb entered the office, she was bent over the fax machine that was printing out an incoming message.

"Is that for me?" he asked, trying to gain her favor with a smile.

Her stony, not-amused expression didn't change.

"Is anyone here to respond to the fax?" he asked, trying to determine if they were alone. The other offices down the hall looked dark.

She was a blank wall.

"Oh, I see," he said. "You're here on a personal matter."

The scarcely veiled accusation by the chief attorney of the United States that she was misappropriating government resources had some effect, and her wrinkled cheeks blushed bright red.

"No, it's not for me. It's just that the Chief of Staff has to look over all the President's correspondence before anyone else."

"...and is Chuck here?"

"No."

He took the paper from her hands and looked it over.

The letterhead was typeset in a sweeping backwards script, probably Arabic. But the message was printed out in English, terse and clear.

"Deliver $20 million to account number 2834457 at the Royal Bank of Riyadh, or I will turn Raymond O. Flowers over to the prosecutor."

The typed signature read, "Osama bin Laden."

Holding the fax, Caleb's fingers turned cold. His knees grew weak. He was looking at a blackmail threat, plain and simple. The world's Number One terrorist organization had struck again. This time right in the middle of the White House. They were using Chinagate to extort money directly from the President. The scumbags!

But did they really have Raymond O. Flowers in their possession? Nothing about the letter indicated proof of his captivity. Then he thought back to Harry Black's phone call the previous night from Atlanta. Someone else had abducted Flowers right from under the CIA contractors' noses. Who else but the captors would know that Flowers was taken?

He stared once again at the typed signature. Osama bin Laden.

Was the President going to negotiate with the terrorist chief? If

Bernard White transferred money to the terrorists' bank account in Saudi Arabia, then he was not only giving in to blackmail, he was digging himself even deeper into a pit.

He felt himself inadvertently licking his lips. The FBI would really have a case against the President then. What more could he ask for? With a little fancy footwork, he could have all the evidence he needed to hold over the President's head. If his men could monitor the bank account in Riyadh, they might come up with the most incriminating evidence against Bernard White of all.

He needed the account number to make his calls and set his plan into motion.

"Gertrude, dear, would you photocopy this fax for me?" he requested.

Which she did with all the professionalism her duties as the nation's First Secretary demanded.

A minute later, he took the copy and repaid her with a smile. "I suggest you contact Chuck Romer on this matter right away," he said. He folded his copy of the fax, slipped it into the inside pocket of his suit coat, and turned on his heels to leave the White House.

He would get Harry Black to document the President's transfer of twenty million dollars into the terrorists' bank account in Riyadh. Then he would send the evidence directly to Stanley Polk and seal the Chinagate case. He had a plan of action. The President was going down, down, down.

Chapter 9

Chuck Romer, the White House Chief of Staff, had to drive through a snowstorm to get to 1600 Pennsylvania Avenue. His wheels slid as he wove through slow traffic and stalled vehicles. The slushy snow lying on a foundation of ice had paralyzed the streets of the nation's capital.

But he was in a hurry and had to take a few risks to get to the White House in time. Gertrude's call from the West Wing had turned his blood to ice. He would have to get to that fax from bin Laden before anybody else.

"Is it a peace deal?" he had asked her hopefully.

"No," she had responded. "Let's just say that he's demanding money. A great deal of it."

Through the blur left on his windshield by overworked wipers, Chuck tried to make out the grooves of tire tracks in the snow. Was the terrorist group changing their tactics, escalating the war, sending over more hijackers? And now they were tying their terrorist actions to specific concessions. That was an eventuality he had hoped would never come about, leaving blood on the hands of the American President if he didn't comply. He had to destroy that fax before it was made public.

For security reasons, parking at the White House was no longer allowed. He would have to park in one of the staff parking lots that encircled the Ellipse. He cursed as he stepped from his car directly into a puddle of melted ice.

He ran under the snow-lined trees, holding his briefcase over his head. How humiliating if the American public saw him like that.

He could hear the chants of protestors in the distance, holding vigil day and night outside the White House. Their chant was clear, "Two Four Six Eight. We don't want no Chinagate."

What morons.

He dug his security badge out of his pocket and held it up for the guard at the black, wrought iron fence.

"You have to wear that thing," the guard said, shivering.

"Just let me through," Chuck snapped. The Secret Service didn't know the meaning of the word security, if al-Qaeda had resorted to blackmailing the President.

But what kind of explosion was bin Laden contemplating next? Did he have a bomb under Washington? The threat alone could leave the entire nation unnerved and bring the capital's business to a sudden halt.

The locked gate buzzed and he entered the grounds of the White House.

He was still brushing snowflakes off his trench coat when he reached Gertrude's workstation just outside the President's office.

He motioned at the closed door of the Oval Office. "Is the President…?"

"No," she said. "Still asleep as far as I know."

That was a relief. He held out his hand for the fax.

She laid it in his palm and turned away, presumably to indicate her disinterest in the subject matter.

His identity badge swung over the sheet as he leaned to sit down opposite her.

Cursing, he whipped the chain over his shoulder and stared at the words.

The fax asked for twenty million dollars; otherwise Raymond O. Flowers would be handed over to the Chinagate special prosecutor.

Then, involuntarily, he found himself laughing. The bastard wasn't threatening mass destruction. And his demands were for a paltry twenty million. What kind of amateurs was he dealing with?

Then he focused on bin Laden's threat. "I will turn Raymond O. Flowers over to the special prosecutor."

Ha! He'd take Flowers any day. Send him Flowers today, and Chuck would have him eliminated once and for all. The Chinagate charade had gone on long enough.

Okay bin Laden, baby. Send me Flowers!

Eventually, his humor wore thin, and more rational thoughts entered his mind. Bin Laden would never surrender Flowers. That was the whole point about terrorism. Terrorists weren't like normal hostage takers or blackmailers. They didn't want something specific in return. That was the theory that Neal Jacobs, the Director of Counterterrorism, had explained during a White House briefing the previous summer. It wasn't that negotiating with terrorists would embolden them to perform acts of greater violence. It was that the terrorists weren't really negotiating at all.

But what if Bernard White did pay the ransom and bin Laden threatened to make the ransom payment public? There was no end to the devastation the bastard could wreak on the United States, not to mention all of their political careers. The Chinagate imbroglio was getting too far out of hand. It was a Beltway game that played right into the hands of terrorists.

It was time to bring in another player to wipe out all the pieces on the game board. Unable to negotiate with the terrorists, he would let the CIA eliminate the Chinagate problem once and for all. He strode briskly into his office and consulted his Rolodex. Did the Director of Counterterrorism take weekends off?

A seasoned CIA hand, Neal Jacobs was indeed at his office in Langley, and took the call immediately. It appeared that the Counterterrorism Director charged with defending Americans around the world never slept.

Chuck cleared his throat. "I can see that your operation to eliminate Raymond O. Flowers has failed."

"How did you know?"

"Recent evidence suggests that Flowers is acting in collusion with known terrorists and is operating out of southern China." Man, he was good, turning Flowers into a national security threat, giving the CIA legal grounds for eliminating him. "The President wants you to deploy ships to patrol the waters there, and increase agents in the major cities of Southeast Asia."

"What specific information are you acting on?" Neal asked, clearly dubious. "If this is a smear campaign against Flowers…"

Chuck felt his face burning. He ruminated for a moment. There was no way in hell he was going to share the fax with Neal.

"We have received backchannel word from terrorists that Flowers has joined their forces." It was a stretch, but not untrue.

"Why would they send you such information?"

By that point Chuck's face was beginning to prickle with heat.

"Just know that the President wants him captured."

"And...?" the Director said leadingly.

And eliminated, Chuck wanted to reply. But he stopped himself short of saying it. Boy, he was wading in treacherous waters, particularly since he was no student of the law. "To testify, of course."

He had to make himself better understood. He would obliquely bring in the covert contract job that the Agency was running to put Flowers on ice.

"I'd like your new assets to work hand in hand with whatever assets you already have on the ground. Their mission is virtually the same."

"Okay, now I think I read you. Whether he testifies or not, you still want him off the streets," Neal said. "But as far as I see it, Flowers didn't perpetrate the Chinagate crimes as part of some elaborate act of terrorism against the United States. I don't see how this links to terrorism."

Chuck wasn't out of the woods yet.

"I can't speak for the motivations of such a man. All I know is we need to get the Pentagon behind this initiative. The President is calling for an all-out blitz."

That seemed good enough for the Director. After all, who was he to contradict an executive order? And, he was hearing it from Chuck Romer, the right hand of God.

Chuck set down the phone with relief. If he was lucky, it would work, and an overt operation to get America's latest terrorist might bear fruit.

Now, all he had to do was scrounge up twenty million bucks. That was the easy part. He picked up the phone again and, from memory, punched in the number of William Ford, chairman of the Party's national committee.

"What the—? Hello?"

"Good morning, William," Chuck said.

"Who the hell is calling this early?"

"It's Chuck at the White House."

"Oh yeah. Hey, what picture won the Oscar?"

"I don't know," Chuck replied. In fact, he hadn't even bothered to stay up and watch the grand finale at the awards presentation. "But I need your help."

"Yeah? Now that you've got my attention..."

"The President needs twenty million dollars from his re-election fund in order to cover some infrastructure costs."

There was a pause. Chuck began cursing himself for not getting a law degree.

"Okay," William said slowly. "Want it in hundreds?"

"No, nothing like that. Here's an account number to transfer it to." And he read off the number from the fax. He glanced around his office. Was there some tape recorder running?

"That's not enough," William said.

"What do you mean?"

"I need the number of the bank to route it to."

Chuck caught his breath. "I don't have the routing number."

"Just the name of the bank will do."

Chuck looked at the sheet of paper in his hands. "Let's just say it's the Royal Bank of Riyadh."

He could feel the silence on the other end of the line.

"Okay," William finally said. "Maybe you should get the Oscar for Best Actor next year."

Chuck hung up and leaned back in his chair. He had a tough job, but lying through his teeth to the Director of Counterterrorism and the Chairman of the Party's national committee took the cake.

Yeah, calling out the Army, Navy, and Marines to rub out that pesky Raymond O. Flowers and his terrorist band, along with eliminating the blackmail threat to the Oval Office, was all in a day's work.

It was amazing to Hiram that the tiny island nation of Purang had an airport at all.

Morning broke quickly for him and the other dozing passengers. The view that met his eyes as he pulled open his window shade was straight out of a travel brochure. Purang was a pancake-shaped island seemingly afloat in a shallow blue sea. They were descending rapidly toward an airstrip that occupied one end of the island. Passing over the land on the way, he could tell that the rest of the island was one big overgrown plantation with the occasional resort built along the beach and a small town mid-island.

White sand rimmed the isle, and that was fringed by palm trees and grassy vegetation. The water was a clear turquoise, and Hiram could see straight to the coral seabed.

The Airbus landed with a small jolt, awakening the other passengers.

"We're here," he told Tiffany, gently shaking his wife by the shoulders.

By the time the plane had taxied up to the small one-story terminal, all the passengers were awake and eagerly grabbing their carry-on luggage. Suddenly, there was a rush to be the first to jump off the plane. Hiram was no exception. He elbowed his way to the overhead compartment that contained his bag, shuffled his feet to orient himself toward the cockpit, and waited.

Tiffany clung to the strap of his shoulder bag. When the door opened, he began to move with the rest of the passengers. At the exit, he was met by a wall of heat that smelled like straw mats that had been drying in the sun. The eight a.m. sunlight met him straight in the eyes, and he had to shade his face to see his way down the metal stairway.

Passengers were walking in a straggly line toward the single building at the airport. A dark-skinned man in a khaki uniform stood inside and watched as they entered. Behind him, a hand-painted sign read "Baggage Claim."

"I guess we wait here," Hiram said. "Immigration wasn't much of a hassle."

"Why can't other countries be more like this?" Tiffany said wistfully.

Hiram could already tell that this was going to be just the vacation they needed.

Many of his fellow passengers had already kicked off their shoes and were stuffing their feet into sandals.

Some were pulling straw hats and sunglasses from their bags. The transition from overworked city dwellers to native islanders was nearly complete.

Two local boys hauled a wagon loaded with suitcases from the cargo bay. It rolled to a halt just short of the building, and passengers pushed their way outside once more to claim their belongings.

Hiram was among the first to pull his two suitcases from the teetering stack.

"C'mon, sweetie," he said, and marched toward an untidy line of decrepit white taxis, rejects from the American used-car market.

The first driver in line worked up his energy to heft the suitcases into the enormous trunk.

Hiram studied the 1970s-era Ford Custom 500. Its trunk was large enough to fit a family of four. "Boy," he remarked to the driver. "Dey don't make dem like dis any more."

The driver looked puzzled. "They don't?" His voice was somewhere between a British and a Hindi accent.

Hiram decided not to burst the man's bubble.

"Take us to da Sandalwood Resort," he said. He thought of asking if the man knew where it was, then realized how ridiculous the question would be to a man who had spent his entire life on the same four square mile island.

The taxi driver swayed around potholes on the uneven road, but kept the Ford going straight despite the fact that they were driving on the wrong side of the road. With a left-hand steering wheel and the car in the left lane, the driver was situated somewhere over the road's shoulder.

The drive took them past a lone fruit stand and dense fields of dry stalks. A butcher by profession, Hiram had hoped to see the local meat supply on hoof, but they were driving through walls of stalks that were higher than the roof of the car.

"What are dey growing here?" he asked the driver.

"Sugar cane."

Tiffany looked up at him. "They're raising cane."

He let out a broad, "Ha!"

The hardy crop spread beyond the fields and was in the process of choking out a cluster of buildings.

"This is our capital," the driver announced proudly.

It was also the only town on the island.

"There is our Ministry of Justice," the man said, pointing to a two-room police station. Presumably one room was the jail cell. "And there's our President's house."

Hiram did a double take. The cottage was a white wooden structure not unlike other houses on the single-road town. Its louvered windows looked out onto a broad patio that circled the house. Wicker chairs faced outward from the center. It wasn't exactly the White House.

"And here's our Embassy," the man said.

"What do you mean *your* Embassy," Tiffany asked. "This is your own country. Why would you have an Embassy in your own country?"

The man seemed puzzled. "This is the only Embassy we have," he tried to explain.

"But it isn't da Purang Embassy," Hiram said.

The man looked at him through the wide rear-view mirror. Obviously Hiram and Tiffany weren't getting it. The cement block building was their Embassy.

Then Hiram caught the words etched into the brass plate affixed to its closed front door. "American Embassy."

Oh. That clarified things.

There was no flag flying from the pole. Perhaps it wasn't occupied year round.

A street sign read 15 MPH. The driver took it at 10. It made the town seem larger than it actually was. Hiram took in the details with interest. There was the island's grocery store and post office all rolled into one. A mosque at either end of town.

Funny, the guidebooks didn't mention Islam's foothold on the island. Surely Christian missionaries had gotten there at some point. Hiram focused on the people milling around the larger mosque as they passed. The men didn't wear skullcaps, and the women's braided black hair was exposed to public view. They weren't exactly fundamentalists.

They passed a library on the outskirts whose granite columns seemed out of place among the clapboard siding and tin roofs of town. Well, at least if tourists got bored, they'd have something to read.

Tiffany looked charmed. Dazzling light reflected on the smile muscles of her cheeks. He envisioned her as Meryl Streep, a colonial landowner surveying her plantation. I had a farm in Purang...

Shortly, they entered a more natural landscape where the flora ranging from flowering bushes to stands of coconut palms that leaned out toward the sea.

Hiram could begin to imagine his wife wearing that surprise she had bought at Victoria's Secret and stashed out of sight. For the next three weeks, the tiny country would be their personal playground.

"And here is your hotel," the driver announced.

A carved wooden sign welcomed them to Sandalwood Resort. They drove over a wooden bridge with rope handrails and circled along a conch-lined drive through a forest of palms.

A portico made from locally harvested timber jutted out to meet them, and several porters stirred themselves inside.

They came to a halt, and Hiram peeled himself off the springy seat.

"What do I owe you, my good man?" he asked.

The driver scratched his head as if calculating the mileage. "That would be three dollars, sir."

"You take American?" Hiram asked.

The man looked confused. "No credit cards."

"No, I mean American greenbacks?"

The man looked even more uncomfortable.

Hiram pulled out a five and tentatively handed it to him.

"Thank you, sir," the driver said and took the money without hesitation.

"Er, keep da change."

Tiffany had rounded the taxi and was standing beside him while two porters whisked their luggage away. He closed his eyes and inhaled deeply. The lush tropical vegetation and pale timbers of the hotel had an exotic and pleasant smell.

"Sandalwood," Tiffany said, reading his mind.

The taxi prowled away and left the two standing alone.

"Shall we, my dear?" he offered, extending an elbow. She took it, and they entered the shaded lobby of the resort. Just beyond that, he could hear the promising sounds of splashing water and laughing people.

Chapter 10

After kissing Lori goodbye at the front door of the White House as she headed out to hail a cab, President Bernard White watched the ragtag group of protesters as they hurled insults from wintry Lafayette Park. If only he, too, could escape his marble prison and flee down the streets of his nation in a cab.

He waved at her as she slipped out the gate, and she tossed back a carefree smile. A second later, she was gone.

Bernard rubbed a forefinger over his lips that still tingled from the touch of her young lips. Did he know what he was getting into, getting hitched to a twenty-something fresh out of college? More importantly, did she know what it meant to marry the President of the United States?

"She's a good kid," a voice said behind him.

Bernard jumped. After three years in the White House, he still wasn't used to strangers creeping around his personal abode.

"Morning, Chuck," he muttered.

"With those poll figures slipping, it's about time to go public with your engagement," Chuck Romer hinted.

"She's not ready for it, yet," he said.

"Ready for what? Glamour, interviews, book deals, national politics, geopolitical psychodrama?"

"No. This," Bernard said, throwing the *New York Times* in his face. A picture of the demolished truck in front of the Kodak Theater dominated the front page.

"Oh, that."

"So who were those terrorists at the Academy Awards anyway?"

Bernard asked, as he headed toward the Oval Office. "I know what they wanted, but I want to put names on their faces."

"Well, they were all al-Jazeera television crew members."

"I know they all were al-Jazeera, but who were they really? Islamic Jihad? Hamas? Hezbollah? Al-Qaeda?" he ticked them off on his fingers.

"I think just actually al-Jazeera TV, sir."

Bernard eyed him closely. "Do you mean to tell me that we just blew up six Arab journalists, and that's all they were?"

"It looks that way, sir."

Bernard paused walking and pinched the bridge of his nose in thought. "No wonder why they hate us."

Then he looked up quickly. A justification had come to mind. "But there was a bomb on the truck."

"Not a large one..."

"But a bomb nonetheless," the President persisted, resuming more confidently down the hall. "What were they going to do with it, nuke insects in their apartments?"

"It was a very common construction site device loaded with dynamite. It could have been planted, sir."

"Planted? By whom?" he asked at the doorway to the office.

Chuck eyed him carefully.

"No, don't tell me," Bernard said, and rushed toward his desk. "I don't want to know."

He collapsed into his chair.

"Do you know why this job is so tough?" he said. "It's all those people who try to be helpful, but only make matters worse."

He threw a pen in the air and caught it.

"They think that a strong al-Qaeda will improve my chances to stay in office. But, by God, I'm not in office for the salary or the power or the prestige. I'd rather have al-Qaeda disappear from the face of the earth than keep this blame job. I'm not hunting terrorists for the sport. I don't need helpful cronies holding up targets so that I can shoot them down."

Chuck pulled up a chair and leaned his elbows against the President's desk. "Do these cronies you're talking about truly intend to be helpful, or do they have their own agenda?"

"I've got plenty of hardliners, and their views are all on the record."

Chuck shook his head. "Other friends."

"Liberals? Are they that underhanded?"

Chuck continued to dolefully shake his head.

"Personal enemies?"

"Name one," Chuck said.

Bernard shrugged. He had done nothing but diligently dole out handouts to political favorites and foes alike throughout his career. "Where does that leave us?"

"I believe someone wants your job, sir."

Bernard sat forward, his blue eyes intense. "Who?"

Chuck studied his shoes, then jutted out his jaw and gave the President a straightforward look. "Attorney General Caleb Perkins, for one."

"Caleb?" Bernard said, sitting back with a frown. "I know that he's ambitious, but I didn't think he had it in him. Bombs in trucks at the Academy Awards? How would that remove me from office?"

"Perhaps when the smoke clears, and the FBI investigates, they will find evidence of its origin, fingerprints if you will."

"Like whose fingerprints?"

"Yours."

Bernard studied Chuck's unnaturally young face. How could his Chief of Staff suspect so much? Suspect in a way that bordered on knowing what happened?

He thought back to the Academy Awards party he had thrown the previous evening. When William Ford had informed Caleb of the foiled terrorist attack, Caleb had suddenly lost all his previous ebullience. He had shut up and turned morose, hostile in fact. He didn't react like a man who had pulled off a successful terrorist attack. He would have been pleased, not hurt.

If anyone, William Ford had been nothing short of ecstatic. If there were fingerprints all over the bomb, they would be William's.

So why was Chuck feeding him all this bull about Caleb?

"This is a serious accusation, Chuck. What direct proof do you have that it's Caleb trying to sabotage me?"

"Ask your secretary how Caleb reacted when bin Laden's fax came in."

Bernard leaned on his intercom button. "Gertrude? Please come in."

She walked in immediately with her clipped stride hampered by a gray, cowbell shaped skirt. "Yes, Mr. President?"

Bernard phrased his question carefully. "Was the Attorney General present when the fax from bin Laden came in?"

"Yes. He was just entering the office when I received it."

"Did he read it?"

"Certainly, sir."

"And what was his reaction?"

"He made a photocopy of it."

Bernard's eyebrows shot up. "And what did he do next?"

"He folded the copy, put it in his pocket, and left the White House, Mr. President."

Bernard lowered his eyes and stared at the lady's polished brown pumps. "Thank you, Gertrude. That will be all."

When the door closed discreetly behind her, he looked up at his Chief of Staff. "Caleb has perpetrated a grave breech of office protocol."

Chuck did not disagree. "Not to mention a security violation or two."

Bernard's mind roamed over what Caleb had done for him recently. He had shuffled the Chinagate investigation over to a special prosecutor awfully fast, rather than burying the investigation within the Justice Department. Was he colluding with the prosecutor, too?

"Should I fire him, or ask for his resignation?"

At that point, Chuck seemed to contradict his earlier stance. "Neither, sir."

"Why not?"

Chuck waved the fax in his face. "Do you want Caleb to go public with this?"

Bernard sank deep in his chair. It seemed like everybody in his Administration had something on him. The U.S. Trade Representative who set up the China oil for WTO concessions deal, those who set up the faked bombing at the Academy Awards, those like Caleb and Chuck who knew the intimate details of bin Laden's blackmail fax...

He had made one small transgression by accepting the Trade Representative's sweetener into his offshore account. Wasn't all business taking place offshore anyway?

But that had left him open to attack from the piranhas. He felt like a giant whale, and the carnivorous fish were keeping him alive only long enough so they could dine on him when the time was right. And with their combined weight hanging onto him, they were dragging him and the entire Party to its doom.

There was only one solution.

"Chuck, schedule a nationally televised address for me Monday evening, prime time."

"You're not going to resign, are you?"

The NCAA Championship Game was just coming on the air, Counterterrorism Director Neal Jacobs realized as he picked up his office phone to make a call. It was a terrible time to bother someone with work, especially when *Sports Illustrated* was the in-flight magazine on Air Force One. The call would poison the entire escapist effect of a good basketball game.

Nevertheless, he went ahead and dialed Assistant Secretary of Defense Max Spelling at home.

"The Commander-in-Chief wants us to expand our horizons aggressively," Neal began at once. "Osama bin Laden owns about twenty ocean-going vessels around the world. We can't afford another *Cole*. We've got to go out there aggressively and find these ships before they pop over the horizon."

Max hesitated. "The Coast Guard doesn't even have the resources it takes to patrol our own ports. We're using naval vessels to assist them. How do you expect me to deploy even more ships around the world?"

"I want you to focus on al-Qaeda-owned vessels."

"I'm not sure the Pentagon knows which ships are al-Qaeda and which aren't. They change their names and country of registration on a daily basis."

Neal shifted around in his seat, and his eyes fell on the young man who was his al-Qaeda investigation expert. "We may have compiled a list of owners of suspected ships, ship profiles, that sort of thing."

"That would help."

"I'll email you that information in the next few hours."

"Hey, Neal, this new cooperation thing really works!" Max said.

"Along the same lines, we believe that Raymond O. Flowers might be colluding with elements of al-Qaeda. That might be our lucky break. You might call Justice and see if they have voiceprints for Raymond O. Flowers. One of your ships just might pick something up."

❖ ❖ ❖

With snow accumulating on the expressway, it took Caleb Perkins over an hour to reach home in Arlington, Virginia. He took the opportunity to develop the plan that he had just formed at the White House. He would have Harry Black monitor the transactions into the terrorists' bank account in Riyadh and then he would send the evidence to Stanley Polk. By the end of the day, the Chinagate prosecutor would have enough evidence to make his case against President Bernard White.

A divorcee for many years, he still had two teenage sons who were home, already glued to the television. Before settling down to watch the championship basketball game, Caleb excused himself from the room and placed a call from the secure line in his study. It was time to gain Harry Black's trust and have him do some work on behalf of the Department of Justice.

"Harry, it's me."

"Good morning, Mr. Attorney General. Do you have any news for me?"

First a tidbit of information to gain Harry's confidence. "Yes, I do. Our men have intercepted transmissions that place Flowers in Eastern Africa," he said, grinning to himself at his manufactured lead. Harry would appreciate the information.

"Can you be more specific?"

"Try this. He's on a photo safari in Kenya."

"Do you have any hotel names?"

"Nothing specific. I'd pick up Flowers' trail in Nairobi, though."

"Good enough. Thank you, sir."

"Ah, there's one more thing I'd like you to do for me," Caleb said.

"Is this part of the contract?"

"You're charging all expenses, right?"

"Yes," Harry said.

"Then this is part of the contract. I want you to monitor a bank account at the Royal Bank of Riyadh. Keep track of who's transferring money in and out of there, and how much. The account number is..." he fished the copy of the fax out of his suit coat pocket. "2834457. Have you got all that?"

"Yes. I'll get right on it, Mr. Attorney General."

"Good. I want you to print out the transaction for evidence."

Caleb hung up before Harry could ask whom the evidence would indict.

He returned to his family room where the two centers were just tipping off. Within minutes, his mind was off the long road to the White House as he was swept away by the electrifying action.

Fully attired in tropical resort wear that Tiffany had purchased for him at Christmas, Hiram slid open the glass door and stepped out onto the hotel room's private deck. They had an air-conditioned ground floor room with a view of the thick bushes and stout tree trunks of the garden.

If he stood up straight and looked between several tree trunks, he could make out the ocean's horizon. The wooden deck was damp from dew, and Spanish moss hung from the thick rope railing. They were in a tropical paradise.

"We've got a coupon for complimentary drinks at the poolside bar," Tiffany said from the doorway.

He turned around.

His redheaded sweetheart was seductively waving the tickets like a fan in one hand and leaning against the doorframe with the other. She wore nothing but a tight white bikini that threatened to turn sheer once wet. Her body was more horizontal than vertical, but that was how he liked her. She was a red-blooded woman of substance, and more of that substance was on display than not.

He fought a surge of blood to his various body parts and turned his attention to the coupons.

"It's not too early to use 'em," he said.

She swayed away from the room and slid the glass door with one swing of her hips. Then she eased herself under one of his arms.

He fought the urge to slip his hand around her bra as they padded barefoot down the garden path toward the sounds of the pool.

They came to the organically shaped pool with its separate wading area and adult lap area. The aquamarine pool was surrounded by white lounge chairs and red-and-white-striped umbrellas, women fussing over their children and men pouring over their newspapers.

But what attracted Hiram's attention most was a lone grass hut between the pool and the beach. A row of four bar stools beckoned to him from the shade of the hut.

They eased themselves into the rattan seats and Tiffany shoved the two coupons across the bar. A bartender, not unlike the taxi driver in physical appearance and stature, finished drying a glass and came over to them.

His long, dark Indian fingers took away the coupon. "What's yours today?" he asked.

Hiram smiled. The guy not only spoke understandable English, but he knew the lingo.

Hiram looked at Tiffany and she allowed him to go ahead and order. "How 'bout somethin' local?" he asked.

"Have you tried our rum and coconut?"

Yeah, that seemed to fit the bill. "Make it two."

Chapter 11

Harry Black wiped the sleep from his eyes, smoothed the wrinkles out of his shirt, and felt the stubble on his chin. He had slept in front of his computer all night at his office in downtown Atlanta. Out his window, the city had woken up to a glaze of ice. He was smart not to have tried to return home to his apartment that night.

He had just ordered Badger and the crew off of Hainan on the double. International flights out of Sanya, China, departed several times a day. He checked the clocks on his office wall. It was just past noon in Atlanta, and predawn in China. Before nightfall, his men would be descending on Nairobi en masse.

He was sorry to make them work on NCAA Championship day. But what did they care? They were earning a thousand bucks a day for essentially lazing around hotel pools, and could watch the game later on tape.

The computer's bare-bones operating system appeared, and he opened Badger's program. Tracing a bank account was a routine that Badger had perfected, using standard off-the-shelf hacker and eavesdropping software. He keyed in the bank's name and the account number and waited. The account appeared onscreen, but thus far there had been no transactions that day.

He kept an eye on any bank transfers that might appear on the computer screen and pulled out the CIA contract that instructed him to track down, neutralize, and deliver Am Cit Raymond O. Flowers to Camp X-Ray at Guantánamo Bay, Cuba.

The Agency's insignia on the letterhead was stunningly plain and simple. An eagle's head, a blank white shield, and a compass rose. And yet, the thousands of operatives the Agency had scattered around the world couldn't find Flowers, and had to rely on a penny ante company like his to do the work.

It was interesting that the FBI could track Flowers down so quickly and in such a remote location.

It did help to have FBI agents stationed around the world, lending criminal tracking capabilities that were sorely lacking in the CIA. The Central Intelligence Agency had been built around the specter of dangerous governments. They didn't have a single criminal detective in their ranks. It would take them years to orient themselves toward tracking down wanted men.

He stared at the blank white shield on the letterhead more thoughtfully.

On the other hand, maybe the CIA still had the right approach. The Agency existed to fill blank white pages with facts and considered analysis on subjects around the world that were vital to America's security and wellbeing. After all, analysis of foreign trends had uncovered the economic woes of the educated Arab public as well as the sentiment of disenfranchisement that had led to the popularity of fundamental Islam among the lower and middle classes. Maybe the root sources of anti-Americanism needed to be addressed, rather than sending out FBI agents on an endless cops and robbers routine that was favored by the gringo gunslingers in Washington. That only seemed to make Muslims around the world angrier.

He looked up at the computer and checked for activity in the account in Riyadh. Still none.

He sat back and mused over the mysterious workings of Washington. How had the FBI found Flowers so quickly? They must have gotten a tip from one of their agents at the Embassy in Kenya. After all, a worldwide alert would send Raymond O. Flowers' photograph to all the FBI field offices around the world.

But he didn't expect the FBI to capture or take out Flowers without the proper authorization from the Kenyan government and without relying on their police or military resources. Besides, the FBI would be working with the special prosecutor and have the opposite mission in mind. They wanted Flowers back in DC to testify against the President.

Well, that wouldn't happen so long as Harry Black was a contractor for the CIA and national security was at stake.

It was against his principles to ice Flowers. His men weren't contract killers. But their mission was to nab him and put him on ice.

That he could live with.

Suddenly numbers flashed across the computer screen. Money was pouring into the account in Riyadh. The computer displayed the transmitting account number, complete with routing information.

Then the amount of dollars in the transaction appeared.

$20,000,000.00.

He pressed the PrintScreen key and the entire transaction began to print out.

The massive al-Qaeda freighter rounded the southern tip of Hainan Island and steamed eastward toward the Philippines. Raymond watched in astonishment as the crew methodically went about the business of creating a new identity for the ship.

Painters leaned far over the railings and created a new stripe around her hull by slopping on orange and black paint. Her two soaring funnels were soon ablaze in orange and black tiger stripes. The skipper hauled the flag off the stern and unfurled a new red, white, and blue checkered flag. Now, what country did that represent?

When the skipper took the old flag back to his cabin, Raymond leaned over the aft railing to watch two scruffy crewmembers paint a new name for the ship. Standing on a platform, they painted the word, "*Ariana.*" Below that, they inscribed her home country: "Panama."

Suddenly, a cry emanated from the captain's cabin. The skipper burst out his door ecstatically waving a sheet of paper in one hand. He did a short dance around the deck, drawing the attention of the entire crew.

They circled around him to find out what had happened.

"Foot soldiers of Allah," he addressed them. "I have good news. We have a new adherent to our cause, Allah be praised. The President of the United States has just joined our ranks."

There was a general gasp of disbelief.

"Trust me, I'm telling the truth. And here is the evidence to prove it." He held up the sheet of paper for all to see. The white page whipped in the wind against a cerulean sky.

Raymond approached, but the words were too far away to read.

"It says," the skipper continued, "that the leader of the Western World, his Excellency Bernard White, President of our sworn enemy, the United States of America, has just deposited twenty million dollars in al-Qaeda's bank account in Saudi Arabia."

The men let out a chorus of cheers, vibrating their tongues to form a piercingly high pitch. Many began to dance around the deck in their bare feet, pounding their naked chests and waving their hands high above their heads.

Raymond felt sick. Watching someone else's selfless devotion to a cause had always made him feel uncomfortable. He had never participated in such displays for any cause. But the reason for celebration made his stomach go weak. He was the reason that the President capitulated. And now the skipper could squash America under his thumb. What would he ask for next?

As if reading his mind, the skipper continued to grind his nose in it. "But we won't stop here. We want more. We want complete submission to Islam!"

The men cheered even more wildly. Victory seemed within their grasp.

The skipper left his men and approached Raymond with easy, confident strides. "There's only one thing left to do before we make our next request."

"What's that?" He was afraid to hear the response.

"They want proof that we have you."

Raymond's shoulders slumped. "I figured it would come to this. What do you want me to do, squat against an anonymous wall surrounded by masked men with submachine guns while you videotape me?"

"Hey," the skipper said, snapping his fingers as if inspired by the idea. "That's great!"

Raymond groaned as he was led past the raucous celebration and to the captain's quarters. The skipper pulled a key from his pocket and unlocked the door.

Raymond had never been inside the cabin before. There were the normal furnishings that a man needed while traveling—a single bed, bathroom, dining table, a couple of metal chairs, and a prayer rug. But there was also a desk with a reading lamp and a personal computer attached to a modem. Beside that sat a radiophone and fax machine. If he could only get his hands on that equipment, he could send out word of his predicament. But to whom? The *New York Times*?

"This will do," the skipper said, pointing to a wall of chipped paint. "You sit here, and I'll get you some guards."

Raymond took a moment to examine the communications equipment. If he could get a hold of the skipper's cabin key, he could surely get word out that he was being held prisoner.

Footsteps approached and he jumped back. The sailor passed, and he was safe, this time.

He squatted down on the cold metal floor. This was pathetic. But it was the only way he could reach the outside world that day.

He saw a ballpoint pen on the desk. He could scribble his location on the palms of his hands and flash them at the camera. No, the cameraman would see that.

There were oily rags in the next room. Perhaps he could form them into letters and words. No, there wasn't enough material.

How about sign language? He could form letters with his fingers. But what could he say to the President who would receive the tape?

Did he really want to communicate anything?

He could get out word of his whereabouts. If the Navy rescued him, he might have a fighting chance of finding his family. On the other hand, the military might come and nab him just to keep him out of the public eye.

If the tape got leaked to the public, it might be worth communicating the state of his health. But who the hell cared? There weren't any close relatives sitting anxiously by the telephone, waiting for news of his fate.

If his family happened to catch him on the tube, they would only be driven sick with anxiety.

The sad truth was that he had nothing to say, and nobody to say it to.

The skipper returned, this time with a digital video camera and tripod and two men who seemed put out by these additional duties. The charade was impressive. Ammunition belts crisscrossed both men's chests. Checkered shawls covered every square inch of their faces, leaving only tiny slits through which to see. Both men held submachine guns indifferently by their sides.

The skipper planted the tripod before Raymond, and then pushed his actors around the stage. Returning to the camera, he looked through the viewfinder.

"This isn't Ingmar Bergman, but it'll do. Now hold your positions."

The only audience worth worrying about was his family. He hoped to God that if they were given access to television news they wouldn't panic. So he held up his face as the skipper hosed the scene with the video camera. He put on his bravest expression, trying to convey the fact that he wasn't in any real danger despite armed terrorists standing over him. He cracked a smile, laughed to himself, and tried to look casually around the room.

The skipper stopped the taping.

"I want you to demonstrate a little more respect," he said. "Act like we're terrorists."

"Okay. I'll try."

The camera was rolling again, and Raymond put on more of a frown. He'd go for serious, with a touch of fear in his eyes. Perhaps Carolyn would detect that he was hamming it up and conclude that he wasn't in any real danger.

After spraying the scene wordlessly for another minute, the skipper clicked off the camera and dismissed his men.

Still irritable, they dumped their ammo belts on the floor and plodded away. Too bad they didn't leave their guns, or Raymond might be able to shoot his way off the ship. He made a mental note to find out where the weapons were stored onboard.

The skipper unscrewed the video camera from the tripod with a broad smile on his bearded face. "Once I send this to the White House, we can proceed with the next phase of our negotiations."

"Which is?"

"Releasing prisoners, of course."

"Like me?"

The skipper studied him seriously for a moment. "Why would they want you? As long as we keep you out of sight and away from the Chinagate investigators, they'll willingly deal with us."

Raymond's shoulders suddenly felt very heavy. "So I guess I'm in for a very long boat ride." He hated the thought that he may have instilled false hope in Carolyn and the children.

Then footsteps padded into the office. It was the first officer reporting from the bridge.

"Captain, it's the Port of Manila. They want us to identify ourselves."

The skipper contemplated the request for a moment.

"We have to reply," the first officer reminded him.

"I know, I know," the skipper said, distractedly. Then his eyes fell on Raymond. "You," he said. "You will speak over the radio."

Raymond picked himself off the floor and followed the two men.

The captain locked his door behind him, and they mounted the stairs to the bridge.

Raymond had never been to the bridge before. Talking on the radio was one more opportunity to get the word out.

Chapter 12

Monday morning, the White House had a full schedule. Chuck Romer had already set up the President's agenda. Early that morning, Bernard White had attended his weekly intelligence briefing presided over by the National Security Advisor and read his daily economic report. At the moment, the President was conducting his weekly meeting with the Congressional leadership.

It was Chuck's chance to sit down at the computer and scan the subject lines of all the urgent messages awaiting him. Email was such a boon to the busy bureaucrat. He didn't need to respond to people in real time. Only when he pleased, when he even bothered to read his email.

One message jumped off the screen. The message header indicated it had been sent from outside the government's intranet, and the sender's name was simply Hamid. It had an attachment that was unusually large, over forty megabytes. And the subject line read "Flowers on Videotape."

For the nerve center of the U.S. Government, Chuck had expected to find a supercomputer on everybody's desk with high-speed, television-quality links to other computers around the world. Instead, he was disappointed to learn his first day on the job, that security concerns had held back the latest shipment of computers, and that he was, in fact, stuck with a Tempest PC dating back several administrations.

The video clip took forever to download. And in the meantime, he couldn't use the computer for other purposes.

He kicked back his chair and considered refilling his coffee cup. But he didn't want to leave his office with Flowers' video displaying on his screen. What to do?

La de da.

His eyes fell on the calendar. On butcher paper taped to his wall, he had written out a highly detailed itinerary of the President's upcoming meetings, speeches, interviews and trips. The meetings were written in blue marker, and included tête-à-têtes with heads of state down to lunches with Lori. The speeches and interviews were marked in green. And trips were highlighted in red, and included official speeches at a bird sanctuary in Florida, a Habitat for Humanity project in Missouri, and a daycare center in Ohio.

Mid August was still surprisingly free. The President had talked about returning to his ranch in California for a few days, so Chuck had left him a week free. It was scheduled just after the opposition Party convention, but before his own Party convention and most likely a moment where the President would take a heavy pounding in the polls.

Why not get married then?

He would propose the idea to the President that morning after the Congressmen vacated the Oval Office.

At last the computer announced proudly "File Transfer Complete." On the screen a new window appeared with a video image.

A man sat cross-legged on the floor directly in front of the camera. Behind him stood two hooded guards.

Chuck leaned in closely to try to identify the man. So that was Raymond O. Flowers. He had only seen the same photograph repeated in newspaper reports. It had depicted an upstanding and open-faced Regional Financial Officer for a major oil company.

The man he saw before him had a light frosting of beard, a ghostly face, bare feet, and a tattered business shirt. His eyes were doing something funny behind his spectacles. Maybe he had a twitch.

The picture swayed back and forth, often blurring the subjects in front of the lens. In the dim lighting, he managed to make out a reasonably detailed image of the captors. They hung loose, holding submachine guns with their heads wrapped in rags.

At first it seemed that there was no audio track. In the silence of the scene, no ransom was demanded. It was just intended to prove that the President was in deep shit.

Chuck turned up the volume on his computer, and picked up faint sounds in the background. He detected voices cheering and whooping in the distance, and a low and dull creaking noise, like metal under stress.

Then the camera suddenly held still, poised firmly on a tripod. Against the paint peeling on the wall, the two terrorists leaned to one side in tandem. They were on a ship!

Then, with a professional dissolve, the video image faded into a handwritten note. "Release all prisoners at Guantánamo Bay, or we will release Flowers."

The threat was concise, even poetic. And it needed no specifics to achieve its effect.

Chuck clicked on "File Save" and stored the clip on his hard drive. He exited the program, picked up his phone, and called Gertrude. "Tell the President to clear the decks. I'm coming in to speak with him privately. Now."

As Chuck entered the Oval Office, the top congressional leaders were still shoving their papers into their briefcases as they were herded out by Gertrude.

He received a particular leer from the House Majority Leader, whose Party sat in opposition to the President.

"Is the Chinagate prosecutor interfering with your normal workload?" the Congressman asked.

"No," Chuck lied. "Not at all."

"Good," the Congressman said. "We don't want to let down our guard on more important matters."

"It's very considerate of you to say that," Chuck said politely.

"In fact, the sooner the whole Chinagate affair is over, the sooner we can turn our full attention back to our jobs."

"Right," Chuck agreed. Where was this guy going with this? If anything, the opposition Party wanted to fan the flames of scandal.

"We wouldn't want any purposeful foot dragging."

"No."

"As that in itself might lead to criminal indictment."

Then the Congressman leaned closer and uttered confidentially. "We wouldn't want the matter as cover for further criminal behavior."

"Meaning what," Chuck said, perhaps a tad too defensively.

"We don't want any mischief under the yellow flag."

Chuck understood the racing allusion. The White House might want to buy time by impeding the special prosecutor's investigation. What sounded like friendly advice came across as intimidation.

When the group of gray-hairs slinked off like attack dogs leaving behind a gnawed bone, Chuck turned to the seated Bernard White.

"I don't like that guy," he said. "He sounds like he's onto something."

"You don't suppose…" President White stopped short of saying the unthinkable. Then said it anyway. "Perhaps Caleb fed them a copy of bin Laden's fax."

"No, he wouldn't do that. It wouldn't be to Caleb's advantage."

The President sank his head in his hands. "So why did you need to see me?"

Chuck gave him a long, solemn look and waited for eye contact.

"Don't tell me. We got another threat."

Chuck nodded. "They're demanding we release prisoners from Guantánamo."

Bernard stood up enraged, his face livid. "They can't play with our national security."

Chuck smiled. "That's what they're all about, sir."

"We've got to nuke the bastards. Do you have any idea where they are?"

"Possibly Southeast Asia. That's the last place we saw Flowers. I can tell you one fact that I ascertained from the video clip that the terrorists sent us. He's being held captive onboard a ship."

"Videotape? Oh, my God."

"Don't worry," Chuck said. "Caleb didn't sneak in and get a copy."

The President circled his desk, a man of action. "I want you to call in our fleet and put a total clamp down on that area. Board and search every ship."

"Doesn't that sound somewhat extreme, sir? We don't even have jurisdiction in those waters."

"Well, what can we do, call in the UN?"

Chuck laughed at the errant barb. "Well, we do have Raymond O. Flowers' voice print…"

"Use eavesdropping, wire taps, whatever it takes. We have to put a stop to this."

"That's brilliant, sir." It didn't hurt to offer a little praise, even though earlier that weekend he had already sent the Navy steaming to the area.

He lingered by the door before leaving the office. "In the meantime, what should we do with the terrorists' demand?"

"Tell 'em to stuff it."

He gave the President a "you can't be serious" look.

"Why not?" Bernard protested.

He returned to the President's desk and folded his arms. "Do you want Flowers testifying that you took kickbacks? Do you want Flowers testifying that you sent a bank transfer of twenty million dollars to a terrorist organization?"

The President's jaw fell slack. The bags under his eyes swelled darkly.

"They're drawing us in further and further," Chuck said, unable to keep the ominous tone from his voice.

The President pursed his lips and leaned against the edge of his desk. "Are the networks ready to carry my speech tonight?" he asked meekly.

Chuck stiffened. "Damn it, Mr. President. Are you going to let these terrorists win? This isn't Spain. This is the United States of America."

"Yeah, and her President is selling out the store."

"You most definitely are not. You are standing up to terrorism!"

Bernard took a moment to consider the idea. Then he said, "Okay, you win. Release the prisoners."

"That's good, sir. That's taking charge!"

Bernard cracked one of his prankish schoolboy smiles. "But only release a handful of them. The terrorists will have to come back to us for more. That'll buy us time to track them down and nuke them."

"That's the spirit, sir!"

Chuck Romer marched directly back to his office, just a few thin walls away from the President, and picked up his phone.

"Get me the Pentagon," he snapped at the White House operator. "I want Assistant Secretary of Defense Max Spelling."

He waited, focusing once more on the vacant week in August. On an impulse, he grabbed a blue felt-tipped marker from his desk and drew tiny wedding bells at the start of the President's summer vacation.

"Yeah, Chuck?" came Spelling's voice over the phone from the quiet of his Pentagon office.

"More word from the top, I'm afraid," Chuck began. "The President is requesting that we release a handful of al-Qaeda suspects from Guantánamo."

"You've got to be kidding."

"And in addition, we want this to be a high profile release. Make sure the press is aware of it."

"Of course they'll be aware of it. Especially when the next car bomb goes off."

"I can't help that," Chuck said. "The President is in a particularly awkward political position at this point, and he needs room to maneuver."

Max still balked. "These are foreign combatants we're talking about. Foreign passport holders. All our American citizen suspects are already back in the U.S."

"Okay, then release a handful of foreigners. What have we got to lose anyway? They're a drop in the bucket compared with the millions of insurgents out there calling for *jihad*."

"We aren't necessarily holding them to prevent them from attacking our interests. We're holding them to gain intelligence."

"You've had years to interview them."

Max didn't have a ready response to that one.

Chuck played the Flowers tape back to the handwritten ransom demand to release all prisoners at Guantánamo Bay, or they would release Flowers. "Do we have any high profile detainees?"

"We haven't given out their names to the public."

"Why not? We want some good publicity here."

"We don't give out names so that the terrorists don't know who we've got and what they're saying. It's a way of getting them to scrap all their current plans."

Chuck stopped to consider that. "Is that why we haven't had any attacks against American interests lately?"

"I'm sure it's a significant reason."

Well, that was just too bad.

"Release a few top al-Qaeda operatives, not the peons, and give their names to the press. We need some good PR."

"You know I'll have to clear it with Kenneth."

"Clear it?" Chuck snapped. The President had ordered the release. Kenneth Spaulding was a wishy-washy Secretary of Defense, a man prone to obsessing over minor legal details such as the Geneva conventions.

"I mean 'discuss it,'" Max rephrased.

"Then discuss it. I want to see action on this by the end of the day."

"Okay. We'll get to work on it," Max said, making no attempt to

135

conceal his reluctance.

Chuck set down the phone, took one last look at the video clip on his computer, then hit the Delete key.

Humming Felix Mendelssohn's *Wedding March*, he returned to the wall calendar that set forth his grand scheme to reelect the President, whether he wanted it or not.

Chapter 13

To her own critical eye, Sandi DiMartino looked striking in a bikini. She examined her physique in the soft lighting of her hotel room. Hainan Island's tropical sun had done wonders for her tan that had faded under Washington, DC's grey skies. Her tan lines had become distinct again, like white cream against smooth, brown muscle.

But her body hadn't been alluring enough to draw Raymond O. Flowers out of his secret world.

She didn't have strong-armed men to whisk him away, as she had seen happen on the beach. She didn't have money with which to entice him. All she had was his trust, and a bottle of Coco Mademoiselle.

If perfume didn't turn his head, he was definitely beyond the appeal of patriotism. In fact, from his disgruntled statements, his loyalty to God and country was all but shot.

Company loyalty seemed strained if not altogether broken.

Raymond had exuded the offhand, uncaring air of someone who was on the run and who had lost his moral compass. She studied her enhanced breasts and tightly toned buns. She should have been the perfect bait.

But she wasn't. Something stronger than his appetites was driving him. And she couldn't venture to guess what it was. It seemed beyond fear of the Feds, anger at his company, and grief over his family. Could it be that Raymond O. Flowers was simply trying to preserve what was left of his self-esteem?

Where did her self-esteem stand those days? She had a good head on her shoulders. A Bachelor's Degree in History from Columbia University. A law degree from Georgetown, clerking for a Federal Judge in San Francisco, joining a team of prosecutors for the Department of Justice, and most recently, heading up the investigative team for the Special Independent Prosecutor, the renowned Stanley Polk, in the Chinagate scandal.

She had a large heart, searching for ways to make America stronger, more pure, and more tightly knit. She had had lovers in college, and again in San Francisco. But those weren't real men. They were callow, half-formed men who latched onto her far more than she needed them.

Some of her buddies back in Washington would argue that she lacked commitment. And her frequent flights from one relationship to another seemed to bear that out. But the way she saw it, she had left a trail of broken hearts only because of her own quest for emotional fulfillment.

Was that a cop-out?

She had to smile. Maybe her friends were right. Sometimes a deranged individual was the last to recognize her own problems.

Raymond had seemed so sincere, mature, and vulnerable. She had found it strangely attractive to lounge with him at poolside and trade observations of life. She had felt herself falling for him, wanting him, trying to dig under his skin and know him better.

But in the end, she had wanted him far more than he had wanted her, and that gave her a painful twinge of sadness.

She slipped into her flip-flops and swung her towel over a shoulder.

Taking one last look at her noble features under her bright, blonde hair, she asked the questioning blue eyes if she was ready to take on the world again.

She was, the eyes assured her. She didn't need Raymond. She just needed somebody before she would head back to Washington.

Due to insurgencies in Indonesia, Thailand, and Malaysia, the Seventh Fleet had already deployed a carrier battle group from San Diego to the area several months before.

Aboard the signals ship *USS Endorse*, Seaman Anthony Carlson was already used to the onboard routine, and beginning to pine for home. He knew that it was still too early in the deployment to contemplate flipping steaks on his backyard grill in his off-base housing, but the voyage was mentally fatiguing, and he needed some sort of break.

For one thing, the voices that his superconductive antennae were picking up weren't speaking a single word of English. The airwaves were awash with languages he'd never heard before.

On Anthony's morning watch, the *USS Endorse* had received a communication from the Pentagon that more voice signature files were on their way. He yawned. It meant a morning of linking up his computer program to the sound wave files so that transmissions he received from radios and cell phones could be matched against known criminals.

The airwaves were singing with communications along all sorts of frequencies, between ships, from ship to shore and back again, among police onshore in the nearby Philippine island of Luzon, between military units on the island, and from ordinary citizens making their cell phone calls from their offices and motor scooters.

Anthony sat straight-backed in the radio room before his bank of computer monitors and watched the latest voice signature files download from the Pentagon. As the long WAV files downloaded, he read over a printout of the new names added to the list. The number of terrorist suspects crept higher each day. Names originating from the Middle East, for the most part. But one striking new name caught his eye—"Raymond O. Flowers." Not only was it an Anglo name, but a notorious one at that.

Now, he didn't follow the Armed Forces News Channel any closer than the rest of his buddies onboard, but even he was aware of the Chinagate investigation that had stalled in Washington due to the disappearance of its key witness.

And among seamen, the name Raymond O. Flowers was a lightning rod for heartfelt political debate. Those who thought the special prosecutor was providing a valuable service to the nation by rooting out corruption in government would like to have Flowers found, put on the stand, and testify against the President.

The far greater majority, who defended the President, would rather not see Flowers ever resurface. And Anthony was among that group rallying around their President, ideological leader, and Commander-in-Chief.

So why was the Pentagon sending them Flowers' WAV file? Was Secretary of Defense Kenneth Spaulding bowing to public pressure and helping out the special independent prosecutor? Was someone in government trying to breathe new life into the Chinagate kangaroo court and bring down the Administration?

He sighed and shook his head dumbfounded. He hoped that he would never get posted to the Pentagon, because as long as he lived, he would never understand the mysterious workings of Washington.

Sandi felt several pairs of eyes following her as she padded across the pool deck in search of a chaise lounge. The women peered over their books and magazines with a mixture of envy and defensiveness. But that didn't stop her from showing a bit of cheesecake and a flash of the forbidden. Men tried to maintain their cool as their breathing came to a halt.

She reached up to tighten the scrunchie that bobbed in her hair, letting the men glimpse the sides of her breasts as they spilled from under the tight neon green top. She squeezed her buttocks consciously as she walked, tightening her calves and flexing her thighs.

She squatted beside a pair of empty lounge chairs, turned on her toes, and observed the tight lines of her legs glistening as hard ridges in the sun.

Then she leaned over to spread out her beach towel, letting her breasts swing free, and catch a breath of ocean breeze where a band of sweat had formed against her skin. She leaned far enough forward to stretch the wedge-shaped bikini bottom far up between her legs.

If there was a real man to find that day, she would draw him out.

She settled down with a copy of the *South China Post* and immediately turned to the international section. The Gulf was showing its contempt for America in new and novel ways. SARS was making a reappearance in Beijing. And Stanley Polk's investigation into the President's misdeeds was stymied. For his part, the President was being romantically linked to some college grad intern. And the Academy Awards had sustained minor damage from a foiled terrorist attack.

A young man approached her.

"Is this chair taken?" he asked in a confident voice.

She lowered her sunglasses.

The man was tall and dark, and his eyes seemed to dance. She could use a man with a hairy chest and a cocksure attitude.

"No, it's free," she said. "Make yourself at home."

He grinned, exposing a healthy row of teeth. Sticking out his hand, he said, "Merle Stevens, with the U.S. Consulate in Shanghai."

She wiped off some tanning oil that had mixed in with newspaper ink, and shook his hand. What a firm, dry grip.

She squirmed against her towel. This guy was more than the average pickup. He was the complete package!

The bearded skipper bounded into the mess hall where Raymond was playing rummy with some of the crew.

"They've conceded," he announced in triumph. "Washington is releasing our men from Guantánamo."

As the other crewmembers emitted a cheer that resounded off the metal walls, Raymond buried his head in his hands. He had become an impediment to national security. No, worse, he had become the most major threat to the United States. As long as President Bernard White held office, the entire country was in the grip of the terrorists.

"What's next?" he groaned.

"What's next?" the skipper repeated. "Next, we will demand that the Americans abandon their hunt for Osama bin Laden and Mullah Omar!"

If Raymond could only go public, that would be his best weapon. He had to forget his own complicity and indictable actions. Who knew how far the terrorists would take this? Would the skipper force the President to roll back homeland security and allow bomb-toting terrorists loose in America?

He threw his cards on the table, face up. The crewmembers he was playing against were no longer interested in the game, as they began clapping and dancing.

Once President White complied with al-Qaeda's demands, he was heading down a one-way street. The President would have to accede to all further demands.

He knew about one-way streets.

His full house staring him in the face, he thought back to his relocation to Shanghai after leaving his family's memory behind.

It did seem strange that he had picked up the pieces of his former life so quickly after their deaths. There he was, back in China, working for the same oil firm. The SARS experience could have changed his life, yet it hadn't. Even with his family gone, he was outwardly the same person, a financial officer with corporate duties to fulfill.

In fact, he *had* changed—only he didn't know it at the time. He had gone back to his company, taking the path of least resistance, in order to give himself time to deal with his anger and grief. He still had many issues to work out.

And it hadn't taken long for his disgust with his company to boil over. His bosses were trying to buy him off with a cushy job, great pay, enhanced expat package, and a very nice three-story house in a gated compound occupied by other foreigners.

But he had had no family to tuck into bed at night. And his job quickly reverted back to handling the illegal funds that he didn't want to touch with a ten-foot pole.

This time it wasn't Chinese bribes sent to the President's offshore account. It was kickbacks from his own company that Raymond directed into the President's account. Was there no end to the man's greed? Once a man took a bribe, he lost all moral compunction about taking another and another.

But in some profound ways, Raymond was not unlike the President. His hands were dirty, too. He had taken the expat package, complete with car, driver, house, club memberships, free recreational travel, free insurance coverage, plush office, and light workload. And then he had done the unthinkable; he had diverted the President's ill-gotten gains into an account of his own.

He had to smile at his own naïveté.

It turned out, by what had to be more than sheer coincidence, that the same diplomat who had helped him in Beijing, the young man named Merle Stevens, had also relocated to Shanghai that summer. And they had met "quite by chance" at the Portman Ritz-Carleton, the latest expatriate watering hole where deals were brokered and China's markets were divvied up. They had shared drinks that first evening, and Merle had shown genuine concern about his ability to handle his family's death so stoically.

Then the diplomat had casually turned the conversation toward the topic of personal savings. Merle had told him that living off a straight government salary, he envied those in Shanghai who were truly raking in the money. If he were in Raymond's position, he would be transferring his life insurance benefits and income straight into a Cayman Islands account and never letting it touch American soil where he would be taxed to death.

Naturally, the topic appealed to Raymond's immediate interests, as he was searching for a way to siphon off some of the "contributions" that his oil company had earmarked for the President.

Merle gave him a tip or two on how to open a Grand Cayman Island account where money is untouchable and untraceable by his company and the U.S. government.

"Hell, half the Taiwanese companies doing business here in China are set up in the GCI," Merle had said.

The expansive, high ceiling of the lobby's bar seemed to impose no limits on Raymond. The drinks were on Merle, and Raymond allowed the rich vapors to work on him.

Sure the Taiwanese were doing it. Even the President of the United States was stashing money in the Caribbean.

He had let the topic rest, and Merle told him soulfully how gratified he felt that Raymond was on the rebound.

Jolted back to the present by loud banging on the tables, Raymond studied the shabby mess hall in which he sat. The sweaty seamen danced on the table before him as if he were a god. The galley was a far cry from the chic restaurants of Shanghai.

He remembered sitting on the 86th floor of the Jin Mao Tower, the world's third tallest building. Elegantly lit, the architectural gems of Shanghai's famous Bund reflected in the Huangpu River. Merle was his companion for the evening, and like most conversations taking place around the private, wood-paneled club, they were back to discussing money.

Over a plate of Shanghainese noodle, cuttlefish, and hairy crab delicacies, Merle blithely revealed to him how he routinely transferred funds for the Consulate's most shady, but highly valuable, contacts. He routed the money through various institutions to secret accounts in offshore banks.

"Actually it's relatively easy," Merle confessed. "You should try it sometime. Send a check to one of these accounts, have their bank issue you a VISA card, and try it out."

"As a financial officer for the Shanghai Branch," Raymond had reminded Merle, "I'm no stranger to shipping funds in and out of the United States. The new anti-terrorist limitations are the big hassle."

"Tell me about it. That's the beauty of my job. I work overseas and ship money from one country to another, circumventing U.S. banks. It's a piece of cake."

"But I've never established my own off-shore account before," he had admitted.

Merle reached for his wallet. "I've got several accounts that I'm not using any longer." He pulled out a VISA card. "Here, you can have this one. There's no name attached to it. It's only a number."

And that card still sat in the wallet in Raymond's pocket.

Sure enough, Raymond had tried the card out the next day, and it worked. He could legally send whatever amount of money he wanted to the bank, no questions asked.

It worked just as well with large sums of money. He transferred a huge amount from his company's pension fund, and that worked as well. A minute later, he returned the money to the pension fund.

It was exhilarating.

Next, he took the latest money his company had designated as a political contribution to the President's reelection campaign. He remembered wagging a finger at the President's personal account number after he typed it in and it appeared on the computer screen. "That's not legal, sir."

Instead of pushing Enter, he changed the account number to read the new account that Merle had so helpfully provided him.

Zap.

Within a nanosecond, the President's black funds totaling $10,000,000 were his, cloaked forever in the secrecy of the Caymans. And the President could never come griping to him. The Chief Executive's only recourse would be to send out enforcers of the waterfront kind, which he highly doubted would happen.

But the President did employ enforcers of the IRS kind. The next day, he had been informed that investigators were on their way to audit his company. They told him to be prepared for "an interview."

That night he had packed his bags and flown to Sanya, Hainan, leaving his lucrative expatriate package behind.

He took a moment to study that decision. Why in the world did he trade a life of bounty for a life on the run?

It had something to do with the fact that his company and the President were partners in crime, and that their misdeeds had cost his family their lives.

So Raymond became a felon of the highest order.

Sanya wasn't a bad refuge. China had some wonderful travel destinations. And look at him now...steaming on a first-class cruise ship across the Pacific. It was even kind of a party ship. His shipmates were rejoicing at the fact that America was up against the ropes.

He shook his head. At the moment, he wouldn't mind talking with the IRS, and telling them everything he knew. In fact, they could come and get him. He'd surrender peacefully.

He looked out the portholes, searching for some recognizable landmass, any land. But all he saw was the vast blue horizon, and their steady wake as they plowed ahead at full speed.

Where the hell were they going so fast?

"I saw you with that guy yesterday," Merle Stevens said.

"Oh him," Sandi said dismissively as she reclined on the poolside lounge chair. She wasn't going to let the ghost of Raymond O. Flowers stand in the way of a little hedonism.

"How well did you know him?"

"He's a very nice man," she said. It was good policy to expect the best of her suitors.

"I'm sure he was," he said, emphasizing the past tense. "What happened to him?"

"Oh, gone home to his family, I suppose," she said, flipping through the paper with no idea of what was on the pages.

He gave a short laugh, more of a sneer.

That drew her interest. A sign of his personality was emerging through the polished veneer. Was he the callous sort?

If so, that could be attractive.

"Why do you laugh?" she asked, setting down the paper.

"Oh, it's just that..." his voice trailed off as his eyes fell on the pool's calm surface. "Care for a swim?"

She had just applied her tanning oil, and the water was bound to be cold that early in the morning. "Sure," she said, tearing the scrunchie from her hair.

He stood and extended a hand, which she took. She allowed him to pull her to her feet. She landed erect, inches from his sculpted body. Instinctively she lay a hand against the thick black swirls of hair on his chest. The pounding under the skin was steady, not racing.

Boy, the guy was cool.

But she liked that.

He led her to the water's edge and turned to lower himself down the ladder step by step.

Aw hell, she thought, and arched herself over the water. She went clear to the bottom of the pool, prowling the depths like a tiger shark.

She spotted his feet stepping off the last rung and his toes touching the bottom. She buried her flowing hair between his legs and slowly drew herself to the surface.

He laughed when her eyes engaged with his.

He tapped her on the nose. "You're it," he said, and plunged away. She swam after him in hot pursuit.

This guy was playing hard to get.

Chapter 14

With the WAV files downloaded from the Pentagon and linked to Seaman Anthony Carlson's computer, he sat back and watched the process at work.

Scanning multiple radio and cell phone transmissions, the highly sensitive antennae on the *USS Endorse* were able to eavesdrop on both official and private communications on sea and shore.

And the airwaves were abuzz. His main terminal was divided into ten windows, each showing another audio print of some conversation taking place. Meanwhile, the computer was humming away, comparing the waveforms with those of known terrorists and internationally sought criminals.

If it found a match, the computer would automatically save the recorded message to a special inbox where Anthony could ship it off electronically to a team of translators at the NSA.

The system worked well, except for two factors. First, there were thousands of transmissions taking place at any given time. Even though the radio room was manned by seven seamen, each with several workstations, they could only analyze seventy conversations at a time. And secondly, in his three years' experience doing such work, Anthony had never once made a voice print match.

So where did he get his thrills? His answer was the hardware and software. They were things of beauty to maintain and watch.

Just as Anthony realized he was letting his thoughts wander, his commanding officer Lieutenant Terrence Whitcomb bounded down the stairs into the room. "Tune in to harbor traffic."

Now, Lt. Terry could be a prick. He had the patience of a gnat and talked in clipped sentences that Anthony still had trouble following. But he was a loyal seaman, ran a tight radio room, and Anthony never found himself working at cross-purposes with him. Hardware geeks seemed to communicate on an extra-personal level on which Anthony felt comfortable.

So when Terry said, "Tune in to harbor traffic," Anthony knew instantly what he meant, even though he would never know the reason behind the order. Terry never gave reasons, just orders...he was a prick.

Then came the surprise of Anthony's life. Terry gave the roomful of techies a sly smile and leaned over a chair to explain.

"I've requested that Manila contact each ship's captain."

Aha! Anthony spun back to his workstation with renewed energy. He tuned into the frequencies dedicated to ship communications, and his computer began to do the voice analysis, checking the voice signatures against those in the database, including those he had recently downloaded.

Lieutenant Terrence Whitcomb was driving the radio traffic to him. Within the next few minutes, he would be hit by a barrage of new voices, each from a different ship.

A single hit would mean that they had located a ship being commanded by a terrorist.

The first officer interrupted Raymond and the skipper while they were dining in the skipper's quarters.

"It's the harbor master once again. He wants to know our coordinates."

The skipper nodded and took a sip of black tea. He would take his time responding.

The first officer withdrew.

This was another chance for Raymond to get heard on the radio. If only the skipper gave him another chance. But he couldn't let the skipper sense how eager he was to alert the authorities to where he and the terrorists were located.

"So why don't you speak on the radio?" Raymond asked over his squid and vegetable stew.

Sometimes their collegiality frightened Raymond. Sure, it was nice to talk with another educated man on a long sea voyage, but he had to take into consideration who his companion was.

Raymond pressed the skipper again. "You could talk with the harbor master yourself."

The skipper waved his hand, crumbs falling off his piece of bread. "We don't use radios or telephones. They know our voices."

"Ha," Raymond said. "Sure they know the voice patterns of the key players in your organization, but surely not everybody. I'm no expert, but they can't monitor every transmission made on earth. I know the NSA has plenty of powerful listening devices and computers, but what's a little radio contact stating your ship's position?"

"We don't talk on radios," the skipper said with finality. "You will do the talking."

Jesus, the guy was obsessive. Who did he think he was, bin Laden? Raymond studied the skipper's soft hands and genteel manner of eating. It must be rare for al-Qaeda to appeal to the Oxford set.

"What brought you into al-Qaeda?" he asked. The question sounded somewhat brash, but maybe the guy liked talking politics. "Did they recruit you?"

"Hardly. Our group existed long before al-Qaeda. They brought our group into contact with other groups and trained some of our men, but al-Qaeda exists because of us."

Raymond didn't detect much enthusiasm for al-Qaeda in the skipper. "You are loyal to al-Qaeda, aren't you?"

"They've become as much a liability as an asset," the skipper remarked. "We could use the funding, but we don't need the publicity. It has made our job far more dangerous."

"What do you mean? You'd rather sit back, discuss revolution with other revolutionaries over tea, then blow up the occasional police station just to feel like you've accomplished something?"

"It's always a hopeless struggle by idealists."

"And now that the populace is stirred up, you may even have a chance of succeeding," Raymond finished his thought. "And that's a frightening prospect to you."

The skipper looked him directly in the eye.

"We are ready to take over," he stated firmly.

"But you don't have a clue what you'll do?"

The skipper laughed. It did not stem from amusement. Rather, Raymond may have touched a nerve.

"*Al Shari'ah*. Isn't that what it's called? Islamic Law. Isn't that what you'll install?"

"Of course. It is a very effective political system..."

"I'm sure at Oxford that's been thoroughly studied."

"...if you leave out the perfectibility aspect that drives governments closer to Islam and further from practicality."

"So you admit it's an imperfect system."

The skipper sucked in his breath and rose from the table. He carefully folded his napkin and looked at Raymond.

"Are you ready to talk on the radio?"

"Sure, why not," Raymond said. His heart began thumping loudly. This was the opportunity he was waiting for.

The last time he had read the ship's coordinates over the radio, he hadn't been able to say his name or slip in a subtle phrase that would otherwise identify him. The skipper had snatched the radio transmitter away from him too quickly.

But this was a second chance to get word out. Simply stating his name over the air would be like a lightning rod, attracting authorities to the evil nexus between the President and al-Qaeda.

Cold from the swim, her nipples stiff, and her bikini plastered to the contours of her body, Sandi lay back under her sun umbrella breathing hard.

Merle seemed no worse for the wear, as he calmly toweled himself off. He called over a pool attendant in Chinese and ordered Cokes for both of them. Then he eased into his lounge chair.

He had nice leg muscles, and very cute toes. Where did this guy come from? She didn't know that the Department of State churned out such hunks.

"I have a confession to make," he said, his voice turning serious.

Oh no. Here it came. He was going to be up-front with her about something that would destroy her fantasy.

She held her emotions in check. "What?" she said affecting as much disinterest as she could muster.

"I knew Raymond O. Flowers," he said, and looked at her to gauge her reaction.

The significance of his statement caught her unprepared, and she let out a laugh, perhaps even a sneer. "Him?" She had long since forgotten about that graying loser with too much personal baggage, and a bad financial record.

He mirrored her smile. "Yes, I do know him well," he said, as if trying to convince her of such an absurd notion. After all, why would a charmer like him, a man on the make, a total dreamboat ever want to make social contact with Raymond O. Flowers?

In fact, she wouldn't have believed him, if he hadn't known Raymond by name. That made her stop and let her investigative instincts take over.

Sponging off the beads of water that rolled about her belly, she casually formulated a question. "How do you know him?"

Merle frowned. The story seemed more complicated than he could relate in the current tone of their conversation. "I'll tell you about him sometime."

"Yeah, sure."

The drinks came, and Merle seemed thirsty. He downed his drink at once, his eyes steady on hers.

For her part, she gently picked up the tall, slender glass and let her lips suck full and moist on the thick straw.

He was still looking at her. She thrust out her breasts with a tremendous sigh and threw back her hair.

"How about dinner tonight?" he asked. "We can talk over a glass of wine and some *pod thai*."

"That would work," she said. She would have to let the matter rest until then.

He set his glass down on a small table between their lounge chairs and flashed her another one of his toothy smiles.

It made her feel like an adolescent before a movie idol.

"I have to be going. I've got some work to do," he said.

"What do you mean? Work on a day like today?" She looked over the ocean and beach below. Nearly all the chairs were occupied, kids were playing volleyball, a paraglider flew past, and young men and ladies strutted around the pool.

"Yeah, hard to believe, isn't it?" he said.

She raised her eyebrows. Did that mean she should be working, too?

"Bye for now," he said. "I'll meet you at the Garden Restaurant at eight."

"Fine. I'll be there."

He stood, picked up his cell phone and towel, and walked away. Sandi traced the V shape of his back down to his slim waist and clinging black swim trunks. She felt helpless, like a small child. She would be putty in his hands. What was she turning into? Where was that cast iron will and enormous ego that had opened doors to her future? Was she going to lie on silk sheets for the rest of her life, a moaning, voluptuous, scented bag of hormones?

"Is this chair taken?"

She focused her eyes on the lounge chair beside her. A skinny teenager wanted to lie beside her and worship her body.

"Get lost," she said, and turned away.

Seaman Anthony Carlson's eyes were already bloodshot. His morning had begun early with the customary calisthenics on the ship's tiny quarterdeck.

That had been followed by flat-tasting scrambled eggs, the same fare he had been served for the past three months. No matter how much salt he poured on them, he couldn't tease out the least bit of flavor. Perhaps the food manufacturer had left out the "essence of egg" seasoning in the egg powder.

Then, watching the new voice files downloading from the Pentagon had burned up two hours of eyeball time. And now, with the entire radio room scanning the ship-to-shore frequencies, it had become a kind of competition among the seven radiomen. Who could spot a terrorist first?

Of course the entire exercise was entirely artificial, as they were as likely to find a terrorist as the Marines were to find bin Laden in Afghanistan.

But the competition did arouse their interest, and dry out his eyes.

Suddenly, a red blotch flashed on one of the tiny subdivisions of his oversized screen. He blinked to clear away the scum in his eyes.

The damn voiceprint was flashing red.

He hid the Record button. "Hit!" he shouted.

Three other seamen had simultaneously jumped out of their seats. "Hit!" "Hit! "Hit!"

They had all won.

The digital voice recording was stored on their hard drives. Anthony donned his headset and listened in.

It was the flat American accent of a man radioing in his ship's name, registration, and general location east of the Philippines.

Anthony's eyes scanned over to the watch list of voices to match. One line was flashing in white. "Raymond O. Flowers."

"Good God," Anthony said. He leaned on the intercom that connected him with Lieutenant Whitcomb's office. "You've got to get down here right away."

Anthony left the recorder going, but there was no further communication.

He slowly removed his earphones and looked at the others. They studied each other in amazement.

Had their system really worked?

Terry Whitcomb came dashing down the stairs.

Anthony stood and saluted. He pulled out his chair for his commanding officer to take and study the results.

Whitcomb glanced at the watch list and rubbed his jaw. Then he pulled on the headset and replayed the transmission.

Anthony couldn't tell from his reaction whether he was stunned by their success or overcome with emotion.

At last Terry spun around, confusion written across his face. "We've caught Flowers," he said to the room at large.

The cheers were muted.

"I'll have to tell the Pentagon."

All of a sudden the full import of the news hit Anthony. They were about to sink their own Commander-in-Chief. He felt a strong resistance rise up within him.

"We can't do that, sir. Maybe the voice print got into our database by accident."

"That's right, sir," another radioman piped up. "The Admiral will shit can us if we get this wrong."

Terry was still rubbing his long jaw.

"I can't avoid it," he said, all emotion drained from his voice. He dragged himself out of Anthony's chair and slowly climbed the stairs.

The others stood and watched him go.

Was he a traitor to turn in a traitor to the President? Or was he just a good soldier?

Chapter 15

Defense Secretary Kenneth Spaulding entered the Cabinet Room at the White House with a grave air.

President Bernard White conducted business for a few minutes, reading off his major points from white index cards.

The entire Cabinet listened dutifully, but their thoughts were elsewhere.

With a divided House and Senate and a Presidential election that year, not much was going to happen by way of legislation. Which meant that it was not a time for new ideas, initiatives, or any sudden change of course. In fact, it was a time to consolidate their gains, package them to the public, and hope that the fickle voters would not vote them out of office.

Then the President went around the room, polling his various Secretaries for political advice. The Secretary of Energy thought it was time to enlist the Saudi's support in holding down oil prices before energy became an election issue. The Director of Central Intelligence offered a bleak assessment of future troop casualties in the Persian Gulf. Attorney General Caleb Perkins seemed to have little to offer except to stay the course. The Secretary of Commerce suggested hopefully that the country could cast their military action in the Gulf states in the light of her pet project of opening up foreign markets.

Then the President turned to Kenneth. "Why so serious today?"

Kenneth had received some remarkable news while in his motorcade crossing the Potomac. But he had spent the entire meeting mulling over how to present it.

"I've got good news and bad news," he said, opting for the trite approach. In fact, by making the President choose between which news he wanted first, Kenneth was distancing himself from being the bearer of bad news.

"I could use some good news," Bernard said.

"Okay, then. Thanks to the inspired work of your Chief of Staff and the Director of Counterterrorism, we've found ourselves a terrorist ship. An al-Qaeda-owned ship, in fact."

The room full of solemn business suits broke out in spontaneous pep rally-type applause. It was a rare moment for a Cabinet meeting.

"We just received information about the vessel: its name, its country of registration, and its whereabouts."

Attorney General Caleb Perkins swiveled toward him and blurted out, "Where is it?"

Kenneth shot him a look. Why was Caleb chomping at the bit? This was no longer an FBI matter. The Navy had located the ship.

Nevertheless, he read from the notes he had scribbled while riding in his official sedan. "It's several hundred nautical miles east of the Philippines."

"In a shipping lane?"

Boy, that Caleb was annoying. Kenneth shook his head. "We don't know where it's coming from or where it's going. It's in relatively uncharted waters where very little exists in the way of land."

Caleb was taking notes. "And its name and country of origin?"

Once again Kenneth referred to his notes. "It's called the *Ariana* and it's sailing under the Panamanian flag."

The President had the most muted praise for the military of the group. "And now for the bad news…"

Kenneth knit his eyebrows and swallowed hard. "It appears that the terrorists have Raymond O. Flowers onboard the ship."

Dead silence reigned. Individually, the members of the Cabinet could shrug off the President's Chinagate scandal. And they were sworn to fighting terrorism around the world. But mixing the two was playing with political dynamite.

Bernard sat back in his seat, a look of resignation on his face. "I knew the time would come," he said.

A mild chorus of support rose up from the room. "You can't quit now. This is just a speed bump. We're one hundred percent behind you."

He waved them off, somewhat heartened by their encouragement, but dread still written all over his heavy features.

Kenneth cleared his throat once more.

"Ah, we do have one option, sir."

No response.

He went on. "We could choose to ignore the ship."

The President looked troubled by the suggestion. "Are you trying to involve me in another scandal, this time letting terrorists off the hook?"

"Not at all," Kenneth said, finding his stride. "The mission of our armed services is a military one. We have no mandate to engage in civilian criminal investigations. Our job is not to hunt down common thieves. How Flowers showed up on that ship I'll never know. But there is no law on the books that compels me to pursue him."

Bernard began nodding. "I think we can strike the last five or so minutes from the record, can't we Jill?"

He looked at the elderly stenographer, who began pounding away on the Backspace key of her laptop.

The President stood, and the rest of the room rose with him. "That'll be all for this morning's business," he said. "Have a good week."

The President brushed past Kenneth as he was gathering his papers. "Nuke the ship," he whispered and left.

Kenneth found himself standing in an empty room. Was the President serious?

Her blonde hair pinned up elegantly for a romantic evening, Sandi DiMartino stood in the lobby of the Garden Restaurant at the Hainan Resort waiting for her dinner date to arrive.

She hadn't seen Merle Stevens around the hotel, pool, or beach all day. What kind of work did a diplomat do at a tropical getaway anyway, and how could she get such a job?

He arrived precisely on the hour. She liked a punctual man. Then her eyes fixed themselves on his dapper blue dinner jacket. He looked down at his attire. "I wore this to match your eyes," he explained.

"Oh," she said, trying to recover from a feeling of being inadequately dressed in her casual, if not slinky, evening gown. "I was just wondering if I'm underdressed."

"Not at all. Less is more."

She didn't mind a man with a subtle sense of humor, even if she was the target of his zingers. They moved as a couple into the restaurant and were shown to a corner table that overlooked the dark restaurant with its straight lines, paper room dividers, square dishes, and elegant hanging light sculptures. Southeast Asian fusion, she concluded.

A pale, gawky Chinese waitress served them ice water with lemon grass swaying among the ice cubes of their glasses.

"May I order?" he asked. "Any preferences?"

She shook her head.

Within a minute, he and the waitress had worked out a suitable fare that would last them well into the evening.

Meanwhile, Sandi watched a trio of Portuguese musicians serenading guests at another table. God, she hoped they wouldn't try that on her. The stiffness of a first date was pressure enough.

Finally, they were alone, with only a dish of stiff, hot spring rolls and her overly exposed breasts between them.

She wanted to ask him more about himself, but they had jumped into the relationship so quickly that it would seem like backtracking to cover such mundane details as his marital status. In truth, she regarded their intimacy as a personal accomplishment and she wouldn't relinquish it by resorting to such mundane topics as their jobs, place of birth, and so on. Although she only wanted to charge ahead, she knew that custom called for them to pass some time together before jumping into bed. She searched desperately for a topic of conversation. She needed to find some intellectual connection between them.

"Tell me about Flowers," she shot out.

He looked at the bouquet on the table, then up at her. Flowers, she got it. The unspoken pun left them with a new intimacy, and left her dazzled by the breadth of his sense of humor, a range that reached from nuanced to sophomoric.

Then he put on a more serious expression. "I knew Raymond in Beijing last spring. His family was struck down by SARS."

He looked up to see if she was following him.

"I wasn't aware..." she said, suddenly moved. Nobody had told her that. Poor Raymond had lost his family less than a year earlier. And what horrible deaths those must have been, struck down on the streets of China by a frightening epidemic!

Apparently concerned by the emotional impact that the news had on her, he tried to venture back onto familiar terrain. "Actually, I have another secret to tell you."

Again the intimacy. She liked that, and needed it at the moment.

"If you want to know the truth, that's only a story. Don't worry. His family is still alive."

That confused her. Either they were alive or they weren't. Raymond wouldn't be just sitting around a resort picking up strange women if he still had a family. "Is he aware that they're still alive?"

Merle shook his head. "No."

"Why don't you tell him, for God's sake?"

He raised a finger to his lips. "Shh."

What was this? A state secret? How could anybody let a fellow human being roam the earth thinking that his family was dead when he knew they weren't? Was Merle actually some cruel kind of monster? "How do you know that they are still alive? Have you seen them?"

"I have," he replied cryptically.

"Then are they still sick?" She tried to imagine an American family languishing in a Chinese ward for respiratory diseases.

"No. Let's just leave it at that."

"But where are they now?" she persisted.

"Still in China."

"You've got to be kidding. And Raymond isn't aware that they're still alive? He's walking around in grief and loss, thinking their dead?"

Merle shrugged his shoulders.

"How could this be?" she breathed, suddenly aware that her breasts were heaving dangerously close to popping out.

He reached across the table for her hand to calm her down.

"I was hoping that you would be relieved to know that they are still alive," he said. "Don't worry about Raymond O. Flowers."

What kind of a diplomat was he anyway? People didn't withhold such information from fellow human beings, much less fellow countrymen! She closed her eyes and tried to let her vision of Raymond's family trapped somewhere in China pass from her mind. The horrifying thought that they were most likely being held against their will, and presumably unable to reach Raymond or tell him of their fate, sickened her. Then she remembered how she had tried to seduce him, and he had resisted. What an admirable man! And how despicable Merle Stevens looked across the table.

She would have to get word out to Raymond that his family was alive. But she wouldn't be able to get very far with this big oaf grinning at her all evening, or worse, not letting her go.

"Don't worry about him," he repeated.

She swept a hand across her face. "He's gone from my mind," she said with her best attempt at a bright smile.

She reopened her eyes and the tall, dark stranger materialized before her with his irresistibly handsome smile. And she had been all set to take him to bed by the end of an evening of intimate talk with great eye contact and strong undercurrents of passion!

Then her cell phone rang.

Attorney General Caleb Perkins couldn't wait until he got back to his fifth-floor suite at the Justice Department. He looked around to make sure that his receptionist and staff weren't listening, then closed the door and took his seat.

He pulled his notes from the Cabinet meeting out of his briefcase and studied them one more time. He had a ship and her fairly specific location. It was his chance to nab Flowers, turn him over to the special prosecutor, and knock the President clean out of the ring and off to Leavenworth.

He snatched his phone, consulted his Rolodex for a card that Stanley Polk had sent him, and dialed the listed cell phone number.

An annoyed female voice answered.

"Sandi?"

"Yes? Who's calling at this hour?"

"This is Caleb Perkins. I have some information that might be of interest to you."

"I'm always ready to hear you out," she said brusquely.

He heard a clatter of dishes and a pen clicking at the other end of the line.

When she was ready, he announced, "It seems that we have located your key witness."

"You mean...?"

"Flowers. The one and only." Caleb read off the ship's name and location in the eastern waters off the Philippines.

When Sandi stopped scribbling, he heard her set her pen down. "To what can I attribute this highly unusual gesture of goodwill between your department and my office?" she asked.

He smiled. "Let's put our gloves down just for one moment," he said. "I've told you where Flowers is, but you have to do the rest."

"Can't you deliver him to me?" she asked.

"That would be nearly impossible. My hands are tied."

"Okay, okay," she said. "I've got the means and I've got my methods."

"Well, *bon appetit*. Good luck to you and your investigation."

"I don't think I'll be eating tonight."

Just before he set his phone down, he heard a young man's perplexed and incensed voice shout at Sandi, "Hey! Where are you going?"

"I don't have time for sex—" he heard her respond before she clicked off.

He set down his phone, the tenderness in his own voice still reverberating in his head. Was he coming on to Stanley Polk's head of investigations?

If he were going to pursue his romantic inclinations, he'd have to date within his own political Party, and well within secure channels.

Sandi didn't have time to change out of her evening dress, more suited for a samba than a series of puddle jumps across Asia.

She caught an eight pm flight to Hong Kong. There, a quick check at the ticket counter revealed a flight to Manila leaving within minutes. Hustling down the long people movers to the far end of the new airport, she flew into the loading ramp just as the doors were sliding closed.

Whew.

She joined a plane half full of bleary-eyed businessmen and lively Filipina ayis eager to get home. She felt somewhere in-between. On the one hand Raymond was pure business, deadly dull in many respects. On the other hand, her body had been primed for a night of action, and she was determined to get it, one way or another.

She arrived in Manila just past midnight, fully expecting to find yet another city that was fast asleep.

She couldn't have been more wrong. The taxi ride downtown from the airport proved to be one of the liveliest experiences of her life.

The skies were dark, but nobody seemed to notice. Along both sides of the slow-moving Roxas Boulevard, neon lit up entire buildings: nightclubs, discos, and restaurants.

Jeepneys, silver-sided remnants from the war in the Pacific were decorated to the hilt with political signs and swirling colors. Riders hopped on and off at will.

Men sported flowery shirts and embroidered sheer barongs that hung over their belts and women, squeezed into tight dresses, clunked around the crowded streets in platform shoes. The crowd was a laughing, smiling, lipstick smeared, highly coiffed, dancing, flirting mixture of men on the make and women out making themselves seen.

The thought of joining the fray exhausted her.

She tried to remember the date. It wasn't a major holiday that she knew of. Could every night be like that?

The sultry air hardly moved, and only a gush of air conditioning from the old taxi's air vents kept her from completely melting away.

Once past the showy clubs, the city relaxed behind walled compounds of single-story bungalows, or slinked down alleyways to compounds of two-story family homes. Trees spread overhead and vegetation pushed against the restraining fingers of myriad gardeners. At last, embedded amidst convenience stores, indoor malls, and potholed streets, several tall hotels sprung up, their rooms glittering like stars against the otherwise dark night sky.

Yet, she didn't intend to sleep long. She had a ship to find.

Chapter 16

The rusty freighter was steaming briskly across the sunny Pacific into the early morning sun when Raymond climbed up to the bridge.

He knocked, and the skipper unlocked the door. He was reviewing nautical charts spread out on a table.

"So, where are we going today?" Raymond asked brightly.

The skipper looked at him without expression.

Once again, Raymond had been rebuffed trying to obtain information on their destination. And the skipper no longer found it funny.

"So I guess we'll just float around out here forever."

He took a moment to study the skipper as he labored over the map. The man was impressive. An Oxford graduate and a revolutionary, how did the guy know so much about ships? A frightening thought entered his mind. The skipper had the kind of raw intelligence, connections, and know-how his oil company craved when hiring employees. How many of these revolutionaries were already embedded in the ranks of international corporations?

The skipper raised his binoculars and scanned the horizon in all directions. Raymond noticed that the radar screen was turned off. Perhaps the skipper was playing it safe and not letting the freighter emit a signal that the authorities could pick up and identify.

The skipper's unusual combination of skills prompted Raymond to want to know more about the man.

"So what is it that drives you?" he asked.

"You are persistent," the skipper said.

"I just want to know. Do you have a personal gripe with some government? Did the Israelis torture your family? Why are you doing all this? Surely killing people isn't in the Koran."

"I'm not killing people," the skipper said fiercely, the first time Raymond saw him lose control of his tightly held emotions.

"Okay," Raymond said. "So you don't kill. Why are you terrorizing people like this?"

"I'm not terrorizing anyone. Look at me. Who am I terrorizing?"

"Okay, so you're not a terrorist. I always thought that term was overused anyway."

"So do I. Our movement is not trying to frighten, harm, or destroy people or civilizations. We're about change."

"So you're the Howard Dean of world politics."

The man laughed. "Perhaps so."

"Back to the question: Why?"

"When we eventually succeed, we will democratize the levers of power in society and the economy. We're fighting for control over our lives."

"What are you, a progressive?"

The skipper looked at him, his expression somewhat hurt.

"What?" Raymond said, unable to withhold a smile. "That's it, isn't it? How frightening. You're a progressive. That's all you are. Ooooh," he said in a wavering voice. "Let's form a Department of Homeland Security, here come the Progressives!"

Suddenly the skipper stiffened. Raymond had struck a nerve. He had gone too far.

"Mark my words," the skipper said evenly, his voice taking on ominous undertones. "Your country will be the first to go. It's the evil weed that is choking out my people. And in the next few days, you will help me pull it out by its roots."

He reached into his briefcase and handed Raymond some papers. "Here. I want you to fill these out."

Raymond glanced over the documents. Once again, the skipper wanted to change the ship's identity. He was holding forms from a company in Vienna, Virginia, that would add their ship to Liberia's open registry.

Meanwhile, the skipper leaned over, opened a small compartment, and pulled out a flag.

He unfurled it, revealing a white star against a blue field in one corner, and red and white stripes covering the rest, not unlike an American flag.

"Today we will turn Liberian," the skipper said.

Raymond looked out at the open sea. Based on its name, Liberia must have been founded on the basis of Liberty. And the skipper was seeking freedom for his entire people at America's expense. If only *he* could be free... The concept seemed so distant and unattainable.

The skipper handed Raymond a pen.

Reflagging, renaming, and re-registering a ship under a different identity every few days must have felt liberating for the skipper. But filling out the forms would only further seal Raymond's fate, the fate of his family, and the fate of his nation.

Dawn broke suddenly and without warning in the tropics as Sandi left her hotel for the Philippine Ports Authority. Her taxi driver steered her expertly through the crowded streets of Manila. How a city could wake up so early after a night of karaoke singing and hip swinging was beyond her.

Men were busy shining shoes, delivering goods, and carrying boxes on their shoulders, their clothes freshly pressed. Children in uniforms walked dutifully to school under the care of older sisters and brothers. Women in flip-flops hurried back and forth across the narrow, potholed lanes.

Sandi's taxi approached a vast, breezy park fringed with palm trees, beyond which lay the widespread crescent of Manila Bay. She caught her breath. Fleecy clouds rimmed the horizon. A lone helicopter crawled across the sky over the empty sea.

It looked like a scene right out of a war movie, where American vessels would steam to the aid of the stricken populace, or Japanese would capture and torture starving soldiers and send them on a death march through Bataan Province. And all the while, they were surrounded by a stunningly beautiful sea and islands that were as lush as gardens.

They passed a long line of people patiently queued up beside the road. They wore baseball caps and Major League jerseys and tight jeans. Was there a ballpark along the shoreline?

Then she did a double take. Above the building flew an American flag. It was the American Embassy and the people had lined up long before opening hours to get their visas. Could it be that Filipinos knew something about America that she didn't?

A few minutes later, the taxi pulled to a halt before the Philippine

Ports Authority building. Twenty *pesos* did the trick. She threw in an extra five for efficient service.

The head of the ports authority was already waiting for her. He was a short man with unctuous manners, a proud bearing, and various military ribbons pinned to his barrel-shaped chest.

"Captain Albano at your service, ma'am."

She introduced herself and shook his hand. He looked ready to kiss it, but must have changed his mind.

Stepping inside, Sandi looked around the large, cluttered office. The captain was the only one wearing his particular kind of green uniform. Perhaps it was a holdover from a previous regime. Then she noticed that just about everyone wore a different style and color of uniform. Perhaps there had been many regime changes, and fashions had a hard time keeping up.

As they walked to Captain Albano's control room, he asked her in a circumspect voice, "Why are you using our radios? Why don't you use that U.S. Navy ship out there patrolling the waters?"

She smiled at the thought. "Let's just say that we're on completely different missions," she said.

He shrugged and gestured to the worn wooden doors that opened onto a control room with a commanding view of the bay.

A row of radio operators communicated with ships as they entered Philippine waters. While the captain set her up with a radio transmitter, she listened in on the heavily accented English of the radio operators who were communicating with the ships. It sounded like most of the ships were just passing through Philippine territorial waters on the heavily traveled sea-lanes that formed the crossroads between East Asia and Southeast Asia and the Americas. Only a few cargo ships sought permission to enter the ports located on the island.

She donned a headset and cupped both earphones over her ears. Transmissions by ship captains were even more difficult to understand.

How did these people understand one another when they had no language in common but English that even a native speaker couldn't make out? No wonder there were so many ferry disasters in the Philippines. And small wonder that there weren't more maritime accidents in the sea-lanes.

Already the air was muggy, and she pulled her blouse away from her perspiring chest. She fought to concentrate.

The radio operators were busy checking ships' positions. To her amazement, there were no radar screens tracking the vessels. Apparently, knowing what ship was where was a far less organized business than tracking airplanes that sent out signals identifying themselves to air traffic controllers.

Suddenly a responding voice on a weak signal caught her attention.

"This is the *Ariana*," the weak, but distinctly American voice announced. Bingo, just as Caleb Perkins had said. It was Raymond O. Flowers.

She smiled. What a darling. What was he doing on that ship? "Hi, Raymond," she interrupted, her finger pressing the microphone's transmit button. "Remember me?"

"Sandi?" Raymond said after a pause for him to remember her voice, shock registering over the crackling airwaves. "What are you doing in the Philippines?"

"I'm looking for you."

There was radio silence on the other end, just half-heard transmissions between other ships.

"There are some people who need you," she said. "Real bad."

"That's the understatement of the year."

"And I need you, too."

"Please state your exact position," a radio operator said.

"Shit. It's 14° 34' North, 130°—" Raymond's voice began relaying the reading on the GPS receiver, but was cut short.

"Please repeat that," the radio operator said.

There was no response. Sandi pressed her earphones tight over her ears and listened to the static for several minutes, but Raymond had once again vanished from her life.

She stomped a heel against the linoleum floor.

Someone had cut off the transmission.

"Reflag immediately!" the skipper barked into the intercom, sending men scrambling up on deck like cockroaches from a fumigated wall.

I'm dead, Raymond told himself as the skipper pried the unplugged transmitter from his fingers, shoved it back into its plastic cradle, and turned off the radio receiver. He had been so close to divulging the *Ariana's* location to someone who could make a difference, who could bring in the Feds.

The skipper hustled him out of the radio room and off the bridge, locking it shut behind him.

How desperate could Raymond be, hoping for the Feds to come to his rescue? Just a few days earlier, he was trying to elude them at all costs.

All it took was one look at the fire in the skipper's eyes and the determination in his furrowed brow. So he didn't call himself a killer or a terrorist. Call him whatever, the man was hell-bent on destroying America and all that she stood for, and Raymond, for one, wasn't going to allow it.

"There's no time. Paint over the name, quick," the skipper bellowed down at the crew.

Paint buckets slopping over, the deckhands rushed to give the ship an instant makeover. The twin funnels lost their tiger stripes, and became glossy black that glistened in the noonday sun.

The skipper climbed down from the bridge and draped the Liberian flag over the stern.

Raymond followed him to watch. Below him, men had been lowered on davits to paint over the name. They had stencils and a spray gun in hand.

"What do we call her?" one man shouted up from below, while the other busily painted over the former name.

Within an hour, the *Ariana* of Panama had become the *Lost Horizon* of Liberia.

Raymond watched the workmen changing the props of their stage drama.

In the same fashion, the Chinese staff at his resort hotel on Hainan Island had done a wonderful job of transforming a colonial-style marble palace into a glitzy Hollywood mogul's mansion.

The night of the pre-Academy Award celebration at Sanya, Sandi had appeared to him like a movie star in a slim, sequined ballroom gown, her backlit hair bouncing with life. She had shed her slinky bikini and was transformed into a romantic vision. She was ready for her close-up.

During their encounter, which consisted of drinks, dancing, and light dining followed by fireworks, she had slipped him her business card. She had been softening him up for the kill.

Now she was zeroing in on him as he floated helplessly in a rust bucket in the middle of the Pacific Ocean.

He reached down and pulled out his wallet. He flipped to her business card. It read Sandi DiMartino, Global Oil Incorporated, and gave her office and cell phone numbers.

What was she doing at the Philippine port, taking down ships' GPS readings? What kind of oil company lawyer did that sort of thing?

Was she friend or foe? He was on the verge of ripping up the business card.

But it didn't matter any longer who got to him first. If she represented the President or the prosecutor, whether he faced a hit squad or life imprisonment, whether he'd ever get a shot at finding his family, first he had to get the terrorists off his back.

He watched the skipper approach with slow, menacing steps. "File those documents immediately," the skipper said, his voice harsh.

Raymond looked down at the papers he would have to transmit to the company in Virginia.

"Come with me. We'll use the fax in my quarters."

In the radio room of the *USS Endorse*, Seaman Anthony Carlson played back the most recent recording that he had made of the conversation between Flowers and the woman in Manila.

"You're sure that's Flowers?" Lieutenant Terrence Whitcomb asked, leaning over his shoulder.

Anthony keyed in the filename of Flowers' voiceprint. He dragged the zigzagging lines across the screen to the voice he had just recorded. The peaks and valleys of the waveform matched exactly.

Terry considered for a moment. "Do you recognize the woman's voice in Manila?" he asked.

Anthony, whose job required that he live by the ear, had a good audible memory, whereas his lieutenant did not. He shook his head. He didn't know the woman his commanding officer was talking about.

"At any rate," Terry said, straightening his back and looking down the long aisle of consoles. "We have to inform the Pentagon that we got another hit and this one included a more accurate reading of Flowers' position."

In his Pentagon office suite, Secretary of Defense Kenneth Spaulding needed to ensure that he had interpreted the President correctly.

It wasn't every day that the Navy blew a foreign freighter out of the water, under any pretext.

He set down the specific GPS coordinates that had just arrived from the Pacific theater, picked up his phone and punched in the number of the White House Chief of Staff.

"Chuck Romer here."

"This is Kenneth," he said in his stentorian voice. "I need to make sure I understand the President correctly about the terrorist ship."

"You brought it up at the meeting," Chuck reminded him.

"Yes, but I want to be clear on our decision. The President asked me to nuke the ship."

"Nuke? That's an expression."

"I figured that. I'm not about to waste a nuclear warhead on a freighter."

"Ha ha. That would be ridiculous."

There was an awkward silence.

So Kenneth tried to clarify further. "So you're saying…"

"Don't you hear me? I'm saying to nuke the ship. Ha. Now, I've got a wedding consultant on hold."

Chuck hung up on him.

Right. One didn't want to be on record making that sort of statement.

Slowly, Kenneth set down the phone and pressed his intercom button. He heard the buzz at his secretary's desk.

"Get me the *USS Endorse*," he requested.

Lieutenant Terrence Whitcomb stared out at the sea dotted with freighters and fishing trawlers of varying profiles and sizes.

The *USS Endorse* had been steaming eastward in an attempt to catch up with the fleeing terrorist ship. It was not an easy task, as the *Endorse* wasn't designed for speed. A floating brick was faster.

But within the past twenty-four hours, Terry calculated, they may have closed half the distance.

The partial GPS reading that Flowers had given out cut a large swath across sea-lanes going in both directions. Some sea-lanes headed north-south, while others headed toward the West Coast of the United States. They would have to identify the ship by sight, however, in the busy waters around the Philippines, how could they figure out which was the *Ariana*?

A visual identification of the terrorist ship would be like finding a specific anchovy in a school of fish. Carefully monitoring ship-to-shore radio transmissions had paid off only to the extent that they were faced with an annoyingly large number of suspects.

"Call from Washington, sir."

Terry jumped at the sound of the radioman's voice.

"Hello?" he said, taking the phone.

"Do you know who this is?"

Terry frowned. Was this some joke? It sounded just like the Secretary of Defense.

"Yes, sir," he replied uncertainly.

"That's Mr. Secretary."

"Yes, Mr. Secretary."

"Do you have the terrorist ship in your sights?"

Terry stared at the fifty ships sprayed across his radarscope. It didn't sound like Secretary Spaulding was in a good mood. Terry had better tell him what he wanted to hear. "Yes, we do, Mr. Secretary."

"Then torpedo it!" the Secretary of Defense shouted.

"Ah, aye aye, sir, Mr. Secretary."

He found himself talking to a dead phone.

"What is it, sir?" radioman Anthony Carlson asked gently.

Terry turned toward the glowing radar screen below him. A long line of freighters lay bow to stern in the wide GPS area that Flowers had indicated.

"We have to torpedo one of those ships," he said, his voice cracking.

"But we don't have torpedoes."

One point of light on the radar screen was a different color. It was a light red, accompanied by a seven-digit code. As opposed to commercial vessels, the military sent out beacons that other naval ships could use to identify them. The computer overlaid the military ship's location over the radar screen, forming a composite display.

Terry pointed to the red dot. Its code indicated all he needed to know. It was the *USS Stuart*, a naval destroyer, equipped to sink everything from submarines to attack ships.

"Our ship doesn't have jack, but *she* can sink the terrorists."

Anthony stared at the crowded scope. "And which one is the *Ariana*?"

CHINA GATE

The Raid

Chapter 17

Hadi Ahmed climbed nimbly up the now-familiar footpath that led to Osama's mountain hideout. He adjusted the knife in his belt and began the climb straight up the final ascent.

His forefathers, the Waziris, had much the same profession as he had that night. They were the robbers and highwaymen who owned the Khyber Pass. They had defeated the other Pathan tribes and the British in the 19th Century. And they were still at it.

A hearty breed of barrel-chested men with handsome physiques, they could take on all comers. But they also knew the hidden trails that allowed them to ambush their prey, then escape and hide so effectively. It was a grim life. His people wore drab, unbuttoned coats, shirts fastened at one shoulder, and long, unfitted trousers. And the women weren't much better off, dressing much the same as the men allowing for the occasional jewelry.

The mountains had made his people strong and gave them their livelihood. Trees grew on the tops of the highest mountains, and the rest was grassy with occasional bushes. Only the few flat valleys were cultivatable. Food came from the accurate firing of a rifle at the unlucky hawk or mountain goat. Allah's providence came mostly from the unsuspecting traveler whom they would accost and mercilessly strip of all their possessions.

It came as no surprise to him why the *jihad* movement had come there for refuge. They could hide and be defended well in the Waziri's natural citadel.

So it struck him as odd that when he reached Osama's cave, he found Osama and his handful of associates packing to leave.

"What news do you bring?" Osama said, his words rushed, as he was busy packing his clothing.

Hadi hastily scrambled up from his prone position to address the great leader of Allah's holy war.

"Your cousin needs final approval. He is ready to stage his raid on Purang when you give him the word."

"He should not be waiting for word from me. He should be going ahead with his plan." Osama glared at Hadi. "I am tired of all these messages. I don't need to know every detail. Allah preserve us, all these messages are dangerous!"

"I am most humbly sorry, sir," Hadi said.

"We are leaving now," Osama said. "We will go with you."

"But it is midnight!" Hadi exclaimed. "The paths are treacherous." He looked dubiously at Osama bin Laden's frail form.

"We will survive the trip if Allah is willing," was all that Osama said. "Now lead us down to Wana."

Hadi saw that all the men were already prepared to leave. One man kicked dirt over the campfire, plunging the cave into darkness.

"Where are you moving to?" Hadi asked. "Wana is not safe. Pakistani troops come and go every few weeks."

"I'm not moving to Wana," Osama said. "I am only going to the airport there."

Hadi knew better to ask any more questions. But he couldn't refrain. "And where to from there?"

"Purang," Osama said simply.

Carolyn Flowers felt herself waking up from a beautiful dream. She tried to chase after the fragments that remained in her memory...

The gushing waterfalls, the kids' distant voices as they played in the shallow natural pool, Raymond's stout forearms lifting something from the water and handing it to her. Holding it close under her chin. The roaring water filled her ears and bounded down a nearby hill. The object felt warm and nuzzled under her.

There was a squeal and the waterfall suddenly stopped thundering.

"Here's Raymond," she heard an old Chinese voice say to her. "Raymond has arrived."

Her eyelids were too heavy to lift open.

Raymond was back?

"Raymond," she said thickly, sounding drugged.

If she couldn't open her eyes, maybe she could lift her arms and embrace him, feel him, smell him close beside her.

Her arms weren't moving, yet she felt warmth against her and heaviness on her chest.

"It's Raymond," the old voice said.

She couldn't move, but that didn't matter. She felt happy, and tears rolled down the sides of her face.

The waterfall resumed its roar, and the dream returned in full color.

The next morning, the *Lost Horizon* looked nothing like its former self, the *Ariana*. And Raymond barely recognized the man who stared at him in the mirror. Perhaps he should clean his glasses.

He ran a trickle of rusty water over his wire-rimmed spectacles, washing off the previous day's sweat and salt spray. Then, using a clean spot on his formerly white shirt, he dried them off.

He took another look in the mirror. No, that was some other man, a crazed and desperate shadow of his former self.

In the tropical heat, he no longer needed his dress shirt. He ripped it off, losing several buttons in the process, and threw it on the floor. That left him in a tank top that was gray with sweat. His firm pectorals and deltoids bulged impressively below the fabric, but his face was a wreck.

He hadn't shaved in days, and the dark beard was beginning to resemble those of the terrorists aboard ship. His eyes were hollow from sleep deprivation, and his cheekbones poked visibly against this skin due to a painful bout of dysentery.

His trousers had become filthy, and he had exchanged them for a pair of fatigues given to him by the terrorists. Aside from his wallet, the multiple pockets were empty.

His feet remained bare, his toes splayed out after several days without shoes. The skin on the tops of his feet was the first to burn, and he couldn't fit the tender blistered skin into shoes even if he wanted to.

It was amazing how thick one's hair became after several days without washing, and how stiff his clothes felt. If only the water pipe in the shower hadn't broken, he might not even smell so bad.

But above everything else he missed, he regretted not having a toothbrush. His breath could stop a Sherman tank.

Okay, so he looked like a wreck, a kind of pirate Rambo. But his situation couldn't be all that bad. After all, the skipper fed him and left him free to roam the ship.

And that was where the freedom ended. He had a big label tattooed to his file from the FBI to Interpol. "TERRORIST." And wherever he went, they were sure to nab him and lock him away for the rest of his life, or worse, shoot him on sight.

Inhaling the refreshing breeze of a new day, he wasn't so sure he wanted to turn himself in. In truth, he neither wanted to keep one step ahead of the White House goon squad, be locked away in a federal penitentiary, or spend the rest of his life in complete frustration aboard a creaking ship. None of the options was a good one. Pitiful as it was, he had a life. He was guilty of nothing.

And who was this Sandi DiMartino, breathlessly seeking him out across oceans, across time? What was her gig?

Surely he wasn't enough of a hunk to distort her radar and drive her off course. Was he?

One more look in the mirror told him otherwise. He was no steal, no bargain. Just damaged goods.

It was amazing to think that a competing oil company would send out an industrial spy to expose him, get his story, and sink his company. Surely Sandi wasn't involved in something that depraved.

So, if she wasn't a sneak or a snitch, then why was she hiding behind that international corporation cover? Worse yet, maybe she wasn't even a lawyer!

Okay, it wasn't as if he hadn't created a few disasters along the way. So he went along with the Chinagate kickback scheme. He could have blown the whistle then, but he was desperate to get his family out of the SARS epidemic.

While living in Shanghai, he shouldn't have siphoned off the President's personal funds from his company either. That was a little ballsy, he had to admit.

But he was an angry man. And those were mere white-collar crimes.

Far worse than that, he had become a catalyst for evil. He had become the terrorist's ticket to blackmailing the most powerful man on earth. If anything, America wanted him destroyed, Chinagate notwithstanding. Hell, if he cared enough, and put himself in the average American's mindset, he'd want himself destroyed, too.

Then the shocking thought struck him.

Every breath he took was only further destroying civilization, the very civilization that his family yearned for. Why even live?

Maybe he was just a caged animal trying to escape. What a stupid, egotistical thing to do as he brought the world down with him.

And say he did escape, unlikely as that seemed under the circumstances. Who would he turn to? Whom could he trust? Who would even trust him?

The message! He had almost thrown it away. He reached down and pulled the torn message from the shirt he had just discarded. Water had blurred the handwriting, but he could still make out the words, "Your family lives."

Due to the dampness of the paper, for the first time he noticed a watermark printed in the paper. It was only the corner of a larger emblem that had the letters "...R A L I N T..."

Who could have written that note? It drove him crazy. Who was playing with his mind? Finding his family was the only reason he needed to escape.

He closed his eyes and took careful stock of the information he had gained about the ship. The bridge was locked, but contained a ship-to-shore radio. The skipper's quarters, also locked, held a computer with a modem, a radiophone, and a fax machine. He had found the arms cache on the second deck, but that was locked as well, and the men whose berths were adjacent to the arms didn't like him poking around. Until he could steal a key or sneak into an unopened room, he was barred from making his whereabouts known or shooting his way to freedom.

Beside the mirror was a porthole. The constant presence of water and sky had a dulling effect on his senses. He rarely looked out to sea anymore.

But this time he did, because an island was just appearing on the horizon, the first sign of civilization that he had seen since leaving China.

"Okay," Lieutenant Terry Whitcomb said, leaning over to study the multiple blips on the radar screen. "We're going to have to use the process of elimination here."

"What," Anthony said. "Sink all of them?"

"I would classify that as a dumb f— answer. I want you to radio each and every ship on that scope and determine which ones are not the *Ariana*. Then we can assume that ship is our target."

"What if they're lying?"

"Then we'll check their names against public registries and the International Maritime Organization."

"What if they don't recognize my authority?"

"Put on a Filipino accent and say you're the port authority."

"Why not ask the port authority to do it?"

"I already asked them once. They won't do it again. We'll be lucky if they keep silent and let us do it. Now, on the double. I'm getting on the horn to the *Stuart*."

Anthony pulled his trackball close and set the crosshairs on the first ship in the GPS area laid out by Raymond O. Flowers. Calculating the exact latitude and longitude reading, he pulled on his microphone headset and dialed the frequency to the civilian maritime channel.

He had heard many accents over the radio in the past half year, and mimicking the local pronunciation came naturally to him.

"Calling on the ship at 15° 56' North, 125° 26' East bearing north by northeast. Please identify yourself."

A minute later, a Japanese accent came over the radio. "This is the *Golden Wave* at 15° 56' North, 125° 26' East bearing north by northeast."

"Calling on the ship at 15° 45' North, 125° 41' East bearing northeast. Please identify yourself."

Within an hour, he had identified half the ships in the target area. He was gradually working his way south and east, away from land and into an area of sparsely scattered islands. The radio signals originated from farther away and were more difficult to hear.

Sometimes he didn't get the ship's name quite right, but wrote down a close approximation. *The Albuflub. The Hole in One. The Kanagaratnam.*

The process went more quickly as time went on. Once radiomen realized that he was zeroing in on their coordinates, they were ready with an answer.

Just as Raymond spotted the island through the porthole, one of the terrorist crewmembers burst into the head and tossed an assault rifle at him. He caught it by the barrel before it hit the metal deck and discharged automatically.

"What's this for?"

A second man reached into the small room and tossed him a gun belt.

"Are we under attack?"

At that moment, the skipper was racing down the passageway. "Get into your gear," he said. "We're making a land assault."

"*We* are?"

"This is *jihad*," the skipper said simply. "It is our duty."

One of the men hauled Raymond onto the sunny deck. In the presence of so many loaded guns, it was probably wise to play along and loop the gun belt over one shoulder. He pointed the muzzle of his gun down and away from the others, aware that he knew nothing about using the awkwardly heavy chunk of metal.

He counted heads. There was a total of fifteen men. The entire crew was on deck, including the galley boy. What were they going to attack?

Several men were preparing to launch the pair of motorized lifeboats and the inflatable raft over the sides of the ship. Beyond them lay a stretch of white sand, the sound of piped-in steel drums floating across the water.

A tourist resort? They were going to kidnap some poor Westerner off the beach?

He set down his gun and began to heft off the load of bullets. Not him. No thank you. Suddenly, he felt a vice-like grip on his shoulder, stopping him cold.

"What do you think you're doing?" the skipper asked.

"What are *you* doing? Those are innocent people out there."

"We're not going ashore to hurt people."

"You're going to kidnap them, just like you kidnapped me."

"Wrong again."

Raymond stared dumbly at the man. "Then why all this ammunition? We're not going grocery shopping."

"Just stick close to me and you'll see what we have in mind."

Raymond thought of shooting off a gun to warn the poor souls on the beach. But, he tended to believe the skipper. They weren't there to take more captives. He was a big enough catch.

Seaman Anthony Carlson tried several times to wake up the radioman at the ship located to the far east of his target zone. He had been talking with the ships for over two hours, and still no names checked out. Each had answered promptly, and his fellow seamen helped him scan the registry databases of the various countries.

In some cases they called the ship back to clarify her name and home country. In each case, the ships responded and their names checked out.

Until now.

"Calling on the vessel at 11° 51' North, 145° 32' East," Anthony repeated for the second time, his voice raspy. "Please identify yourself."

Again no response.

He looked up at the men around him. "Someone tell the lieutenant. We might have found our target."

As the seaman departed, he studied the farthest east blip on his radar screen. It was far south of a main shipping route, and the Doppler reported no movement. Against the blank blue field, it looked dead in the water.

He pressed a few keys on his computer keyboard and brought up an overlay of landmasses. Sure enough, the blip seemed to be just off the shore of a tiny island labeled "Purang."

"Maybe it's anchored there," one radioman speculated.

"Sure is a damned small island," another said. "It didn't even show up on the radar."

Lieutenant Whitcomb came jumping down the stairs into the radio room.

"What did you find?"

Anthony wiped his bloodshot eyes, trying to focus on the screen one last time. "This ship," he said, pointing to the small white blip. "It doesn't respond. All the others check out."

"We'll need a visual ID," Terry said. "And it's too far away for us to reach."

Anthony considered the distance involved. It would take the *USS Endorse* another twenty hours to reach the spot, and the destroyer *USS Stuart* could only reach it in ten.

"The *Stuart* has a helipad," Terry informed them. "And she's expecting a troop of Marines to land on her shortly. I'll have them redirect to that island."

"Purang," Anthony said.

"What?"

"It's the name of the island. Purang."

"Whatever."

"Don't you think we should establish whose sovereignty the island falls under?" Anthony asked.

Terry seemed annoyed by the seeming irrelevance of the question. He stared at the screen and spelled the name out loud. Then he turned and disappeared up the ladder.

"Where's he going?" one radioman wondered aloud.

"Off to call his buddy, the Secretary of Defense."

Anthony closed his eyes and smiled. "I only meant that we could call up the island by telephone and have someone there tell us the name of the ship."

"Cool. You have a phone. Do it."

Anthony accepted the challenge.

He leaned forward in his seat and pulled up a program that looked just like a cell phone on the screen. He clicked on a directory assistance button and waited. After a few seconds, the phone rang on the other end and an automated voice recognition system kicked in.

"You have dialed a pay service," the computer said. "If you wish to continue, your call will be charged to your account depending on the distance called. Please state whether you would like to reach a person, place, or company."

"Place," Anthony said.

"Thank you. What is the name of the place?"

"Purang."

"Thank you. Can you be more specific?"

"The United States Embassy in Purang."

"Thank you. Here is the number..."

So it wasn't a territory of the United States, but it was big enough to merit an embassy. Anthony typed the number into an onscreen notepad.

"I will now connect to the United States Embassy in Purang," the computerized voice said. "The total charge for this directory assisted call is $24.55."

Anthony rolled his eyes and waited for the phone to ring on the other end. After several connection delays, the phone began to ring in Purang.

There was no answer.

He had reached a dead end. He didn't even know that the American government had diplomats living on that speck of land. And now that he needed them, they weren't there.

He clicked off the phone and shook his head at the others whose eyes were fixed on him. He may have accepted their challenge, but he was damned if he would bilk the Navy another $24.55 by placing another call.

The Secretary of Defense had long since put his Pentagon office far behind him for the infinitely greater tranquility of dinner and a good night's sleep at his residence in McLean, Virginia. But it only took the Ops Center a matter of seconds to catch up with him.

Kenneth Spaulding was accustomed to receiving calls in the middle of the night. He shook off the cobwebs and reached for the secure phone installed beside his bed.

It was Lieutenant Terrence Whitcomb of the *USS Endorse*. "Yes, Lieutenant. Did you sink the ship?"

"Not yet, sir. We're only now confirming its identity."

"What? I thought you had it nailed."

"It's a big ocean, Mr. Secretary. We're flying Marines over to Purang right now to check it out."

"Purang? Don't we have an Embassy there?"

"I'm not aware of that, Mr. Secretary."

"Okay, I'll get the Ops Center to track down our Ambassador and have him check out the ship. Anything else?"

"Uh, no, Mr. Secretary."

"Okay, then stick with the mission."

Kenneth sat up beside the bed and turned on his dimmer switch to see the keypad. He pressed the Ops Center button and waited.

After identifying himself to the operator, he asked to be patched through to the Secretary of State. That took a full minute.

The wheels of government turned slowly after midnight.

Eventually, he had Secretary of State Lyle Hamilton on the horn. He explained the problem and asked the Secretary to ask the embassy in Purang to check out the suspected terrorist ship and inform his point man, Whitcomb on the *USS Endorse*.

The moment his head hit the pillow, Kenneth fell asleep again, fully assured that the State Department wouldn't fumble the ball.

The State Department Ops center had no more luck reaching the tiny embassy in Purang than did Seaman Anthony Carlson.

A quick check of holidays around the world revealed, however, that it was Purangian Independence Day, surely a day of celebration on the tiny island nation.

The Pacific Island Desk at the Department pulled up a cable from two days before stating the officially filed travel plans of the Embassy staff during the holiday.

According to the cable, it appeared that the Ambassador and his Deputy were deep-sea fishing at the moment.

Hiram had spent many a July 4th watching the Plainfield Independence Day Parade.

He had cheered on many fire trucks polished like a new penny, balloon men pushing their carts along the curb, religious dance troupes strutting their stuff, soccer league teams dribbling down the street, flags twirling, souped-up cars flashing their lights, policemen performing figure-eights with their motorcycles, and juggling clowns on stilts. But Independence Day in Purang was a completely different thing.

First, there was the celebration of the harvest. And, as sugar cane was the primary crop, rum was the primary libation.

Rum and coke, corkscrews, daiquiris, piña coladas, rum on ice cream, pure Bacardi from the bottle.

Next came the roast boar, turning slowly on the hotel's spit. Along with that came native Polynesian women in grass skirts swaying their hips to and fro. It made his eyes swim trying to keep up with their gyrations.

The entire island was celebrating.

Down the shore, another resort was setting off strings of firecrackers. All the fishing boats were pulled up on shore. Even the fish got a break that day.

Tiffany was dancing with the hotel staff, which seemed to have totally abandoned the restrictions of the social hierarchy. The chef was a Frenchman, and he stood out among the guests whirling around in his tall white hat.

Hiram was holding a clipboard, judging limbo contestants on the beach. Most fell flat on their backs in drunken laughter. He gave them a second chance.

Steel drums throbbed over the speakers, encouraging the dancing and limbo and general spirit of wild celebration.

A pair of guards stood stiffly at the edge of the property with flower necklaces framing their berets, shoulder boards, and frowns. Their stiff demeanor seemed at odds with the carefree atmosphere.

"Come on," Hiram told one guard. "Lighten up. What you got here is South Pacific!"

Then he looked up and saw what the men were watching. A cargo ship had anchored half a mile out to sea, and tiny skiffs were making their way to the island.

"Rumba!" Hiram cried, offering a bottle of rum to the approaching visitors.

Chapter 18

Raymond O. Flowers was certainly no terrorist, but he looked the part.

Their faces grim, his shipmates were focused on the task at hand. They had the government of an island nation to overthrow in the name of Allah.

Their intensity was impressive, the muscles of their forearms twitching, their combat boots squared and ready to pounce from the ship.

As they drew near to shore, their plan of attack became more apparent to Raymond. An accomplice onshore had lined up three vans to transport the invaders across the island to the capital.

But why the music? Why all the blaring loudspeakers along the shore? Perhaps the plan was to distract the unsuspecting natives.

Within a hundred yards of shore, he made out fleshy white tourists in Hawaiian shirts and Bermuda shorts, native girls in grass skirts, and some middle-aged women trying to bend under a limbo pole. It seemed like a drunken orgy, and his fellow terrorists looked on with interest.

However, the moment their boats' hulls struck dry sand, the terrorists were all business. They piled out in formation. Thrust forward, Raymond crawled awkwardly to the front of the boat.

As soon as his bare feet struck sand, he felt a whirling sensation and almost fell backward. It was the first time he'd stood on firm ground in days. He wanted to sink to his knees and embrace the earth.

But war drums were throbbing, and like the coordinated mechanism of a clock, the terrorists divided into groups and boarded the windowless minivans. Raymond looked wildly about for an avenue of escape.

"You stay with me," the skipper told him and squeezed him into the middle of the front seat of a van. The skipper jumped behind the wheel and they peeled off down the road.

It was a left-hand drive, American model van, but the road signs faced backwards. The stop sign was on the left side of the road.

Leaving their landing crafts far behind, the terrorists zoomed past cane fields and eventually reached a two-lane road. One vehicle split off to the right, while the skipper's van led the other van to the left into what looked like a sleepy hamlet.

They paused at a building that looked much like a mosque. It had a crescent on the dome, but none of the merrymakers out front wore religious headgear. Rather, they were dressed in party clothes. Some even toted bottles of alcohol.

Three terrorists jumped out of the rear van and scrambled, weapons pointed upward toward the building.

As the skipper pulled away, bursts of automatic gunfire ripped through the air. Crowds of people cheered along the side of the road. Perhaps they thought it was firecrackers.

You poor sops, Raymond thought soberly. You don't know what's going down.

Hiram only realized that something was truly amiss when he made out the guns on the landing crafts.

The three groups of men poised to spring from the boats were armed to the teeth. Their battle fatigues, ammo belts, helmets, and AK-47s were like a scene out of a war movie, completely out of context during Purang's Independence Day celebrations.

At first he thought they might be part of a reenactment of the liberation of Purang. He checked the shoreline. He would have expected onlookers to line the shore in order to witness the event, perhaps taking a snapshot or two.

Instead, only three white vans with no markings were waiting for the soldiers.

"Is dat yous army?" he asked one of the guards, whose large eyes were following the scene.

"No. We don't have an army," he said.

Then abruptly, the two guards ducked and ran to the edge of the beachfront property and took up defensive positions along a property line, defined only by hedges. They held up wooden sticks in self-defense.

"Tiffany!" Hiram shouted to his wife.

She couldn't hear him over all the noise and dance music. He watched her shake her booty with the hotel staff. Let her enjoy herself until he had a chance to check things out.

He raced back to their hotel room, which they customarily left unlocked in the informal atmosphere of island life. There he found the number of the local police in the phone book and dialed them.

"Hello," a cheery voice responded. There was music in the background.

"Yeah, is dis da Purang police department?"

"Yes, it is."

"I'm calling from da Sandalwood Resort. I just sawr several motorboats, you know, land on de island from a freighta off da shore. De men onboard, dey was all packin' machine guns."

"I don't believe that's possible, sir."

"No, I just sawr dem wit' my own eyes. Dey landed and drove away in dees tree white vans. Were you expecting dem guys?"

"Not to my knowledge. Sir, have you been drinking?"

"Of course. But I'm telling ya, I saw it for real. And dey looked like mercenaries. Dat's what I'm saying."

"Well, we'll check it out. Thanks for ringing."

Hiram hung up the phone, unconvinced that the man had any intention of checking it out. And given the diminutive size of the island, he might have been speaking with the entire police force.

Suddenly, the island getaway seemed frighteningly vulnerable. He checked the zippered compartment of his suitcase. His airplane tickets were still there. Given the price he paid for them, surely they were not restricted by date. Perhaps he and Tiffany could make a break for the airport and catch an earlier flight.

Their three-week vacation would be cut short to a mere three days.

As he sat on the edge of his bed in the darkened room, his mind roamed over the various facilities in town. What were the mercenaries going after?

The American Embassy? That would be an easy target if they were terrorists.

He fumbled through the telephone directory and found the number for the American Embassy.

He dialed them at once.

The phone rang for a full minute and nobody answered. Of course, it was a national holiday. Nobody was at work!

He had to get Tiffany to the airport.

Throwing every loose scrap of clothing and their toiletries into their suitcases, he cleared out their hotel room.

It was a struggle to zip the luggage closed.

"Tiffany!" he called out the open door. Of course she couldn't hear him.

He lugged the two enormous suitcases out onto the patio. He couldn't see his wife from there. Struggling, he entered a narrow pathway that cut through bushes, hiked over an arched bridge, and stumbled through some fan palms to the dance area.

He dropped the suitcases and called again. "Tiffany, come here. We gots ta leave!"

She turned and spotted him. Her jaw fell open. "Rammy, what are you doing?"

He motioned for her to follow him, and he wheeled around and began hauling the suitcases back to the lobby.

She caught up with him in a matter of seconds.

"Hiram. What on God's green earth are you trying to do? Have you completely lost your mind?"

"Sweetie, we got ourselves terrorists on dis here island. We gots to get to da airport at once."

"Are you hallucinating? I don't see any terrorists."

"I sawr 'em der on da beach. I tell ya, dey're invading da island."

"Oh, Rammy," she said, her face suddenly transformed with compassion. She wiped the sweat from his forehead. "You've been worrying too much. There are no terrorists here. That was in New York."

He wasn't getting through to her. Much as he had resisted the inclination all his life, it was time to play the dominant male.

"I'm leavin', and you're coming wit' me."

Horror seemed to grip her. Then tears. He was going to ruin their vacation!

For a moment, he saw the folly in that. Hell, even if there were terrorists, it was happening all over the world, right? What was wrong with a little terrorism on Purang? The hotel had its own guards.

Then the instinct for flight took over again.

"Sweetie, dey snatch average people off da beach. Dey lop off deir heads an' leave 'em for dead in da jungle. Dat's what we're lookin' at."

Sobbing, she fell against him. She beat against his large chest with her tiny fists. "I don't want this. I can't take this anymore."

He looked around frantically. He seemed to be the only one who was panicking. Maybe it was better not to fly off the handle.

"Okay, look, sweetie," he said, finally relenting. He spaced out his words as if talking to a child. "Let me take you back to da bar. Der you can be happy, listen to da music, and let me just check tings out a little."

She looked yearningly at the pool bar alongside the beach.

"Okay," she said in a small voice.

He grasped her by her shaking shoulders and guided her past the pool to a barstool. "Now, what will you have?"

Her eyes were wide open, but she didn't seem to be seeing anything.

"She'll have one of dose coconut drinks, der," he told the bartender. "An' talk to her, will ya?"

He felt bad about leaving her, but a quick scan of the beach told him that the soldiers were no longer marauding along the sands.

He hustled the suitcases back into his room, and made for the front desk.

"So what have you heard about da attack?" he asked the young Purangian woman behind the desk.

She looked thrown by the question.

"What, don't yous have radios?" he asked.

She pointed to a portable radio behind her.

"Good. Now tune in da local news report and tell da guards what ya hear. I'm tellin' ya, der are soldiers on dis here island."

She stared at him, her eyes wide.

"Will ya do it?" he thundered, then hurried for the doorman. "Go fetch me a buncha guards," he told the man.

The man went away, and Hiram jumped behind the wheel of the hotel's official car. He stared at the steering wheel. Everything was backward. Even the keys dangling from the ignition were on the left side of the steering column. What about all those who were right-handed? And who left their keys in the car anyway? Suddenly, the lax security of the island had a disturbing effect on him. The island was wide open for attack.

The two guards from the beach rushed up. "Jump in here," Hiram yelled. "We gots to wake up da cops."

He scooted over and let one of the guards take the wheel.

Shortly, they were off, weaving through a cane field. Then Hiram gritted his teeth. A white van was careening down the middle of the road right at them.

Lieutenant Terry Whitcomb felt like he was in the hot seat, wedged between the Secretary of Defense, the State Department, and the *USS Stuart*. He was the pivot man in the operation to take out the terrorists. He hadn't heard back from the Secretary of Defense in half an hour and was nervously picking at his nails. The operation wasn't moving ahead, and he felt responsible. What was he to do?

He phoned the *USS Stuart* to see if they had received any instructions from Washington.

Like him, they had heard nothing from the Pentagon. But the chopper full of Marines had arrived on the *Stuart*, and the Marines were standing by while the helicopter underwent weapons checks and refueling.

Just then, Terry heard a beep on the line from another call. "Can you hold on?"

He switched from the *USS Stuart* to the other line.

"This is the State Department Ops Center," a man said. "We are unable to contact our Embassy in Purang. I'm afraid nobody's answering the phone over there. We'll have to rely on you to send over a plane and make visual contact with the ship. I'm sorry that we can't be of any help."

"Thanks anyway." Terry managed to say. Useless pinstriped twerps. He switched back to the *USS Stuart*.

"Nobody in Washington can identify the ship," he said. "You're gonna have to go in and investigate. Apparently Raymond O. Flowers is among the terrorists, and we have permission to take him out. In fact it sounded more like an order."

"Roger that."

And that was the last Terry Whitcomb heard from the *Stuart*.

He sat back and caught his breath. Had he just given the Marines the go-ahead to kill Flowers?

Hiram stared at the white van bearing down on their hotel car. Couldn't the van stay on its own side of the road?

For his part, the guard at the wheel wasn't doing much to avoid the impending collision. If anything, he was ensuring their demise by frantically weaving all over the road.

The white van had no way to avoid them.

"Don't you know how to drive?" Hiram yelled. "Stay left."

"I've never driven before," the guard confessed, gunning the engine when he should have been hitting the brakes.

The van had no way to squeak through. Both drivers jerked their steering wheels too hard and too late, and they rammed broadside into each other. The result was catastrophic.

Metal slammed against metal in a thunderous impact that ripped Hiram's seatbelt clear out of the seat.

He was aware of sliding across asphalt on a sheet of metal that created a shower of sparks. Behind him, debris from the vehicles scattered in all directions, squealing and rubbing auto parts, tumbling bodies, and exploding shards of glass.

Lying on his side and still moving, he realized that he was still clinging to the handle of his car door. He struggled to keep his head and limbs away from the ground as he slid down the road and spun to a halt.

He lay in the sudden quiet, eyes closed, waiting for the car or van to explode.

It never happened.

"Hey there," a voice said.

He felt a foot nudging him in the side.

"You okay? Get up."

He opened hi eyes.

A group of teenage boys was standing over him.

"No problem," one said. "You okay now."

Where was he? In the hospital? How much time had elapsed?

He looked around him.

He had slaughtered animals and chopped meat his entire life, but he had never seen anything as gruesome as the scene before him. Bodies lay torn apart and strewn across the road. Rifles lay on the pavement, hand grenades rolled to a stop, and vehicle parts were distributed up and down the road.

He had survived a collision with a van loaded with weapons.

"It's okay, mister," the boy repeated. "You can get up now."

These people sure had a whoopsy-daisy attitude toward automobile accidents. He pulled himself into a seated position. To his amazement, his head felt clear. He checked out his clothes for blood. He hadn't sustained a single injury. How could he have emerged from the disaster unscathed? Was this a miracle?

He rose to his feet and wiped off his bare knees. Even that was unnecessary.

Meanwhile, the two guards from his car lay prone on the road, and one of the heavily armed mercenaries sat up in the grass, rubbing his shaggy black beard.

The shockwave hit first, sending Hiram flying to the ground. Then the sound reached his ears. The mercenaries' van exploded in all directions, sending a fireball upward, and bullets screaming past him.

The heat struck next, singeing Hiram's shorts, shirt, and curly black hair. He clutched the ground as several large mortar shells exploded and rocked the ground. He squeezed his eyes tight and uttered a series of Hail Marys. All he could think of was Tiffany.

He prayed that she wasn't watching this.

Then he heard other voices, like a chattering flock of birds. They were near him, warbling away.

He opened one eye.

Bathed in the orange glow of the nearby fire, the Purang boys had fallen by his side and, like him, were praying. "Allah have mercy on me."

The heat dissipated quickly, but Hiram slapped his clothes to make sure he was not on fire. Several boys had to roll in the dirt to put out flames on their clothing. The air smelled like a barbeque gone wrong.

The mercenary in the weeds lay prone on his back, his face transformed to cinders.

Gritting his teeth in anger, Hiram rose to his feet. He was standing in a giant pit of devastation carved into the beautiful, lush island. He was the only man alive in a heap of weapons.

The guard had effectively taken out the white van. But they had yet to save the day, for he had seen two other vans on the beach. The armed invaders were on the march elsewhere on the island.

And that made him very angry.

The brave guards were mutilated chunks of severed limbs. He had to turn to the boys for help. He sucked in his breath, a feeling of omnipotence coursing through his veins.

"Der are more soldiers on dis here island. Which of you wants to help me get da bastards?" he asked.

They brushed off their hands and knees and got to their feet.

Hiram picked up a pair of assault rifles that lay nearby. He threw one to the nearest boy, who caught it and looked it over, clearly never having seen such a weapon before.

Hiram threw the other rifle to the next boy, and one to each of the other four.

He had himself an army.

Pocketing the unexploded hand grenades, a small regiment was taking shape. The oldest was their leader, and Hiram became their supreme commander.

"Which way to town?" he asked, disoriented.

The oldest boy pointed ahead of them, and they began their silent march toward town.

On the horizon, Hiram made out a plume of black smoke trailing skyward. Then he saw another. Shortly thereafter came a loud thud of exploding ordinance followed by the chatter of machine gun fire.

Chapter 19

Raymond found himself in a pitched battle the moment the two vans came to a halt in town.

With terrifying ferocity, the terrorists flung the van's back doors wide open and jumped to the street, guns ablaze. They poured hot lead into a three-story stucco building. From the sandstone embellishments on the façade, it looked like some sort of local palace, which was rapidly being chipped away by bullets.

There was some weak resistance by single-shot pistols and semi-automatic weapons, but soon hostile fire ceased returning from the place, and it didn't take long for the terrorists to seize the building.

Hauling him into the courtyard, the skipper proclaimed, "Purang is ours!"

Just then a submachine gun rattled in the far corner of the courtyard. A last holdout.

Raymond bolted behind a wall.

One terrorist hurled a hand grenade at the source of the shots. The explosion resounded around the walls of the courtyard then inside Raymond's ears. God, he was nearly deaf.

He peered around the corner. A guard had fallen off the wall into the middle of the courtyard. Behind him, black smoke billowed from an exploded arms cache.

He turned away from the corpse. Death was no stranger to him, but it bothered him viscerally. He sank to the tiles underfoot and leaned a cheek against a cold wall that glistened with dampness.

There came another cry, sounding distant and muffled in his damaged ears. He barely reacted when another huge explosion rocked the building.

Nothing about war was good.

He thought for a moment of shooting his way out of the building and throwing himself on the mercy of the natives. But they no longer controlled their own island.

An unsuccessful attempt to escape from the terrorists might land him in even more trouble.

But damn it, he wasn't going to take part in the incursion.

Then, as he saw the terrorists stealthily infiltrate the higher stories of the building, a thought occurred to him. He was in a unique position to foil their plans.

Shaped like a scorpion with its two sets of rotating blades, the CH-46 Sea Knight helicopter transferred its weight from its landing gear to its rotating blades and grudgingly lifted off the *USS Stuart*. Gunnery Sergeant Hank Rove noted that it was 1200 hours, a mere five minutes after they had received orders to find the *Ariana* and take out the terrorists and Raymond O. Flowers.

Seated around him, the twelve-man unit of Marines was strapping themselves back into the transport chopper, each armed for hand-to-hand combat. Fully refueled, the chopper spun midair and began her swift journey across the cobalt sea.

Hank reflected that they were defended only by him and the other aerial gunner sitting back to back, chained to their machine gun mounts. A transport helicopter was hardly the proper equipment to gash a hole in the hull of a freighter. They would have to assault the ship by hand.

But first he would spray the terrorist ship with gunfire to cover his unit as they boarded her. There was no stopping a determined band of Marines. As he examined his ammo supply inside the closed fuselage cargo compartment, he speculated about how big the catch would be that day.

Every strike against terrorists offered a chance at bringing down one of the top al-Qaeda leaders. Boy, could he use the reward money for bin Laden. After a year hunting down fleeting ghosts across southern Afghanistan, he was ready for a target that sat still. And there was nothing more vulnerable than a ship at sea. And nobody as merciless as he was that moment.

He wanted the strike to go well, and then he wanted to go home. A yearlong deployment under hostile fire had been more than any soldier should be forced to handle. And now his return flight through Japan to the U.S. had been diverted for a maritime escapade. It had better pay off.

"Fan out and capture all government figures," the skipper ordered.

His men bashed doors open and scrambled up staircases.

Raymond fingered the trigger of his gun as he followed the skipper to the upper floors. The man's back kept spinning about as he turned at staircase landings. The skipper's boots echoed farther and farther ahead in the muffled deadness of his ears.

Finally Raymond came to an open door. He stepped through and came across an office with a ceiling fan and dusty file cabinets. The skipper wasn't there. Crouching and ready to attack the skipper, he crept past a council room and what looked like guards' quarters, but those rooms were also unoccupied. The skipper was gone.

Then a hand reached from behind him and ripped the AK-47 from his grip. What the hell? Raymond hadn't heard anyone approach from behind. He rose and turned around.

The skipper seemed disappointed as he raised Raymond's gun between them.

"I wasn't trying anything," Raymond protested.

The skipper's hand tightened around the trigger.

"Honest, I wasn't," he said, images of summary executions passing through his mind.

The muzzle rose deep and dark, level with Raymond's eyes. Beyond that, he saw the skipper's trigger finger pull.

He closed his eyes. Carolyn!

A metallic click echoed down the empty chamber.

He opened his eyes, puzzled.

The skipper laughed as he tossed the assault rifle away.

"We gave you one with an empty clip," he said, with a derisive laugh.

Okay, Raymond could take a little humiliation. He could swallow his pride.

"How could we have miscalculated?" the skipper wondered aloud, and turned to face the bare rooms. "There's nobody here. If we don't jail their government, we'll risk an uprising."

Raymond was still in the process of letting out his breath, and wasn't ready to help the skipper just yet.

"I certainly wouldn't resist you guys," he offered.

It seemed like a small, happy country. The government didn't bother to show up for work in the middle of the week, they didn't seem to have touched their filing cabinets in months, and their people walked around in festive clothing. Had he stumbled upon the Shangri-la of the South Pacific, where everybody was content, and there was no political strife? If so, the skipper's full-armored assault seemed a tad excessive.

"Aren't the people supposed to greet you with sweets and flowers?" Raymond asked a bit sarcastically.

"That's the theory," the skipper said. "But you never can tell."

Raymond was still trying to get over his near-death experience. He limped over to the President's leather office chair. There, he spun the globe that sat on the desk. Were the terrorists playing Russian roulette with countries? When the globe came to a stop, he stared at the first country he saw, the U.S.S.R. The Union of Soviet Socialist Republics wasn't still intact. Nor was Yugoslavia. Hadn't Zaire changed its name, and hadn't Hong Kong turned red like China?

The Purang flag was priceless, a single palm tree against a blue field. It looked like a child's drawing.

And the note left on the President's desk could hardly have been serious. "Remember to call the pool boy for Friday. Love, Rennie."

Then he realized that his smile didn't derive from ridicule. Rather, it stemmed from a desire he had long since forgotten he had. He wanted the world to be simple again.

The Marine helicopter circled behind the cargo ship, steering well away from its freight crane, tower, and twin funnels.

Hank made out the name on the stern, just below the Liberian flag. "*Lost Horizon.*"

"That's not the *Ariana*," came the pilot's voice over the headset. "I'll radio the *Endorse.*"

They circled closer while the pilot made his report. Hank didn't see a soul onboard. It was just a rusty tub, the paint on its deck having peeled away in large, dark spots.

Then something caught his eye on the horizon.

"Smoke at two o'clock!" he shouted over his mouthpiece.

The chopper shuddered and straightened. They changed course

and headed across the waves toward land. From his new angle, Hank lost sight of the twin pillars of black smoke.

"Looks like there's a battle underway," the pilot reported. "Prepare your combat gear. We're going in."

Hank made sure that his seat belt was firmly fastened, then kicked open the cargo door. In the rush of air sucked out of the belly of the chopper, he held on tight to his mounted gun and swiveled it out over the yellow fields dotted with orange-blossomed flame trees. From the air, it looked like a sleepy place.

But you could never be sure.

He flicked off the safety and began to seek out targets.

It didn't take long for Hiram to put together what was happening around the government palace.

He and his armed squad of local boys stepped off the island's single bus and took up positions across the street from the building. Smoke still rose from its roof. Gunmen in military fatigues, the same men he had seen land on the beach, hung out of several windows, aiming their weapons down at the street.

The palace seemed to have two entrances. One was an office entrance, and the other was an arched entryway leading to an inner courtyard. He watched in horror as two gunmen carried out the limp remains of two guards and heaved them onto the street where they settled in a cloud of dust.

It was high noon in Purang, and Hiram felt strangely out of place. He had never served in the military. He'd never held a gun in his hand. Now, suddenly, he was forced into a role he had only seen in the occasional movie.

What would they have done in *The Dirty Dozen*?

He trained his assault rifle on the back of one of the terrorists as he wiped his hands and turned to reenter the palace.

Staring through the very precise scope, he found a spot right between the man's shoulders.

He curled an index finger around the trigger and waited for his heart to stop pounding. He timed the man's stride, then gently squeezed.

Nothing happened.

He tried again. Nothing. This was a submachine gun. Maybe he had to hold down the trigger.

Through his other eye, he caught a glimpse of someone reaching under the stock of his gun. It was a tiny hand, from one of his Army boys. He felt a switch flip.

Suddenly, the gun went off, firing several volleys under his hands, pounding repeatedly against the top of his shoulder. The barrel rose involuntarily, spraying the front of the palace with bullets, shattering glass that showered the street.

He removed his finger from the trigger, and the firing stopped.

Ouch. He lowered the gun and rubbed his throbbing shoulder. He hadn't expected such a violent recoil. Ahead of him, the two terrorists ran back into the courtyard unharmed.

Several of the other boys opened fire next, their guns exploding from behind cars parked on the street. Some of their bullets entered the blown-out windows. Others bounced off the sides of the building, flecking off pieces of white plaster.

Then flashes of light signaled bursts of machine gun fire from inside the building. Windows shattered around him. The bastards were returning fire.

Hiram spun around and threw himself into the nearest shop. Meat was swinging against his shoulders, beating at him. He came to a stop and found himself face to face with a pig's head, its dead eyes locked on his.

He wrenched his attention back to the shop. His hand had landed on a butcher's block. On it lay a meat cleaver and several carving knives with stout wooden handles. He picked one up, pig blood still dripping from its blade, and hefted it expertly in the palm of his hand.

He was an expert with the knife and suddenly, he knew what he had to do.

The moment his office window shattered, Raymond hit the floor. And with the breaking of glass came the shattering of his illusion that Purang was a peaceful place, a place that would offer no violent resistance.

The President's office was ripped apart by erratic gunfire. The national flag toppled and landed on his head.

He let the fabric cover him as glass splinters sailed across the room, their jagged edges potentially more harmful than the bullets.

He lay whimpering under the banner, his eyes squeezed tight.

Why me? What on earth had he done to deserve all this? Now, he would surely die, holed up in a government building like Butch Cassidy and the Sundance Kid. He wasn't even trying to take over the government.

All he wanted was to find his family and get on with his life.

Gunfire erupted sporadically from several directions. The building was surrounded. Even if he wanted to shoot his way out of the building, there were no bullets in his gun.

And how could the terrorists hold out forever against such full-scale resistance? Where did Purang get such a professional army?

Then a whistling, whirling sound flew through the broken window. He peered from under the flag in time to see a butcher's knife spinning through the air, coming right at him, and embedding itself in the President's bulletin board just above his head.

The skipper sprang to the window and responded with rifle fire. The mechanical chattering sound seemed increasingly distant to Raymond. Then he felt liquid splatter on his forehead.

He reached up and wiped off droplets of blood. Looking up, he found its source. Animal blood still dripped from the handle of the butcher's knife.

He needed that knife!

He lifted a hand and reached toward the bulletin board where the blade still quivered. He gripped the wet handle and pulled the knife free.

Unnoticed by the skipper, he slipped the knife under the flag and hid it there. It was his only weapon. His only way of breaking free.

The terrorists truly were in a desperate situation. Could they make it back to the ship? Perhaps they could slink away into the watery wasteland, never to be seen again, only to emerge months later as a Kuwaiti-flagged merchant ship in Norway.

But all exits were blocked. They had no vehicle to ram their way out of the building. The only thing the terrorists could do was negotiate their way out of the huge, miscalculated mess.

How could the skipper have been so dumb?

Then his eyes fell on a cord lying under the President's desk. He had access to a telephone.

Reaching one hand up out of the fabric of the flag, he felt around the top of the desk, knocking over a pen set and sending a round paperweight crashing down on his head.

Annoyed, he yanked on the telephone cord and the entire phone fell to the Presidential carpet. He pulled it under the flag and dialed

"0."

"This is the operator," a woman said with a British accent. "How may I help you?"

Raymond closed his eyes in thanks. "I'm an American citizen," he whispered. "I'm being held by terrorists at the government building."

"Let me connect you with the police," she said, maintaining her businesslike tone.

Moments later, the phone picked up on the other end.

"Hello," a man's cheery voice answered, again with a British accent. Live music rose from the street in the background.

"Is this the police?"

"Yes, it is."

"They've got me captive in the government building. I'm in the President's office."

"Excuse me, but who has got you?"

"The terrorists. The terrorists!"

"I wasn't aware of any terrorists..."

"Then who's shooting back at us?"

"Someone is firing a gun?"

"Not some*one*. Hundreds of people. We're under siege at the government building. I'm being held hostage in the President's office."

"Sir, have you been drinking?"

"No I haven't. Get an earful of this!" He held the phone away from his mouth to pick up the sounds of machine gun fire. "Does it sound like I'm making this up?"

"Those are firecrackers."

"No they aren't. They're weapons. Bullets are flying everywhere." He was beginning to speak so loudly that the skipper might hear him above his own gunfire. He lowered his voice and said coldly, "Aren't you aware that your island is under attack?"

"Not to my knowledge. Sir, I'm going to have to write a report."

"No you won't. You will pick up your gun, get your police force together and free me from this building."

"Well, I'll send someone to check it out. Thanks for ringing."

Raymond slammed down the phone.

He was doomed. There was no way out. He sank lower until his cheek touched the floor. Let the terrorists battle it out. Maybe they'd use up all their ammunition and have to surrender. Then another horrifying thought struck him. He might end up spending the rest of his life in a Purang prison cell, with only that dunce of a police chief for company.

Then, imperceptibly at first, a distant throbbing entered his perception. It was only an insignificant noise in the battle raging below.

But when he heard terrorists begin to cry out in fear from within the building, he realized that something big was up.

The din of gunfire ceased, and the throbbing drowned out all sounds. It was pounding through his open window.

"Americans!" one of the terrorists yelled from deep within the building.

He peeled back the flag and hazarded a glance.

Casting a shadow over the buildings across the road, a Marine helicopter came into view, its fuselage door open, a soldier seated behind a machine gun firing away. They were here to save him! For the first time in days, he saw light at the end of the tunnel. And bathed in the light was a vision of his family.

The skipper ran across the room and crouched down behind the desk, just feet away from Raymond, who remained half-covered for protection.

The terrorist leader was sweating profusely, with the smell of gunpowder on his hairy arms. He still held his smoldering weapon in one hand. His eyes scanned the room searching for something. At last they fell on Raymond.

"You!" he exclaimed.

"What me? Not me. I didn't do anything."

The skipper pointed to the phone.

"I didn't call in the Americans. Honest I didn't."

"I'm not saying you did," the skipper said, spacing out his words evenly. "I want you to pick up that phone and call the police and tell them that we have you captive."

"No, not the police. The guy's brain-dead."

Surprise appeared in the skipper's eyes. That was quickly replaced by anger, anger at Raymond's betrayal. "You talked to the police?"

"Only briefly. Believe me, the guy's not altogether there."

"I don't have time for this!" the skipper screamed. The chopper edged closer. With a good pair of binoculars, the Marines could make out who remained in the government building. "Dial the phone!"

Raymond drew the phone closer and dialed the operator. Within moments, he was connected with the police station.

"It's me again," Raymond said.

"How can I help you today."

"It's *me. Me!*" As if his previous call had never happened.

He decided to resort to the polite approach. "Here's someone who'd like to talk with you."

He handed the phone over.

"Hello," the skipper began. "In the name of Allah, I have taken control of your government. You will now lay down your arms, and rejoice in His liberation."

Raymond watched as the skipper's face turned beet red. Trembling with fury, he smashed the phone down. He jumped to his feet and raised the stock of his rifle to his shoulder, taking careful aim out the window. He was going to pick off Raymond's rescuers.

No, you don't, you bastard. Raymond scrambled out from under the flag, clutching the bloody butcher's knife in one hand. As he rose, he could see out the window clearly. Marines were shimmying down a rope onto a rooftop opposite them.

The skipper had aimed his AK-47 at the chopper and was blazing away. The room seemed oddly silent to Raymond's ears. The louder the noise, the quieter his world became, and the more focused he grew.

He didn't have to think about it. He just did it.

He reached the knife back as if he were preparing to throw a baseball, then rammed the blade forward into the skipper's back. He continued to push forward even after making contact. The firing submachine gun pressed the skipper's body back against him, and he countered with the force of the knife. The tip glanced off of bone and hit the skipper's spinal cord. Raymond winced, but still kept the knife moving. With a last yank of his arm, he twisted the handle and severed the man's spine.

The skipper dropped the gun, took several uncontrolled steps backward, and fell into the Presidential chair. His weight pushed the tip of the knife through his chest wall until it protruded through his uniform. Then he went slack, his dilated eyes staring up toward heaven.

Swimming through his silent world, Raymond felt dizzy and nauseous. He never wanted to see another terrorist, and he wasn't going to die in that hellhole.

He turned and hurled himself through the doorway into the corridor. The terrorists were busy firing weapons elsewhere in the building.

Numbly, he jumped down the stairs three at a time and reached the ground level. He stood wavering, his knees weak. Then he stepped from the building, his hands high above his head.

He took several steps into the street.

He didn't care if the terrorists shot him. He didn't care if the guy tossing knives into the building hit him.

A few more steps.

He didn't even care if the Justice Department got him and locked him away for embezzlement. Yeah, he could pull out his China card, and spill the beans on the President's Chinagate transactions, and perhaps even win immunity.

Halfway across the street.

But he didn't care about all that.

He just wanted the bloodshed to end.

He reached the shadows of the far side of the street.

A beefy guy in Bermuda shorts stepped out of a butcher shop. He held a submachine gun in one hand and stopped him with a cautionary hand.

"I don't have a bomb strapped to me," Raymond said.

"Yous American!" the man said.

"Raymond O. Flowers. You may take me away now."

The heavy-set guy looked confused as he hustled Raymond off the street and out the back door of the shop. There, a group of Marines in full combat gear stood in the blustery downdraft of their chopper.

"Dis here's an American," the overweight man said. "Goes by Ray."

"Raymond O. Flowers," Raymond introduced himself again.

The Marine studied his face. He seemed to recognize him. Then he nodded and said something into his lip mike. Time passed, and bursts of machine gun fire broke through the slicing blades of the chopper.

At last the Marine held a hand to one ear, listened, then nodded, and motioned for Raymond to go up into the chopper.

"How can I get up there?" he asked. It wasn't like there was a staircase. The only way up was by a thick rope that dangled from the hovering beast.

A Marine showed him how to slip his foot into a loop in the rope and hold on with both hands.

"And I want to do this?" he shouted.

The beefy guy slapped him on the shoulder. "It's either dat or dis." He rattled his gun and returned into the butcher shop to polish off the terrorists.

Raymond fit one foot into the noose, but his bloody fingers slipped on the rope. He hugged it with both arms.

Moments later, the chopper began whisking him away from the dusty town, and the dwindling gunfire below. As they flew away, the rope winched upward until he was pulled into the fuselage. There, a pair of strong hands pulled him to safety.

The soldier wrestled him onto one of the benches that lined the metal walls of the cabin and strapped him to his seat. He gripped the bench with both hands and closed his eyes.

Thank God the American military had come to his rescue. And not a moment too soon. A few minutes later and he would have perished among the terrorists being slaughtered.

The Army sure was fearless, facing such firepower to get him out alive.

He envisioned a few newspaper headlines bearing his name, a few pictures of him smiling before Capital Hill. But he didn't want to be a hero.

He just wanted his family back.

He just wanted a suburban house, a shopping mall, a camera store, a nice food court. It didn't matter if the Chinese fast food wasn't real, or the air was ionized. He just wanted a normal job, perhaps selling shoes at a strip mall. That would satisfy him.

He'd settle for anything that America could offer, and he wouldn't utter a word of what had happened between the President and the Chinese. He didn't need to testify. He'd strike a deal with the government. He didn't know anything. Honest.

All he wanted was a small bungalow, far away from terrorism. Perhaps along the Chesapeake. No, it could be in Green Acres. He didn't care. As long as the kids had running around room and he had bacon for breakfast.

He opened his eyes. The cargo door was closed, but pure blue sky poured in through the large window opposite him.

The machine gunner sat beside him, a dreamy look on his face.

"Where are you going?" Raymond asked, his voice sounding distant.

The Marine pointed to himself. "Me? I'm going home."

Raymond could only make out what he was saying by reading his lips. "That's nice," he said. "Been a long time?"

"Over a year in Iraq."

"Huh?" He cupped a hand to his ear.

"*It's been over a year.*"

Raymond nodded. He could understand that.

"Do you know where they're taking me?" he asked.

The nearest port of entry would be fine. All he needed was to obtain a new passport and visa and book a return flight to China.

"Yeah," the Marine said, not offering much information.

"Where are they taking me?"

The Marine raised an eyebrow, then a shadow of sympathy crossed his face as they locked eyes.

"You're going to Gitmo, by way of Hawaii."

"What?"

"*Gitmo.*"

"Where's that?"

"Guantánamo Bay, Cuba."

Raymond wasn't sure he heard correctly.

CHINA GATE

The Interrogation

Chapter 20

Hiram Klug was exhausted. The Marines had managed to round up ten terrorists from what was left of the governmental palace. Another five gunmen were found dead, including the one he was staring at. The tall bearded man sat with a knife plunged gruesomely through his back as he sat at the President's desk. It looked like one of the butcher's knives he had tossed through the window.

Just then the Marines' unit commander stepped through the doorway into the office, broken glass crunching beneath his boots. "More terrorists just landed at the airport."

"We gots ta stop 'em," Hiram said.

"We don't have the manpower. We don't even have the resources to take care of these prisoners of war."

Out the window, a second Marine helicopter approached the same place that the previous chopper had hovered.

"I'll tell ya what," Hiram said, feeling the need to be decisive. "Lock da prisoners in a closet and I'll take care of dem. I've still got some time left on my vacation, but I'm sure you guys gots plenty of other tings ta do. So why don't ya clear yourselves outta here, and I'll wake up da police station and we'll go down to da airport an' mop up dose last remaining terrorists."

The Marine looked incredulously at him. But Hiram was insistent.

"Yous guys have done a great job, saved my vacation and all. Now I'm sure I can take it from here. Honest."

"Well..." the strong young man equivocated. "I suppose they're no longer a threat."

"Yeah, yous got dat Flowers guy ta take care of. I'm sure you gots ta hustle him off ta somewhere." He walked with the Marine out of the Presidential office, but paused for one last look around the place. It was a cozy little office for a Head of State. It was sunny and could be cheerful, if you tidied it up a bit.

"So tell me about dose terrorists dat just landed."

"We got a mayday from the control tower on our military frequency. Apparently the plane landed without clearance and the customs inspector found them unloading a cache of AK-47s, grenade launchers, and plenty of ammo."

"Are dey still at da airport?"

"No, they got past security and are heading into town."

Hiram had to laugh. His memory of airport security at Purang's international airport was that it didn't exist.

"I know the road there. I'll take my boys toward the airport and intercept dem. Not a problem."

He was already halfway down the stairs to the street. There, he rounded up his gang of youngsters who still held their rifles upright as if guarding the building.

"We got lots to do, boys," he announced. "Follow me."

When Carolyn Flowers woke up, it felt like she hadn't dreamt for a long while. In fact, her mind was completely devoid of memories.

Questions slowly drifted into her consciousness. Where was she? Who was she? At first, she didn't try to answer them.

She opened her eyes in search of clues.

There was a clear, straight line where wall met ceiling. A medical examination lamp swung away and turned off.

An old man was straightening his back, turned away from her, several long needles dangling from his fingers.

Who was that man? And what was with the needles?

Slowly she became aware of a thick bundle resting against her chest. The white rolled-up form rose and fell with her every breath.

And then it moved. The fringes of the sheet pushed back, and a tiny hand poked out, quivering as if struggling to reach out to her.

"It's Raymond," the old man said, his Chinese accent soft and kind.

Carolyn pulled one of her hands out from under the sheets and reached for the newborn child. Her fingers were bloated and lacked feeling, but she was able to pull the wrap away from the small form and reveal a face. It was beet red, all puckered up and pinched in the tight bundle that enclosed him. He looked like a pudgy old man, full of personality and wisdom.

Then his eyes opened, coated by antibiotic gel. He couldn't possibly see much, but the large eyes, shaded deep blue like a clear sky, were looking her way.

The doctor was smiling kindly, and she nodded at him in thanks. His joy was also evident. Beyond him, there was nobody else in the small, barren room.

Then her eyes returned to the child. She understood.

"So they call you Raymond," she said. The doctor had interpreted her screams for her husband as calling out to the child about to be born.

So, the little boy was named Raymond. That was okay with her.

Her memory of who she was and where she was being interned began to come back to her, subtly making their presence known. But she gently held the memories, laden with all their anger and concern, at bay. She was beholding the magic of a new life, and the little baby was curling his fingers, with dangerously long fingernails, around her extended index finger.

My, what a grip!

The February sun had yet to rise over a chilly Virginia as Secretary of Defense Kenneth Spaulding set down the phone in his darkened office suite at the Pentagon. The caller had been the Commandant of the Marine Corps with some positive news from Purang.

"We have not only foiled a terrorist plot," the Commandant had said, "we have captured Raymond O. Flowers to boot."

"He's still alive? You were supposed to sink his ship."

"He wasn't on the ship. We caught him red-handed trying to take over the government of Purang."

Kenneth had had to think quickly. Everyone from the President on down hoped that vaporizing the ship would make the problem go away. Apparently things weren't going to be that simple.

"So where do we take him?" the Commandant had asked.

In the end, he had to fall back on an old international legal loophole. "Take him straight to Guantánamo," Kenneth said.

"Roger that."

In the oblique light shed from the corridor, Kenneth contemplated his next call. He didn't want to hold the political hot potato for long. At the very least, he needed political cover. He groped in the dim light for the White House button on the dial pad. Within seconds, he was connected directly to White House Chief of Staff Chuck Romer.

"Chuck," he said at once. "We've got Flowers."

"Are they lilac?"

"What?" Had the guy gone insane? How could he joke at a time like this? Here a Marine helicopter was transporting the Chinagate special prosecutor's key witness that could bring down the entire Administration.

"I had hoped for mauve, but lilac would do," Chuck said.

Kenneth couldn't think up a reply, witty or otherwise.

"Lori wants purple, so I think I'm leaning in her direction."

"Chuck, will you get a hold of yourself? This is the DoD, not the FTD. We've got Raymond O. Flowers in our custody in the Pacific Ocean."

"Oh, that kind of Flowers," Chuck said, seemingly unfazed. "You didn't sink his boat?"

"That wasn't an option. We wound up with him in our hot little hands."

Chuck paused, then came back in a severe voice. "You do know what to do with him, don't you?"

"He's an American citizen. He does have rights, you know."

"Fewer rights if he's not around."

Kenneth couldn't believe his ears. "Are you talking about eliminating him?"

"Did I say that?" Chuck replied testily.

"Oh, you mean keep him off American soil? Well, I've directed to have him flown to Guantánamo Bay."

"That should work. But I'm no lawyer. You work out the details."

"I'll consult my General Counsel."

"You do that. And no leaks. No press visits to the base. I want a complete information blackout."

"We can ensure that." Was Chuck asking too much?

"Now one more question. Do you think the President would look good in a lilac cummerbund? That would go with Lori and the bridesmaids' bouquets."

❖ ❖ ❖

Waiting for his General Counsel to arrive from the Defense Legal Services Agency, Kenneth Spaulding sat back at his desk and reflected on what he had just done.

He had just ordered his troops to place Raymond O. Flowers in the Joint Task Force GTMO's detention facility. The idea was to isolate suspected terrorists off American soil, to deny them the protection of American law, specifically the Bill of Rights, which granted detainees a speedy trial and the right to an attorney.

The Administration's policy in that case was to purposely ignore the Geneva Convention for the treatment of prisoners of war, based on a Department of Justice finding that terrorists weren't combatants of a state that was a signatory to that convention. This policy enabled the military interrogators and the private contractors they hired to use more coercive methods than were normally possible to elicit information. He knew well, as he had personally authorized the use of threats such as drowning and attack by dogs, as well as approved stress position, loud music, strobe light, and sensory deprivation techniques on the least forthcoming unlawful combatants.

However, one thing bothered him greatly. It was his understanding that the U.S. only sent foreign nationals to Guantánamo Bay detention facilities. And Flowers was an American citizen.

There was a polite knock at his door and Ivan Nemroff entered. Ivan's agency, the DLSA, provided legal advice and services to the defense agencies and could get Kenneth out of just about any pickle.

"Mind if I turn on the lights?" Ivan asked as he entered.

"Fine," Kenneth said with a wave of the hand.

Ivan flipped on the overhead lights, revealing a fit man with a thick brown mustache and goatee. Kenneth offered him a seat, which he took.

"Today's problem," Kenneth said, sitting back behind his massive desk, "is Raymond O. Flowers."

He looked at Ivan, who nodded, already well aware of the problem with which Kenneth was wrestling.

"The White House wants him out of sight, which means detained somewhere off American soil...indefinitely."

"So you told me."

Kenneth admired Ivan's circumspect approach to ticklish political matters that frequently cropped up in the Secretary's office. After all, they were forging a new way to prosecute a war, as their enemy had shifted from conventional armies to slime bucket individuals wielding an inordinate amount of power.

"I'm not sure we can intern Flowers at GTMO because he's an American," Kenneth explained. "So far, we've transferred all American terrorists to military bases in the States where they are on trial for treason by military tribunals. I see you shaking your head. Is that not the case?"

"Not exactly, Mr. Secretary. There are two conditions that must be true in order for us to transfer a prisoner to Guantánamo and detain him there. First, he must be a foreign national, and second, he must have received training from a terrorist group such as al-Qaeda or was in command of three hundred or more enemy soldiers."

"Start with the first condition. Clearly Flowers is an American citizen," Kenneth said.

Ivan hesitated. "We do have ways of changing that."

Kenneth frowned. "I thought the Supreme Court upheld a person's right to citizenship. We can't just take it away."

"That's absolutely true. But I've checked out Flowers. He is an orphan, and many details that automatically confer citizenship onto a child are unknown in his case. For example, was he born on American soil? Were his parents American citizens? Did he spend at least five years of his youth in America? Unless he can prove at least one of these things, he may not be an American citizen."

"What if he has a valid U.S. passport?"

"You need to be a U.S. citizen to obtain a U.S. passport, but possession of a U.S. passport is not sufficient proof of U.S. citizenship."

Kenneth felt a chill in his veins. This guy was good.

"How about the second condition, the terrorist connection?"

"We're on more solid ground there, Mr. Secretary. According to the White House, he has been acting in collusion with terrorists."

"And how can they prove that?"

"I haven't seen their evidence. But Flowers was picked up during a terrorist strike on Purang. Guilt by association is adequate grounds to put him away."

"Okay," Kenneth said, trying to sum up. "So given that he needs to be detained indefinitely for the good of the American people, what are our options?"

"Under our current policy, you have two options," Ivan replied, as if reading from prepared notes. "Number One, if you are unsure of the legal grounds for holding him, you could render him to a foreign power, say Egypt or Morocco, where the authorities could interrogate him using their own methods and therein detain him. Or, if you are more comfortable with the legal grounds that I have just enumerated, you could order him detained at Guantánamo, which is the legal equivalent of outer space."

"Okay," Kenneth said, making a snap decision. "On the basis of his disputed nationality and terrorist connections, let's stick him in Guantánamo. Maybe we can force some al-Qaeda names out of him while he's there."

"That would be most appropriate, Mr. Secretary. This is America, but we do have ways of making people incriminate themselves, or at the very least discredit themselves."

"Guantánamo Bay?" Raymond repeated to himself, incredulous. Why were they sending him to Guantánamo Bay? There wouldn't be any press corps waiting to take down his story.

Perhaps it was just a normal debriefing location, sort of like how they took former hostages from Beirut to U.S. Army hospitals in Germany for mental and physical checkups.

The government had learned from Vietnam not to dump released POWs back on the streets of America without significant psychological help with their adjustment.

He had to laugh. On the whole, the terrorists had treated him humanely, even courteously. It was the Americans who were shooting back and throwing knives while he was holed up in the government palace. They weren't afraid of spilling his blood. What more impersonal acts were they capable of? Then the images of bloody, tortured, and sexually humiliated prisoners in Abu Ghraib prison outside Baghdad came to mind. Americans could dehumanize and put the screws to prisoners as well as anybody.

Did the guy really say Guantánamo?

He recalled images from the Chinese press of Taliban and al-Qaeda detainees wearing blacked-out goggles and kneeling in cages in the brutal sun. Hadn't several of them tried to hang themselves in captivity? And hadn't the U.S. Army court-martialed prison chaplains who were trying to assist them?

Thank God, he was an American. The military would never pull such a stunt on him.

And thank God that they weren't taking *him* as a prisoner of war. After all, the Marine onboard the chopper had given him a cup of coffee and made him feel as comfortable and welcome as one could aboard a noisy, vibrating military helicopter.

Yeah, it was good to be one of the boys again.

As he contemplated the calm ocean surface below, his mind drifted into the future. In the end, he didn't want to testify against the President of the United States. Why bring down the leader of a proud nation, who fostered such a genuinely moral army? After all, the machine gunner was a fine reflection of the American people. Raymond was proud to be American.

If he could avoid a subpoena by the Chinagate special prosecutor, he'd do so. Deals were always being struck in Washington. Some smart cookie would think up something. Maybe even that Sandi DiMartino would materialize again. She seemed interested in his case. Whomever she worked for might be sympathetic to his cause. Heck, it might have been she who had called in the cavalry to rescue him.

He shifted in his thinly cushioned seat. Yup, his wallet was still there with her business card. He pulled it out and examined it with its Global Oil Incorporated logo and address. He had to laugh. She was no corporate lawyer. She had real connections.

He examined her telephone number. It was a Houston number, probably fictitious. Then he noticed her cell phone number. It was all sixes followed by all ones. How coincidental could that be? Clearly another fake number.

The helicopter gradually pitched back, unsettling a circular area of waves. They were approaching a landing pad.

Boy, he could use a little less sea and a little more terra firma. A cottage along the Chesapeake would do him just fine.

Chapter 21

Harry Black was a frustrated man on his flight from Atlanta to Washington. His men had been tearing Nairobi apart, unable to find any trace of Raymond O. Flowers.

Badger had sounded both puzzled and angry over the phone. "Just show me one line of computer data placing him here," he had said. "Without a byte trail, I don't believe a thing. Just get me my computer back."

Harry had done his best to assure him that the Attorney General himself had given him the tip.

"But the field agents don't know a thing about it," Badger had retorted. "If they don't know, how does the freaking Attorney General know?"

At that point, something had snapped in Harry. He had gone from defending his source, namely Caleb Perkins, the Attorney General of the United States, to siding with his crew.

"I'll go to Washington and work on the problem from there," he had assured Badger.

"Great, because this new Embassy here in Nairobi is giving me the creeps," Badger had said. "The terrorists bombed the last one off the face of the earth."

As soon as the commercial liner touched down at Ronald Reagan Washington National Airport, Harry hit the pavement. His first stop was to be an unannounced call on Caleb Perkins at the Department of Justice.

The Diamond cab took him down Pennsylvania Avenue and detoured around Lafayette Park where a vocal mob of protesters was screaming "We can't wait for Chinagate!" at the White House. Harry had to laugh. The Chinagate investigation would go nowhere if he was able to find Flowers and yank him off the streets.

At the Department of Justice headquarters, he gave his name to the guard behind the security desk and waited as he phoned upstairs. A prominent display showed that the terrorist threat level was orange, "High."

What had caused the threat level to rise from yellow up to orange?

The guard stepped around the desk and proceeded to pat him down and run a wand over him and under his arms and between his legs. If Harry hadn't grown used to such treatment at airports, he might have felt more offended.

The briefcase was next. It went through a bomb detection device. As if he wouldn't have already exploded the bomb by then just standing in the lobby.

"You may proceed, sir," the guard told him, sliding an identification badge toward him over the counter. "Through that scanning chamber."

That was also new to Harry. He waited for the first door to slide open, then stepped inside. The door slid shut behind him, and he was shut into a small room.

Some unseen machine zapped him with invisible rays, and some perverted guard behind the wall examined his physique.

Harry waved at the blank walls.

Then the far door slid open, and he stepped through.

Wasn't there something in the Constitution about being innocent before being found guilty, and a person's right to privacy? It seemed as if recent security measures had encroached on those concepts. Perhaps those who decided such things had determined that it was time to cross out a few lines in the Bill of Rights.

The elevator took him straight to the fifth floor, where another security guard greeted him, this one with an attack dog.

A little paranoid, aren't we?

At last he was shown to the Attorney General's suite, an opulent use of space in a city that had little room to spare. But, overseeing the Federal Bureau of Investigation and the Drug Enforcement Agency and the Bureau of Alcohol, Tobacco, Firearms, and Explosives and the Bureau of Prisons as well as all federal prosecutors did entitle one to some measure of grandeur.

"Hi, Harry," Caleb said, striding forward eagerly to greet him at the door.

"What's with the smile on your face?" Harry asked. "You know why I'm here. You deliberately misled me about Flowers' whereabouts."

"Please, take a seat," Caleb said. "I think some explanation is in order."

Harry remained standing.

Leaning awkwardly against his desk, the rotund Attorney General tried to ease the tension with a laugh. "It's really quite embarrassing. The Marines have picked up Flowers on a small island in the Pacific."

"Not in Kenya."

"No. He turned up elsewhere."

"He didn't turn up where you told me he would be. You sent my men on a wild game safari in Africa."

"Let me remind you that you're under contract."

Harry stiffened. "I may be under contract, but only to see after America's security needs. I am under contract the same way that you are under contract to see after the justice of the nation. As far as I see it, there is no distinction between civilians and government officials in this case."

"Yeah, but I put my hand on a Bible and swore an oath to office."

Harry bristled. "Religion and mere words are not thicker than blood. My men put their lives on the line every day, and I'm determined that it will not be for some political game played here in Washington."

"This isn't politics, honest."

When the Attorney General had to plead for someone's trust, Harry knew there was big trouble.

Now that Flowers was in the hands of the military, the operation was essentially over. And so was the secrecy. It was only a matter of time before the press and protesters would catch wind of the military operation and demand that Flowers testify in the Chinagate case. "I'm curious where he goes from here."

The Attorney General remained expressionless. "Why naturally, the Pentagon should hand him over to the special prosecutor."

"You don't sound the least bit unhappy."

He caught the Attorney General casting a glance down Pennsylvania Avenue at the White House.

Suddenly Harry understood the change in tactics. With Flowers' capture, the problem had turned from a security issue into a political one. "This is going your way, isn't it," Harry said. "It's playing right into your hands. That's why you had the CIA send me out to find Flowers. You want Flowers to testify. You want the President out of the race."

He looked around the spacious office, replete with sports trophies along with diplomas and pictures of the Administration with his face prominent among them. But there were no "Caleb for Prez" banners up yet.

"It's not exactly going my way," Caleb said. "The Marines are taking Flowers to Guantánamo, and you know what that means."

Harry understood. That had been the plan all along, to muzzle him forever. "But if you want a different outcome, you're still the Attorney General. Can't the Department of Justice demand his extradition to America?"

"One can't be that blatant in Washington," Caleb said. "I don't want to alienate the Party and the voter base."

Harry was having a hard time keeping up with Caleb's train of thought. Caleb Perkins had executed a complete about face. He wanted to turn the Flowers case into a political opportunity. And for that to happen, he needed Flowers freed, and his testimony made public. Harry wasn't so sure he saw Flowers' testimony as a good thing.

Perhaps sensing that Harry wasn't completely behind him, Caleb circled his desk and produced another manila envelope marked "TOP SECRET."

What was this? A payoff?

"Take it. This is another contract for your company."

It *was* a payoff.

Harry made up his mind not to take it. But that didn't mean he wasn't curious. "Contract for what?"

"To interrogate Raymond O. Flowers. To reveal the truth."

"I don't know anything about Chinagate and financial dealings…"

"No. I'm sorry. Perhaps you weren't aware…the Pentagon is holding him on *terrorism* charges."

"Terrorism? How did they come up with that one?" He knew that the Pentagon had to try and smear Flowers, but wasn't terrorism a bit extreme?

Caleb threw up his hands. "They found him on an al-Qaeda ship in the Pacific during a military coup."

"Right," Harry said with a laugh.

But Caleb's face remained serious, and troubled.

Harry let out a low whistle and looked at the envelope in Caleb's hands. "Whose name is on the contract, yours or the Agency's?"

"It's the Pentagon this time," Caleb said, handing him the envelope. "It includes military orders."

Harry sighed. As long as it was still a security issue...

"But of course it's important to do more than just interrogate him. I want you to set him free."

So it was more than security work. Caleb wanted him to do his dirty work and sink the President.

"I'm sorry. I can't—"

"Take your time. Look into the case. Talk with him. I'm sure you're a good man and you'll realize how Flowers has been terribly wronged by his country."

Oh shit. Now Caleb was appealing to his sense of honor.

He took the envelope.

Caleb offered a handshake as well. "Is it a deal?" he asked.

Harry shook the hand. "I'm only doing this for Flowers. And if it turns out that he's a terrorist, I'll tear up the contract."

"You're a good man. I'm sure you'll fulfill the contract."

But Caleb pressed his palm longer than usual. His blue eyes penetrated into Harry's, searching for a commitment beyond the written contract.

Harry fought back the impulse to look away. It was like staring into the eyes of a self-righteous man that he knew was stupid, ill-informed, and misguided. It was a look designed to form a bond of trust. Harry looked back directly, but didn't return the Attorney General's smile.

He left the suite, the guard with the dog, the scanner machine, and the terrorism threat display far behind. He left the Department of Justice shaking his head. If this was how America intended to operate, she would need to write a new Constitution.

One that was far less noble.

The last thing Hiram saw of the Marines as he and his young recruits trotted toward the outskirts of the capital was a second helicopter swooping away with a long rope of soldiers hanging from the cargo door. They looked like the day's catch on a fishing line. As the chopper hauled the men in, it swung away from the town, plunging the island in silence.

This was soon broken by the roar of jet engines. Ahead of him, a passenger jet was just taking off and rising above the cane fields. Hiram squinted as it banked into the midday sun. Then, as it circled over the island and headed west, he made out the white tail fin and green flag of a Pakistan International Airlines jet.

"Look out, sir," one of the boys shouted. "Here come the terrorists!"

Hiram looked up the two-lane highway, tall cane rising on either side. Sure enough, the boys were right. Another anonymous white van was hurtling down the road straight at them.

He flicked off his safety switch. "Into the fields on the right!" he shouted.

The boys dropped low and scooted across the road, the assault rifles dangling from their hands.

The white van's driver must have suspected an ambush and suddenly hit the brakes, some fifty yards from Hiram's position.

The vehicle came to a complete stop and waited.

"Now what?" one of the boys whispered.

The van was too far away to hit with accuracy. Hiram felt vulnerable, shielded from sight but not from bullets.

"Half you guys stay put, and I'll take two boys with me." He picked the two youngest in the group. "If dey try to drive past you, shoot out der tires."

He motioned for the two youngsters to follow him through the field. It was tough going, the cane shoots sharp and unforgiving underfoot. They circled wide but in the general direction of the back of the van. Fortunately they soon reached a tire-rutted track that roughly paralleled the highway. They began to trot.

Listening for gunfire at first, then for voices, he put a finger to his lips. The boys were even stealthier than he was as they left the track and approached the highway.

He heard a door click. Still no voices.

They settled into a crouch and held their positions.

The enemy's feet landed on the pavement just ahead.

Hiram strained to see through the long, yellow leaves that fluttered gently in the humid air.

The voices were guttural, and in a language he had never heard before, unless perhaps it was on television. They sounded frightened and suspicious.

Hiram advanced on his elbows and knees, keeping his rifle ahead of him and aimed at the voices. From his new position, he could make out the passengers who had alighted from the van. Instead of taking up defensive positions, they were standing straight, looking about themselves in confusion. Their long robes and unkempt beards seemed out of place on the tropical island. Several men wore thick glasses. One man stood out as taller than the rest. He had a calm, priestly look on his face.

They sure looked like odd birds, but certainly were no terrorists. Only one man held a gun in his hands. He was a small man with what looked like an unbuttoned coat, a floppy gray turban, and strange, coarsely woven shoes. That was the one to watch out for.

Hiram raised his rifle and peered down the long barrel. He lined up the muscular man in his sights.

"Drop da gun," he shouted coolly.

The men froze in position, but the gunman turned his assault rifle Hiram's way.

"Drop da gun, or I'll blow yer head off," he repeated, this time with more authority in his voice.

The tall man's face dropped, then he motioned to the gunman to lower his weapon.

"On da road der," Hiram shouted.

The man placed the gun on the simmering hot pavement.

"Now step away from the van."

Like a herd of timid deer, the group moved away from the van. The men seemed to form a protective shield around the tall man among them.

"Hands high in da air," Hiram said. "And spread out."

The group complied.

Hiram rose to his feet and walked slowly out of the thick wall of cane. "So what do we have here?" he asked, studying the men closely. He circled behind the van and looked inside. It was empty.

"Okay, you can come out, men," he shouted to his troops.

From up and down the road, the band of tiny boys stepped out of the sugar cane field. The captives' jaws dropped.

Hiram picked up the rifle that lay in the road and passed it to one of his troops.

"I don't know who you are, or what you're doing here," he finally announced. "But I don't like the look of yous guys."

A car had been steadily approaching from the town. It finally squealed to a halt, and a man in a uniform stepped out.

"I'm the police chief here," he said. "What are you doing with that gun?"

Suddenly the tall captive broke out in laughter, his glaring eyes cutting through to Hiram's core. Clearly the chief of police of Purang had no idea that his island was at the epicenter of Islamic *jihad*. His government had nearly been taken over by mercenaries, and he was worried about a man standing in a field with a gun.

Hiram didn't like the laugh, or the triumphant look in the man's eyes. He fought to regain control of the situation.

"You," he pointed to the police chief, the man who had mocked him on the phone for being drunk. The man who refused to lift a finger when confronted by news of an invasion. "You're fired."

The smile had vanished from the face of the tall terrorist, and his searing look once again clouded over.

Hiram's boys were pulling boxes of weapons and ammunition out of the van. It looked like dangerous stuff.

"What's this?" the police chief said, addressing Hiram, alarmed by the sudden profusion of weapons. "Are you trying to take over the island?"

Hiram gave a twisted smile. "Yeah. I'm da boss now. I'm taking over dis place. And you're under arrest."

One of the boys approached the police chief and stripped him of his hip holster and gun. Slowly the man raised his hands over his head.

The other boys spread out before the line of terrorists. Each held a prisoner at gunpoint. Hiram counted the number of men again. One was missing!

He picked up the rustle of sugar cane in the distance. The small, muscular one had escaped.

The smile had returned on the face of the tall stranger.

"I don't know who yous guys are," Hiram said, angry with himself for letting the man escape right from under his nose. "But I'm putting the lot of you behind bars."

Hoarse from talking on the radio, Sandi DiMartino placed her headset on the desk before her at Manila's port authority. A huge wave of heat blew in from a worn, sandy lawn behind the facility.

Captain Albano appeared and set a cup of black tea beside her.

"Thank you so much," she said. She took a sip and let its warm vapors soothe the back of her throat. She felt the ring of perspiration just below her hairline begin to evaporate. How a hot beverage could feel so good on a simmering day, with the sun directly over the Philippines, she might never know.

The sound of Raymond O. Flower's voice had completely vanished from the airwaves, no matter how urgently she had repeated his name.

Realizing that he still might be held captive by the men on the beach, she had tried to give him some hope to go on.

She had repeatedly tried to inform him that his family was alive. They had not died from SARS, were safe, and were held prisoner in China. He had to trust her, and she would work for their release.

But after an hour of jamming the frequency with her desperate pleas, she had given up.

And then she had heard some other harbormaster demanding that ships at specific coordinates identify themselves. The guy must have had some sort of radar. She had listened to each ship responding, hoping that one might be Raymond. But that search had ended in vain.

Maybe the terrorists had caught him on the radio. Her only hope was that he could escape them and trust her and find some way to contact her.

She checked her cell phone for any missed calls. There were none. People back at Stanley Polk's office must have also lost hope in her investigation. Their case against the President would have to take a different tack, or be dropped altogether, because she wasn't bringing a witness home.

Her radio headset lay beside her teacup, unused.

"Say," she said. "Do you suppose any of those ships out there are American Navy?"

The captain shrugged his shoulders. "I'm sure some are," he said and stuffed his green shirt back neatly under his bulging belt. "But you would have to reach them on a military frequency."

"Then I'll do that," she decided. She was desperate enough to try anything.

The captain tuned in to a frequency commonly used by naval vessels. "There you go, madam."

Sandi closed her eyes and composed her thoughts, then said, "Calling any American naval ship in the eastern waters off the Philippines. This is the Philippine Ports Authority. Please come in."

All of a sudden, the radio blared with dozens of voices responding to her call.

"Have any of you come across Raymond O. Flowers?"

Utter silence.

Damn. She had tipped her hand. Now she wouldn't get a word out of any of them. The name "Raymond O. Flowers" seemed synonymous with "treason" to many Americans, not the least of whom must be the men and women in uniform.

Then a telephone rang beside the desk. A Philippine officer picked it up, spoke briefly, and handed it to Sandi. "It's for you."

She pressed the phone to her ear.

"Did you say that Flowers' family is still alive?" came a young American male voice.

"Yes, I did," she replied. "Do you know his whereabouts?"

There was some hesitation, then the voice came back whispering, "I do. Mr. Flowers has been apprehended."

"Do you have him with you?" she returned in a whisper.

"Negative. We were the ones to locate him on Purang. We called for the *USS Stuart* to arrange the capture."

"Is Raymond in good condition?"

"I wouldn't know that, ma'am."

Sandi concentrated on her next sentence, willing the response to come out, even if it meant a court-martial for the brave informant calling her.

"Where are you taking him?"

"That would be GTMO, ma'am."

"Thank you," she responded. "Thank you so much."

Now all she needed to do was hustle her butt back to Washington. And figure out what "GTMO" was.

Chapter 22

The C-17 military transport plane banked tightly for its final approach to the United States Naval Station at Guantánamo Bay, Cuba. The dry, hilly scrubland below became visible out Raymond's window, and he found himself looking down at a set of Florida-style tract houses, beaches, and a golf course. All the trappings of home. This wouldn't be so bad, even with his hands cuffed uncomfortably in his lap.

Early in the flight, he had been rudely awakened to his new status, and it was only now beginning to sink in. Somehow along the way, he had changed from being a rescued hostage to a prisoner of war. It had to be a bureaucratic foul-up on the part of the Navy. Sooner or later, Washington would sort things out, take the handcuffs off him, and set him free.

As the plane descended sharply, they passed over uniformly spaced rectangular cottages that faced the ocean between two beautiful white sand beaches. It would not be a bad life for Cubans. However, an American flag was fluttering from the flagpole.

He had once read that Guantánamo Bay was the oldest U.S. base on foreign land, and the only one located in a Communist country. Located on the far eastern tip of Cuba, as far away from Havana as possible, it was a mere fifty miles across the water from Haiti. He remembered seeing pictures of tens of thousands of Haitian boat people who had been plucked out of the Caribbean by U.S. Navy ships and brought to languish in cinderblock houses that were hastily constructed on the base at Guantánamo. Poor souls.

Then the plane glided low over a complex of buildings surrounded by wire fences. The buildings were newly constructed, but looked menacing, with guards posted on all corners. Who lived there? Certainly they didn't make soldiers live under such tight security without much of a view.

The plane skimmed low over the gentle, clear water and made a marvelous landing on one of the dual landing strips. Raymond would have applauded the pilot's skill if his wrists hadn't been chained together.

The young Military Policeman assigned to guarding him helped him unfasten his seat belt and rise to his feet. It felt good to stretch his legs after a long flight across the Pacific and the Gulf of Mexico. When the exit door opened, he felt a waft of fragrant, humid sea breeze. He was in Cuba, American style.

As they said in Washington, bring it on.

Since he was the only detainee to step off the plane, he received personal attention. A military bus took him a short distance to a ferry that conveyed passengers eastward across the bay. He stepped onto the bobbing boat with a sad smile. Not another boat. He wouldn't mind a house on the beach overlooking the turquoise water, but he could do without another boat ride anytime soon.

The engine chugged to life and he instinctively reached for the railing. Ouch! It had become burning hot under the direct sunlight.

Strange that a pair of gray speedboats with manned machine guns escorted them across the sparkling water. It seemed like a scene stolen from *Miami Vice*, augmented by Cuban troops stationed just beyond the heavily fortified and patrolled no-man's land, Cuban gunships plying the waters, and angry Taliban and al-Qaeda terrorists beating their prison walls.

Okay, so he could see the need for a couple of armed ships keeping a close watch.

The trip began on a winding channel through a growth of bushes and short trees. Lurking among the mangroves might be a sniper or desperado al-Qaeda escapee. Raymond kept his eyes peeled.

The ferry droned on at a crawl. He turned to the Military Police Corps soldier who remained close by his side the entire trip from Hawaii. "Can't we speed it up a little?"

The grim young man shook his head, his white helmet reflecting the sun in his eyes. "Manatees," he said.

Raymond looked carefully among the tree branches that dipped into the water. What was a manatee, anyway? Some sort of local revolutionary?

The MP seemed to sense his confusion. He pointed down into the water.

A fish? Were they stinging jellyfish, like the famous man-o'-war? Suddenly he remembered the jellyfish that he had stepped on at the beach in Hainan. Maybe he had been stung, and he had gone unconscious, and the last few days had all been a terrible nightmare. But he didn't need to pinch himself to make sure this was really happening. The handcuffs seemed real enough.

But he didn't see any huge jellyfish in the clear water.

"Sea cow," the MP said.

"What?"

"A manatee is a sea cow."

Raymond frowned. "You mean to tell me that we're slowing down these gunboats here in Cuba because of a sea cow?"

"Hey, they're an endangered species. The propellers could mangle them up."

He could hardly believe that a soldier was lecturing him on the environment. Go figure.

At last the narrow channel widened into the open bay that, curiously, was devoid of ships. Having successfully avoided the manatee menace, the ferry picked up speed. In the wheelhouse, the captain rammed headlong into the waves that buffeted the unwieldy ship. He supposed navy types lived for that sort of thing.

Even his motorboat ride along the eastern shore of Hainan Island in the South China Sea didn't bring on such nausea. The blunt prow of the ferry flew high and plunged low with each wave.

Setting foot on shore was the highlight of Raymond's day. He survived the crossing without losing his lunch. But a mild headache persisted as he boarded another bus at the landing. Such service.

And look at that, a grocery store, Golden Arches, an outdoor movie theater, a high school, a church, a baseball field, suburban houses. Was he mistaken? He had arrived in southern Florida, not some hardscrabble outpost where American soldiers held a death grip on Cuba's last vestige of freedom, with Colonel Jack Nicholson's hardened face bearing down on his troops, forging them into men of iron.

And a red and green stoplight at a place called Camp Delta. He had to let out a laugh. He bet the Taliban and al-Qaeda got a good laugh out of that one. The long, peaked white buildings that looked like a prefab trailers would serve as their new torture chambers.

Raymond glanced around the busy intersection where olive-drab cars and buses pulled out of a camp surrounded by razor wire and entered the main road that stretched off into the dusty distance.

"Where's Camp X-Ray?" he asked the MP.

"Abandoned a few years back," came the tight-lipped response.

Raymond raised an eyebrow. They had certainly moved the prisoners up a few notches. This Camp Delta looked like a Marriott compared with the iron cages of Camp X-Ray that he had seen pictured in the *China Daily*.

"Take one last look around," the MP said. "This will be your new home."

A heavily armed soldier in battle fatigues swung the gate open, and the bus turned into the camp. Slowly it began to dawn on Raymond that the prison camp was meant for him.

Harry Black couldn't wait to leave Washington. He would rather be in Guantánamo and find some way to free Flowers, even before his Piedmont Personnel team arrived from Africa to begin interrogations.

As Harry walked toward his departure gate at Dulles International Airport, a newly arrived flight was just emptying its passengers onto the carpeted terminal. He swam against the current of brown, oriental faces. Where had they all come from?

A Caucasian woman stood out in the crowd. She was a foot taller than the rest. Her shoulder-length blonde hair caught the afternoon light just right.

She was a knockout in her wraparound sunglasses, baby blue business suit, and long, lean calves. If he could, he would have hired her on the spot.

But he was in a rush to make his flight to Miami, from which he would transfer to a military flight down to Guantánamo Bay.

Ticket in hand, he jumped into a bus-like vehicle. It chugged to life and began to transport him across snowplowed taxiways out to the far terminal.

Only when he reached the departure gate did he learn that the flight had been delayed and would leave fifteen minutes late. This was going to be a long day spent in airport terminals. He might as well use the extra time wisely and do some research on the Web.

Seated at the boarding gate, he lifted the cover of his laptop and it woke up. He gave the computer a minute to find the Internet hotspot and log him into the net.

First stop on his cyber journey was the *Washington Post* site. Even though he was right there in Washington, the connection was slow. At last the front page appeared in its onscreen format.

The big story was about the President's announced engagement. Under that item was another story titled, "Kudos for Administration's Strong Response to Oscar Night Terrorists." He skipped both articles.

He clicked on the search box and typed in "Raymond O. Flowers" and pushed Enter.

The list of recent articles on him was nothing short of astounding. His name appeared in twenty *Post* articles and editorials in the previous two weeks. Man, this guy was a hot item.

The subjects of some headlines were already well known to him.

President's Fate Rides with Flowers
Flowers Must Have Something to Hide
Immunity for Testimony?
Are Chinese Harboring Flowers?

One headline in particular caught his attention. It raised an issue he hadn't considered before, that Raymond O. Flowers was implicated in the same crime as the President.

Why Did Flowers Do It?

"Flight 1047 to Miami is now boarding…"

He clicked on all the articles he could find in order to download them to his computer. The process was finished in five minutes, just as the last passengers were boarding.

"You'll have to turn off your computer until after takeoff," a gate attendant told him as she handed back the stub of his boarding pass.

"Oh, right." He hit the Off button and snapped the screen closed before passing through the gate.

That would give him plenty of in-flight reading.

Sandi DiMartino felt like she was back on familiar turf as she entered her office building in Rosslyn, Virginia.

And the men were so gorgeous in Washington, she thought as she rode up a full elevator to the fifteenth floor. Her libido had been rekindled the moment she had stepped off the airplane at Dulles, and she had walked into a crowd of handsome, well-coiffed men.

On her way, she glanced briefly at the dark hulk of Stanley Polk, the Chinagate special prosecutor, sequestered in his gloomy office.

She glanced out the window at the ice-fringed Potomac River and made her way through the sea of desks to her own pile of papers.

Pulling along her luggage as she walked, she attracted stares, young lawyers and clerks rising to their feet.

She stopped at her desk, removed her winter coat, and rifled through the huge stack of documents and memos in her inbox.

At last she turned around, and was met by a sea of inquiring faces.

"Well, what?" she asked.

"What do you mean what?" her assistant asked. "That's what we want to know. Did you find Flowers?"

She put on a stumped look. "Yeah, in a way."

"Well, where is he?" Ralph, the chief litigator, asked.

"I wish I knew." Then she shot out, "Does anyone know what GTMO is?"

The staff looked at each other as if she were talking in tongues.

"GTMO," she repeated. "You know, some place where the military flies former hostages."

It still didn't ring a bell.

"Oh, hell," she said, and picked up her phone. She dialed a friend in Alaska who served in the Air Force. "What's GTMO?"

"Honey, I don't have the vaguest idea, but it's sure nice of you to call."

She needed a better lead.

Wait, the guy on the ship that she had radioed must have been in the Navy. Maybe someone in the Navy would know.

She consulted her little black book and found the number of Charlie Swain, a friend she had made back in college. He was in ROTC. They had never dated, but had stayed in touch over the years, probably because they had never dated.

"You want to know what GTMO is," Charlie repeated from his law office. "Are you sure you want to know?"

"Sure as shooting. I'm going to storm over there right away."

"Sandi, planes don't fly to GTMO," he said. "And I'm not so sure you'd want to go anywhere near the place."

"Why's that?" she asked, suddenly concerned that her plan of attack would fall through.

"Because GTMO is our Navy base at Guantánamo Bay, Cuba."

"Oh."

"It's a place where pillboxes outnumber palm trees," he said.

"I'm not worried about the guns," she said. "I'm just worried about getting in to see my client. He's being detained there."

"Sandi, the last thing in the world I would like to be is a defense attorney for a terrorist held down at Gitmo. Believe me, he's got zero rights down there, and you're going to face a military tribunal. Are you up to speed on your military law?"

"I don't know a thing about it."

"Neither do I. They operate by their own Military Law, of which I haven't even read Chapter One."

"Thanks for your help, Charlie," she said, setting down the phone.

Raymond was off limits to her and the rest of the world. He might as well be on Mars.

After takeoff, with details of the snow-filled Virginia countryside receding below him and passengers stripping down to their tennis outfits and Spring Break gear, Harry Black hauled out his laptop, placed it on his tray table and booted up.

The headline "Why Did Flowers Do It?" was facing him on the screen.

Scanning through the article, he gleaned a few details of Flower's former life as a financial officer and family man.

The father of two elementary school students and husband of a professional fashion designer, Raymond O. Flowers had a rich and rewarding family life. His company paid for all his overseas trips, including two round trips home for his entire family each year. Furthermore, his company provided him with a car and driver, a house, and school tuition at the expensive International School of Beijing.

But that was not to say that Raymond was financially dependent on his company. He had an annual income topping $150,000, in addition to health and property insurance benefits. More than half his salary wasn't taxable, as he didn't live in the United States.

Flowers was already a happy, wealthy man. Why would he feel the need to take part in a criminal enterprise?

The article went on to speculate that perhaps Flowers was heavily in debt, but that could not be substantiated in any way. He might have been an avid supporter of the President and therefore was facilitating the kickbacks to the President as a means of supporting his re-election. But Flowers wasn't even a registered voter in his home district in Maryland. Perhaps Flowers sought a political appointment from the President, such as the Ambassadorship to China. Again, not likely as Flowers was characterized by colleagues and former classmates as politically naïve.

If Flowers had no reason to seek out padding the President's pockets, then he must have been after the money. After all, wasn't he, as a financial officer, intimately familiar with banking procedures? Harry had to concede that anyone who worked solely with money all day must have some interest in or fascination with money. But then, there was no indication that Flowers siphoned off any of the money for himself.

That left only one answer. Flowers had been coerced.

The article explored the possibility that Flowers had been forced by his company to perform the illegal act of sending kickbacks to the President's Cayman Islands offshore bank account. But the special prosecutor had subpoenaed the entire hierarchy of his corporation, and could come up with no one who professed knowledge of the crime.

Besides, how could they have coerced Flowers to perform such a clearly illegal act? Surely they wouldn't threaten to take away his job, otherwise Flowers would have gone straight to the FBI. Then maybe someone had threatened something other than his job, say, for instance, his legal status in China, his company benefits, or even his or his family's life.

That was where Harry found himself nodding in agreement.

The article speculated on the highly coincidental fact that the kickbacks occurred well into the period when SARS was running rampant on the streets of Beijing, and most travelers and expatriates had long since fled the country. Yet Flowers' family had remained. Not only remained, but caught the SARS virus and died.

Why would Raymond have remained in Beijing so long, exposing his family to such danger?

Had someone forced them to stay? In which case, Flowers was doubly a victim of the kickback scandal in that it implicated him legally and it cost him his family's life. In effect, wasn't Raymond O. Flowers a victim, rather than the perpetrator of a crime?

The newspaper article ended with a sad depiction of a lone man attending the burial of his wife, daughter, and son in a Maryland cemetery shortly before the Chinagate scandal broke.

Whatever had caused Raymond O. Flowers to wire kickbacks to the President of the United States was not worth his family's death.

Harry snapped the laptop shut, and his eyes filled with tears.

And to think that his company, Piedmont Personnel, had just spent a week trying to track down Flowers and deep six him for the CIA. What kind of bastards was he working for?

He made a decision on the spot, as the young woman beside him slipped out of her sweater to reveal a braless tank top.

He resolved to resurrect both Flowers and his reputation.

Chapter 23

Gradually, as if scales were falling from Raymond's eyes, the Army's intentions became all too clear.

First two guards clad in camouflage fatigues took him to a maximum-security prison and told him to strip. There in the long hallway of padlocked steel wire doors and not a single voice to be heard but their own, he pulled off the civilian clothes that the Marines had given him.

"Underwear, too," one of the two guards commanded.

What was this, Abu Ghraib Prison? Raymond checked the guards for digital cameras, but they weren't taking pictures. And their expressions were all business. So he slipped out of his briefs.

"And your eyeglasses."

"These?" Raymond said, pointing to his thin, harmless wire rims.

The guard nodded solemnly.

Raymond folded the spectacles, careful not to scratch the lenses, and handed them over. This meant going blind. He had to squint to make out the guards' faces.

Only after he was stripped of every last possession including his dignity, a guard unlocked a door to one of the cells that was halfway down the hall.

"Step this way."

It was a neat, spare little chamber with white corrugated walls, a four-foot by four-foot steel wire window facing a small recreation yard, a metal bed bolted to the wall, a floor toilet, and a square metal sink with running water. An arrow was painted on the floor for no apparent reason. Perhaps it pointed toward Mecca. On the bed lay a thin foam pad, a blanket, and a prison uniform.

He slipped on the orange shorts and pants, then pulled on the orange shirt. Carolyn would hardly approve of the design or color scheme. It made him look like a walking traffic cone.

He squinted at the pair of flip-flops. He hadn't worn shoes in days, but slipped his toes into them anyway. After all, his feet were growing cold on the concrete floor.

Then he fumbled through the hospitality kit provided by the prison. There were a couple of towels, a washcloth, a prayer cap, a half-inch thick prayer mat, a book in Arabic that he took a wild guess was the Koran, and a bar of soap.

Despite those homey touches, he was hardly grateful. The army had stuck him in solitary confinement.

"Hey," he cried. He began to beat his fists against his cell door. The sound echoed down the long, high corridor. "Don't I get to call a lawyer?"

When his voice stopped reverberating around the cellblock, he heard a pair of guards chuckling in the blurry distance.

He turned back and sat on the corner of the bed, still unable to grasp the full enormity of his plight.

"I am a prisoner," he whispered to himself. And who knew or cared?

Harry Black observed the arid Guantánamo Bay landscape with interest as the military bus chugged toward Camp America, the living quarters for troops assigned to Camp Delta.

Leaving the airport and harbor behind, he spotted two naval ships at anchor, hidden from the sea. Grinding its way eastward, the olive drab bus proceeded past a group of hurricane shelters. Fortunately, it was the dry season, and he wouldn't need to worry about crippling storms.

He spotted various signs that pointed to a cemetery, the military training area, and bunkers. They kicked up dust as they passed a trailer park that stretched along the road. He grinned at the irony of the name, Green Acres. Other signs pointed northward to the high school and golf course.

The terrain grew rougher, and the road twisted to get around steep hills that were punctuated by scrub brush. Beyond the immediate landscape, a much higher mountain range rose out of the haze. Those had to be in Cuba proper, yet he still couldn't see the famous fence that divided the American troops from Fidel Castro's troops.

There were many tactical groups assigned to Gitmo, such as drug interdiction, forward logistics supply, training, and prisoner detention, but the underlying reason for the base was to give the Cubans a show of strength.

Border patrols wore combat uniforms, helmets and bulletproof vests, setting a serious tone for other units operating at the base.

After Castro cut off the water and electrical supply in 1964 in response to the Bay of Pigs invasion, the base had to create a desalinization plant and generate its own electricity. As the challenges escalated, the Americans seemed even more determined to remain and thumb their noses at the Cubans.

Turning southward down Kittery Beach Road, Harry began to get a sense of the famed Cuban beaches. The bus stopped briefly at a traffic light near a heavily guarded complex of sterile new buildings called Camp Delta. He took the opportunity to case the place. Somewhere inside, Raymond O. Flowers must already be familiar with the prison routine.

Then they chugged onward, finally dipping downward to a sprawling complex of offices and living quarters. With Kittery Beach on the left and Windmill Beach on the right, he had arrived at the Guantánamo Riviera.

"Command Post for Interrogations," the bus driver announced, and the bus ground to a halt.

Squinting in the bright sunlight, Harry looked for the command post. All he saw was miles of identical plywood houses strung along a single road. Side by side, their peaked roofs looked like an unending wave of temporary housing.

Then he spotted a sign under one of the eaves. It had the Defense Intelligence Agency insignia on it, a globe spinning on a torch.

He stepped inside the room. It was a mere fifteen by thirty-foot rectangle packed with naval personnel, working with quiet and efficient purpose. He looked down at his business suit. It not only jarred with the starched uniforms around him, it hardly impressed.

Even though he had served eight years in the Marines, throwing a salute wouldn't work while wearing civvies.

"I'm Harry Black, reporting for duty," he said to the female yeoman, and handed over his orders.

"Welcome to Camp America, sir," she said without looking up.

She examined the papers briefly, and a worried look crossed her face. "Were we expecting you?"

"Yes, my company has a contract to interrogate one of your detainees. I arrived as soon as I could."

"Very well. Come with me."

She led him to a closed office door and knocked.

"Enter," came a smart, if curt, response.

She smiled and handed Harry the orders. "Good luck," she whispered.

What could he do but enter?

A tall, dark-haired young commissioned officer rose behind the desk. Harry repeated who he was and why he was there.

"I'm Commander Jack O'Shay," he said, offering his hand. "I'm in charge of setting up the interrogation teams at Camp Delta. I understand that you have been assigned to the Flowers case."

"That's correct, sir." He shook the officer's bony hand.

"Well, we have all sorts of teams coming and going…CIA, DIA, State Department, Israelis, interpreters. It's like Grand Central Station around here."

"I hope that Raymond O. Flowers is kept well away from the other prisoners."

"Yes, we got word. He is in one of the vacant detention blocks in Camp 3. We haven't had many new detainees recently. Maybe we've mopped up all the terrorists."

"Or can't sort out the terrorists from the insurgents."

"That could be, too. Thank God they don't send them all here."

Harry looked around uncomfortably. "How do I get started?" he asked.

"Okay, first the ground rules. All interrogators such as you must have taken the Military Rules of Interrogation course."

Harry had anticipated this requirement. "I took that back in the Marines," he lied.

"Good."

Harry wasn't surprised that the commander didn't bother to double-check this fact in his service records. Which explained a lot about how things got so screwed up in the prisons of Afghanistan and Iraq, not to mention Guantánamo. And showed how little had changed since then.

Commander O'Shay went on to his next point. "Second, no use of MPs as any part of your interrogation process, that is, to soften up the prisoners before you interrogate them. The MPs are under a separate command and there's a firewall between them and us."

"Understood." At least that new rule had been hammered home.

"Good. Now about your housing. I understand that you have requested bunks for ten men."

"That's correct."

"Well, I'm sorry, but all the refurbished housing facilities at Tierra Kay are occupied at the moment. We've been gradually moving troops out of the sea huts to make room for offices and storage. However, we do have a nice unit just two doors down that will house ten soldiers comfortably."

"Are you talking about barracks?"

Commander O'Shay nodded. "We call them sea huts, with a great view of the sand and breaking waves."

"That'll do."

As if rushing to bolster the image of the place, he added. "We've got food served daily at the Seaside Gallery, with air-conditioning."

Free food. That made up for the substandard accommodations.

"There's a large mini mart in the parking lot of the mess hall. We've got a Navy Exchange down the road, and complete workout facilities in one of the bubbles, a telephone and Internet hut, a bar and lounge hut…"

He wasn't about to live the life of a private, making three free fifteen-minute morale calls per week, and standing in line to get onto the Internet. "And office space?"

There the captain winced. "You'll have to work out space with Camp Delta Facilities Command for that. Sorry."

Harry understood.

"Now, can someone show me to my quarters?"

Two minutes later, he stood at the front door of his building that smelled of fresh plywood. There was something wrong with the place, but he couldn't put his finger on it. Then he realized what was bothering him—there was no lock on the door. He pushed the door open and scanned the dark room. It was in fact dormitory-style barracks. He and Badger and the men were about to get to know each other very well.

He entered and shut the door. The insulated walls muffled the sound of the waves against rocks. It was hot in there, so he flipped on the light, found the air conditioning unit, and turned it on full blast. With a loud creak, he sat down before the cool breeze it created.

He was sitting on one of ten wood-framed beds that stood side-by-side and filled the entire room. He knocked over a stack of white pillows behind him, lay back, and stared at the crossbeams above.

Could he operate covertly, expose Flowers to the public, and get off the base alive?

He hadn't felt the restrictions and single-minded purpose of boot camp in over twenty years. Yet the sensation came back to him in all its dehumanizing crudeness, constricting his chest. His fingertips rubbed against the coarse wool blanket beneath him.

Under the circumstances, with the lack of privacy, the surrounding razor-wire fence and the flood of memories of his youthful devotion to his country, it would be doubly hard to commit an act of treason.

Sandi dragged herself into her cozy Georgian townhouse in Ballston, Virginia. It was only a short Metro commute from Rosslyn, and an equally quick walk from the station to her quiet street, but she felt like she had been running a marathon and getting nowhere.

She turned on a table lamp, threw off her overcoat, flopped into the first armchair she found, and stared at the blank, white wall that confronted her.

It had been a long day. The sun had risen at midnight, mid-flight between Manila and Los Angeles. And she had eaten lunch somewhere over Kansas.

In her office that afternoon, she had learned that she would have to become an expert in military tribunals in order to gain access to Flowers. Then she had learned that the military claimed no knowledge of Flowers' whereabouts.

She was being stonewalled by the Pentagon. She had ordered her staff to fire off a freedom of information act request to ascertain his whereabouts. But knowing where he was didn't guarantee that she could visit him.

In that regard, she was even more stymied. If he were at Guantánamo Bay, there was no way she could enter the base, much less interrogate Flowers and get his deposition in the Chinagate case.

She had only two options left. She could try to represent him and thereby gain access to the base, or she could search for a legal maneuver to spring him from military custody and bring him to the United States where his full rights as a citizen would have to be observed as he faced a civil trial.

Her mind spun with the enormous roadblocks to both of her solutions. If she were allowed to represent Raymond, she couldn't possibly learn the ropes in time to represent him at a military tribunal. Like her friend Charlie Swain, she hadn't even cracked the Military Law book open to the first page.

Or, how could she bring him to the States? She had absolutely no experience in extradition matters, and her client would be an American prisoner of war possibly facing charges of treason. If anything, she would be a liability to her client and might even get him the electric chair. Even bringing down the President wasn't worth executing a decent, innocent man.

As she unpeeled her winter coat and kicked off her wet boots, she remembered how simple life had been at the resort in Hainan.

She had reclined by the pool alongside Flowers discussing his company's "asshole hustlers" as he had called them. He couldn't hide his bitterness.

He had blamed them for corporate scandals as well as corruption reaching "all the way up to the White House."

She had felt a tingle of delight when he had said those words. He was her man. He had much to tell, and enough anger to tell it, under the proper circumstances. Unfortunately, being held by the military and subject to their justice system effectively prevented him from testifying against the Commander-in-Chief.

At last, she stood and checked her mail slot. Many newspapers, envelopes, and packages had spilled onto the floor behind the front door. But first, she needed a bath.

Hauling herself upstairs, she pulled off one item of clothing after another. She turned on the hot and cold water faucets and watched steam begin to rise from the Jacuzzi. She emptied a few drops of bath oil into the tub, and inhaled the aroma of jasmine that subsequently infused the room.

The water ran slowly, and she had a few minutes to kill. In her bra and panties, she returned to the living room and made herself a martini from the wet bar.

Raymond O. Flowers had liked to drink...what was it? Some hopelessly tame drink.

She sipped from her triangular glass and screwed up her face with pleasure. It was nice and dry.

Yeah, Raymond had ordered them both daiquiris, without even asking her. Almost as if she were his wife and he was used to ordering for them both.

Well, she wasn't his wife, and the daiquiri nearly made her vomit, but she had stuck with him and played along long enough to glean a few more vital details from him, and plant the idea of his retaining her legal services, although he had no idea that she actually worked for the independent prosecutor.

In fact, drinks had lowered the inhibitions of both of them. Flipping through her mail as she sprawled on her divan, she sorted her bills from her personal mail.

What had she asked him pointblank? "Do you believe the President's guilty of taking kickbacks?" Boy, she had been bold. In retrospect, she may have blown her cover.

A smile crept across her lips. Raymond had nearly choked on his drink when she had mentioned the kickback scandal.

Two players heavily involved in the Chinagate affair, both tiptoeing around the subject, neither admitting to be a part of it, was a pretty funny scene. But, luring a man out of China and into the lion's den of Washington was proving to be a challenge.

Raymond had left no doubt that he had incontrovertible proof of the President's guilt. What had Raymond said? Something about making Saddam Hussein blush. And at that point, he had divulged that he had worked for Core Petroleum.

And that was as close as Raymond had gotten to confessing his involvement in the crime.

She thought she had him on the hook by then, and the Academy Awards bash thrown by the resort had served to bring them even closer. Looking down her long, slender limbs, evinced a wistful thought or two. Raymond would have made a move on her that evening, but something had held him back.

Most single men wouldn't have turned her down, but Raymond had. Did he know that his family was still alive, and that jumping her would be an act of infidelity? Probably not. He was bitter and suffering, not busy trying to track them down.

If she had known at that time that his wife and kids were still alive, she wouldn't have made a move on him. She would have broken her cover and told him who she was and why she needed him. After all, he had touched a sensitive spot in her, a vulnerability for mistreated souls. And in the end, she was glad that they hadn't coupled the night away, and just left it with a tender kiss.

Curled up around a throw pillow, she found herself squeezing it for warmth and comfort. Suddenly, prosecuting the President no longer seemed important. She merely wanted to help Raymond get his family back.

Just then, her eyes fell on a buff envelope the size and shape of a Hallmark card. The name on the return address read, "The White House."

She tore it open at once, and pulled out a wedding invitation. President Bernard White wished to invite her to his nuptials with Loretta Blythe Crawford that August.

Sandi had never expected to receive any invitation to the White House for any reason. Bernard White was masterful at charming his adversaries and throwing them off balance.

But what floored her was the name of his fiancée. Lori Crawford had been her roommate at Columbia!

What was that tart doing with the President?

Then it hit her. Lori was an intern at the White House. Of course, that's how she would have met the old man. And knowing Lori's fresh-faced innocence combined with her considerable talent at displaying her charms, the President's fate must have been sealed the moment she walked into 1600 Pennsylvania Avenue.

A smile came to her lips. So Bernard White wasn't inviting her to the wedding. It was Lori, rounding up old college chums to fill her half of the church.

She almost overlooked one other letter that she had sorted with the bills. It was in a plain white envelope, had no stamp, and bore some official seal that she usually disregarded. But not finding a return address, she examined this one more closely. The Defense Legal Services Agency name struck a chord. These were the guys she was up against. The JAGs.

She tore open the envelope and found a hand-written note inside. It was a personal invitation for her to meet with Ivan Nemroff, General Counsel to the Secretary of Defense. The note requested that she meet him at 6:30 the next morning at Pierce Mill for a jog through Rock Creek Park.

How did he know she was a jogger? She vaguely knew the meeting place from infrequent weekend workouts in that area. The District wasn't her normal territory, but it might be where Ivan lived. In any case, she would jump at the chance to interrogate him directly, and to hear him out.

At that moment, she remembered her bath running upstairs.

She threw down the pillow and invitation and charged up the stairs to the bathroom. Steam was billowing into the hallway.

She had to fight through the perfumed cloud to find the faucet. She could turn off the cold handle, but the hot side nearly burned her hand. She reached for a towel and wrapped it around the handle and managed to turn it off.

Thankfully the water hadn't overflowed. She stripped completely, waded through the steam, and dipped her toes in the water. It was just perfect. The humid air clinging to her skin, she slowly slipped into the scented water.

And then the questions began to flood her mind. Why did the General Counsel of the Defense Department want to meet with her? What kind of man was Ivan Nemroff? And should she wear her sexy pink shorts?

Rolling a two-wheeled cart in front of him, a prison guard entered Raymond's block from the darkness of the evening.

Raymond unstuck himself from the bed and watched through the white mesh as the soldier walked down the corridor.

"How long are you going to keep me in this cage?" he asked as the guard approached his cell.

"We don't call these cages," the guy said tersely. "They're enclosures."

"Okay, enclosure then. How long?"

"I am not at liberty to discuss your case with you," he said by rote, then stopped the cart and began to work on Raymond's meal.

He peeled back the paper cover of the dinner, which Raymond recognized as an army-issue MRE, a Meal, Ready to Eat. The guard set to work inspecting the contents of the box, picking off any suspicious looking flecks from the meat and dusting off the plastic juice cup. He removed some folded squares of toilet paper and threw them away in a plastic bag.

"Hey," Raymond said. "I might need that."

The guard shook his head. "You wouldn't guess what people try to kill themselves with."

That shut him up. Suicide by toilet paper? What could make one that desperate?

The guard removed the plastic wrapper from the spoon and threw away the vinaigrette dressing.

"Choking hazards?" Raymond asked.

The guard looked at him, but wouldn't reply.

Next, several packs of salt went into the trash, leaving one for Raymond. He supposed that prisoners could induce vomiting and get themselves taken out of jail to a hospital.

"Where's the nearest emergency room?" he asked. "Havana?"

"Funny. We have a twenty-bed medical facility right here in Camp Delta. It's got all the latest equipment. So don't try anything."

He let out a low whistle. Twenty beds. There had to be far more prisoners stashed away in the camp.

"Why am I all alone in this cell block?"

The guard pushed what remained of the package through a slot and handed it to Raymond. "I'll pick that up when you're done."

He took the hot dinner and stood there. He didn't want to let the guard go. It was the first human he'd seen since his detention began. "Just tell me what kind of routine I can expect."

The guard stopped his cart. "You get three culturally appropriate meals a day. You get exercise in the recreation/exercise area once a day. You get two fifteen-minute showers a week at which time we issue you a new suit. That's the routine."

"What do you want me for? Why are you even holding me?"

"I'm an MP. If you want to chat, talk with the interrogators."

"Is someone coming to ask me questions? I've got plenty to say."

The guard moved on without response. Raymond would just have to satisfy himself with his dinner.

"I'll be back to account for the material in your meal," the guard called, and departed into the blur.

Raymond had no table, and had to settle for eating the meal on his bed. The chicken breast and noodle dish, accompanied by green salad, dinner roll, margarine, and fruit gelatin dessert reminded him of airline food. He took a few nibbles. It wasn't Thai Airways. More like China Eastern. But as long as he ignored the decor, it was almost palatable.

The guard had only stirred up more issues in Raymond's mind. Foremost was the question, why was he alone?

He looked around at the empty cells, and began to imagine Afghan Taliban and al-Qaeda terrorists hanging by their bed sheets.

Maybe he had better just count himself lucky to be alone.

He took a bite out of his roll. It was a bit dry, but he couldn't complain...and he could use real butter.

He had plenty to tell an interrogator. He had reason to believe his family was still alive. The terrorists had captured him; he hadn't joined them. And he had been robbed of all his money.

But how much should he divulge of what they really wanted to know? He wasn't associated with the terrorists in any way. In fact, he had personally killed the terrorist leader. But if they tried to wring a confession out of him about Chinagate, he might have to hold back. Did he really want to implicate their Commander-in-Chief?

Suddenly it occurred to him why he was alone. The Army didn't want information out of him. They wanted to prevent him from spilling the beans.

The United States government was afraid of him.

Chapter 24

Harry Black awoke to the blare of a bugle playing reveille. He jumped out of bed, and his feet landed on the crude wooden floor.

Outside, soldiers would be raising the flag. It was another day at an American military base. And Harry's memories of reveille in Georgia's Ft. Gordon, Missouri's Whiteman Air Force Base, and Camp Butler in Okinawa came back to him with fondness.

Of course, military duty at those camps was easier as the world was far less complicated to a young man. But at the current stage of his career, he was faced with far more painful decisions and thorny predicaments.

He would trade it all in for a few days of cleaning engines, sentry duty, and flight school!

The air conditioner had been droning on all night. He thought he would give it a break. He turned it off and opened the door that faced the sea.

Distant whitecaps replaced the constant drone of the air conditioner. The fresh morning breeze was cool enough for him.

Pulling on a jersey and a pair of running shorts, he prepared for a jog along the beach. Maybe he could even get to the patrolled border with Cuba. How picturesque.

He stepped outside and stretched for five minutes, unknotting the leg muscles that had grown cramped in airplane seats and relaxing the lungs and heart muscles that had tensed up as he entered Washington.

There was no access to a beach from his location, so he needed to work his way past the sea huts. He took one last look at his building number to submit it to memory, then set out along the paved street. The morning sun at his back threw everything in sharp relief. He passed the flagpole where soldiers had already raised the stars and stripes. He ambled past the Seaside Galley, his legs stretching more freely. Soon he was past the last sea hut, and a marvelous beach stretched out to his left.

He cut through bushes and ground his way across the powdery white sand toward the water. Far out at sea, waves formed in long breakers that rolled intact all the way to shore. Beyond the breakers, a handful of fishing boats rocked in the water. Ernest Hemingway might have been on one fifty years earlier.

He was alone on the long strand of beach. Alone to the world and alone to his thoughts. He never forced himself to think very deeply while jogging. It was a time to commune with nature.

In the back of his mind, he knew what he had to accomplish with Raymond O. Flowers. Either spring him free, or get his voice heard.

But what was his plan?

He jogged a half mile before the question came back to haunt him more relentlessly.

What was his plan?

Nearing the end of the beach, he came to a halt. A bright pink conch lay in the sand. He picked it up and held it to his ear.

The wind whipped up granules of sand that prickled his face, and the smell of the sea was even stronger in the large, spiral shell. The roar of waves seemed magnified as he held the opening over his ear, but he was actually hearing the flow of his own blood.

Cuba was a far cry from icy Atlanta and snowy Washington. It was a timeless place, stuck in the late 1950s. If only the world were as simple as it was back then.

But was it so simple then? Were the missile crisis and the threat of being obliterated by nuclear war any less complicated than a world awash with terrorists?

He set the shell down and turned to face the sun. Its rays broke into millions of fragments across the sea's surface and bore down directly in his eyes and hot against his face.

It felt like Cuba was turning a giant spotlight on him. The return trip would not be so pleasant.

And as his running shoes pounded against the wet sand, the same question returned, repeating itself with every stride.

What was his plan? What was his plan?

Halfway home along the beach, he broke his rhythm and slowed to a walk.

That day, in his role as an interrogator, he would try to meet with Raymond and take down his deposition.

He imagined himself flying back to Washington with a piece of paper bearing Raymond's signature. That evidence alone would allow the special prosecutor to subpoena the witness and thus force the military to release him.

Yes, a piece of paper with Raymond's testimony was all he needed to sink President White, who had lined his pockets at the expense of such dupes as Raymond.

The more he dwelled on the injustice done to Raymond, the faster his heart pumped, and soon he found himself sprinting at full tilt down the beach and inland past the sea huts to his own place.

He arrived as a total wreck, his clothing saturated with sweat but his manner demonstrating a new determination.

Sandi did not need to set an alarm that evening. Her jet-lagged body turned over listlessly in her sheets all night. In the morning, she doubted if she had slept at all.

Dawn was just breaking as she slipped into her workout attire. Her pink jogging outfit gave her a shiver of pleasure. The anticipation of streaking through the icy stillness of Rock Creek Parkway in the early morning appealed to her.

Nonetheless, it was wintertime in Washington, and a pity that she had to wear more. As she pulled on a loose Georgetown sweat suit, it felt like she was covering a bottle of wine with a paper bag.

She folded her work clothes into a gym bag, grabbed her briefcase and wool-lined trench coat, and locked the door behind her. She found her old, reliable Toyota still parked alongside the icy brick sidewalk, and piled everything in.

Shuddering from the cold, she started up the engine and turned the heat on full blast. Waiting for the engine to warm up, she ran the windshield wipers to clear off the last traces of snow.

Thank God she didn't need to climb out of the car and chip away at the windshield by hand.

Her breath was steaming up the windows, so she switched from Heat to Defrost. The warm flow of air blew over the windshield and against her face. She was ready to go.

She couldn't take the drive very quickly as the previous day's slush had solidified overnight into frozen ridges of ice. Under gray skies, traffic crept along the expressway into the District. And the bridge was especially slick.

Beyond the bridge railing, she noticed that the Potomac flowed freely out to sea. Perhaps winter was ebbing as well.

Driving up the Parkway that early was still possible, but on her way, she passed a truckload of workmen heading south to place traffic cones behind her and shut off vehicular traffic from that direction.

She pulled into the Pierce Mill parking lot precisely at 6:30. There were no other cars parked alongside the 18th Century gristmill.

She had just begun stretching exercises beside her car when a middle-aged man, sleek and slim in his Lycra leggings and warm-up jacket jogged up.

"You must be Sandi," he said, his breath escaping from under a trim mustache and beard in a frosty plume of steam.

"Ivan Nemroff?"

He stuck out his gloved hand and she shook it. Her cold knuckles felt warmer under his touch. His dark brown eyes were full of self-confidence. She liked that.

"Let's head out first," he suggested. "We can talk later."

"Fine with me."

Striding side by side with the lean athlete gave her an exhilarating thrill. They skirted the Mill and headed northeast past crystalline glades and through arched tunnels of white tree branches.

Ivan was as fine a runner as his body promised. They laughed as they ducked under branches and alerted each other to upcoming icy patches.

Her initial concern that she wasn't adequately fit to keep up with him proved unwarranted. He turned out to be more of a trotter than a quarter horse, keeping a steady gait that she had no trouble matching.

They were in high spirits when they eventually drew to a halt and turned around to head back.

"Let's walk for a few minutes and catch our breath," he suggested. "The rest is all downhill."

"I'll have to be honest," she said, hoping to capitalize on their bonding experience. "I feel frustrated under the rules in which you have incarcerated Raymond O. Flowers. It denies me access to him, and denies him repatriation to the United States."

"He's a very dangerous man."

"To whom? Only the President, as far as I can tell."

Ivan didn't respond, letting her frustration dissipate. He seemed to be biding his time, but for what?

She couldn't be the only person who knew that Raymond O. Flowers was being held on the island of Cuba. Was she? Who had told her? It was that voice on the military band in the Philippines. Perhaps only the U.S. military knew of his whereabouts, and her knowledge of his whereabouts made her a target of the Administration. She wished that she had told others in her office. Why was she keeping it all to herself? To garner all the glory when she produced the star witness?

Suddenly she felt all alone in the vast, wintry park.

She remembered recent newspaper stories of unsolved kidnappings in the park. Surely, he didn't mean to abduct her.

She studied him carefully. He wasn't capable of murder, was he?

She kept a lookout for escape routes off the winding path and into the woods. Maybe she should continue to ply him with questions, throw him off balance.

"You have suspended Flowers' Third, Fourth, and Sixth Amendment rights."

He was letting her pummel him left and right. But he was absorbing the blows without the slightest reaction. He was a good lawyer. He knew how to make his opponent reveal her case.

What gave him the upper hand was that he was also the judge and jury.

"But all those legal rights don't matter to you, do they?" she said, rubbing her nose for warmth. "You do this all the time down in Guantánamo."

"Not for those who collaborate in embezzlement schemes," he said.

"Then on what charge are you holding him?"

Ivan continued a few steps and looked at her out of the corner of his eye. "Terrorism."

Sandi erupted in laughter. "Raymond, a terrorist? That's too funny for words. No really, what are the charges?"

"I told you, terrorism. We picked him up on the Pacific island nation of Purang while we were mopping up a terrorist operation there. He's one of al-Qaeda's chief financial officers. In fact, we have since uncovered evidence that in addition to trying to extort money from the White House, he has engaged in reflagging al-Qaeda-owned vessels and conspiring to topple the Purang government."

Sandi stopped dead in her tracks. "Raymond? Do you mean to tell me that Raymond is one of *them*?"

She had to admit that the idea had never crossed her mind. First of all, was the special prosecutor Stanley Polk unwittingly playing into the hands of terrorists? After all, Chinagate could be no more than an elaborate scheme to put pressure on the White House, allowing terrorists to blackmail the President. Raymond couldn't be behind all that. He didn't have a mean bone in his body. On the contrary, he was upset by the corruption he discovered leading to the White House.

"I have to state for the record," she said carefully, "that I, for one, believe Raymond O. Flowers is no terrorist."

Ivan spread out his hands. "We have ample evidence to the contrary. Do you want to see it?"

She shuddered, becoming acutely aware of the cold morning. This Ivan the Terrible was a master at casting doubt. No wonder that he was the Pentagon's top legal counsel. Suddenly all her spirit had been dashed from her. "No, I don't need to see any evidence," she said under her breath. "Let's go."

Ivan's smile was not unkind. "Race you home?"

She didn't know how to feel. Her fear for her own life had been immediately replaced by Ivan's sledgehammering her plans to access and rescue Raymond. He had Raymond in custody for terrorism! This guy was creepy. Suddenly, all she wanted was to get away from him.

Letting her legs carry her back to her car, she resolved not to talk business with Ivan for the rest of the run, and never to speak with him for the rest of her life.

Maybe Ivan wasn't out to get her, but she wouldn't let him get what he did want, to skewer Raymond O. Flowers. If she were ever to save Raymond's skin, it was now abundantly clear that she needed to skirt the Pentagon by a wide margin.

She needed to find another means of accessing him.

At midmorning, Harry found the Defense Intelligence Agency command post at Camp America where he had checked in the previous day.

He squeezed into the sea hut and nodded to the yeoman he had met the day before. She thumbed him in the direction of the commander, not bothering to take him back there herself.

Harry knocked first.

"Enter," the commander's voice sounded behind his office door.

Harry poked his head inside. The lanky commander didn't bother to stand and greet him. "I thought I sent you to the Camp Delta command post."

"Yes, Commander, you did," Harry said, taking a step inside. "But I'm wondering about the status of my team. They should have arrived by now. I've been expecting them all morning."

"Oh, them," the young man said, and set down the report he was reading. "It seems that the Pentagon won't be cutting their orders. They won't be coming."

"They're part of our contract to interrogate the prisoner."

"Well, I guess that just won't be happening, will it."

Harry was floored.

"Where are they now?"

The commander regarded him as if he were lecturing a schoolboy. "I told you to set up your own office. Without an office, you don't have a phone number, an email account, a mailing address. How can people get this information to you if you treat this place like a hotel? Now, I'm not the manager, I just work here. Go figure these things out for yourself."

Harry had never felt so belittled in his life, if he discounted boot camp. He was not used to being put in his place, and his first impulse was to pull the young man's granny glasses off his nose and bash his fist into his face.

But that would be a waste of fist.

He stormed out of the office and through the hut door. Outside, he tried to get his racing heart under control. Someone was pulling the plug on his operation. He needed to act fast, before the Pentagon caught up with him and shipped him out of Guantánamo.

He flipped out his satellite-equipped mobile phone and placed a call to Badger McGlade. Several satellite links later, Badger picked up in what sounded like a busy store.

"Where the hell are you?" Harry shouted.

"At Baskin Robbins," Badger replied. "We're stuck in Kadena Air Base in Okinawa, and the brass won't put us on a plane to Gitmo."

"Yeah," Harry concurred. "It sounds like they're trying to prevent us from interviewing Flowers. You sit tight there, and I'll try to get in to see Flowers right away."

"You haven't seen him yet?"

Once again, Harry felt himself being scolded, but this time for good cause. What had given him the impression that he had the luxury of time on his side?

"I'll be in touch," he said and switched off the phone.

He marched back to his sea hut where he rifled through his briefcase. He pulled out his orders and a pen and notepad and jogged out to the main road.

A bus was just pulling up, and he climbed aboard. "You going to Delta?" he asked.

"Yes, sir. Next stop."

The bus arrived at the traffic light and then entered the main gate at Camp Delta.

Harry jumped out and showed the guard his orders.

"You may proceed to the camp commander," the guard said. "You will find him located in the next office block down the road."

Harry strode past the trailer park of detention buildings. Some orange-clad prisoners were kicking a soccer ball in a small, enclosed field adjacent to their cells. He checked their faces. Flowers wasn't one of them. Soldiers walked in pairs from building to building, their black boots padding softly on long rubber mats as they did their rounds.

So these were unlawful combatants, a term that was undefined in the Geneva conventions. They were common criminals fighting for a stateless foe against the entire United States. That certainly gave them special status. Or no status at all.

How could Raymond O. Flowers be regarded as a foe of the United States?

He burst into the camp's office building, a single-story bungalow. "Show me to the camp commandant," he barked at the staff sergeant at the reception desk.

Apparently more accustomed to mealy-mouthed intelligence types, the sergeant jumped to his feet.

"Yes, sir," he said and threw a salute.

Fresh off the boat from Nebraska.

At that moment, a tall, broad-shouldered Hispanic lieutenant colonel strolled out of his office. "May I help you?"

"I'm Harry Black, on orders from the DoD to interrogate Raymond O. Flowers."

"Lieutenant Colonel Rodriguez," the officer introduced himself. He had a comfortable grip, but a standoffish smile.

"I need to see Flowers right away," Harry said.

The lieutenant colonel glanced at his orders and grimaced.

"I'm afraid that won't be possible," he said. "I can't grant access to the prisoner until I'm given the go-ahead from the Pentagon."

"Who's running this camp anyway? Raymond O. Flowers has information that's vital to our national security. I've come all the way from Washington, only to find that the Pentagon has thrown up roadblocks to the rest of my team."

"Sir," the lieutenant colonel said, clearing his throat. "These orders state that you are to interrogate him on criminal matters. That would be fine, except that the Pentagon is undergoing a simultaneous investigation into his terrorist links. He's being charged with treason."

Harry paused a moment. What terrorist links? Had the military really found him on an al-Qaeda ship as Caleb Perkins had said?

"You can't be serious," he said.

"Oh yes," the lieutenant colonel said. "We're very serious."

"Then let me at him. I'll find out what you need to know."

Rodriguez wavered, but held firm. "I'll have to order you to stand down until further notice. You won't interrogate the detainee today."

Harry glared at the man who stood flat-footed, a huge obstacle to his plans to obtain a deposition.

Was the Pentagon onto him? And what was with the terrorism links and treason charges? Everybody knew that Flowers was just a glorified accountant.

"I'll go back to my quarters and wait this one out," he said at last. "But I am not a patient man."

He left his mobile phone number with the sergeant. "Here's my office number. Call me as soon as I can go to work on the prisoner."

The two men watched him leave the office in a huff, their faces a blank wall.

As he stormed down the paved road back to the guard booth, Harry wondered if he had played it all wrong. He had come to Guantánamo expecting to find dusty cages and prisoners with heatstroke under 24-hour arc lights. Instead he found air-conditioned cellblocks, recreation areas, paved streets, and traffic lights. Interrogators probably even read prisoners their Miranda rights these days. His bluster seemed out of step with the times.

Was the war on terrorism being waged by lawyers in pinstripes?

❖ ❖ ❖

Like his dinner, Raymond's lunch was also on the dry side, but the quiche did offer a robust mixture of cheeses. He did note the lack of ham, but considering that most prisoners were Muslim, it was understandable. The chef had done a wonderful job of substituting pepper and other fresh vegetables. And the flakey crust was nothing short of superb.

Eating with a plastic spoon, however, did detract.

He pushed the tray aside when he was finished and turned to the dense crisscross pattern of wires that formed his window.

Were they going to hold him there forever? So far, nobody had come to see him. He had not even seen an officer. Did anyone in the outside world know he was there?

As he studied the deep blue sky, his mind turned to thoughts of freedom. Say he was released from prison. Say he spoke before a special prosecutor, then an impeachment committee, and the press finally left him alone to start a new life. How could he get back to China? He had no money.

His money in the Caymans was no longer flowing into his VISA account. His luggage was presumably still waiting by the taxi stand at the resort in Hainan. Without his papers, he wasn't even sure what his bank account number was. Only what's-his-name, the State Department officer might know that.

The name "Merle Stevens" came back to him. Merle could help him, but Merle could hurt him, too. That was it! The only person who could have possibly cleaned out his account was someone who knew the secret account number. And that was Merle!

How could that angel of mercy, who had helped him through trying times in Beijing as his family was swallowed up by a SARS ward, have done such a slimy thing to him?

He remembered back to Nigerian con games whereby unwitting dupes transferred their money into the conmen's bank accounts thinking they were participating in a get-rich-quick scheme.

How could he have fallen for that?

Or was there more to it than that? From the moment he had met Merle, his life had gone into a death spiral. From his desperation to his family's supposed death, to his life on the run, to his sudden financial ruin, Merle had been there coaching him every step of the way, guiding him through unfamiliar shoals and offering shady financial advice.

Had Merle set him up and made him disappear? Had Merle taken his family?

Merle had magically appeared at the airport as his family was whisked away, conveniently leaving him behind. Merle had used his position to obtain news from hospitals about his family. Merle had handed him their remains. Merle had moved to Shanghai where he was trying to start a new life. Merle had given him a secret account in which he could stash his own money.

He had set Raymond up! But maybe not just for the money. Was something more involved?

Perhaps Merle was leading him astray for some darker purpose. Maybe he wanted him to be on the run, to disappear from the scrutiny of the media and the Chinagate special prosecutor. It was becoming increasingly apparent that Merle was a government agent trying to make him disappear. And Merle had held his hand throughout the entire process. How could Raymond have been so gullible?

The prison guard was just entering the cellblock to collect the remains of his lunch. Raymond angrily shoved his tray out the slot.

The young soldier didn't leave until he had picked through the remains to account for everything.

If Merle was trying to railroad him into a life on the run, he had succeeded. However, people like Sandi, the lawyer in Hainan and on the radio in Manila, were busy trying to track him down. She wasn't trying to hide him from the public eye, like Merle was. Instead, she was trying to bring him out into the open. And that was just what he needed, someone to hear the tiny voice locked away inside the iron cage at Guantánamo Bay.

Then he remembered Sandi's business card that he had carried in his wallet. She had been reaching out to him.

He stood up irately and addressed the MP. "Don't I have a right to an attorney?"

"Do you see any lawyers walking around here?"

"I'm not trying to be funny. Don't all prisoners get at least one phone call?"

The MP merely laughed. "They barely even let *me* make phone calls from here."

"Well, tell your superior," Raymond said, his voice trembling. "I want to make a phone call."

Where was his wallet with the business card? Oh yes, the guards had taken that with his fake passport and the rest of his clothes. His fake passport!

Oh, God. This didn't look good.

Okay, concentrate. Without the business card, he'd have to recall the number by heart. It had a lot of sixes and ones in it.

As the guard's boots padded down the cellblock, he closed his eyes and tried to visualize the number on her card.

Chapter 25

So Raymond O. Flowers wanted to make a phone call.

Lieutenant Colonel Rodriguez, the Commandant of Camp Delta, had to chuckle when the guard relayed the prisoner's request.

Not long after Rodriguez dismissed the guard, however, he got to thinking. Was he denying the prisoner a right "consistent with the spirit of the Geneva conventions?"

He'd have to check with the legal shop.

Within a minute he was on the line to Ivan Nemroff at the General Counsel's office at the Pentagon.

Before relaying Raymond O. Flowers' request, he needed some guidance on what to do with the interrogator on special assignment for the Pentagon.

Ivan's voice conveyed an expansive mood, as if he had just enjoyed great sex with a terrific broad. "What interrogator?"

"His name is Harry Black."

"I've heard of him. He's a private contractor, former marine. What's he doing interviewing prisoners?"

"I've never met him before," Rodriguez said. "But he talks tough. And Intelligence has been running short of interrogators lately."

"Actually, this could be good. Let Harry talk to the prisoner, only I want you to tape record their meeting. I want to hear what both men have to say."

"I doubt if Harry Black has much to say," Rodriguez said. "He's from the old school of hooking people up to car batteries and the like."

"Maybe so, but you know about contractors. I want to make sure he's looking out for our best interests. So send me the tape."

"Sir, ever since Iraq, we don't allow cameras or any other kind of recording equipment in cell blocks."

"Then find some place else where they can talk and you can record them," Ivan suggested.

That sounded reasonable enough. Camp Echo came to mind, a set of buildings where prisoners could talk to their attorneys just before being sent to a tribunal. He'd have to get his electronics security team to rig up some unobtrusive eavesdropping there.

"And I've got another question," Rodriguez continued. "The detainee has expressed a desire to make a phone call."

"What else does he want? Television?"

"I know, sir. It sounds funny. But I just want to adhere to our policy, so I'm relaying his request to you."

"Let him make it."

"What?"

"Let him make the call, but listen in. I'd be interested to learn who the detainee calls and what they discuss."

Lieutenant Colonel Rodriguez sucked in his breath. These Pentagon types certainly played hardball.

"Roger that, sir. I'll send you a tape."

He set down the receiver. Now he was going to tap his own phones.

His stomach was growling, but before heading off to lunch, he spent fifteen minutes discussing eavesdropping arrangements with his engineers. It was fascinating to hear how they could make use of the limited materials they had on hand. They were simply going to install the web cam from the Internet café in a knothole in the ceiling of Camp Echo's visitation room. As for the telephone bug, they would simply tape record the conversation on an extension line unbeknownst to Flowers.

Satisfied that all would work according to plan, he pulled Harry Black's mobile phone number closer and dialed him. He would let Harry interrogate the prisoner that afternoon.

If the Pentagon were going to put up roadblocks, then Sandi would have to approach Raymond O. Flowers from a different direction. Say, the White House.

Sitting in her car with the engine idling and the heater on full blast, Sandi tugged off her ski cap, rubbed some feeling back into her raw cheeks, and headed downtown to the YMCA for a quick shower and to change into her business attire.

She shifted her car into reverse and spun the tires on the icy parking lot. Pulling into the flow of cars that crept cautiously down the slick parkway, she tried to visualize Lori Crawford.

At Columbia, she and Lori had attended many of the same history classes, even competing head to head with her at times. Beginning college as a serious student, Lori and Sandi were cut from the same cloth, and the two attended movies and explored the city together, methodically selecting a different district each weekend.

But one fall term, Lori had returned from a wild summer love affair, and the prim, bespectacled scholar had undergone a magical transformation. For one thing, Lori had let her hair grow out into a bushy frizz. Her clothes changed dramatically from the embroidered blouses, argyle sweaters, and pleated skirts to men's shirts and vests and baggy trousers. She hung around guys and even lit up a cigarette on occasion.

From that point on, competition increased between them, driving each to spend more time flirting with different boys than studying with each other. But it had always been a low-key rivalry, and Sandi owed much to her friend for drawing her out into the social scene, where she had remained stuck, spinning her wheels, to that very day.

Now Lori had raised the bar considerably. Marrying the President of the United States took their competition to a whole new level.

Pulling into a public garage down the street from the YMCA, Sandi reflected on how Lori's life was changing from paying parking lot attendants to whistling for the chauffeur. It was a life she could get used to, herself.

She slogged down the sidewalk, her gym bag drooping from one hand. She hadn't talked with Lori Crawford in several years. Thinking back, it might have been as long ago as the Commencement Exercises at Columbia's Low Library.

How could she let so much water go under the bridge? Was she as fickle with her female friends as she was with her male friends? She didn't have many lifelong pals to draw upon if she ever did have a wedding. Her empty half of the church would be a sad sight indeed.

She pushed into the front door of the public-smelling YMCA and headed upstairs to the locker room. A quick shower would put things right. And for a while, the hot steam soaked her skin and soothed her soul.

She returned to her locker and slowly drew on her panties and stockings. She reached into her bag for her bra and felt the phone. Damn it, she needed to call Lori and get back in touch. If not for the sake of Raymond O. Flowers, then at least for the sake of their friendship.

She checked the number on the RSVP line of the invitation and punched it in.

"This is the White House. How may I help you?"

Lori already had a telephone receptionist.

"I'm trying to reach Lori Crawford to accept her wedding invitation."

"One moment please…"

It didn't take long for Lori to pick up the phone. "This is Lori."

An unexpectedly sweet voice floated over the line, summoning back Sandi's memories of her college years—her days spent with Lori loafing around art galleries in SoHo, looking for John Lennon's apartment building, exploring the hidden chambers of St. John's Cathedral. From the soft, girlish sound of her voice, Lori had either regressed all the way back to freshman year, or purposely jettisoned the sultry sound for that of the ingénue.

"Hi Lori, it's me, Sandi."

"Sandi! I was hoping you would call. Where are you?"

Sandi looked around her. She was sitting half-naked in an empty locker room, while the rest of the world was at work.

"I'm here in DC." That was as specific as she would get. "And I understand that you're getting married."

"Isn't that so exciting?" She could have sounded stuck-up or flighty, but she didn't, and that was appealing.

Sandi picked at her fingernails. Was it too early in their reunion to take advantage of Lori? What the hell…

"Say," Sandi said, as if on a whim. "Would you like to get together and talk?" She held her breath.

"I sure would, but I hope you don't try to give me wedding advice," Lori said. "I'm getting it from all sides, all the way from my Mom to Dear Abby."

"Hardly. I'm the last one to talk about marriage. I live in self-imposed spinsterhood."

"Good. Then why don't you come over here for lunch?"

Sandi nearly dropped the phone.

"Here? As in the White House?"

"Sure. We've got lots of great food."

Sandi let out her breath. "Why not? That would be great."

She turned off her phone, slid on her watch, and checked the time. She had just enough time to drop by the Edward Bennett Williams Law Library at Georgetown and pick up a few books on military tribunals.

She couldn't get over the feeling that it was just like old times. Hitting the books and having lunch with her old buddy Lori Crawford.

Harry was looking over the abundant, but mediocre, buffet offering at the battalion-sized mess hall when his mobile phone rang.

It was Lieutenant Colonel Rodriguez from Camp Delta.

"Word just came down from Washington," Rodriguez said. "In their infinite wisdom, the Pentagon has authorized you to interrogate the prisoner. "

"That's why I'm here."

"You will report this afternoon at 15:00 hours to Camp Echo."

"Roger that," Harry said.

Lieutenant Colonel Rodriguez went on. "You are not permitted to bring a camera, video recorder, tape recorder, writing instrument or any other recording device, electronic or otherwise. Do I make myself clear?"

"I am here to elicit information from him."

The commandant stood firm. "No recording. No writing."

"Fine. Have it your way. And when will you allow my men here to assist me?"

"I haven't determined if and when they can gain access to the base. If they show up, they show up. *Comprendo?*"

"Yeah, I understand."

He clicked his phone off, mystified. Maybe his bluster had gotten through to the commandant after all.

But how do you take down a deposition without a pen?

Sandi walked the short distance from a cab to the White House for lunch with Lori. Police restrained loud protestors who were hurling abuse at the White House from behind a barricade across the new, brown, crushed rock pedestrian plaza that covered the stretch of Pennsylvania Avenue between 15th and 17th Streets.

When she was just steps from the White House gate, her cell phone rang.

Distracted, she picked it up.

"This is Ray Flowers."

"What? I'm sorry, I'm at the White House and I can't hear you." She hustled behind a quaint old light post that could shield her call from the noisy protesters. "Raymond?"

"I'm calling from a prison cell, and I want to report to the authorities that I was set up."

"Set up? By whom?"

"By an American diplomat in Shanghai named Merle."

"Merle Stevens? I know him."

"These guys aren't playing fair," Raymond said. "I don't even have the right to an attorney."

"No kidding. You've been denied your Fourth, Fifth, and Sixth Amendment rights."

It was amazing that Raymond had called her at all, after she'd spent all morning searching for some legal means to reach him. Had he been sprung free?

"Aren't you still in the military prison at Guantánamo?"

"Yeah. The MPs let me make this one call. I don't know who you really work for, but I decided that you could help me the most. Actually, you're the only one I can turn to."

"Well, you called the right person. Now I want you to listen to me carefully. I have some good news to tell you. Your wife and kids are still alive. They never died from SARS. Merle Stevens told me that they are being held against their will somewhere in China."

There was a very long pause, fraught with emotional turmoil and confusion. "How do you know Merle?"

"He was at the resort in Hainan. He confessed the whole thing to me."

Raymond's voice quavered. "If Merle was there, then he's the one who left me the message."

"What message?"

"Saying that my family is still alive. He's the only one who would know."

"The bastard."

Raymond returned with a note of awe. "Who are you anyway?"

"I work for the Chinagate special prosecutor. I tracked you down to Hainan Island for information you had on the oil deal in Beijing. You are the chief witness in our case against the President."

"Then why am I being held?"

"You're being held by the military as a terrorist. I have been searching for legal means of reaching you, Raymond, but the President apparently wants you there, safely out of sight from public scrutiny, as well as out of the special prosecutor's hands."

"I don't care about the President," Raymond's voice came back, suddenly choked with tears. "All I want is my wife and kids."

Lieutenant Colonel Rodriguez, the Camp Delta commander, gently returned the telephone receiver to its cradle. It was tough listening to a man confess, no matter how hideous the crime. A true confession came from deep within the soul.

But Raymond O. Flowers had something other than a confession. Some jerk had told him that his family was dead. Raymond's true heartache only became apparent when he was faced with confirmation that they were still alive.

He had to bring this to Ivan's attention. Within a minute, he had the Defense Secretary's General Counsel on the line.

For some reason, Rodriguez found himself talking in lowered tones. "Flowers just got off the phone. I heard the whole thing."

"Who did he call?" Ivan asked at once. His voice was also a near whisper.

"He talked to the investigator for the Chinagate special prosecutor!" Rodriguez related. "I didn't catch her name."

"Sandi DiMartino. I know her," Ivan said. "I've been trying to keep her out of the loop. And if my instincts are correct, she doesn't have either the guts or the pull she needs to get Flowers' testimony."

"Sir, if I'm not mistaken, he called her at the White House."

"Good God. What is she doing there?"

Lieutenant Colonel Rodriguez set down the phone. "Have a nice day," he said with a smile. It was becoming clear to him that Raymond was something of a hero, if not a national icon, and anyone who wished him ill was not only malicious, but downright unpatriotic.

Chapter 26

The Secret Service checked their guest list at the White House gate, and Sandi DiMartino's name was on it. Lori Crawford had the place running like a well-oiled clock.

The terse guard confiscated Sandi's cell phone and handed her a numbered tag to retrieve it later. Then he gave her a visitor's badge and sent her on her way up the circular drive. It was supposed to be the official entrance to the home, and must have been so in the days of horse and buggy. But with the advent of helicopters, the President seemed to come and go mainly from the South Lawn.

How was Lori going to do her grocery shopping...by Huey?

A Marine stood by the front door. Despite the fact that he stood in his full dress uniform with no overcoat, he was not shivering in the cold. He glanced at her badge and jumped to open the door for her.

She would have found the gesture charming, had it not been for the pistol in his hip holster, the heavy-duty black boots, and the brisk efficiency of his manner. Instead of being welcomed into the executive mansion, she felt ushered into a high-level meeting of the government.

It took her breath away to consider that if the Chinagate affair played out correctly, she would be ousting the President from that very house, thus changing the makeup of the most powerful government of the world.

Maybe she'd just stick with her social engagement with Lori that day.

Directly inside the door, the receptionist told her that Lori was already at the cafeteria.

"The White House has a cafeteria?"

"It's a functioning government office as well as a house," the lady reminded her. "Shall I have a guide take you to the cafeteria?"

"Sure."

The way there was labyrinthine, and she was glad she had a guide. Otherwise, she might have found herself wandering through the kitchen.

"Sandi!" came an excited voice from across a long room full of tables.

It was easy to spot Lori, a profusion of red lipstick and bouncy red hair in a sea of black suits. Sandi had wondered if their reunion would be stiff and clumsy. She was immediately set at ease by the future First Lady, who bounded across the room and threw her arms around her.

Within seconds, they were perched together on the bench of a cafeteria table sharing their life stories. Sandi decided to leave out the fact that she was working for the special prosecutor who was on the verge of kicking Lori's future husband out of the White House and into jail.

And somehow, that seemed irrelevant at the time. Renewing a lost friendship was one of those moments that made life worth living.

A dapper man in his mid-fifties joined Lori with his lunch tray. Sandi recognized him at once as the President's Chief of Staff.

She supposed that even busy Chiefs of Staff had to eat lunch. But it was no ordinary school lunch. It looked like the chefs had been slaving away over his chicken parmesan for hours, arranging the sprigs of parsley just so.

"Chuck," Lori said. "I'd like you to meet my old pal Sandi. Sandi will be coming to the wedding."

She expected indifference, but the guy's previously huffy demeanor changed radically.

As soon as he heard the word "wedding," he turned effusive and extended his hand. "We're arranging seating today." He pulled a piece of paper from his coat pocket. It was a series of circles with people's names printed around their circumferences. "Who would you like to sit beside?"

They poured over the names for several minutes, the chicken crying out to be eaten. It was just Sandi's luck that Lori was on a diet and forgot to offer her food.

Sandi pointed to the chart and picked a seat at the same table as the President of South Africa, and Lori clapped with joy. "Now I'll have you meet another charming buddy of mine. Here's the Attorney General."

Sandi raised her eyes, and there stood Caleb Perkins. This was like a kind of country club. Only it wasn't like some small town's pretentious country club. This was *the* country club.

"Hello, Mr. Attorney General," she said, standing and taking his proffered hand. "I'm honored to finally meet you."

"You know him already?" Chuck Romer asked, his political radar apparently picking up suspicious signals.

"Only by reputation," she said, trying to gloss over the fact that Caleb Perkins had called her personally from his ivory tower at the Department of Justice to propose a détente and to offer information leading to Raymond's whereabouts in the South Seas.

"Oh, by reputation," Chuck said, and resumed talking business with the President's fiancée.

Sandi turned to the slightly rotund, but formerly athletic Attorney General, and they moved away from the others.

"So, Caleb," she said, and suddenly wondered where along the line she had gone from a fledgling federal prosecutor-turned special investigator to being on a first name basis with the chief lawyer in the land. She checked his blue eyes that nearly matched her own. He didn't seem to mind the informality. In fact, his smile appeared to encourage it. "You won't guess who I just talked to."

"Who?" he asked, as if unable to solve a riddle.

"Raymond O. Flowers," she said, keeping her tone low.

He didn't look fazed in the least. If anything, he seemed on top of the situation. "I just sent a private contractor named Harry Black down to Gitmo to interrogate Flowers," he offered.

"And why might you do that? To shut him up?"

"On the contrary, young lady," he said, his voice gruff when he whispered. "With the intention of exposing the story and getting Flowers' Chinagate deposition."

"You wouldn't," she whispered back in disbelief. "That's exactly what *I'm* trying to do. Have you had any success?"

"He's down there right now. I don't know if he's getting anywhere, but he has every opportunity to do so."

She lowered her voice even more. "Isn't that a bit underhanded?" she asked, looking around the white-walled edifice in which they stood.

"On the contrary. I am a patriot. Learn the truth, and the truth shall set you free."

"And the truth shall make you the next President."

Suddenly Caleb Perkins took on a whole new aura of desirability.

Sandi looked across the room at Lori, who was bubbling over with excitement as she discussed her future with the rest of the White House's inner circle. A fantasy momentarily took hold in her imagination.

She snagged Caleb's arm and escorted him back to the aromatic lure of the food line. "Would you be free for drinks tonight?" she asked.

"I think I could arrange that."

Later that afternoon, Sandi returned to her office in Rosslyn, only to find the place lifeless and demoralized.

"Where have you been all day?" demanded one of the researchers as Sandi entered the large open room of desks.

"Oh, first I had to visit the Pentagon's General Counsel."

"Whoa. Stop right there," came the voice of their congressional liaison. "What does the Pentagon have to do with this?"

"They're holding him," she said. She began to advance on her desk, throwing comments over her shoulder. Stanley Polk was hunkered down in his office, and hadn't appeared before his staff, much less the public, in days.

"As a matter of fact, the military is holding him on terrorism charges. It appears that Raymond is also mixed up with al-Qaeda."

A general groan rose from several corners of the room.

"So I went over to the White House."

She heard the staff perk up at their desks. A book fell to the floor.

"Did the President talk?" came a voice.

"No," she said with a self-effacing laugh. "But the Attorney General did."

She could sense the staff moving in closer.

"And what did he say, pray tell?"

She felt their breath against the back of her neck and spun around. They all fell into the nearest place of repose. Some found an empty spot on a desktop, a chair, or a comfortable location by the water cooler.

Her eyes roved from face to face. She seemed to be offering their doomed case its only ray of hope.

"Well, he acknowledged that the Justice Department is aware that Raymond is in the hands of the military at Guantánamo Bay. And he has sent an interrogator down there to take Raymond's deposition."

The room erupted with a scream. She instinctively ducked, only to realize that it was a scream for joy. She had managed to unleash their energy and renew their sense of purpose.

"But," she cautioned, trying to quiet them down. "We're not one hundred percent sure this will work."

"Let's go to the press with it!" the public relations man shouted.

"Don't let a word of this leak out," she returned with a savage snarl. "The Attorney General's interrogator has to do his work in utter secrecy, otherwise he'll never get within a hundred miles of the prison."

The group of lawyers and clerks looked at each other in sudden realization. They were entering a very crucial phase that demanded their complete confidentiality.

"All we can do is wait and hope that the Attorney General can get word out of Guantánamo," Sandi said.

"The Attorney General is part of the Administration." It was a basso voice, one the average citizen knew from television coverage of the case. It was Stanley Polk. "How can you be sure that he'll share the information with us?"

Sandi looked into the red-rimmed eyes of her boss.

"Because I have a date with him tonight."

Harry Black peered at his watch in the glaring mid-afternoon light. It was fifteen hundred hours, the time the camp commander had appointed for him to visit Raymond O. Flowers.

Approaching the heavy security at Camp Echo to interrogate Flowers, he felt ill equipped. He didn't have a pen or tape recorder. He had no way of taking down Raymond's testimony, much less a sworn deposition.

And what incentive did Flowers have to talk? Certainly Harry wasn't going to beat it out of him. The most Harry could say was that he'd do everything he could to get him released from prison.

Lieutenant Colonel Rodriguez was standing beyond the guard booth waiting for him.

Once the lieutenant colonel led him past the razor wire and double guards posted there, Harry was startled to be looking at a set of one-story tract houses. The camp had none of the bluesy Folsom Prison ambience, the Leavenworth institutionalism, or the desolation of San Quentin he had expected. But what did he know?

"What is this place, a halfway house?"

It looked like they were in a tidy working class neighborhood. Each bungalow had large windows and a gently slanting roof.

"Once the President of the United States has selected a detainee for the Military Commission," the lieutenant colonel explained, "we take him here where he is allowed access to his attorneys."

"I'm not his attorney," Harry objected. "And I'm sure the President wouldn't select him for anything. I just want to interrogate him in private."

"You'll get to interrogate him," the lieutenant colonel assured him. He said nothing about privacy.

They approached the first house in the camp and mounted the three steps. From there, Rodriguez opened the front door, leading him into a place that was subdivided into two rooms.

One room was for Harry, and the other, clearly was a prison cell, guarded by an alert-looking MP.

Through the steel mesh, Harry made out a recently shaven prisoner garbed in orange. His light brown hair with receding hairline and his squinting light brown eyes contrasted sharply with the swarthy, wild-eyed features he had come to associate with terrorists.

He was looking at a family man from Middle America, someone he might meet at the hardware store, except that his hands and feet were shackled and bolted to the floor.

"How about some privacy?" he requested, indicating the military policeman standing beside Raymond's cell.

"He'll come with me. You have half an hour."

Harry checked his watch again. What could he say in half an hour?

"Fall in," the lieutenant colonel ordered, and the guard marched with him out the front door.

Harry studied the man behind bars, the half-blind guy he was supposed to pistol-whip into submission, and from whom he was supposed to extract a confession.

After recent cases of prisoner abuse, the heavy metal gate seemed more to protect the prisoner from him than the reverse. He knew that the prison scandals had forced the Pentagon to revise its doctrine and rules of interrogation. But making him talk to Flowers through bars was going a bit too far.

He glanced around the room and looked for surveillance devices. Alas, there were far too many pipes, cracks, nooks and crannies where such a device might be hidden. He had to assume that they were being closely monitored, if not recorded.

This was going to be one useless meeting. He could not press Raymond with important questions, much less have the answers written down and signed under oath as an affidavit.

Damn, he was two feet away from Flowers, but couldn't get the information he needed.

He thought of shaking hands, but that, too, was not possible.

In the end, it was Flowers who made the first move, whispering tentatively, "Glasses."

"Huh?"

"They've got my glasses."

"Oh," Harry said. That explained the squinting. "I'll check on them."

"Are you my lawyer?" Raymond asked, as if afraid to open his mouth.

"No. I'm the guy who's going to spring you free."

Raymond took a deep breath and his rigid shoulders fell into a more relaxed position.

The images and voices of Harry Black and Raymond O. Flowers came crisp and clear under the lawn through a wire onto Lieutenant Colonel Rodriguez's computer screen.

From there, the images and voices continued over a cable and were transmitted by satellite to the Pentagon, where Ivan and his team of Judge Advocate General Corps lawyers were recording every last word.

Rodriguez nodded as he watched the conversation unfold. It became clear to his discerning eye that Harry Black suspected that the interrogation was being recorded, so he remained tight-lipped except to gradually fill Flowers in on what charges he faced.

"They tell me you got picked up on an al-Qaeda ship in the Pacific," Harry began.

Rodriguez recognized the deliberate approach to interrogation, whereby the interrogator befriends the detainee.

"Not really," Raymond's voice came from behind the bars.

"So you're denying the terrorism charge?"

"They're charging me with terrorism?" Raymond let out a laugh that seemed to dispel the anxiety in his previous demeanor. "If that's all it is…"

"Terrorism against America is a serious charge and can result in capital punishment."

Rodriguez continued nodding. The switch to dire threat. By this point Flowers would have to cling to Harry Black for help.

And, true to the interrogation manual's prediction, Flowers came forward, entreating his new friend for help.

"You gotta get me out of here," he pleaded. "I've got a family that I haven't seen in over a year. I thought they were dead and buried. I can't go on like this. I'm not a criminal. I never harbored the slightest intention of harming America. I only got kidnapped by some terrorists and they used me. I tried to resist, but they made me pose in a videotape to the White House. I swear, I was under duress."

Rodriguez watched the screen carefully as Harry Black stood up, showing mild interest. "You sent a videotape to the White House? What did it say?"

"The terrorists threatened to release me to the Chinagate prosecution if the President didn't release al-Qaeda prisoners."

"Did the President release any prisoners?"

"Of course he did. The terrorists never released me to the prosecutor. If they had, I wouldn't be sitting in this prison."

Rodriguez began nodding to himself. It all fit now. That explained why Washington had suddenly and without explanation ripped his prize prisoners out of Camp Delta, never to return them. The White House was taking its marching orders from al-Qaeda.

"What's this about your family?" Harry asked, his voice low, confidential, but easily picked up by the microphone.

"I received a message about a week ago that they were still alive. I've being trying to get to Beijing ever since to track them down. The commander here let me place a call, so I called a friend that I had made in China. It turns out she is an investigator for the special prosecutor. And she informed me that the Administration faked my family's death by blaming it on SARS. Once I had sent the kickbacks to the President, the government systematically began trying to demoralize me."

The telephone rang on Rodriguez's desk. It was Ivan, his voice trembling over the phone. "Stop the camera! Stop the interrogation at once!"

"Yes, sir. At once, sir."

"And destroy the tape!"

"Understood, sir."

He replaced the receiver and smiled at the screen. Then he reached behind the CPU and yanked out the transmission cable that was sending the images and sound across the satellite link to the Pentagon.

On-screen, the interrogation proceeded apace.

Flowers was whining about some State Department diplomat who had steered him toward absconding with his oil company's illegal contributions to the President.

"I took the money," Flowers confessed. "I did take the money. But those were illegal funds. In effect, I was protecting the President by never letting the money get into his offshore bank account."

An incredulous smile spread across Rodriguez's broad face. The testimony couldn't have been more damaging for the President. If the implications weren't so devastating for the nation, it would be comical.

When the half hour was over, Harry thanked Flowers politely, and reassured him that he would find a way to help him.

"You are my lawyer, aren't you?" Flowers said, completely comfortable with his relationship with Harry Black.

"No, I never said that," Harry told him. "I'm just here to interrogate you."

That left Flowers stunned. He had just spilled his entire life's story to a military interrogator.

"But don't worry about it," Harry said, shaking the prisoner's limp hand through the bars. "I'm here to help."

Rodriguez clicked the Save button and rose from his chair. He quickly rushed across the lawn to escort Harry out of Camp Echo. It was a brief opportunity to talk with the handsome interrogator in private.

"I'd like to invite you to a round of golf at the Officer's Club," he told Harry as they stepped outside.

Harry appeared dazed and disoriented, as if hit by too much disconcerting information all at once. He stared vacantly at Rodriguez as if he were a mere distraction.

"I think I can help you," Rodriguez offered.

At that, Harry's eyes locked on his. For the first time since the two men had met, Harry lost his stiff, military manner.

"Sure," Harry said. "I'll take you up on it."

Rodriguez saw him off on the base bus.

"I'll send my car to pick you up at oh-nine hundred hours," he called out, and Harry waved from the steps of the bus.

Chapter 27

Waiting at the bar of the China Dragon restaurant, Sandi reviewed her plan. She swiveled about in the rattan barstool and stared in the mirror at her elegant silhouette, her delicate jaw, her wide-set eyes, and the errant strands of blonde hair in a halo of pin lights. She had to win Caleb over to the special prosecutor, but she had little to work with—little to offer, little to throw at him.

In the end, she needed Caleb to hand over Raymond's testimony. But he would have strong reasons for holding onto it. He might be planning an internal investigation by the FBI. Furthermore, by going public with the testimony, he would be jeopardizing the career, if not life, of his own source, that brave interrogator at Guantánamo.

She also had history working against her. She had to remind herself that the Justice Department did not have a glorious record of sharing information with independent prosecutors. But she would change all that tonight. She would form a personal bond between the two shops.

The bar at the Old Post Office was the perfect place to create such an unholy union. The Washington gossip hounds that dogged every agency of every branch of the government thrived on such spottings. To that end, they hung around the classic watering holes of Washington, such as the Monocle stuffed with Capital Hill insiders, the Taburna on I and 18th exclusively serving globetrotters, and the Hay-Adams Hotel across the street from the First Family. No Washington insider would ever be caught dead at such a tourist site as the Old Post Office.

When Caleb strode in, he had already checked his overcoat and was attired in a double-breasted suit, crisp white shirt, and a red bow tie.

"You changed your outfit," Sandi said, admiring his impeccable taste in apparel.

"Just for you," he said with an intimate wink.

She was impressed, not to mention flattered. The trip from the Justice Department was a mere two-minute walk up Pennsylvania Avenue, yet clearly he had taken a detour.

"You went home to change?"

He smiled, abashed. "No. I keep several suits at my office."

Oh, of course. How stupid of her to inquire.

"I'm trying the plum wine," she said, grasping for another subject. "Care to try some?"

He leaned in close as she held the pewter cup to him. His thick lips were not that unattractive. At least they were moist and had substance.

"Yum," he cooed. "Very tasty."

Sandi noticed him glancing down the bar as he stood back. He didn't seem comfortable taking a seat.

Perhaps even the sleepy restaurant tucked in the shadows of the Old Post Office lobby was a bit too exposed for him.

"What say we take the elevator up to the bells?" she suggested.

He looked up at the glass ceiling several stories above them. Beyond that, the night was black and clear.

"Why not?"

Perhaps he had a yearning for the romantic as well.

Sandi paid the bar tender and let Caleb escort her to the elevator. The ticket agent explained to them that two tickets bought them a guided tour of the Congress Bells. Or they could just do it on their own.

She looked at him.

"On our own," they said in unison.

That brought out a happy laugh from him.

She was doing fine, she reassured herself. His stellar career was at risk if he were discovered giving her the deposition. She would have to provide him something in return. He looked like a powerful enough man to take whatever he wanted, to pluck any flower he saw, but he seemed romantic enough to sniff it first.

The ride took them high above the Old Post Office stores and restaurants, past the glass ceiling, and into the distinctive, pointed bell tower that rose nearly as high as the statue on the Capitol dome.

Inside, they walked around the ropes that bell ringers could pull to chime the change ringing bells, some of the largest in North America.

She felt his hand on the small of her back, guiding her past the goggling tourists and up a set of stairs. They stepped out into the cold night.

The sound of the bells would carry up the hollow tower and out to the city from where they stood. She looked down. What a magnificent view from two hundred and seventy feet! In the chill of the evening, the weather was clear and sounds and lights prickled the air. The Mall spread out at their feet like an unreal movie set, with the illuminated National Archives containing the Constitution, the Declaration of Independence, and the Bill of Rights just across Federal Triangle. The various well-known monuments to democracy appeared like children's models beneath them, and the vast black Potomac River snaked through the countryside to the south.

Liberty never rang so clear, and she felt a shiver.

They were alone for the moment, and Caleb drew his arms around her and embraced her. His lips closed in on hers. She let him explore her lips and find her tongue. They dueled in silence for a while, their clothes crushed together.

Suddenly she heard a fluttering of feathers. She jumped back to look.

Caleb started laughing. A dove had flown out of its perch and was winging its way across the Mall. It soared high above the ice skaters at the temporary ice rink, and over the strolling couples on the crushed rock paths. It wheeled about and flapped toward the White House just up the street.

"That has got to be one of the loveliest mansions in America," she said, barely conscious of the wistfulness in her voice.

Caleb didn't answer. It was his dream as well.

Sandi took note of their continued privacy. It was time to share a little more than saliva.

"I can't wait to see Raymond again," she said. "Did you know that his family is still alive? They never died from SARS. In fact, they're being held captive somewhere in China."

"No," Caleb said sympathetically, as if commiserating over a sick pet. "You're kidding."

"Nope. I learned this from a State Department diplomat based in Shanghai. The guy's a spook. He says the Chinese are holding Raymond's family somewhere in their country."

"Whatever for?" Caleb was beginning to sound genuinely intrigued.

"Trying to drive him to drink, soften him up, set him up, frame him, and put him on the defensive."

Caleb was listening closely, a flash of recognition lighting his eyes. "What's the diplomat's name?"

"He called himself Merle Stevens. He's a very slick operator."

"I know him."

"You're kidding," she said. Did Caleb play some part in the crime?

Caleb explained himself. "I'm aware that the Agency tried to frame Raymond by giving him access to a huge volume of illegal funds, a payoff from the Chinese to Bernard White."

"And Raymond took the bait?"

"Apparently so."

"So that explains why Raymond is on the run and unwilling to come to the United States to testify. The poor guy. He thinks he's a common criminal."

"I guess the Agency plants men like Stevens in the State Department to perform the dirty work."

"Telling someone his family is dead is more than dirty," she said.

Caleb shook his head. "That's all the more reason to set Raymond free."

She examined him with newfound appreciation. Caleb might push the law and stretch the truth at times, but he would never incriminate an innocent man and destroy his family.

"My office is receptive to anything you can share with us," she said, her lips slightly parted.

"Don't worry, honey," he said. "It's coming very soon."

And once more she found herself, a recent law school graduate, being kissed by the chief attorney of the land, high above Washington, under the stars. She felt like she had just aced the bar.

"I think I have an idea," Caleb said, pulling away and gazing fondly in her eyes.

"What kind of idea?" She wasn't quite ready for a marriage proposal.

"An idea to take care of Merle Stevens and reunite Raymond with his family."

Sandi liked the cocked eyebrow and sly smile Caleb was beaming her way. He was capable of initiating an idea on his own, he didn't need permission to set a plan in motion, and he didn't need a Chief of Staff to lecture him on how to court a lady.

Then he shot her a question that she couldn't immediately put in context. "Say, have you ever slept in the Lincoln Bedroom?"

Chapter 28

Caleb Perkins awoke early the next morning, fresh from the previous evening's romantic dinner date with Sandi DiMartino.

After shipping his kids off to the school bus, he returned to the empty house and his youngest son's room. Rifling through his sports magazines and computer games, he found the boy's cell phone.

It was plastic and felt like a toy.

He punched in a cell phone number and waited.

The line connected. "This is Harry Black."

"This is Caleb. I've got a plan. Can we talk?" He could hear seagulls crying and waves crashing in the distance.

"Yeah, I'm out for my morning jog," Harry said, evidently slowing down to listen.

"Good. Last night I learned something very interesting. It turns out that Raymond O. Flowers' family is still alive and being held in China. It seems the Agency wanted to rough him up so bad he'd commit a crime and be forever beholden to them."

"I'm way ahead of you," Harry said. "I talked with Flowers yesterday. But I didn't get the specifics."

"I did. And I think there's something we can do about it. There's an American diplomat in Shanghai named Merle Stevens. Why don't you send your team there and beat the stuffing out of him. He's the one who whisked Flowers' family away from him and set him up with funds to abscond."

"Thanks for the tip. I'll send my men to deal with him. I won't need a contract from you for this one. It's on the house."

"He can tell us where Flowers' family is being kept."

"So much the better. My men have been in a holding pattern on Okinawa. I'll send them to Shanghai right away."

"There's only one roadblock to getting Flowers reunited with his family," Caleb said, the dark menace of terrorism filling his thoughts.

"Yeah, it's called Guantánamo Bay," Harry said. "They don't let prisoners just waltz out of here. If possession is nine tenths of the law, the U.S. military has nothing to worry about. The swarm of lawyers on the special prosecutor's staff look like only so many gnats."

"That's not what's keeping Flowers put. I've been informed that the Pentagon his holding him pending terrorism charges. And they've got evidence to boot."

"That's bullshit according to Flowers. And let me assure you, he is no terrorist."

That was a relief. Suddenly, he got the feeling that he was doing something illegal as well. "I've gotta go," he said, looking anxiously around his empty house.

"Can't you bring this up with the Secretary of Defense? They'll let Flowers go once they hear his story."

"Kenneth Spaulding is not on our side."

"How about Spaulding's legal office?" Harry said, sounding desperate.

"I'm sure they're busy at this very moment putting the case together *against* Flowers."

"So what can we do?" Harry asked, a note of desperation entering into his voice.

"*I* can't do anything," Caleb said, "except hang up."

"Tell the Pentagon they can take a flying—"

Caleb shut off the phone. It was a child's phone, after all.

Rodriguez exhibited powerful form while driving the ball.

Harry watched the lieutenant colonel's Top-Flite sail nearly out of sight on the first tee. He would have some pretty stiff competition that morning. It seemed clear that the top brass at Guantánamo had little else to do with their spare time than perfect their golf game.

He moved his head over the ball, and drew back his club, remembering to bend his left knee ever so slightly inward. He released a blast designed to leave little doubt in Rodriguez's mind that he had picked a formidable foe. The white speck dribbled down the middle of the fairway some twenty yards beyond the lieutenant colonel's lie.

Harry stuffed his driver back into his golf bag, and the two men strode off together down the hill.

"I like your swing," Rodriguez admitted. "Where did you pick it up?"

"You can't grow up a good ol' boy in the shadows of the Masters without dreams of wearing the Green Jacket."

"You're from Georgia?"

"Can't you tell by the way I talk?"

Rodriguez shook his head. "Your words come out more like a blend of Ivy League and military speak. Your accent could come from anywhere—from California to the Gulf Stream Waters."

Harry grinned. "I guess Yale and the Marines bred the Georgia out of me."

They paused at Rodriguez's ball, and Harry stood back to let him make his approach shot.

The course stood out in the dry terrain. It lacked many trees, but compensated with other hazards such as small lakes and lush bushes.

Rodriguez unleashed a controlled four iron that found the front fringe of the green.

"Where does the groundskeeper get all this water?" Harry asked. He set down his bag and selected a five iron. "Surely not from the tap."

"That's right," Rodriguez said, as Harry lined up his shot.

He took a back swing.

"From sewage."

Harry's grip slipped on the downswing, and the ball sliced straight into a sand trap to the right.

He shot Rodriguez a fierce glare, only to find the officer trying to muffle a snicker. So that was how this game would be played.

A deft attack with a sand wedge and a nice six-footer with no break moved Harry back into the game, and Rodriguez two-putted to make par.

They approached the second tee on even terms.

After a pair of straight drives on a par four dogleg, Harry let Rodriguez start up the conversation again.

The lieutenant colonel seemed to have more on his mind than fouling up Harry's game.

"I think we may have something in common with respect to Flowers," Rodriguez began.

Harry sensed that he was feeling him out.

"That would be nice," Harry said, taking a risk. "He's wrongfully accused."

"That's how I see it," Rodriguez said, a bold statement coming from a man who wasn't exactly at the top of his chain of command. "I deal with hardened terrorists every day. The kind that blows the limbs off children, and would blow their own brains out for their cause. I'm used to dealing with inmates that would rather hang themselves than squeal on a brother. These are the nuts I have to crack. It's serious business, and it saves many lives. So I don't have time for these games Washington is trying to play with Flowers."

"I'm glad to hear you saying that," Harry said, relieved to hear such candor. His fear that he had repelled Rodriguez two days before with his initial bluster was put to rest. They seemed to share a common view of Flowers.

Rodriguez continued talking as he eyed his approach shot around a stand of palm trees. "So, in that regard, I'm willing to hand Flowers over to you if you're willing to take him."

Harry felt the blood drain from his face. His legs felt bolted to the fairway. The breeze wanted to lift him off the earth, yet he was chained to the ground.

"Boy, wouldn't I love to take him," he admitted. "But I can't just bring him to Washington."

Rodriguez swung neatly through the ball with a tidy little click on impact.

"Keep playing," he said under his breath.

Harry walked up to his ball that sat lightly on the thick turf. He needed a two-iron for his next shot.

"To hell with Washington," Rodriguez said behind him. "Take him straight to his family."

Harry stood upright and stared back at the officer. "You know about his family? Were you eavesdropping on our conversation?"

"I had to. Orders from above."

Harry took a wild whack at the ball. He was giving up information to Rodriguez with every admission on his part. Was the guy trying to sucker information out of him? He decided to clam up.

Taking long strides to catch up with Harry, Rodriguez resumed the conversation. "I've reviewed your military record. You are a certified pilot on several types of aircraft. I understand that you have time on the B-2 Weapon System Trainer at Whiteman. I have a bird ready and waiting if you are willing to fly Flowers out of here."

Harry decided not to give up anything. Let the fool talk all he wanted. Harry Black wasn't going to hang himself.

"You got a mike in your golf bag, too?" he asked.

Rodriguez stopped. "Hey, you. I'm not setting you up. I'm here to help you."

"Yeah, prove it," Harry said, ready to throw off his golf bag and land a punch.

Rodriguez held up both gloved hands. "Hey, I'm not trying to start anything. I'm here to help you if you need me."

"You bugging my mobile phone, too?" Harry demanded to know.

"Not at all," the officer said, apparently aware that he had lost his credibility. "Let's just play golf."

Harry would have loved to take up Rodriguez on his offer. In fact, it sounded too good to be true. A flight out of Guantánamo with Flowers felt a bit like *The Great Escape*. But he didn't trust in or plan on feats of heroism. He was too methodical for that.

When the nine holes were up, and a badly defeated Lieutenant Colonel Rodriguez had dropped him off at his sea hut, Harry went right to work.

Still clad in his casual golf shirt and slacks, he walked out onto the boulders that formed the waterfront and found a secluded spot where the seagulls hadn't yet whitewashed the rocks.

He dialed Badger, and checked his watch while he waited for the connection to go through. It was just before the men would hit the sack in Japan.

"I need you to hustle the team over to Shanghai ASAP," he ordered Badger as soon as the tired voice came on the line. "There's a man with the U.S. Consulate there named Merle Stevens."

He went on to describe Merle's inhumane act of faking the deaths of Flowers' family just to keep the President off the hook. "What we still don't know and what we need you to find out from Stevens is where he stashed the family."

"Sounds like just asking him wouldn't be very productive," Badger said.

"You'll have to figure out what will make the guy sing. I'll approve any methods you can come up with."

"He sounds like a real a-hole. Don't worry, we'll take care of him and find the family."

"Stay in touch," Harry said, and clicked off.

He stood up in the small hollow that was protected from the wind. The salty sea breeze caught him full in the face.

Now he had to decide on how to spring Flowers out of Guantánamo. How he wished he could trust the lieutenant colonel.

Harry had gone to flight school with the Marines and had toiled away in flight simulators for many hours. He was a bit rusty, but he was sure it would all come back to him in a hurry.

What worried him more was that Rodriguez was onto him.

Out at sea, several local fishing boats were plowing home with their catch. He couldn't see any way to commandeer a boat and sneak Flowers off the base and into Cuba. Even if he did, he would be delivering Flowers into the hands of Castro, which was no better than turning him over to al-Qaeda once more. Flowers was still political dynamite.

He climbed over the rocks back up to the row of sea huts, that neat line of military uniformity that stretched as far as the eye could see. Flowers was held under constant guard in a protected detention camp within a naval base fortified against the Cuban Communist regime. Springing Flowers from captivity would be an overwhelming challenge in itself. And frankly, he was feeling somewhat bankrupt for creative solutions.

Even if Rodriguez was giving him enough rope to hang himself, how far would the lieutenant colonel go with his ploy? Take him to the airstrip? Provide a long-range jet? He could play along as far as he could without getting into trouble. And, if Rodriguez wasn't careful, an opportunity to escape might crop up.

By the time he reached his hut, he had made up his mind to call back Rodriguez and sound him out further.

But as soon as he opened the door to the plain wooden building, Harry abruptly sucked in his breath. There would be no need to contact Rodriguez. A dark, menacing pillar of power, the lieutenant colonel stood waiting for him in the gloom of the hut. And seated on the bed beside him was Raymond O. Flowers, a pair of shiny glasses plastered to his face, as if having them back demonstrated an act of good faith on the lieutenant colonel's part.

"What's this?" Harry asked, sniffing the air for some sort of sting.

"Hey, will you stow away your boxing gloves?" Rodriguez said. "You're as stiff as a Sunday preacher. I'm giving you Flowers. I figured you didn't believe me on the golf course, so here he is. He's yours."

"And how do I get him out of here?"

"Tonight I'll have the *Spirit of Kansas* waiting at the Air Terminal on Leeward Side."

"A B-2? The stealth bomber?"

Rodriguez nodded. "The Joint Task Force has her deployed here for drug surveillance in South America. She's yours. I figure you might like to take her to China, so she's fueled as far as Guam. You can refuel there and take her as far as you like."

"I can't fly continuously that far by myself." He tried to calculate the number of hours the trip would take, crammed in a cockpit manning the complex plane.

"I'll assign a co-pilot to the mission."

Harry tried to think up other reasons not to fly the stealth bomber into China, but couldn't.

"I won't ask any questions," Rodriguez said. "But I do need her back in one piece."

Harry examined the Marine officer's proud bearing. "You could lose your commission over this, if not be drummed out of the service."

"That doesn't matter enough. Anyway, the way I figure it, if you do your job right, the top brass will hand out promotions all around. In any event, I'm on a first-name basis with half the JAGs in the military."

That sealed it. Harry would accept the offer, contingent on the lieutenant colonel coming through with the stealth bomber and not pulling any stunts along the way. "So how soon before we can leave?"

"I'll have your leave papers ready by six, and I'll have the MPs escort you to the airport at seven."

It was a relief to hear that Rodriguez was sticking his neck out by providing official orders and transportation, both of which would be documented in paper on the base.

Rodriguez turned to Raymond. "In the meantime, I suggest that you do not leave these barracks. It might be better to keep a low profile."

Raymond O. Flowers smiled. "I'm good at keeping a low profile," he said, and stood to thank the officer who had released him from jail.

An awkward handshake followed, then Rodriguez turned and left.

Harry faced his new charge. "Well, what's it feel like to be a free man?"

Flowers looked around the room at the ten beds arranged in two neat rows. "Somehow it doesn't feel like freedom yet."

CHINA GATE

The Verdict

Chapter 29

Hadi Ahmed had never been in such a sticky and sweltering climate. He felt dangerously close to passing out as he approached the large mosque on the edge of Purang. He was drawn to the white-domed building because his instincts told him he could find sanctuary there.

In his tribal clothes, designed for the snow-capped Hindu Kush, he stood out from others in the tropics. And his instincts told him that he had to blend in. He alone had survived that big brute's ambush of Osama and his key associates. And he alone could seek to free Osama and seek revenge for his capture. He was horrified to think of the mighty leader of the holy war languishing in a prison cell, and he needed to pull together a band of similar-minded brothers and storm the police station where the group was jailed. He might find the support he needed in the mosque.

He passed the normal array of widows, limbless, and impoverished as he approached the marble building. He didn't have any of the local currency with him to donate, and besides, these people didn't look so bad off. It was he who should be lying on the pavement begging. If he didn't obtain food that day, he would have to steal some from one of those numerous bakeries along the main road in town.

At the front steps of the mosque, he kicked off his woven grass shoes and entered the building.

Thankfully it was cool inside. His brothers were assembling in throngs for Friday prayer, and he followed them to the large hall. He was happy to know that he was among East Pakistanis who resembled him in their accent, appearance, and demeanor. Should he confront one now and ask questions?

They seemed all business as they entered the lofty hall. Either they were pious and their minds were centered on Allah, or they were in a rush to get the service over with. Hadi couldn't tell which.

They grabbed rolled up straw mats stacked against the wall and lined up in rows to face Mecca. Hadi unrolled his mat, fell to his knees with the others and bowed low to offer a prayer.

"Mighty Allah, help me to free the great leader of your crusade for Islam. Help me to assemble the brothers I need to do your work."

Shortly, a robed imam appeared before them. Hadi listened closely to the oratory and prayers as the old guy rambled on about the harvest of cane and influx of tourists. He didn't hear a word about *jihad* and injustices brought upon their people.

Hadi was more than disappointed; it threw all his plans in disarray. He peeked at his brethren about him. Who were these guys? If they weren't going to the mosque to seek guidance in doing Mohammad's unfinished work, then why were they there? To ask for more money?

He wouldn't find *jihad*-ists at the mosque.

After the imam reached the end of a long Koranic reading, he launched into a prayer in English that caught Hadi's attention.

"May the almighty Allah watch over our former President and his family as they seek a new life in the carpet business. And may He bless the giant hero who saved our island from terrorists who sought to destroy our way of life here on Purang."

What? This guy was against the invasion? What infidels!

Hadi lifted his head off the floor. These weren't sacred stones. These were the chambers of the coerced. He tried to close his ears to spare Allah the painful words he was hearing. But he couldn't resist continuing to listen.

"Bestow your grace on the mighty Hiram Klug and his beloved wife Tiffany as they strive to bring reconciliation to our island home. Lavish on them great riches at their humble abode. Grant them your wisdom, we beseech you."

Blasphemy! They were praying for the infidel of all infidels, the man who held a gun to Osama's head and took him prisoner!

He couldn't wait for the prayer service to conclude. He rolled up his prayer mat and threw it on the heap. Turning to the young man who had prayed beside him, he felt compelled to open his mouth and speak.

"Where is Hiram Klug's *humble abode?*"

The young man looked at him, startled that Hadi needed to ask. "He is staying at the Sandalwood Resort."

"Of course," Hadi said, recovering himself. "Thank you, brother."

As he emerged into the bright day, the throng dispersed in all directions, seeking shelter from the hot sun. Hadi came to a decision. It was a decision that his forefathers would have reached without thought, and came naturally to him.

He would seek revenge.

An armed Chinese soldier escorted Carolyn Flowers and her newborn baby down the dim passageway back to her cell. It was hardly the homecoming that she would wish for a child being brought into this life.

They passed cages filled with North Korean families that stopped their normal chatter and stared at her.

They had all heard the sounds of childbirth. She could read into their eyes that they had vicariously felt her pain.

But catching a glimpse of the newborn brought instant joy to their faces. In cell after cell, the families began rising to their feet to catch sight of the new miracle in the midst of their desperate lives.

Caught attempting to escape into foreign embassies in Beijing, the political and economic refugees from North Korea had found themselves slammed from one brutal existence, that of underground asylum seekers, to prisoners in a Public Security Bureau jail. Frankly, she could tell from the ease of their gestures that neither had been as bad as starvation and freezing to death in Pyongyang.

Unexpectedly, a prisoner began clapping, the toothless gaps in his smile indicating his age. That provoked several more people to cheer and join in the clapping.

Before Carolyn was halfway back to her children's cell, she was holding up the newborn Raymond O. Flowers, Jr., for all to see. It felt more like a victory parade with police escort, and perhaps that was how her fellow captives felt. She had achieved a small victory that they could all share.

Jane and Sammy had thrust their small heads between the bars of their cell to see what was causing all the celebration.

"Mommy!" they cried, repeating her name again and again.

"I'm back." She approached their humble abode with a broad smile. It infuriated her that the guard took so long to find the right key to unlock the gate and let her in.

"You brought us a baby!" Jane shouted.

"Can we keep him?" Sammy asked, pulling his sister back to get a look.

Carolyn knelt between her children and soaked up their enthusiasm. It was clear that they had weathered her absence well, or at least forgotten about it in the blink of an eye. Which was good. She hadn't enjoyed being separated from them all that much.

But the baby was the new focus of their lives.

"Is he a brother?" Sammy asked.

Carolyn nodded. "His name is Raymond."

Jane began to giggle. "He doesn't look much like Daddy," she said. Her ponytail flipped around as she laughed, and she reached back to tighten the rubber band that held her hair together. When had Jane become so mature?

Carolyn regarded Sammy, who was petting little Raymond's cheeks. And when had Sammy grown capable of sharing his mother's affection?

Little Raymond began to screw up his features.

"Oh oh, Mommy," Jane said with concern. "What is the problem?"

"I'm not sure," Carolyn said.

Then the small body contorted, his face turning bright red.

"Mommy, look!" Sammy said. "He moves!"

"Is he going to cry?"

Jane's question was answered within seconds as Raymond belted out an angry wail that resounded throughout the prison.

"I think he's trying to tell us he's hungry," Carolyn said, beginning to unbutton her blouse. "I'll have to nurse him."

Sammy reached down to his own shirt and began unfastening the buttons. "Can I help?"

"No, big guy. That's Mommy's job."

Jane's eyes grew wide with wonder.

"Boy, Mommy, how did those get so big?"

That night precisely at seven, just as the orange sun slipped beyond the bay and behind the Cuban mountain range, Harry Black heard a U.S. Army Humvee pull up to the sea hut.

Earlier that day, Harry had bought Raymond some civvies at the

Navy Exchange, including shoes, casual wear, and a windbreaker.

"You go first," Harry whispered to his companion.

Raymond scampered into the Humvee and ducked out of sight. Then Harry strode toward the awaiting vehicle with all the confidence he could muster. As soon as the two men settled down on a bench seat, the car lurched forward, heading for the airport.

U.S. Naval Base Guantánamo Bay was an eerie place at night. Most lights were turned off for security reasons, and the buildings were few and far between. Riding in the quiet of the open road, Harry absorbed for the last time the sights and smells of the lonely American footprint on Cuban soil. Maybe someday, the Cuban nation would be able to live the good life as well, and Americans could come down to the sandy shores of the Queen of the Antilles and soak up her unique beauty.

He thought he could hear a Cuban salsa pulsating in the distance, or perhaps it was only his imagination. Could it be that the American soldiers and seamen were getting into the Cuban groove?

Certainly Lieutenant Colonel Rodriguez had overstepped his bounds, flirting with treasonous acts in a naval base that was meant as a showplace of military might.

But sometimes listening to the tunes of another country and listening to one's inner voice amounted to the most patriotic acts possible. And Lord knows, Harry had thrown out the rulebook on the assignment and was winging it strictly on personal intuition.

The ferry ride back to the Leeward side of the bay was calm, as the earlier sea breeze had died down, leaving a moonlit crossing on gentle swells.

Raymond O. Flowers was absorbed in his own thoughts for the entire trip, perhaps trying to cope with his radical change in fortune. Harry let him be. If they found and released his family, that would be an emotional milestone Harry was not even sure that he could take. And Harry didn't even have a family.

As Rodriguez had promised, the leave papers were all in order and he found himself striding across the apron toward an elegant stingray of an aircraft. The B-2's ground crew was just finishing its fueling and final inspection.

"You jump in," Harry said. He wanted to check out the plane.

He walked around the sleek flying wing that seemed too aerodynamically unstable to fly, with its weight well aft of the center of lift. Indeed, it was able to keep airborne only by the constant juggling of wing surfaces by onboard computers. A human pilot could never get the thing off the ground.

Harry had to admire the bold shape of the black aircraft, a design that Jack Northrup had conceived of in the early 1940s. Northrup had even built some test planes employing the flying-wing concept. The sleek lines of the aircraft when viewed from the side derived from the fact that it was all curves, but not constant curves. In order not to reflect radar energy toward any one spot, each curve had a continuously changing radius. In fact, there was little distinction between wing and body, as the dorsal hump and engines rose like sand dunes out of the wing, and the belly was a gradual swell originating at the wingtips.

Harry had flown his fair share of B-2 simulator missions at flight school, and the entire process was ridiculously easy. Even easier than trying to fly the F-117A Nighthawk stealth fighter jet. Pulling a pickup into traffic was a more difficult and hazardous maneuver than taking off in a B-2.

On the other hand, if things went wrong, there wasn't much a pilot could do about it, with the exception of bailing out. And that was never fun.

Oh sure, he had flown simulations, but only the best pilots in the military were allowed to do what he was about to do. He ran his fingers over the radar-absorbing carbon-fiber composite skin, walked back and forth beneath the full fifty-two-meter wingspan, and finally climbed up into her belly.

He found a nervous-looking co-pilot already standing with Raymond in the cramped ten-foot by ten-foot cockpit.

"This civilian tells me you want to fly to China," the co-pilot said, nervously fingering the helmet by his side.

Harry nodded. "That's right. And you're going to help me get there."

"Not on your life," the co-pilot croaked, apparently unaccustomed to asserting himself. "I'll take her as far as Guam, but if you want to sneak her into Communist China, you're on your own."

"So you refuse to comply with Lieutenant Colonel Rodriguez's orders?"

"He never told me that you intended to fly to China," the man whined. He let his helmet slip from his agitated fingers. Looking around in a panic, he turned to leave.

Raymond's eyes looked pleadingly at Harry.

"Hey, buddy," Harry said, grabbing the young pilot by his shoulders and turning him around. "You sit down and follow orders, or I'll make you. Do I make myself clear?"

The man looked fearfully into Harry's glowering eyes. "I won't be held responsible—"

Harry slapped him across the face. The man cringed, blood draining rapidly from his face. Then his eyes rolled back and his knees buckled.

Harry caught his slumping form.

"Was that necessary?" Raymond asked, visibly upset.

"What did I do?" Harry asked. "The guy fainted on me." He began to drag the body toward the stairwell.

"You aren't going to dump him on the tarmac!" Raymond exclaimed in shock.

"Hardly. We'll need him later. Grab that lounge chair, will you? And set it up out here."

Raymond did as he was told, squeezing past the two men and unfolding the chair that had been stowed on the flight deck. He pushed it into a tight position beside the staircase that was sealed inside the aircraft.

"Close quarters," he commented.

Harry dropped the limp body onto the chair and closed the cabin door behind him.

"Will he get enough oxygen back there?" Raymond asked.

Harry examined the seal around the cabin door. It was loosely fitted on its hinges, unlike the titanium-reinforced doors to the cockpits of commercial airliners. But, like commercial jets, the door was lockable from inside. He flipped the door latch in place, effectively imprisoning the unconscious man.

"He'll get plenty of air to breath. And he'll be far more comfortable than I will. He took my bed. Now put on your helmet."

He stepped over the chemical toilet and pushed past Raymond, who was trying to figure out how to fit his helmet over his head. Harry adjusted the padding for him and pounded it on his head. Then he lowered himself reverently beside Raymond in the flight commander's seat.

The CRT displays and amber readouts flickered with nervous energy. It was time to say goodbye to Guantánamo Bay.

He slipped on his helmet with its built-in microphone, earphones, and Head-Up Display. He threw a salute to the ground crew, and pressed the self-power switch.

Beneath him, the four General Electric engines rumbled to life.

Out of the corner of his eye, he caught a line of military vehicles barreling toward the tarmac.

Oh, my God. Either Rodriguez had double-crossed them, or the base commander was onto him. The blue lights flashed as they headed onto the airfield from the nearest gate. Harry's ground crew was calling him off, the signalman motioning for him to turn off his engines.

Like hell he would.

"Hold on tight," he said into his built-in mike. "We're going for a ride."

The multibillion-dollar Pentagon investment in state-of-the-art stealth swung under his gentle touch so that her nose pointed at a right angle to the first runway.

"Request permission to take off," Harry said over the airwaves to the control tower.

"That would be a negative," the reply came back. "Please return to your hangar."

Harry boosted the turbo, and felt himself flatten against the back of his seat. The longitudinal accelerometer recorded their rapidly increasing speed.

The trucks and troop carriers were angling toward him, threatening a runway incursion given his current course and velocity.

He extended the control surfaces to reduce speed and swerved the front wheel hard into the line of vehicles. The last blue light swirled under the nose of the jet, as Harry managed to weave his landing gear behind the moving obstacles.

The vehicles swerved in cascading order and pursued him in his new path. Harry headed for the next taxiway turnoff to the runway, some twenty-five yards from the normal threshold. He'd have to use every inch of runway left to get her in the air.

Not to let the aircraft lose momentum, he went to full throttle, felt himself thrown back against his seat, swung the aircraft onto the runway and eased her nose over the centerline of the strip.

Only two vehicles were still able to keep up with him. Heading for the far end of the field, they hoped to meet up with him, and catch themselves in his wheels just at the moment of takeoff.

He jabbed in both afterburners and locked in the takeoff profile. If he could manhandle the yoke himself, he would pull up her nose before the approaching vehicles. But as she was designed, he had to rely on the *Spirit of Kansas's* preprogrammed flight control system to execute the takeoff in its own deliberate way.

This was sheer madness. He could see the vehicles converging on him at far too sharp an angle. They would broadside him before he could get airborne. They were throwing their lives in his path in order to stop him. How could anything be worth paying the ultimate price?

He nudged the nose slightly to the portside, veering off the center of the runway. Perhaps he could angle behind the vehicles and still remain on the runway, taking off before he struck dirt and weeds.

They had the speed for liftoff, but the damn computer was taking its sweet time lowering the six elevons and beavertail assembly for lift. He couldn't take her any closer to the edge of the runway without the rear wheels striking dirt. The two vehicles, one a Humvee and the other a pickup were straddling the two sides of the centerline. He couldn't split the difference. The flying wing was about to take a nosedive into the grass.

The pickup suddenly began to fishtail. In an instant, Harry saw why. They were all about to ram into the fence at the end of the runway.

The truck's rear wheels slid right, giving Harry just enough room to squeeze by on the left.

Did the computer realize that they were at the end of the airstrip? Even a weak takeoff might leave them crashing into the nearby range of mountains in Cuba. Wouldn't a $2.1 billion B-2 Stealth Bomber be a prize for the Cubans!

Up, up, he tried to will the nose into the air. Both vehicles disappeared beneath his starboard wing, unable to screech to a halt before ramming into the chain link fence in a ball of fire.

A grinding sound came from the trailing edge of the flying wing. Slowly, the elevons began moving into position. And not a moment too soon. Grudgingly, the front landing gear released its grip on the tarmac. The nose popped up into the air.

Could the rear wheels get off the ground in time to clear the fence? Harry pressed the button to retract the landing gear, then sat back and watched with horrified fascination. More grumbled roaring of engines to either side of the aircraft. Undercarriage grinding their way up into the fuselage. Stealth, bah. This was the loudest rumbling, vibrating takeoff he had ever experienced.

They were sinking lower!

Then he caught smoke rising from behind the port wing. His eyes flashed to the console. No blinking red on the temperature indicators.

The flight surfaces pulled the aircraft higher. Finally, reluctantly, the rear wheels let go of the earth, and the smoke instantly stopped.

He hadn't even cleared the ground and he had retracted the landing gear! What a dope! The wing wasn't on fire. Harry had steered off the runway, and the rear wheels were kicking up dust!

He could no longer see the runway lights or the fence ahead, only the black sky above. The jet climbed steadily. There was no crash of debris in the rear.

They had broken free of Guantánamo, but the sheer sides of a mountain range loomed in the wraparound cockpit window. Harry had to take back control of the jet, the takeoff having cycled through its program.

He checked the afterburners. Still on full. Forcing the controls hard to port, he kicked the two drag rudders into a tight spinout midair. The jet didn't like that, the wing shuddering under the maneuver.

But Harry didn't want to be shot down by the Cubans, much less crash and burn in their mountains. The aerodynamically dubious craft sheered to the starboard, but found traction again and banked as necessary to brake the forward motion into Cuba.

Harry glanced beyond Raymond out his starboard window. A long illuminated stretch of fence ran parallel to his flight path. He was flying on the American base's border with Cuba. At any moment, anti-aircraft fire might spray up from either side below. He hugged the fence, trying to ease further back into the base. Then bam! The illuminated fence was gone.

Had he drifted into Cuban airspace? Where had the fence veered?

There were no ground lights on either side of the cockpit. He checked the bearing indicator projected inside his helmet. He was heading due south. Then he realized where he was.

He was over the Caribbean Sea. He had broken free.

He spoke into his helmet microphone, "Are you still with me, Raymond?"

"Ugh," came a weak response.

Harry smiled. Raymond had survived. The rest of the flight would be a dream compared with the takeoff.

Just then he heard a knocking noise coming from behind him. Was there a loose part or some kind of mechanical glitch? He couldn't identify the source of the sound, and pulled off his helmet to hear better.

It was rhythmic, growing louder.

He checked his cockpit display. There were no emergency indicators flashing. Had he clipped one of the military vehicles that had given chase?

Then he heard a muffled cry. "Let me out of here!"

It was the hapless co-pilot in the stairwell. Harry smiled grimly as he donned his helmet once more. He would need the guy later to fly the bird out of China. Having the co-pilot take over for him when he grew tired during the long flight would be an asset, but given the man's questionable attitude, he might pose a hazard on the flight deck.

"What was that?" Raymond was asking over the helmet microphone.

"Just our passenger making a fuss."

Raymond sat back and looked out the windscreen contemplatively. "What if the military tries to shoot us down?" he asked, looking warily out the window at the moonlit sky.

"How can they see us?" Harry said. "We're invisible to radar and infrared, difficult to detect by eye or ear, and we leave reduced smoke and contrail. Besides, they wouldn't begin to contemplate shooting down one of these babies, considering how expensive she is."

"Unless they thought we were terrorists..."

Harry swallowed hard. That was a possibility. He didn't want to think of what terrorists could accomplish with one of these birds.

He consulted his computerized world map and punched in a set of coordinates.

"We're heading for Guam," he said. "I suggest you sit back and try to relax."

"Won't they try to stop us in Guam, too?" Raymond asked.

Harry closed his eyes. Of course they would. The military would be alerted and waiting to stop them the moment they landed at the naval base in Guam.

They were aloft with nowhere to land.

Chapter 30

Badger McGlade was a high-tech kind of guy. And any kind of high-tech kind of guy was bound to love Shanghai's Magnetic Levitation train that zipped passengers from the far-flung Shanghai Pudong International Airport downtown in a mere seven minutes and twenty seconds.

He had three men and Carmen with him as he stepped onto the open train car and placed himself in one of the individual blue seats, much like a padded airplane seat.

Catching a magnetic wave, the train elevated a few inches and began a quiet, continuous forward acceleration. Soon they were racing alongside a highway. The train banked and he found himself looking straight down at cars and trucks that seemed to be standing still. He checked the speedometer on the wall. It wavered between 430 and 431 kilometers per hour and maintained that speed. Calculating swiftly in his mind, he yelled out, "Folks, we're going 270 miles an hour!"

Zipping by at ground level, it felt like they were taking off and landing in an airplane, only faster and quieter.

After a few minutes of fields, canals, water towns and greenhouses, the modern skyline of Shanghai's Pudong district came into sharp relief. Badger's heart beat even faster. What a futuristic kind of place!

He led the others out of the Longyang Road Metro Station and took a short taxi ride to the riverfront in Pudong. There they alighted, surrounded by high-rise office buildings of every conceivable shape. Several looked like rocket ships attached to launch pad towers. Others had windows that reflected in different colors and directions. One place resembled a pink needle not unlike the Eiffel Tower updated to the 21st Century.

Modern cars obeyed traffic laws and were dwarfed by the wide boulevards and immense skyscrapers. But Badger felt grandiose. He was walking through an entirely man-made environment that seemed to be the product of a single imagination.

He summoned the team around him. "Here's where we earn our pay," he said. From his briefcase, he pulled a photo of Merle Stevens and passed it around for the team to submit to memory. "Our mission is to find Stevens and get him to tell us where Raymond O. Flowers' family has been hidden away here in China."

"What's our plan of action?" a tall young man asked. Skilled in several Oriental languages at the Defense Language Institute in Monterey, Boris Vukic had been their resident translator.

"I'll call the Consulate and set up a meeting with Merle," Badger explained. "From that moment on, we'll monitor his movements. So first, we have to get to the Consulate."

He handed around pocket maps of Shanghai, each with the Consulate's location marked with a red dot. He continued, "My hope is that he'll meet me for lunch, and we can question him there. Remember that he's not likely to give us the information without some form of coercion. At this point, I'd stop at nothing to get him to spill the beans."

The others nodded, like a team in a huddle.

"Now you wait here," Badger said, "and I'll make the call."

He wandered away from the others and found a concrete bench on which to sit. He had done his preparation the night before and was armed with as much information as his contacts at the Agency could supply him. Briefly, Shanghai was on the vanguard of change in China. Its industry, infrastructure, policies, and economy were on the cutting edge. Like the days of old, anything was possible in Shanghai, as long as one didn't cross the line politically. So the American Consulate followed suit. Its mission was chiefly to foster change, openness, and strong interrelations between Chinese and American institutions such as businesses, universities, and the like.

After thinking it over for several hours during a sophomoric American movie on the closed circuit TV at Kadena Air Base, he thought he had come up with the perfect angle to create a meeting with Merle Stevens, who was nominally an economic officer at the

Consulate.

Badger would pose as a documentary filmmaker seeking background economic information on Shanghai. In his experience, those know-it-alls who worked at Embassies and Consulates and lived in the foreign environment were only too happy to show off how much they knew. Perhaps this stemmed from Washington not caring enough to read their daily reports.

So, changing his persona to that of a documentary filmmaker, he picked up his mobile phone and jabbed at the number for the Consulate that he had already programmed.

An operator answered and directed his call to Mr. Steven's desk.

"Hello, this is Merle Stevens," came the voice that Badger could only describe as handsome.

"Morning, Mr. Stevens," Badger began with his best California dude-talk. "My name is Aric Birch. That's Aric with an A. I'm producing an American documentary on Shanghai and I was looking for an expert in the economics of the city. I was given your name by a, uh. By... I'm sorry, I've forgotten his name. Some dude from the Academy of Motion Pictures who spoke highly of you. He said to pass along his high fives and look you up. So here I am."

"Well, Mr. Birch. Welcome to Shanghai," Merle said without missing a beat.

"Say, are you free for lunch today?" Badger inquired. "You pick the place and I'll treat. And think beyond Big Macs; I'm on my boss's expense account."

"Yeah, sure. Have you ever been to M on the Bund?"

"Never heard of it, but hey, that doesn't mean it doesn't exist, right?"

"It's on the steep side, but gives you a great perspective on the city."

"That's excellent, Merle. I'll make it happen, for two at say nooner?"

"No sooner."

"Ha," Badger said. "Cool."

He turned off his phone and closed his eyes in thanks. So far so good. Now all he had to do was to make reservations for M on the Bund in two hours.

❖ ❖ ❖

Harry checked the B-2's Navstar GPS navigation readout displayed on the visor of his helmet. He was only two hours away from Guam and closing in at near sonic speed.

But they couldn't land on the tiny island without being permanently grounded. Harry recalled that the B-2 Spirits had a range of nine thousand six hundred kilometers unrefueled. It could be refueled in flight by the boom method, thus making it more than an intercontinental threat. It was a global threat. But he also realized that, given the Gitmo troops' hostile reaction to their leaving, no fuel tanker was likely to come up and help them.

He couldn't wait forever for Badger's call.

"What's that?" Harry asked.

Flowers had produced a CD from his shirt pocket.

"It's a recording that the camp commander back in Guantánamo gave me. It's our conversation in prison."

Harry grabbed the shiny disc. "Do you know what this represents?" he asked, waving it in the air.

Amber reflections played in Raymond's face.

"This is more powerful than any number of bombs we could be carrying in our weapons bay. This could sink the Administration."

"How?" Raymond asked.

Harry had to smile. The guy could be so naïve. "It's your testimony. This is what the special prosecutor needs in order to make their case against the President."

"Do you mean that I won't need to go to Washington in person to testify?"

"My guess is that this is potent enough evidence to bring Chinagate slamming shut in the President's face."

He looked down at the equipment arrayed before him. He had millions of dollars of weapons and navigational hardware before him, but where was the CD player?

"We'll have to ship this to the Department of Justice the moment we touch down."

"If we ever touch down," Raymond said.

Harry corrected himself. Maybe Raymond wasn't so naïve after all.

Badger McGlade guessed from the name that M on the Bund would be a trendy spot. But he was not prepared for the dramatic impact of its location.

It was right on the historic curtain of buildings that fronted the old side of Shanghai. Shivering, he stood on the terrace of M and looked down the long, curving stretch of banks and customs houses that both created and illustrated Shanghai's success at the turn of the century.

Beyond the four-lane road and riverfront promenade lay the Huangpu River. A wide, muddy river, it was a superhighway for ships of all kinds, primarily barges, cargo ships, and ferries. The Huangpu flowed down from the mighty Yangtze, China's major artery that carried products and raw materials from deep within the country out to the world at large.

Then, his eyes lifted to the new area of Pudong from which he had just arrived by taxi through a long tunnel. The modern skyline stood in stark contrast to the sooty old buildings around him. It didn't take long to see where China was headed, and fast!

"You must be Aric with an A," came a baritone voice behind him.

Badger turned around, a hand extended. "Just call me 'A on the Bund.'"

The diplomat laughed. From his hearty handshake, Badger decided to eliminate physical coercion as one of his options. He'd have to rely on the rest of his team for that.

"Let's eat!" Badger said. "We've got lots to discuss."

A few minutes later, a bottle of smooth, sophisticated white wine from Australia's Margaret River region sat open between them and they were clinking glasses and celebrating the glorious view.

Seated inside to avoid the cold, they could still appreciate a blue sky high above the city. "Enjoy the weather," Merle was saying. "Days as clear as this are rare."

"I wish I had my camera rolling right now."

"So what kind of a documentary are you contemplating?"

Badger was prepared for the question, and gave a one-paragraph response, in effect saying that he would like to draw on Merle's experience for background on the city. "Essentially, what I want to know is, are the Americans screwing the Chinese, or are the Chinese screwing the Americans?"

Merle laughed heartily. "Now, that's the great unanswered question, isn't it?"

The baba ganoush and hummus arrived in record time, served by a pleasant young woman with perfect tableside English. Badger wouldn't mind finding out her bedside manners either.

He spread some dip on a cracker and momentarily lost track of why he was there, even where he was. He felt transported out of time and space. Nothing like tasty Middle Eastern food served by a scrumptious Chinese waitress on a rooftop high above colonial Shanghai to disorient an American like him.

Alas, Middle Eastern food was basically a thing of the past, as he hadn't dared to enter such a restaurant anywhere in the world for some time. He couldn't help but think of all he was missing in the Middle Eastern cultures, not the least of which was the food.

The thought of terrorism snapped him back to reality. His job was to put the screws to Merle Stevens. The young diplomat should never have set foot in Badger's Middle Eastern den that noon. His forty thieves were waiting in the kitchen, knives bared.

Well, not exactly, but close.

Then his Casablanca chicken arrived, and the staff delivered Merle his char-grilled marinated king prawns. Badger lost himself in the richly textured flavors of the chicken. He never knew that you could do such a thing to a fowl. He would never look at chicken the same way again.

And what could M do for dessert? He decided to top off his meal with flourless chocolate cake with whipped cream and raspberries. Merle opted for a hot apricot soufflé with almond brittle ice cream.

It was with deep regret that Badger finally called for the bill.

"I thank you for this lunch," Merle said formally. "And I wish you great success in your endeavor."

Merle was a well-tanned, well-built man with a commanding air and easy demeanor. It was too bad that his feathers would be so ruffled by the time his elevator reached street level.

They entered the dark elevator lobby reserved exclusively for the restaurant. Badger watched his guest snatch a matchbook and slip it dexterously into his pocket while they waited.

The elevator was slow in coming. Badger filled the awkward time once again thanking Merle for his assistance.

"The pleasure was all mine," Merle replied.

The elevator door finally opened, a black hole lined by a pair of Western men in leather jackets.

Merle hesitated at first, but Badger cordially invited him to enter. Merle took several steps inside and turned to jab the lobby button.

Badger didn't move, and let the elevator doors slide shut before him. He heard the car lurch downward through the antiquated building, then suddenly come to a halt between floors.

He returned to the restaurant and strolled out to the terrace for fresh air. By the time the elevator reached ground level, his men would have some answers concerning Raymond O. Flowers' family.

The river traffic hadn't thinned over the lunch hour. It looked like a gritty life on the Huangpu. It would be even more so with the addition of a floating corpse.

He shook his head. He didn't want to know what techniques his team was employing.

Looking directly down at the street, he couldn't see his men anywhere. They must not have emerged from the building. The icy breeze was beginning to numb his exposed skin. Boy, had he been seduced by the sunny warmth of Hainan Island in China's south. In truth, the country could be damned cold, and Flowers' family was probably frozen to death in some godforsaken prison.

He shot another look downward, but no luck.

Then his mobile phone rang. He put it to his ear.

"This is Boris. We got what we needed and he got what he deserved."

"Where are you?" Badger asked, confused. He hadn't seen them leave the building.

"Look down at the riverfront."

Badger saw a small family barge pulling away from the Bund, a body in a business suit spread-eagled on the deck. It was Merle Stevens.

"So, did he sing?" Badger asked.

"Like a songbird."

"Where is Raymond O. Flowers' family?" Badger wanted to know.

"Outside of Harbin, in a state prison in the woods. I have the name of the place, but I couldn't pronounce it."

"Where's Harbin?" Badger asked.

"Have you ever heard of Vladivostok?"

Badger shuddered at the name. It was Russia's Far Eastern capital, a chilly, remote seaport. "Yes I know about Vladivostok."

"Well, Harbin is in Manchuria, due north of Vladivostok, about four hundred and fifty clicks inland. That's where the Chinese prison is located."

"Lovely. I'll meet you downstairs in a few minutes."

He took a last look at Merle Stevens' inert body that lay on the fast-disappearing barge. Soon the barge merged with the heavy volume of ships that plied the waters. "*Sayonara*, Mr. Stevens."

Badger slipped back through the restaurant with its elegant mixture of Eastern and Western furniture and art. The Chinese waitress smiled at him as he left.

For the first time he thought he detected a look of triumph behind that inscrutable Oriental smile. Had he calculated the dollar-renmenbi conversion correctly? It brought to mind his first question to Merle. Perhaps the Chinese were screwing the Americans in ways he had never considered.

Chapter 31

Bleary-eyed, Harry Black stared at the tops of puffy pink clouds. He had flown on the edge of dusk the entire way. Chasing the day would be futile, and the fleeing sun had remained just beyond the horizon. He had been flying in twilight for eighteen hours. He wanted to remove his helmet and rub his eyes, but he needed to watch the HUD, Head-Up Display, indicators projected on his visor.

His fuel was running low. There was no way he could reach the eastern fringes of Asia on one tank of gas.

Raymond was dozing in the seat opposite him, unaware of the pinch they were in.

Then Harry felt a vibration in his pants pocket. It was his satellite-equipped mobile phone ringing. Thank God the signal could pass through the skin of the aircraft.

He slipped off his helmet and dumped it in his lap.

"Yes?"

"Harry, this is Badger, calling from Shanghai."

"What did you find out?"

Badger's voice sounded jubilant. "Merle Stevens informed our men that Flowers' family is being held at a Chinese prison in Harbin, which is in far northeastern China."

Harry didn't know the place. "I'll look it up on the navigational computer. I hope they have an airport."

"They do. I'm going to fly there this afternoon. How are you getting there?"

"By military aircraft."

"Are you being escorted? Do you have official clearance to enter Chinese airspace?"

"Hell no. I'm on my own," Harry said.

"The Chinese will try to intercept you," Badger warned. "Are you sure you want another EP-3 spy plane incident. They could hold you hostage for several weeks."

"I don't intend to knock any of them out of the sky. Incidentally, I'm flying a B-2 *Stealth* bomber. I don't think they'll ever see us."

"Holy shit! A B-2? Don't let the Chinese get their hands on one of those babies. The Pentagon would throw you in the brig for divulging state secrets."

"I don't intend to hand it over."

"Good," Badger said with a shiver. "By the way, there's some sort of cold snap happening here. You'd better bring a coat."

"You've been slumming around the tropics too long."

"I'm serious. Wear a parka. Once you get to Harbin, let's coordinate. The team and I are on our way to Hongqiao Airport in Shanghai. I hope to make Harbin before nightfall."

"I may beat you there," Harry said. He signed off and placed his helmet back over his head.

He immediately checked one of the CRTs below eyelevel. He flipped through map projections until he had a spherical globe centered on the Pacific.

Indeed, Harbin lay inland, northwest of Vladivostok, though still in Chinese territory where Manchuria met Siberia.

At the moment, he and Raymond were passing over Guam, the southernmost island in the Mariana Islands, far northwest of Hawaii. His flight path would take him straight to the Philippines.

The fuel indicator told him otherwise. He had a mere fifteen minutes of flight time at his currently reduced speed. The jet's engines were sucking the last droplets out of her fuel tanks.

He reached for the radio transmitter. "Andersen Air Force Base come in," he said in as calm a voice as he could muster. "This is the *Spirit of Kansas*. I need in-flight refueling over Guam immediately."

"*Spirit of Kansas*, this is Andersen Air Force Base. Request denied. Land your aircraft at once."

"I'm prepared to ditch this bird at sea unless you provide prompt in-flight refueling," Harry announced. Then he read off his coordinates. "Unless you want to be responsible for losing a B-2, you'd better scramble a tanker now."

After a moment's wait, the base in Guam came back. "I'm sorry. We can't get a tanker aloft that fast. You'll just have to land here."

The ruse wouldn't work.

"I'm lowering altitude to 25,000 feet in preparation for ejection," Harry said. His HUD flashed the amount of fuel remaining and the time and distance left at current speed and fuel consumption. He had ten minutes until they dropped out of the sky.

"It's a large, dark sea you're jumping into," came back a different voice, this one sterner.

"I'll take my chances," Harry said. "Two point one billion dollars," he reminded the base. "Lowering to 20,000 feet."

"This is the base commander. You'll spend the rest of your life behind bars if you lose that aircraft."

"Now, where's the ejection button..."

"I order you to touch down at Andersen AFB on the double."

"Sorry, gotta go. 15,000 feet. We jump at ten thousand."

Static crackled over the radio. Raymond was wide awake by this point and threw a wild look at Harry. "I don't know how to parachute," he said.

Harry winked. The *Spirit of Kansas* was descending rapidly. Five minutes left give or take a minute or two. He strapped on his helmet and switched to the helmet's communications system.

"Prepare to eject," Harry commanded over the microphone, making sure the radio was transmitting his comments to Guam. "Adjust your harness over each shoulder..."

The base commander came back on the air. "If you look directly above you, we've positioned a tanker to refuel you." His voice had a defeated tone.

Harry glanced up and sure enough, a Hercules refueling tanker was arriving overhead, a fuel boom lowering toward the top of his fuselage.

He switched off the radio. "Eureka! It worked. Now, to get hooked up."

His jet was running on autopilot, maintaining a steady speed and altitude. He would have to switch over to manual for the fine adjustments needed to guide the fuel line into the opening above him. He pressed the button to open the fuel door, and then clicked off the autopilot, taking control of the fully digital quadruplex fly-by-wire flight control system.

"Easy does it," he whispered to himself, guiding the touchy aircraft slightly higher, but losing momentary control of the pitch. He watched an electronic indicator show the beavertail assembly just behind him on the centerline of the flying wing struggle to keep the nose pointed horizontally.

Less than a minute of fuel remained in the tanks.

Harry heard the angled boom slip into his tank.

"Contact. Please refuel at once. I have no fuel left, repeat no fuel left." He had trouble keeping the tension out of his voice. He had practiced a stall on the simulator once, but didn't want to experience one now.

"Releasing fuel," the tanker pilot announced over the airwaves.

Harry checked the HUD, both hands steady on the yoke. The fuel indicator ceased to drop and held steady. Each drop of new fuel was being consumed at the rate in which it was delivered. He couldn't fly all that way to China.

"Pump it faster," he said. "I'm only barely staying up here."

"Roger that. Increasing fuel."

The HUD's fuel indicator steadily climbed.

"Are we going to make it?" Raymond whispered over the headset.

Harry nodded reassuringly, not taking his eyes off the computerized horizon that he was trying to maintain.

It took twenty minutes of nerve-wracking adjustments to keep the two aircraft coupled midair. When at last the boom withdrew from the tank, Harry closed the fuel door, punched in new coordinates for Harbin, switched to autopilot, and felt the acceleration press him back in his seat.

He looked at Raymond. "You take over for a while. I need a nap."

Raymond sat bolt upright and shot him a look as Harry eased his seatback into a reclining position.

Harry wasn't aware of what happened next, because he was fast asleep.

Hiram Klug couldn't believe their good fortune. The resort wasn't charging them for lodging or dining or even the bar. The vacation was entirely on them.

Hiram decided to make good on their offer by taking Tiffany to the beachside restaurant for a full-course anniversary dinner.

No skimping for them any longer.

It seemed incredible to him as he strolled along jungle path illuminated by light bulbs underfoot. The people of the island were so thankful to him for doing what he considered the only thing a rational human could do—defend his wife and help maintain order on the island.

"Ya know," he told her, thinking aloud. "I'm kinda embarrassed by all dis attention."

"Nonsense," she told him. "You soak it up."

"I have ta admit, I don't mind the free-bees."

"Me either," she said, her CPA training shining through. "I wouldn't want to calculate all that we've spent. It's like we're guests on some reality TV show, with all expenses paid."

"I did appreciate da statues and rugs dey gave us. They would look kinda nice in da family room."

"And I thought the jewelry might go well next time we go to the movies."

"Hell, Sweets. I gots bigger plans for us."

They reached the restaurant. A highly respectful *maitre d'* recognized them at once, and his dark face grew radiant from the pleasure of serving them. They found a suitable table along the water's edge. Lights hung from the bow of shrimp boats that bobbed far out at sea.

"Bigger plans?" she picked up their conversation where they had left off. "Like what?"

"Sweetie, picture this." He leaned back and drew a large frame around his idea. "The Paper Mill Playhouse. Season's tickets!"

She simply shook her head dumbfounded and full of respect for her husband. It was all too much, even for him to comprehend at times.

Their server arrived, a young woman who couldn't keep her enormous eyes off of Hiram. The deference in her voice made him want to giver her a noogie. Enough with all this respect, already.

They placed an order for King Crab and the catch of the day. She promised them that they wouldn't be disappointed.

Their highballs arrived immediately, and they drank a toast to the island. Nothing further needed to be said.

Several waiters hung about in the shadows of the candle-lit restaurant. A sea breeze gently stirred the air. The speakers were piping in Henry Mancini. The evening couldn't have been more perfect.

He looked into his wife's lovely sapphire eyes. She looked twenty years younger.

"Hiram," she said at last. "You shouldn't have taken such a risk."

He knew what she was referring to, and it wasn't the Paper Mill Playhouse.

"Listen, that's all over now. I did what I did, and it's done, okay?"

"But, I mean, shooting a gun?"

"Yeah, but I had to. You shoulda seen dese guys. Dey were trying ta kill people, average people like you and me!"

"I know. It's so horrible, but why did you have to be the hero?"

Hiram heaved a sigh. "I guess some people get all the luck."

It had been an enormous risk. Maybe he wasn't using his brains.

"Well, at least dese guys, whoever dey are, are all behind bars."

"Did the police ever figure out who they are?"

"I tink the police chief is on permanent leave." He reflected on how the loser had avoided the final standoff with the terrorists. "And I certainly don't know who those guys in robes are. Dey are all a bunch of hoods, if you ask me, and I don't have no time for 'em. They can rot in da Purang prison as far as I care."

"Without a trial?"

"Hey," he said, gesturing around him grandly at the resort, where a band was warming up beside the pool, and at the line of coconut palm trees that fringed the sand- and seashell-covered beach, then out at the enormous sleeping black sea. "What more evidence do you need? Dey and deir guns was trying to destroy da peace."

Just then a muffled, distant boom came from overhead. Hiram looked beyond the restaurant's awning, but saw nothing in the black night sky. It must have been some sort of invisible, supersonic jet flying high above the Pacific Ocean.

The waiters were assembling their food at the far side of the restaurant. Three men lined up and carried in all the dishes at once.

The first man presented Tiffany with her King Crab. Would you like me to pour butter on that for you?"

She assented.

"Your catch of the day, sir," the second waiter said deferentially, setting the large round platter on the table before him.

Hiram looked up at the third and last waiter, who stood trembling with a white cloth over his forearm. "Yes?" he asked.

He wondered where he had seen that man's face before. Certainly not at the resort. He was too light-skinned, and he seemed too broad chested to be an islander.

The man removed the white cloth and revealed a carving knife in his hand.

Hiram didn't need his fish carved. He looked down at his meal. "Dese are fillets."

"Hiram!" Tiffany's voice rose from her throat.

He glanced up, reflexively raising an elbow to shield himself. The waiter had turned the knife on Hiram and lunged toward him as he sat in his seat.

Jumping to his feet, Hiram slipped under the short man's arm and caught him full on the face with his elbow.

Women screamed around the restaurant. Chairs squeaked in the sand.

The man took a second pass at him. The knife sliced through the air, this time under Hiram's arm, toward his stomach. Hiram turned his assailant away with his elbow, sending the man off kilter. His short arms couldn't reach far enough to get the knife close to Hiram.

He felt the blade slash through the fabric of his new batik shirt. This was totally unacceptable, not only ruining his anniversary dinner with his wife, but also ruining his newly bought outfit! Trying to frighten off the man, he rushed the guy, sending him to the sand. The knife flipped harmlessly from his hand. Unable to stop his forward momentum, Hiram stumbled over his assailant and landed squarely on the man's chest. That produced a strange sounding, "Oof."

"Hiram!" Tiffany said, a note of censure in her voice.

He struggled back to his feet to explain himself. "Sweetie, he tried ta stab me."

"I know but…"

The waiter had regained his feet, his fingers fumbling for the knife.

"Hiram!" Tiffany said, this time with a shriek of alarm.

He raised his hands in self-defense. But there was no need.

The young man grasped the knife with both hands and pointed it inward. "*Allahu Akbar!*" he shouted and plunged the blade deep into his own chest, pulling it upward into this heart.

Blood spurted everywhere.

A woman beside their table began to choke on her food.

Tiffany was speechless.

Hiram looked into the man's eyes. Whatever possessed the guy?

The erstwhile attacker fell to the sand at his feet. And with him went the answers to all the questions that were forming in Hiram's mind. Who was this guy? Why did he want Hiram dead? And what in the world was worth killing oneself for?

318

Tiffany was clinging to him, her body trembling as she gazed horrified at the spectacle at their feet.

"Dat's okay, sweetie," he said, turning her soft, round shoulders away. They rocked together and looked out at the vast, protective sea. "I tink we got 'em all, now."

Night had fallen by the time Harry glided down toward Harbin Airport.

Below him, the landscape was cloaked in blackness. It was the Chinese countryside, with little electricity, forested, and buried under snow.

If the approach beacon at the airport's VOR station wasn't strong enough, Harry would have to set his glideslope based on dead reckoning. And that was not what he preferred.

"Mayday, Mayday, Mayday," Harry shouted. "This is an American military aircraft requesting permission to make an emergency landing at Harbin Airport. Come in?"

"Dis ia Harbin Airpor. We don hava you on radah. Plea idena, plea idenfy yousel."

"I repeat, this is an American military aircraft. This is an emergency. Request permission to land at Harbin Airport."

"Okay, fine. You clea to runway 02, wind ata 030."

Harry let out his breath and checked that he was locked in correctly to the beacon that seemed to magically guide the air wing lower and closer to its destination. It was almost as if the Chinese were leading them in on a silk thread.

He saw Raymond gripping his seat, his knuckles white.

"You can relax, Raymond," he said, lowering the landing gear. "This is all automatic. Have you ever been to Harbin before?"

Raymond shook his head. "Ice festival."

"What's that?"

"Harbin holds an annual ice festival, but I never saw it."

How nice. A town halfway in Siberia celebrating ice. Now that was a stroke of merchandising genius.

The *Spirit of Kansas* found its way through the pitch black toward a lighted runway two miles in the distance. Harry watched approvingly as she maneuvered herself with tiny adjustments.

Just wait until the control tower took a gander at her unusual shape. The local military brigade was probably already on its way, preparing to storm the plane and take her crew captive.

But there was no such reception committee. As they glided into the pink glow of the arc lights, he spotted an Aeroflot Russian Airlines jet and a Air Koryo North Korean jet parked on the tarmac. But no tanks or military vehicles.

The wheels touched down on snow-swept concrete. Harry turned in the drag rudders to form an air brake. They rushed through the gloom, pressed against their seat harnesses until they came to a rolling stop.

Harry gunned the twin engines and turned the nose back toward the terminal. It was a large building, and unusually modern looking. What was a model airport doing in the middle of nowhere?

He couldn't find ground control on any frequency, so he steered for a position near the Russian commercial liner.

"Well, Raymond, we're back," he said as they rolled along. "Ready to look for your family?"

Raymond lifted off his headgear. He looked like a new man, young and vigorous. Perhaps he finally felt delivered from imprisonment.

"This is my country," he said. "These are my people. Ready for a few *chung-guo ren*?"

"What's that? Chop suey?"

"No, it's the Chinese people. A sea of one point three billion faces. And I love 'em all."

"I'm glad to hear it," Harry said, spinning down the engine and coming to a halt. "They might be spending the rest of their lives there."

He released his seat harness and removed his helmet. "Let's go!"

On his way to unlocking the co-pilot from the stairwell, he reached for his travel bag in the back of the cockpit.

"It looks cold out there," he said.

"Cold?" Raymond said, taking a proffered sweater. "You don't know cold."

Harry unlatched the cabin door. The young airman was standing at an angle, holding his crotch.

"The lavatory is unoccupied now," Harry said, gesturing to the portable toilet in the cockpit. But I suggest you make it quick and fly this bird back to Guam as quick as you can."

The man rushed past them, unzipping his flight suit.

Harry lowered the air stair and stepped out of the fuselage, only to feel his business suit seize up and clamp around him.

An even wind was howling over the tarmac. He felt his eyelashes instantly freeze.

Across the airfield, he saw a pair of vehicles racing toward the plane. The People's Liberation Army had arrived to liberate the plane.

He heard the stairway close behind him with a thud. He and Raymond were on their own.

They set their legs in motion toward the terminal where a warm light emanated from behind an airlock of double doors. Incredibly, nobody stood waiting inside.

Behind them, the B-2's engines roared to life. The sudden gust of wind nearly sucked the saliva out of Harry's mouth. He clamped his jaw shut to retain the moisture in his body.

The two vehicles that sped past them looked like troop carriers. The *Spirit of Kansas* was already taxiing away. The trucks gunned their engines in hot pursuit, their unit commander barking out orders. White-clad soldiers hung out of the back of the truck to get their first look at the flying wing.

It wouldn't be long before they figured out what was about to slip through their fingers—state-of-the-art technology, much of which had been literally invented to create the bomber. It would probably have been the largest technology transfer of all time.

But it would take longer for them to fully appreciate their good luck that evening. The Chinese government had just gained a bargaining chip worth trillions in favorable trade deals and incalculable value to their own political and international aspirations. And it wasn't an airplane. It was a man named Raymond O. Flowers, express delivered into their cold little hands.

By the time Harry reached the terminal, his ears felt brittle and two columns of ice had formed beneath his nostrils. There had better not be any press waiting to snap his picture.

Not surprisingly, it would take some time for the Chinese bureaucracy to catch up with the two intruders.

Even the spanking new immigration booths were empty and the two men walked right into China as if entering someone's living room.

"Care to pick up some tourist information?" Harry asked, pointing to a rack of maps and brochures.

"No, let's keep going," Raymond said.

Sure, Harry understood.

As they stepped out of the terminal, a booming roar passed overhead, pursued by a barrage of automatic gunfire. The *Spirit of Kansas* had taken wing once more.

Harry found a few taxis waiting just outside the terminal. He rested his hand on the tinny roof of one car, a far cry from the high-tech mode of transport that was disappearing in the blackness above.

"You talk to the driver," he said. "I have no idea where we're going. Let's just get out of here."

"*Women yao qu Harbin,*" Raymond said, sliding into the back seat.

Harry jumped in just as the taxi driver prepared to speed off.

As they swung around the airport terminal, Harry glanced out his window. There the afterburners of the *Spirit of Kansas* glowed like two small fires in the east.

Then he turned his attention to the man huddled behind the wheel, vigorously scraping frost off the windshield with a debit card as they raced off into the darkened countryside.

In the back seat of the taxi, Harry reached for his mobile phone. It was a miracle that two American mobile phones could communicate with each other in China. But it worked. Badger picked up on the other end.

"We just arrived at the airport and we're taking a cab into the city," Harry said. "Where are you?"

"Just checked into the Gloria Inn here in downtown Harbin. I've got a room for you and Raymond to share."

Harry shifted hands holding the phone, as one hand had already grown stiff with cold. "Okay, what's the room number?"

"1214."

"Got it."

"Harry, how in the hell did you get through Chinese security?"

Harry grinned. "A little luck, a little chutzpah, and a little confusion on the part of the Chinese."

"Do they know you're here?"

"It will take them a while to figure it out. They certainly don't know either of our identities."

"Okay," Badger said dubiously, drawing in his breath. "It takes an hour to reach the city from the airport."

"An hour? Why so long?"

"It's a long way away. Enjoy the ride."

"Just heat up the room for me, will you? All I have is a suit coat."

"I'll send the men out to buy you some parkas and winter gear. This isn't Cuba, you know."

"I figured that out."

Harry hung up the phone and smiled at Raymond. "They'll have parkas for us," he said.

Raymond nodded, but his thoughts were elsewhere. He was sitting on the edge of the bench seat, not so much anxious at the speed demon's driving. More like full of anticipation.

Chapter 32

Entering Harbin, all Harry Black could think was, "What ice festival?"

Factories and warehouses were scattered indiscriminately on the outskirts of town. Huge, serious-looking construction equipment roamed up and down the highway. A cloverleaf spiraled them downward off a bridge and onto the main street lined with apartment buildings. The austere architecture felt more like Moscow than China.

Then the colors began to appear. Sculptures had carved glistening gateposts and statues out of ice. Red, green, and yellow lights glowed within the "ice lanterns." The frozen streets and snow-packed sidewalks were lined with the colorful works of art.

Pedestrians slid about on the streets, making their way to restaurants and bars. As they laughed, plumes of steam rose from their lips.

Marked by several such ice lanterns, the Gloria Inn extended a welcoming portico to greet them.

"Uh-oh. Cab fare," Harry said.

"Try dollars," Raymond suggested. "Harbin is a fairly international place."

Harry pulled a twenty from his pocket. The cabbie was squeezed in a plastic compartment that surrounded his seat. He had to reach a hand up to the ceiling to grab it. He examined the bill for a moment, held it up to the light, then nodded. He pushed a lever down and printed out a receipt, which Raymond nabbed on their way out the cab.

"Who are you going to charge this one to?" Harry asked.

Outside, he picked up some Italian and French being spoken. Then a chic Russian couple walked by, and someone spoke with a Boston accent. Filling in the gaps were the Asian languages, similar in their clipped style, all unintelligible to his ear. The place was definitely on the map.

A doorman with a Fu Manchu mustache let them in. Facial hair on Chinese was a rare sight. Perhaps there was a Mongolian influence to the place.

They wandered the wide hallways for a minute before finding Room 1214.

Badger was inside waiting for them with a tray of steaming spring rolls.

"Care for an appetizer?" he asked.

Harry whisked Raymond into the room and quickly shut the door.

Then he grabbed for a spring roll. He cupped both hands around it and tried to warm up his fingers.

"Hey!" Badger said. "Those are for eating."

"I'm not sure what's worse right now, my hunger or the cold," Harry tried to explain.

Then he remembered Raymond standing by the door.

"This is Badger McGlade who works for my company," Harry said. "Badger, meet Raymond O. Flowers."

"Guantánamo Ray." Badger held out the tray. "I'm a big fan of yours."

Raymond looked confused. "How do you know anything about me?"

"Ha! I know everything about you," Badger said. He set down the tray and flipped his laptop open. Several news headlines appeared on the screen. He flipped from article to article.

Mystery Man Eludes Marines
Brief Sighting by Butcher
Polk Seeks Flowers to Clinch Case
Flowers 'Private Man' Says Neighbor

Raymond seemed fascinated. "All this because of me?"

"You bet," Badger said. "You're the man of the hour."

"Jeez, all I want is my family back."

"I'm afraid you're going to have to get used to the fact that everyone in the world wants you for one reason or another," Harry informed him.

"And what's *your* angle?" Raymond asked, looking Harry directly in the eye.

"I don't like what they did to you," Harry said slowly. "It's a case of the cover-up being worse than the crime. I don't care what bribe you accepted for the President. I don't care what terrorist organizations you belong to. The Feds should never have taken your family away from you."

Raymond sank to the edge of a double bed. His feet shoved into Harry's old jogging sneakers, he toed the threadbare Persian carpet. He sank his face into his hands. "If you can help me get my family back," he said, "I'd willingly go to prison."

"Don't you worry," Harry told him. "We won't let that happen either." And he finally shoved the spring roll in his mouth.

It was the best damned food he had ever eaten. Suddenly he realized that he hadn't touched a crumb all day.

"Oh, and before I forget," he said. "Badger, can you email this video to Caleb Perkins at the Department of Justice?" He pulled Raymond's CD-ROM from his pocket.

"Sure thing," Badger said, turning to his notebook and sliding out the CD tray. "What is it?"

"Raymond's testimony for the Chinagate investigation."

"Way cool!" Badger exclaimed, and nearly dropped it on the floor.

"Be careful, will ya?"

Twenty minutes later, Badger's file transfer was complete.

Toweling off from a hot shower, Harry placed a call from the hotel phone to Caleb Perkins' office at the Department of Justice.

The office hadn't yet opened and the department's internal telephone system asked him to leave a voice message.

"Check your email," Harry told the recording. "I just uploaded a video clip for you." He wanted to keep the message vague and brief in case anyone in Washington was scanning incoming calls for his voiceprint.

"Tell them it's okay to open the attachment," Badger whispered. "It's not a virus."

"Too late," Harry said. "I already hung up."

"You know how the Justice Department is coming down hard on spyware and worms and spam and other security issues," Badger explained.

"I know all about the Justice Department and security," he said, remembering the threat level display, the body scanner chamber, and the attack dogs guarding the Attorney General. "Caleb Perkins will want to hear Raymond's testimony."

He flipped a dry towel to Raymond.

"Your turn in the shower."

Caleb Perkins reached his office at the Justice Department at seven-thirty a.m.

His secretary, an astute paralegal with twenty years in the civil service, met him at the door. "You just received a phone message from Harry Black," she said discreetly. "He called to tell you to check your email. He sent you a video clip."

"Fire up my machine," Caleb said. He didn't have the vaguest idea how the computer worked, much less how to download a video clip via email. "And get that video clip on the screen, will you?"

A few minutes later, his technology savvy secretary had him all set up in his office to view the clip.

"That will be all. I can take it from here," he said, dismissing her from the room.

Seconds later, he was staring at a scene that had his Inaugural Address written all over it. The image showed Harry interviewing Flowers behind a prison door. Each word that spilled from Flowers' lips was a further indictment of the sitting President. "This is political dynamite," he said to himself. "Bernard White is toast."

Before the testimony had finished playing, he reached for his desk phone and dialed Sandi DiMartino's cell phone.

"Hi, baby," he said. "Sorry if I woke you up."

"No, I'm in the office, Caleb," she said in a disappointingly formal way. "What's up?"

She'd be putty in his hands after he told her the news. But, maybe he could approach this with some subtlety and indirection.

"Do you have an email address?" he asked.

"Sure, why? Want to email me a belated Valentine?" she teased.

He frowned. It wasn't the reaction he was hoping for. He felt like blurting out the news of the clip.

Sandi gave him her email address over the phone, and he jotted it down. He had her repeat it several times, to make sure he had the capitalization and punctuation correct.

Each time she recited it, he savored the low, patient tones of her voice, the aspirated vowels, the sibilant consonants. "S-S-S-Sandi…"

"Okay, I think I've got it," he said at last. "Check your email in a few minutes."

He tried to restore the composure on his face and called his secretary back into the office. "I'd like you to send this video clip to the following email address…"

He handed the slip of paper on which he had written Sandi's email address.

"When you're finished," he said, "Delete the clip and shred that piece of paper."

She nodded and left the office, shutting the door behind her.

He turned off his computer and stared at the briefings on his desk. He had a day of meetings lined up on his calendar, but what he really wanted to do was to leave the drudgery of running a government department behind him, and deal with more pressing public issues, like preparing to walk down the red carpet to the tune of "Hail to the Chief."

And what would complete the picture was Sandi walking down the carpet clutching his arm.

Surrounded by her staff, Sandi leaned over her computer screen to watch the long file download. She was conscious that her short business skirt revealed a bit of thigh, but she couldn't worry about that now. Soon the file transfer was 100% complete. It was on her machine.

"I've got it!" she said announced.

The staff erupted with a victorious cheer.

Stanley Polk emerged from his office as the roomful of lawyers rejoiced and congratulated their lead investigator. Sandi was accepting kudos from all quarters.

"Do you mind if I watch that thing?" Stanley said in his low, penetrating voice.

"Not at all," Sandi said, stepping away from her desk. "Have a seat."

Stanley eased his large frame into her swivel chair and Sandi clicked the "Play" button for him.

It was standing room only to watch and hear the voice of the elusive key witness to their case. Sandi had to pinch her arm to remind herself that the moment was real. Raymond's face was clearly visible behind the prison door as he talked at length about the President accepting kickbacks from China and the oil company. She only saw the thick brown hair on the back of his head, but the stranger interrogating him seemed calm, his voice gentle, his manner receptive.

When the clip finally ended, there was no doubt in anyone's mind as to the President's guilt.

But Sandi was not sure about one thing. "Will this be admissible as evidence?" she asked, directing her question at Stanley Polk.

As he swiveled around in the chair to face her, she could clearly see that all his despondency during the preparation phase of the case had melted away. "Hell, yes, it's admissible. And it's incriminating as anything we could have hoped for."

The room let out a cheer, with Sandi the focus. She was afraid that they were going to try and lift her on their shoulders and parade her around, which wouldn't be decent given the shortness of her skirt.

But Stanley Polk rose to his feet, asserting his authority. "Good work, Sandi. I want this statement prepared as a deposition in court. Jack, I want you to personally transcribe the tape. We will ask the court to admit the tape and transcript as evidence during the trial. Fred, call *The Washington Post* and make a statement attributable to an anonymous source within the investigation. Do it now."

"Sir?" Sandi said, looking at the frozen image on the computer screen. "This evidence was supplied to us by the Attorney General of the United States. I wish to request that you drop any charges against Caleb and not move to subpoena him."

"Understood," Stanley said, in a rare moment of magnanimity.

"I've got one more piece of evidence to investigate," Sandi said, hoping the one last piece would seal the special prosecutor's case. "Did Raymond's family really die as the State Department claimed, or are they covering something up?"

Stanley stared at her. "I don't want you to bring up the question unless you can prove that they were lying," he cautioned.

"We'll ask for a warrant to dig up his family's remains in Maryland. If it turns out that's not their remains, we'll have further proof of a cover-up on the part of the Administration."

"Okay, find out who is buried in the family plot," Stanley said. "But keep it low key in case that line of inquiry leads us nowhere."

The roomful of lawyers and legal aids stood around expectantly, waiting for further orders.

"Okay everyone, into your groups and get to work," Stanley said. "We have no time to lose. I'm filing this in court tomorrow."

He walked back to his office, a bounce having returned to his stride.

Sandi turned to a colleague in the investigations unit. "Prepare a warrant request for the judge in Maryland asking to dig up the family's remains."

"Right away. We might have a warrant by this afternoon."

Later that morning, as she sat at her desk and waited for the judge to issue a search warrant to open up the Flowers family plot, Sandi's eyes were glued to the television screen, savoring every moment of the victory.

Stanley Polk was an impressive speaker, and looked the part of an impartial prosecutor as he issued a statement to reporters in a hastily staged press conference at the National Press Club.

"We have just obtained incontrovertible evidence of misdeeds by various elements within the Executive Branch. Our prosecution team will file for an indictment in Federal Court tomorrow morning. This could lead promptly to a criminal trial. I'll take questions now."

A reporter asked what was foremost on everyone's mind.

"Will you seek to indict the President?"

Stanley turned to the seasoned reporter who had asked the question and glared down at him over his reading glasses. "Yes, we will."

The press buzzed with the news that hit like a bombshell. The President would be indicted. Some rushed out of the room to file the story with their bureaus. The rest pressed him with more questions.

Finally Stanley picked out a young woman standing in the front row.

"Does the evidence you just mentioned point to the President?"

Stanley took his time answering, thus building anticipation.

"Yes, it does."

The reporters scribbled down the prosecutor's exact words. It was even difficult for Sandi to contemplate—they had solid evidence that linked the President directly to the scandal. More questions followed. Stanley picked out a reporter, who hoarsely called from the back row, "Is it Raymond O. Flowers' testimony?"

The room grew so quiet, reporters appeared to have stopped breathing.

Stanley Polk leaned into the bank of microphones.

"Yes, it is."

A telephone rang in the office, and the young lawyer that Sandi had assigned to exhuming the remains answered it. He spoke briefly, then thanked the other party, hung up, and raced over to her.

"We just got the warrant," he said, breathlessly. "We can dig up the remains."

The case was definitely gaining traction.

Sandi stood and turned off the television. "Call up the local sheriff in Maryland and the cemetery groundskeepers. I want to see this for myself."

Chapter 33

The next morning, Harry Black fought off hunger pangs as he led Raymond O. Flowers, Badger and the rest of his team down to the breakfast buffet. In a large, high-ceilinged room offset from the hotel lobby, they began to stuff their faces. The warm *dou jiang* soymilk, heated red bean paste buns, and bacon and eggs went down well. They would bolster Harry for a search through the high-rises and endless apartment compounds of snowy Harbin.

Beyond the elegantly arched windows that spoke of a European influence, families and couples streamed in a single direction.

"Where are they going?" Harry asked.

Raymond pointed to a giant inflated statue of Mickey Mouse at the end of the street. "That looks like the entrance to the Ice Festival."

Suddenly, Badger stopped eating and the blood seemed to drain from his face. He pointed a croissant at someone beyond the frosty window. "There goes Merle."

A tall, well-built man in a fur coat limped against the crowd, searching the faces.

"Hey," Badger called to the rest of the team seated at another table. "I thought you took care of him."

"We did take care of him," Boris responded.

"I meant *take care* of him."

"We did *take care* of him."

"Well then, what do you call *that*?"

"Okay, stop this," Harry said, rising. "We're not the mafia."

Merle Stevens was just turning to enter the hotel.

"Carmen!" Harry ordered under his breath.

The young woman, who could play the role of Filipina ingénue flawlessly, excused herself from the table, skirted around the outer tables of the restaurant and approached Merle with a clipped stride from a different direction. Merle's eyes were drawn to her and he removed his Russian fur hat.

Meanwhile, the rest of the team slipped out of the restaurant and took the elevator up to their adjoining rooms.

"How are we going to work this?" Badger asked Harry once they were safely back in their room. The rest of the team stood around the walls and listened. "He'll recognize Raymond, the men, and me."

Harry considered their predicament. This could be an opportunity, as Merle could lead them to the prison. They needed Merle alive and intact.

"We've got trouble," one of the men said, looking down through the arc of the window. "Chinese police are crawling all over the street, and they look serious. They have sidearms."

There was a knock at the door.

"It's Carmen," the voice said on the other side. "Let me in."

Badger eased the door open, and she came flying into the room.

"I came back for my coat," she explained. "I told him that I'd help him find his friend."

"Well, tell him to take his police buddies with him," Harry said. "They've surrounded the hotel."

"I told him that I never saw the man he was looking for. I think he's looking for you," she said, pointing at Badger.

"Whatever you do," Harry said, "lead him and the police away from this hotel. We need some freedom to find the prison."

"Okay," she said, her cheeks already flushed from the thrill of the challenge. She turned to leave.

Harry stood beside the searing hot radiator watching the police carefully. They were big, lean types, in long, dark blue overcoats. They wore gun belts in plain sight. Their rigid stance and alert eyes made them appear to be more like some Federal force than local cops.

"Okay, the police are heading back to the festival," he called out. "And Carmen's taking Merle back there, too." Carmen had emerged with Merle Stevens from the front door, both holding foot-long kebabs of candied fruit. "He's a real romantic. He seems to be taking her on a date to the Ice Festival."

"I doubt my family is there," Raymond said, a note of disappointment in his voice.

Boris had been busy pecking with his long, slender fingers at the keyboard on Badger's laptop. "I found a few maps in the CIA collection," he said.

Harry leaned over his back to check out the screen.

Harbin was built along a broad river that froze over in wintertime. Across the river sat an Island called Sun Island. There were no major cities near Harbin proper, but there was a tiger preserve a few miles out of town.

"Tigers?" Harry asked. "I thought they lived in jungles. We're on the Arctic Circle."

"Haven't you ever heard of Siberian tigers," Boris asked. "Huge white cats."

Harry shrugged. "What's this?" he asked, pointing to an enclosed space just beside the tiger preserve. Boris clicked to zoom in on the area. The CIA had designated the compound as PSB Psn 14.

"What could that possibly mean?" Harry asked the room at large. He repeated the name aloud.

"PSB might stand for the Public Security Bureau," Raymond suggested. "They're the Interior Ministry's enforcement arm."

"Could 'Psn 14' denote a prison?" Badger wondered aloud, looking to Raymond for an answer.

"I can't think of any other reason why the PSB would maintain a facility so far from a city," Raymond responded. He nudged Boris aside and looked at the screen. Could that be the place where his family had been held for nearly a year?

"Okay, we're losing time," Harry said. "Let's split up. I want Badger and Raymond to take the team and check out the PSB facility. Maybe the family is there. Boris and I will isolate Merle and find out from him where he's keeping the family."

Badger quickly prepared his team. They donned their warmest clothing and passed around clubs made from the legs broken off wooden tables. They had no other weapons and would have to be resourceful. Then they departed from the room.

That left Harry alone with Boris. "Would Merle recognize you?" he asked his language expert who was shutting off the computer.

"No," Boris replied. "I didn't rough him up in Shanghai."

"Okay. Let's see where Merle leads us."

❖ ❖ ❖

At six pm in Maryland, two groundskeepers hacked with spades into the frozen earth.

Sandi stared at the single tombstone, lovingly placed there by a grief-stricken father. The names on the stones seemed to come to life for her, because they truly were alive. She whispered the names to herself "Carolyn Stone, Wife of Raymond O. Flowers," "Jane Anne, Daughter," and "Samuel Alexander, Son."

How empty one would feel to bury their entire family all at once.

The spadework was not easy going, but it turned out that the grave wasn't deep. Half an hour into the digging, the workmen unearthed three urns.

The pathologist wrapped them in plastic, handling them like a piece of evidence. He taped the plastic bag shut and labeled it with a code number related to the special prosecutor's case.

"I'll take these to the lab, now, ma'am," the pathologist said. "We'll do a DNA analysis. Do you have any hair or saliva samples to check against?"

"Do you need to compare the ashes with something? I thought you could just figure out who it was."

"I'm sorry, ma'am. It's not that easy. I can tell a few things if I have an excellent sample, but these are burnt remains, so what I can deduce from them is limited."

"Well, do what you can," she said. "I doubt if there are any hair samples left."

"Sure thing. I'll get a report to you within a few days."

"That would be great."

The workmen didn't bother to fill in the hole. Most likely they thought the ashes would be re-interred shortly.

If Sandi's hunch was correct, there would be no need to bury them again.

The winter parkas and Russian fur hats that Badger had bought were perfect for the arctic air, as Harry and Boris stepped out of the Gloria Inn and headed toward the annual Harbin Ice Festival, the city's main attraction built upon the wide, frozen Songhua River.

Harry spotted life-sized buildings built out of blocks of ice below the embankment. Included were a welcoming Arc de Triomphe, followed by a Great Wall, Pyramid, Matterhorn, and Lhasa Buddhist Monastery. Children and their parents were sliding down the riverbank on discarded tires. Harry took the stairs.

In addition to the huge ice edifices, he took in delicately carved ice creations, including colored ice "paintings."

Groupings of Chinese tourists walked in silent wonder, dwarfed by the creations around them. But Merle and the blue-clad police were nowhere in sight.

After an hour in the snow, Harry needed to thaw out. Boris found them a small restaurant, a square one-room structure built on ice in the middle of the river, with all the comradely ambiance of a ski hut. A cup of steaming coffee hit the spot, and Harry began to rethink their strategy.

They couldn't just walk around the North Pole like frozen zombies without obtaining any information.

"We've taken up an entire hour and only passed a quarter of the ice sculptures. He could be anywhere and we'd never find him."

Boris agreed. "I could ask the waitress."

He signaled her, and the petite young lady came over. It seemed to be a family-run business, with her husband opening the beverage bottles and heating the coffee.

She and Boris exchanged a few clipped phrases, and she left the table.

"Well, what did she say?"

Boris had a sneaky look on his long, angular face. "We should look over there inside the mountain. The police were just here."

Harry had his gloves back on his hands before Boris finished his sentence.

Outside, he spotted an entrance to a tunnel in a mountain of piled up snow. "Let's check this out first."

They left the brilliant sunlight and entered a blue world carved out of the snow. Bending slightly to fit in the tunnel, Harry climbed up slippery steps that took him higher into the mountain. Occasionally, they passed intersections where other tunnels crossed theirs.

At one point, Harry stopped. Footsteps were crunching in the snow, receding down one of the branches of their tunnel. He heard no voices, only the chilly echo of feet.

"This way," he whispered.

They emerged from the darkness, only to find themselves high above an icy crevasse with a slatted wooden bridge spanning the gap. Balancing himself and careful not to let his street shoes slip on the bridge, Harry began to creep across.

He steadied himself midway over the empty space. He knew enough not to look down, but he had to keep an eye on where to place his next step. Why couldn't he be back in Georgia where he belonged? He took another step, his street shoes sliding all over the board before he found his balance. Couldn't Badger have bought him boots? Leather-soled shoes were less than worthless in the slippery and cold conditions. He had to continue before his toes froze.

He took a deep breath, which he regretted immediately. It filled the last pockets of warmth in his chest. He felt one of those dry hacking coughs coming on. He clasped a gloved hand over his mouth and skittered across the remaining three boards to safety.

Boris walked casually across the bridge and joined him.

"Not big on winter sports?" he asked.

Harry shook his head. "I'd rather be wrestling an alligator."

Then he put a finger to his lips and listened. The group was leading them through more ice tunnels and up and down more stairs on a trek through the huge mountain. Harry remained several corners out of sight, listening for any clues to who the silent party was.

Harry saw daylight around one corner, and paused to peer carefully around it. Several Chinese police were sliding on their backs down a final slippery tunnel that led to the ground.

He summoned Boris closer to have a look.

As the troops reassembled, Harry could see six pairs of fur-lined military boots through the small opening. Their leader gave a brief command that echoed up the tunnel.

Harry turned to Boris for a translation.

"They're spreading out further, into groups of two. They're looking for four male foreigners, and they have sketches of their faces."

"Well, they don't have your face or mine," Harry said. "But we are male foreigners, and almost everyone else seems to be Chinese around here."

A full minute after the last set of boots tramped out of view, Harry prepared to exit the mountain. He wedged his feet against the corners of the tunnel and tried to work his way down without falling, but one foot gave way immediately, and he found himself sliding on his back, feet first. He arrived at the bottom flushed with embarrassment, sprawling in front of a crowd of young couples.

Amid their laughter, he turned to look back and make out the shape of the mountain he had just left. He had been crawling through an enormous statue of Buddha, its round belly and bald head forming the bulk of the mountain of snow.

The group suddenly let out a scream, and Boris came barreling down the tunnel, emerging from the Buddha's navel. His boots rammed directly into Harry's side. The group scattered in all directions for safety, leaving Harry and Boris groaning and writhing in the snow.

The group's scream had attracted the attention of all who were in the area. Two foreigners on their backs in the ice must have made a funny sight.

But not to Harry.

"Let's go," he whispered. He regained his feet and clutched the bruise in his side where Boris had hit him. He staggered toward a row of townhouses elaborately carved out of ice blocks to form a warren of white buildings.

Suddenly a shot rang out and echoed around the frozen structures. Harry felt the heat of the bullet searing the air just overhead. He didn't wait to find out where it had come from.

He ducked into the nearest doorway and pulled Boris with him.

One look at the sparkling ice formations and he got the theme. There was a three-story Great Hall of the People, a towering replica of the Kremlin, and a detailed ice sculpture of the White House.

He looked above him. "10." He was at the Prime Minister's residence in London.

Unfortunately, the door wasn't real, and there was no escape through the building. They were precariously exposed. They would have to flee along Downing Street.

"Aim for the White House," he said, then launched himself into plain sight. Two more shots rang out. Kicking up chunks of snow, he slid several doors down the alley and came to a stop behind a pillar.

He had to shade his eyes in the glinting rays of sun. The White House was whiter than the real one.

Gasping for breath, Boris joined him behind the next pillar. "The shots are coming from the Kremlin," he whispered fiercely.

Harry could make out the onion-shaped domes, but not the rest of the building.

"Let's circle behind the Great Hall of the People," he suggested. They could make their way closer to the police without being seen. Maybe they could attack from behind and disarm the men. He could do with a weapon or two.

They slipped between the White House and the Great Hall of the

People, then alongside the long, pillared building past a replica of the statue on Tiananmen Square. Even the ice underfoot was etched into the large stones that made up the famous square. When they came into view of the Kremlin, he could make out a pair of policemen aiming their pistols along Downing Street.

"Now," Harry ordered under his breath and pointed to the two policemen. He and Boris walked briskly up to the tower behind which the men stood, and they chopped each policeman behind the neck. The two men crumpled to the snow without a sound.

Harry grabbed the pistol that had landed in the snow. It was a GLOCK 17, a locked breach, short recoil 9mm with a capacity of seventeen rounds of ammunition in the grip. He unfastened one belt holster, and Boris removed the other.

Two of the six police had been felled.

He looked at the fur-lined boots for a moment. He could sure use them. But he ordered himself to snap out of it. Time was more important. Boris was reloading one pistol and handed it to Harry, retaining the other.

They strapped on the fallen policemen's holsters, giving them dozens more rounds of ammunition.

"Watch out!" Boris whispered as he straightened his back and buckled his belt holster.

A sudden cry burst in Harry's eardrum from the direction of the Luxor and Pyramid exhibit. He heard a boot turning in the snow, and he ducked to the icy ground.

A moment later, a policeman plowed into him. Harry rose and buried an elbow into the man's solar plexus. The policeman fell on his face and didn't move. Harry stepped around the corner and saw three other policemen sliding and reeled to a halt as they tried to reverse direction. Boris plugged one of them in the leg.

"After them," Harry cried. He picked up the policeman's Glock and emptied the compartment of spare bullets from the man's belt into one hand.

They had dropped four of the six policemen, and hadn't even gotten to Carmen and Merle yet.

They broke into the open and took after the pair of fleeing policemen. The men stretched their legs to reach the mighty pillars of Luxor. There, two more figures joined them as they bounded for safety behind the tall ice columns.

One was limping badly.

"That's Stevens!" Boris said huffing in the bone-dry air.

"The other must be Carmen," Harry surmised. He fired a shot over their heads to force them to turn back.

The pair and their police companions veered away from the fifty-foot pillars and made for open ground.

Why were they risking exposure?

Harry and Boris took chase. But they didn't gain much ground as they passed a large rectangle cut into the ice. It was the size and shape of an Olympic-sized swimming pool. Water flowed swiftly under the opening. Out of the corner of his eye, Harry caught several bobbing swimming caps. A group of old men was swimming bare-chested in the cold water. Their sure, even strokes kept them in place as they swam against the swift current.

Then Harry looked forward at Carmen's group. They were sprinting away from the cover of the ice sculptures. He fired another shot above their heads, and they veered like a group of antelope.

Then he saw where they were headed. Glistening in the sunlight like a string of pearls, a line of gondolas was heading out over the frozen river.

"They're headed for Sun Island," he breathed.

Merle, Carmen, and the two policemen piled into a gondola. Just as Harry arrived, the door slid shut and locked in place. An arm reached out the open gondola window.

"Run for cover," Harry cried, and they plunged into a snowdrift behind the station.

The policemen began pouring lead into the snow around Harry and Boris. The two weren't alone. Several families joined them trying to escape the mad gunfire. In the distance, the gondola swung back and forth as it vanished into the sunlight.

Using his Chinese, Boris threw some questions at the people huddled beside him. They answered in frightened voices.

"There's another way across," he translated. "Dog sled."

Then Harry spotted a team of Huskies just beyond the station. "Let's go!"

The two men commandeered the sled, with Harry taking the reins. Sensing a pair of riders, the dogs sprang to their feet. A solid flick of the reigns across their backs sent them flying on their fixed route across the river.

Squatting to lower his center of balance, Harry trained his eyes on the swinging gondola. Hunched in the front of the sled, Boris fired away at the gondola, but his shots flew erratically off the mark.

The gunshots only served to frighten the dogs, which ran faster. They jumped over snowdrifts while Harry fought for balance on the wooden sleigh.

Ice pellets spat up around them. The policemen had spotted the sleigh and were emptying their clips on them. Harry heard Carmen's screams from within the gondola. Gunpowder stung the air.

The dog sled was faster than the gondola, but it didn't take long for Harry to realize that the dogs weren't headed in exactly the same direction as the gondola. The frightened dogs were veering under it!

Within seconds, they would pass directly beneath it, and Harry had no way of stopping the dog team.

As they approached the gondola, Boris's pistol appeared to jam. The policemen's firing also came to a halt. In the eerie quiet, all Harry heard was the dogs' rhythmic breathing, their soft paw steps, and the smooth blades of the sled against the snow.

A man's face appeared at the window just above them.

"Do you know what you're doing?" the man shouted in English. It was Merle Stevens.

"I'm trying to find Flowers' family."

"No, you're trying to throw the Presidential elections for the terrorists, just like in Spain. You're trying to kick us out of the Middle East."

"I'm just trying to kick a crook out of the White House."

At that point, the sled passed under the gondola, which glided along, suspended forty feet overhead.

Merle didn't try to communicate after that. Instead, a hail of bullets sprayed the snow in front of them as the valiant Huskies emerged on the other side.

"Mush!" Harry cried as they raced for the banks of Sun Island.

Chapter 34

Sandi DiMartino returned to the Chinagate special prosecutor's office from the Maryland cemetery and heaped her trench coat over the back of her desk chair. She was determined to help review the final brief that Stanley Polk would present to the federal judge. Suddenly, her female assistant signaled her from across the room.

"It's the coroner," the assistant shouted, pointing to the phone.

"Don't you mean pathologist?"

The woman shrugged and handed her the phone. Sandi was right. It was the pathologist.

"I could go ahead with the examination of the DNA," the man began. "But I thought I'd draw something to your attention at the outset."

"Go on," Sandi said, and took her seat. She wasn't picking up positive vibes from the man's tone of voice.

"As soon as I returned to the lab, I opened the urn."

"Yes?"

"There were bones in there. You know how foreign countries haven't quite perfected cremation yet, and they leave lots of bones."

"No, but go on."

"Well, it's clear at first glance—these are not human bones."

"What do you mean?"

"One thing is for certain. These are not human remains."

"That's great news," Sandi said, letting out her breath with relief. But she quickly regained her composure. "Can you write that up in a report and have it to my office by the start of business tomorrow?"

She could include it as evidence in the brief.

"Sure thing. Not a problem."

She thanked the man, and set the phone down with a smile. It was a tired, happy smile. Raymond's family was still somewhere out there.

On his way to checking out the suspicious PSB Psn 14 site, Badger McGlade passed through downtown Harbin. It was a thriving city with a substantial downtown. Near the highway, some gleaming highrises overlooked immediate countryside. A computer geek, he was impressed by the heartiness of the human race as people went about their daily routines, such as shopping, working, riding their bicycle carts, gathering trash in their garbage trucks, and hauling mounds of crushed rock in oversized dump trucks.

The taxi sped along the ice-covered highway on bald tires with no chains. Not even studs. Badger could visualize them skidding into a ditch and never reaching the prison.

The landscape was flat with cropland on the south side of the highway, and forests to the north.

The defroster either wasn't working or had never been installed. Badger kept shaving frost off the windshield for the driver, who was content to peer through a tiny peephole that he scraped for himself.

The sun rimmed the horizon that day, casting long shadows over the snow. But the sky was bright blue and the golden glow was cheery.

"There's the wild tiger preserve," Raymond O. Flowers called from the back seat.

Badger cleared a spot to look out his window. The gateway around the entrance reminded him of a wild animal safari park in the States.

The driver was grunting, slowing down, and heading for the shoulder.

"No! Keep going!" Badger shouted.

"*Qing jixu. Jixu wang qian zou,*" Raymond called from the back seat. Keep going straight ahead.

At least someone spoke Chinese.

The driver resumed his former speed and direction, leaving Badger sweating at the armpits.

A minute later, Raymond cried out, "There it is! *Ting che!*"

This time, the driver didn't seem to want to stop. Perhaps he felt burned by his last attempt to stop the car.

"Stop the freaking car!" Badger shouted.

The driver cowered, but drove on.

Badger tried to reach around the driver's plastic protective cage to grab the wheel but couldn't.

"*Ting che!*" everyone was yelling from the back seat.

The driver took one look at the facility and kept plowing ahead.

"Oh, man," Badger said. "This ain't gonna work. He doesn't want to go there. How do we stop the car?"

Raymond pried his door open, ready to jump out, but the speed was too great. The open door threw off the driver's trajectory, and they began skidding toward a high snow bank on the near shoulder.

"Brace yourselves!" Badger yelled.

But how could they? There were no seatbelts, and Raymond was hanging halfway out of the taxi.

The collision sent Badger's shoulder into the windshield. Likewise, the driver flew forward, engaging himself in the steering wheel and landing hard on the horn.

Badger heard a torso slam into the driver's cage, and the other team member knocked over the back of his passenger's seat. Raymond was nowhere in sight.

The taxi kept moving after impact, flipping onto its side and sliding down the highway. Meanwhile, a huge yellow road grader barreled down on them. Turned on his side and lying on a cracked window, Badger had only a moment to brace for the ensuing impact.

His seat was wedged up against him by one of the team. His face was pressed to the windshield. The yellow grader loomed above him.

Raymond's door came slamming shut on top of the car.

Blaring his horn, the road grader streaked inches from the windshield, its blade catching the taxi's trunk. Badger held onto the dashboard as they spun in nauseating circles down the road on their side.

The driver flopped lifelessly in his cage. Behind Badger, there was silence. Was he the lone survivor? And where was Raymond?

The taxi finally came to a halt with one final, bone-jarring jolt. Badger squeezed his eyes shut and braced himself, but went flying through the air with a windshield's worth of shattered glass. He landed on his back atop a snowdrift, several yards from the highway.

He might as well keep his eyes closed. And make angels in the snow.

❖ ❖ ❖

Badger McGlade gradually regained consciousness, but couldn't open his heavy eyelids. He was on a cold surface. God, Harbin was cold. Everything about it was cold.

But he wasn't lying on snow. It felt hard, like a table.

Then he noticed that the sun shone directly overhead. How could that be possible? He was in the far north, unless someone had transported him to the Equator. He felt slight warmth from the light above him. Perhaps he was back on Hainan Island.

If so, he had died and gone to heaven.

At last, he pried his eyes open, slowly letting his new environment seep into his consciousness.

That was no sun directly overhead. It was some sort of medical light in an operating theater.

"Easy now," came an old man's heavily accented voice.

In the lamp's reflector, Badger made out a familiar face next to him. It was the famed Raymond O. Flowers, his eyes closed as if he were asleep, his body laid out on a second slab. Along the side of his face, poor Raymond had sustained a bruise that was just beginning to puff out and turn colors.

Then Badger smelled the strong odor of garlic. He looked overhead. An old Chinese doctor was leaning over him, breathing in his face.

"You're a lucky man," the doctor said in English.

Badger couldn't believe his ears.

The doctor laughed nervously beneath his white surgical mask. "Oh, don't worry. You're still in China. See?"

He pulled off his thick eyeglasses and revealed two oriental eyes.

"I speak English because I learned Special English over the years on VOA and BBC. And you're a lucky man. All of you foreigners survived the crash, but the taxi driver did not."

Badger tried to sit up and look at Raymond.

"I can't move," he said.

The doctor laughed again. "That's because your brain needs time to fully recover."

"Am I paralyzed?"

"Not at all. But you're still in shock."

Did the doctor learn medicine over the radio as well? "Am I hurt? I can't feel a thing."

"Good," the doctor said, and reached toward Badger's temples with a pair of long, thin needles.

"No!" Badger cried.

But he couldn't move, and the acupuncture needles only felt like a pair of thumbs pressed lightly against his temples. The effect of the needles was instantaneous. Feeling rushed to his toes. He wiggled them.

"More!" he shouted. "Give me more needles!"

The doctor laughed, his facemask billowing in and out with every labored breath. "You still need your rest."

Two pins approached just above Badger's eyebrows.

"These will help you sleep."

The room blurred as his eyes crossed. He knew he was in good hands, and fell into a peaceful slumber.

Harry Black and Boris spilled out of the dogsled as they came to a halt at the far side of the frozen Songhua River.

A hundred yards to Harry's left, the gondola disappeared among the trees.

Rubbing the soreness from his arms, he dragged himself up a path through the snow toward the sound of voices. Who else would be out on the frozen island?

He emerged from the woods with Boris and had to blink several times to believe what he saw. He was surrounded by frosty white architectural edifices, elephants, giraffes, wolves, and mermaids carved out of solid chunks of snow.

He stumbled about. Was he in a trance?

Crowds of spectators milled about the feet of the statues. They frolicked in the foot-deep snow amidst the awe-inspiring sculptures that rose up around them.

Flags from different nations fluttered in the snow beside the gleaming sculptures. Harry approached the American team that was hard at work on an amorphous blob carved out of blocks of snow. Perhaps they had seen Merle and Carmen and the policemen.

"Hi," he said.

The two men didn't look up, but responded in a friendly way. "Are you enjoying yourselves?" one asked as he carved some snake scales into the rear end of the blob.

"Somewhat," Harry said. "Seen any other Americans around

here?"

"We're the only ones for miles around," the other man said. "We're the only American team here in Harbin. Brad's from Arizona and I'm here from Chicago, where we love the cold."

"I see," Harry said, looking past the men for any sign of the Public Security Bureau police.

It was hard to take his eyes off the strange, horned head that the other man was sculpting fifteen feet in the air.

He circled under the head to get a better look. "What in the world are you making?"

"We're doing a half-buffalo and half-snake creature," the young man from Arizona said enthusiastically. "It has symbolic meaning to the Chinese."

Boris looked dubious. "Okay."

"Well, good luck," Harry said.

Stomping his feet for warmth, Harry ran from sculpture to sculpture. Peering ahead through the smooth edged lines of ice, he looked for any sign of Merle and the Chinese. But all he found was a continuous stream of happy tourists wandering through the forest wonderland.

The cold was getting to him. His face began to hurt. It felt squeezed by some cryogenic technique, and pinched in such a way that he would look distorted for the rest of his life. The world was out of focus, and his head pounded.

"There they are!" Boris rasped under his breath. "Near the gondola station."

Sure enough, the last pair of policemen was standing in line to take a gondola back to the city. Guarding them at the rear were Merle and Carmen, their backs to the station, a pistol in Merle's hand.

They stood beside a grizzly bear rearing on its icy hind legs. Harry could see Carmen glancing around alertly.

Harry summoned Boris to follow him. He circled through the crowd and then through a stand of trees to the far side of the grizzly bear statue. A team from Singapore was patching on fur icicles and adding some final touches to the precariously tall beast.

Harry removed a glove and gripped the Glock in his pocket. In the minus twenty-degree chill, his exposed fingers had frozen around the grip.

Great. He was frozen to his gun.

Peeling his fingers away would be painful. Then Carmen turned his way. Her back was to Merle, and Harry could see the anxiety written on her face. He signaled her with a half-wave, and their eyes locked. She instantly relaxed and forced a wink.

The two policemen in their navy blue overcoats were piling into a gondola, leaving Merle and Carmen alone.

Harry advanced to the shadows of the bear and pulled the Glock halfway from his pocket, enough for her to see it. She nodded.

Spinning around on the toes of her boots, she kicked out at the pistol that extended from Merle's hand. The dull black gun arced out of his hand, and Harry jumped out from behind the bear.

"Freeze!" he yelled, the blunt muzzle of his Glock pointed squarely at Merle's head.

"What an unfortunate use of terms," Merle said, suave despite his predicament.

Carmen tore herself free of him, picked up Merle's firearm, and ran to Boris. The Singaporeans paused in their work to watch the two men facing off.

"Now what?" Merle asked, eyeing Harry suspiciously and trying to circle away.

"Now you take us to Raymond's family."

Merle ruefully shook his head, as if Harry didn't understand. "Don't you see? As long as the Chinese hold them, the President is safe. You release them, and the entire Administration will go down."

"I don't care about the Administration," Harry said. "And something tells me you don't either. So don't try to wrap yourself in the flag."

"I am an officer of the United States Government," Merle said impressively, if not defiantly. "You don't understand what's at stake here."

"Yeah, I know what's at stake. Your scam, that's what you stand to lose. But I'm here to tell you something else, buddy. You stand to face life behind bars for covering this one up for the President. And I'm thinking Guantánamo is too good for you."

Merle's grin was frozen on his face. "Why? Is Raymond O. Flowers enjoying his time there?"

"Make that past tense," Harry said. "He's here with me in Harbin. And he wants his family back. And there's nothing you can say that will change that."

"He seemed to be getting along quite well without them," Merle said with a lewd twinkle in his eyes.

"On the contrary, you brought him to his knees with their supposed deaths. You turned him into a common criminal, not unlike yourself. Now you'll show us where you're keeping the family, or..."

"Or what? You'll shoot me?"

Harry hesitated.

"Or what?" Merle taunted, edging closer to the gondola. "If I die, you'll never find his family. You need me."

Bone-dry wind whipped out of the blue sky and whistled through the barren trees. Harry turned to Boris. "Get me a bucket of water from the cable car station."

Merle's handsome eyes focused on Harry, who was having a hard time keeping his head from exploding in the cold.

"You don't have the right to do anything to me," Merle said. "Killing a federal officer is a capital offense."

"Give me your coat." Harry reached out and began unzipping Merle's coat. Merle grinned in his face, as Harry pulled off the parka and threw it against a low snow wall built around another exhibit.

Boris arrived with a bucket from which steam was rising.

"Pour it over him," Harry ordered. "We'll turn him into a living ice sculpture. That ought to take the prize."

Boris lifted the bucket over Merle's head.

Curious onlookers closed in on the small group. Perhaps it was some sort of demonstration, whereby a man could survive despite wearing a sheet of ice.

"Give me my coat," Merle grumbled in resignation, unable to keep the shiver out of his voice. "I'll take you to his family."

Boris lowered the bucket halfway.

"First tell us where they are," Harry demanded.

"They're in a prison just beyond the tiger park," Merle said, clutching his arms for warmth. "But knowing that won't do you any good."

"Why not?"

Merle's beautiful teeth were chattering audibly. "They won't give up the prisoners unless I authorize their release. You have to take me with you."

"Let's go, then," Harry said, waving his free hand at Boris. "Grab his coat and let's go."

Boris set the bucket down in the snow. A disappointed groan rose from the crowd.

"There's a shuttle bus," Merle said. "That'll take us there."

Boris scooped up the coat and threw it to Carmen, and they began to trudge through the dispersing crowd. Merle took them to a vast, icy parking lot where exhaust rose from cars and buses as they nudged toward the single exit.

Merle took them to a twenty-seater, its windows steamed up from a heater inside.

"Good enough," Harry said, and directed the small team and captive there. The warmth sucked them up at once, and the driver slammed the door shut behind them.

Harry could barely balance on his frozen feet. He pushed Merle into the seat opposite the driver, and stood rocking over him. "Tell him where to go."

Merle spoke in Chinese to the driver, who responded in what sounded like an explosion of shrieking expletives.

Merle calmly indicated the gun in Harry's frozen hand.

Wordlessly, the driver put the bus in gear and began to angle them between cars toward the exit.

Chapter 35

Raymond O. Flowers stirred comfortably on the examination table. All his body parts were sending back pleasurable reports, and his skin tingled reassuringly.

He adjusted his glasses and rolled his head to one side. Lying there was the man they called Badger McGlade. His shirt and pants had all been rolled back, exposing an entire body punctured by needles, as if he were some sort of voodoo doll. And the strange thing was the smile on the poor guy's face!

Then his eyes fell on a pack of paper diapers, the tiny kind that only the smallest babies used. He hadn't seen diapers like that in five years.

The next thing that entered his awareness was the sound of firecrackers. Someone was celebrating outside the building.

What sort of a building was it, anyway? The bright, overhead lamp looked like it belonged in a dentist's office or hospital operating room.

Then the car crash came back to him in fragmented images. He associated no pain with the event as he had smashed into the back of the taxi driver's cage.

Badger had been sitting in the front passenger's seat, and the two members from Harry's team were sitting in the back seat beside him. Where had they gone?

He rolled his head in the other direction. Two prone bodies lay crammed between a cabinet and his examination table. Their heads were wrapped in bandages, and IV tubes dripped into their forearms. They were either asleep or still passed out.

He studied the interior of the room. It was a rudimentary examination room, turned into a sickbay.

So why the continuous string of firecrackers?

A door opened to the outside and he heard men shouting in Chinese. Boots stomped into the building along with the rustle of coats and some heavy breathing.

The firecrackers began to sound more like automatic weapons. Then the door whooshed closed. Several soldiers in green wool overcoats hauled a wounded comrade into the room, and an old man in a lab coat directed them where to lay the victim on the floor. Blood was oozing from the poor man's mouth that was contorted with pain.

Raymond eased himself into a sitting position. "Badger," he whispered. "Wake up!"

He reached over and shook Badger's arm. Then he noticed that his own arms were exposed. Both forearms were covered with tiny needles as were his calves, making him look like he had been attacked by a porcupine. More likely he was part of some diabolical doctor's experiment. He began to pluck the prickly needles out of his skin.

"Take it easy," the doctor said, rushing over to help Raymond.

"What are all these needles for?"

"To relieve the pain," the doctor explained, his voice kind, but weary.

"Am I injured?" Raymond asked, testing out his arms and legs.

"No bone damage. Just some stitches here and there."

Again, the front door opened in the corridor. This time Raymond could tell for sure that a battle was raging outside.

Two Chinese soldiers charged into the small room. One was carrying a makeshift white flag. He thrust it into Raymond's hands and pulled him to the edge of his table. The doctor began helping Raymond put on his shoes.

Badger was beginning to stir as if reluctant to give up a pleasant dream.

"Badger, what are they doing to us?" Raymond shouted.

The poor guy seemed so out of it, he wouldn't know any more than Raymond did. So he had to leave Badger lying prostrate on the other examination table. As he was pulled to his feet, Raymond got a better look at the two other members of Harry Black's team. They had fared worse in the car crash, having flown into the front seat and against the windshield.

Raymond turned to the doctor as his shoes hit the floor. "Where's my family?"

The old man offered a kind smile and turned his head, indicating the back of the building.

"I won't go anywhere without them!" Raymond cried.

"Leave, please," the doctor said, holding out his hands imploringly.

"Is my family okay?" Raymond shouted over his shoulder as the soldiers shoved him out of the room.

"In perfect health!" the doctor called after him.

All concerns for his safety disappeared. They were still alive!

The soldiers pushed at the front door, exposing him to the cold air and din of battle.

He could see soldiers crouching at positions along the top of a wall and firing toward the roadway. Shots volleyed back just as fast.

He tried to hold onto the doorframe. Wooden splinters gouged into his fingers, calloused from a week at sea. After coming so far, he wasn't going to die in a hailstorm of bullets and leave his family to fend for themselves.

A firm hand, thick as a farmer's, tried to pry his fingers away from the building.

Raymond leaned into the back of the soldier's hand and sank his teeth into the flesh. The man howled with pain and leaped back.

"That's for holding my family in this freezing dump," Raymond said, and spat a chunk of skin back at the man who was doubled over in pain.

Several rounds of hot lead flew through the air and seared into the door behind his head. He turned with his improvised white flag to strike the next soldier in line.

But the man grimly caught his arm, blunted the blow, and wrested the crude weapon away. Raymond could tell from the fear in his eyes, that the man wanted him out of the prison in order to stop the bloodshed.

"Go on, Raymond," came a shout through gritted teeth. Raymond looked back and saw Badger McGlade, his distant form leaning against the darkened hallway. Even Badger wanted to bring the senseless violence to an end.

A soldier screamed in agony and fell from the compound wall, landing with a bone-breaking crunch at Raymond's feet.

Raymond felt his resistance quickly ebbing away.

He allowed the grim soldier to hustle him across the compound.

The guy thrust the white flag back in his hands. Another soldier opened a small wooden door beside a larger swinging gate for vehicles.

Raymond closed his eyes and pushed the white flag out through the parted door. The gunfire came to a temporary stop. He looked back at the soldiers. Relief was etched in their broad, Manchurian features.

"It's me," Raymond called across the expanse of snow that was packed hard by tire tracks. A dilapidated tourist bus stood smoldering twenty yards away. "Hold your fire."

"Come out!" a familiar voice rang from behind the bus. It was Harry Black.

It was a voice he could trust.

He took a step out the door, then another. Waving the flag above his head, he advanced toward the bus. As he neared it, he could see that it was riddled with bullet holes. Halfway there, he broke into a run and ducked for cover behind the engine block. There, Harry threw a parka around him.

"Ouch!"

"What?"

Raymond removed the coat to show both arms, still covered with the gleaming needles.

"Why all the needles?" Harry asked.

"There's a doctor in there who thinks acupuncture is the cure for everything."

Harry rolled his eyes. Carmen stepped around him and began picking the needles out of his skin.

"Who else is in there?" Harry asked impatiently.

"Badger and your other two men. They appear hurt, but at least they survived."

"Survived what?" asked Boris, the tall member of the team.

"We had a major accident on the highway. Our car overturned, and apparently the prison guards carried us here to see their doctor. I spoke with the old guy and he confirmed that my family is being held inside—"

Just then his eyes fell on a fourth person that he recognized—Merle Stevens. The strapping young diplomat was standing unarmed with his back to the bus, hoping not to be recognized.

His cover blown, Merle produced a broad smile—the same reassuring smile that he had displayed when he picked Raymond off the pavement at the Beijing Airport, when he handed Raymond his family's ashes, when they had met again in Shanghai, and when he had given Raymond the account number where he could stash the President's ill-gotten gains.

The only thing Raymond was reassured of now was the bastard's guilt.

With a sudden, terrible vengeance that he had never felt before, Raymond ran toward the supercilious secret agent and threw a shoulder into his chest. Merle staggered sideways, his feet scraping futilely on the ice, and landed far from the rear of the bus.

An eruption of gunfire from the compound tore the agent's body apart. It spun in pinwheels of blood that sprayed in spirals across the snow. Merle's body finally came to rest twenty feet away, sprawled on its back for all the world to see, the limbs unmoving, steam no longer emerging from the lips.

"Way to go, Raymond!" Carmen said.

"They've got my family!" Raymond cried, turning on the prison with an overpowering sense of rage.

"Easy now, Superman," Harry said, preventing him from leaving the protection of the bus.

Just then a woman's cry arose from the rear of the compound. That was followed by the screams of two children as they were forced to fall a great distance.

At first, they sounded vaguely familiar, like an auditory hallucination. They were cries he had heard so long ago, coming from the back of an ambulance, that they couldn't be real. Nor could anybody still exist who uttered them. Yet, in his heart, he recognized the voices instantly. And they came piercing through his consciousness like a spasm of pleasure. The individual personality of each cry was so familiar to him, he could visualize the fear on their faces. His family was calling out to him in need.

"What's on the other side of that metal fence?" he asked the others.

Harry looked at Boris, then Carmen, then directly at him. Deep growls emanated from the neighboring property as the family thrashed through trees and stumbled across the snow.

"Your family's in a Siberian tiger preserve," Harry told Raymond, as if his wind had been knocked out of him.

Chapter 36

Harry Black listened to the sounds and voices of a woman and two children thrashing through trees on the opposite side of the fence. There was also what sounded like a tiny baby's cry rising in the frozen air. Then there came the deep growl of hungry tigers. He was under no illusions as to their safety. They had jumped out of a prison and into the jungle.

"The prison guards released your family into a wild tiger preserve," he tried to explain calmly to Raymond O. Flowers. His wife and children were in danger of being torn apart by fangs and claws.

"Where did that little cry come from?" the disoriented Raymond cried.

Harry thought for a moment. He and his men were pinned down behind a bus by prison guards. There was no way to clear the tiger preserve fence from their position. They would have to drive around on the icy highway to the entrance of the preserve.

He looked hopelessly around for some means of escape.

Suddenly gunfire erupted from inside the prison compound. A truck's engine coughed several times, then started up inside. No bullets whizzed in their direction or embedded themselves in the side of the bus.

"What the—" Harry said.

Gunfire crackled in the brittle air, temporarily covering the roar of the frenzied tigers.

"It's Badger and your men!" Raymond exclaimed. "They're breaking out. Hold your fire!"

At that very moment, a Chinese personnel carrier broke through the front gate of the prison. It was pursued by a hail of bullets from guards along the wall of the compound.

Badger's head was bent down for cover behind the steering wheel. The two other heavily bandaged team members sat beside him, one firing back through an open window.

Harry made out the distant sound of scores of people scrambling over a wall at the back of the prison, away from the tiger preserve. Who were they?

Badger was about to zoom past him.

Harry jumped out from behind the bus and waved his arms. Badger saw him and jammed on the brakes, sliding several yards to a halt beside the punctured shell of the bus.

Harry made a mental note to give Badger a raise the next pay period.

He waved for Raymond, Carmen, and Boris to follow him. Carmen and Boris rushed in front of the personnel carrier for protection, but Raymond lingered behind.

What was keeping him?

Then Harry saw why.

Raymond stood slump-shouldered over the body of Merle Stevens. With a vicious kick, he struck deep into the fallen spy's side. The only response was a dull thud, not even an involuntary muscle twitch. The bastard was a corpse.

Satisfied that he had finally laid the cause of his nightmares to rest, Raymond came loping back. A rueful, pained expression filled his face. Behind a violent flurry of loud smacking bullets that ripped into the sides of the personnel carrier, Harry led the team at a trot toward the highway.

The moving truck proved a perfect shield for blocking bullets, and they reached the four-lane without injury. At that great distance from the prison, gunfire no longer sought them out.

"I'll drive," he said. "Everybody else in back."

He opened the shredded canvas flap at the back of the personnel carrier. In the dwindling light, his team members scrambled out of the cab and up into the enclosed flatbed. Bandaged and contorted in pain, they had suffered from no additional injuries. He gave Raymond, Carmen, and Boris a boost and they all piled in.

Then he circled around to the front where Badger had already moved into the passenger seat.

"Good job, old man," Harry told the youngster.

Like Raymond, Badger was wearing a layer of needles, and they didn't look very comfortable. He needed Carmen's gentle touch to remove them.

"You jump in back, too, and have Carmen treat you. I'm taking us into the tiger preserve."

Raymond O. Flowers reached out and hauled Badger McGlade into the rear of the personnel carrier. Then the truck fishtailed across a sheet of ice as they raced to the entrance of the tiger preserve.

"Did you see Raymond's family?" Carmen calmly asked the young Badger.

"Yes, I did see them," Badger replied, as he settled into the wooden bench and let Carmen pluck the needles out of his skin.

Raymond closed his eyes. Finally...human contact with his family, proof that they still lived. He nodded to Badger in thanks.

But that was ten long minutes ago. Were they still alive in the dangerous tiger preserve?

"The Chinese are desperately trying to get rid of all the evidence," Badger explained. "We have to get inside the tiger preserve and pick them up."

"Can tigers climb trees?" Raymond asked, trying to visualize how his family might escape danger.

"I don't know," Badger said, the thought lingering in the icy air.

A sudden swerve brought half the occupants flying toward the other side of the truck. Harry was sparing nothing in his determination to save Raymond's family.

The rumble of their tires drowned out any sound of tigers.

Raymond felt sick with anxiety. Not since he first received the mysterious message in his hotel room in Hainan had he felt such desire to see them. And the closer he got to them, the stronger the craving became.

Perhaps, as before in Beijing, it was his own presence that endangered them.

He shook off the thought. He watched through the open flap in the canvas at the back of the personnel carrier as they swung off the highway. They began to streak through sparse, wind-gnarled conifer trees that poked up randomly as if a child had stuck matchsticks in the snow. They were not trees his family could climb to safety.

Then the high fence came into view, like a cheap, snowy version of Jurassic Park. Somewhere within that enclosure, the wild cats were circling Carolyn, Jane and Sammy...drawing closer.

In an extremely short day, the long shadows were disappearing in the dusk.

Raymond pulled off the last remaining needles from his legs and rolled his pants down. The short, stabbing pain of the needles was nothing compared with what Carolyn must be going through. He would gladly endure greater pain to spring his family free. He would throw himself into the path of a tiger.

The personnel carrier took a sudden turn and veered toward the fence. Harry was picking up more speed.

"Hold on tight!" Badger shouted.

A moment later, Raymond heard wood cracking, then splintering. Wires scraped against the sides of the vehicle.

They had bashed through the front gate.

Harry gunned the engine and Raymond was rocked back by another collision. Then he heard a same scraping sound of wire, some tearing apart the canvas roof overhead.

Raymond held the rear flap open. The shattered remains of a double-entrance gate lay in twisted tatters in the snow.

They were inside the park!

"Carolyn!" Raymond screamed. "Jane! Sammy!"

His voice vanished quickly in the open land. The others kept silent, letting their ears search for a response.

Through the rear flap, he made out a huge tiger licking blood from his paws. His breath was icy, but he seemed utterly warm in his coat of orange, black, and white stripes.

There were more tigers, stretching their gargantuan lengths against the trunks of trees. Others prowled, heads lowered, their noses seeking out their next dinner. A white Siberian tiger, stood out against the darkening sky, its bright chest catching the last glow of warmth from the sun.

He had never seen so many tigers in his entire life, much less in one place. The compound, with its stripped-down trees and artificial mountains, was crawling with the creatures, which were clearly in their element.

Still no sound of his family!

As the personnel carrier rumbled over a snowy track in the general direction of the prison, a tiger charged them. It aimed right at Raymond's position by the back flap. For a heart-stopping moment, he tried to tie the canvas flap down. The tiger's claws ripped through the fabric with a malicious swipe.

The foul breath of the beast felt hot on Raymond's face. One of the team drew out a pistol, but never fired. Through the ripped covering, Raymond could see the exhausted tiger pull up short, confident that he had frightened off the intruding vehicle.

Oh, where were Carolyn and the kids?

They passed one big cat in a gully feasting his catch. Raymond stood up to look as it sank its teeth into the flesh. It came up with a mouth full of chicken feathers.

He sank back onto the floor with relief.

Suddenly a weapon discharged from the cabin. It was Harry, shooting madly out the window.

"Hey, you!" Harry screamed, trying to shoo some large beast away.

Had he found some tigers stalking his family? If so, that meant that his wife and kids were still alive!

Raymond could feel his heart racing in his chest. His adrenaline had reached a new peak. He was on the verge of rescuing the loves of his life.

The personnel carrier lurched off the level track and began to grind up a snowy slope. The bumps threw Raymond and the others into the air. His foot came crashing down atop someone else's boot, and he slipped sideways, hitting the floor hard on one elbow. The next bump shook him into a sitting position on the compartment floor. Badger dragged him up onto the bench.

The gunfire continued unabated from the front cabin.

Raymond rushed forward in the troop compartment and tried to catch a glimpse of what was happening up ahead. A piece of plywood had been screwed into the former window's frame. He couldn't view into the cab. He yanked at the board with his fingers.

Then he felt someone else helping. It was Boris. Working together, they tore the wood away, revealing the back of Harry's head. In front of him, through the frosted window, he made out a swaying, swerving landscape of muted white with the occasional shadow of a tree.

Harry was aiming his semi-automatic pistol straight down into the snow. Raymond could see why. A tiger was trying to sink its teeth into the truck's front left tire. Harry was screaming at another tiger that was bounding along on its wide, padded paws keeping pace with the truck.

They ground higher up the slope, at times sliding back a few feet before finding better traction elsewhere.

"Why are we going up there?" Raymond shouted through the opening.

"Can't you see them?" Harry yelled. He took his hand off the steering wheel for only a second to point directly ahead.

Raymond had trouble focusing on the distance. The windshield was all but covered with ice, and anything beyond that was a blur of motion.

Then he saw a small cluster of black shapes clawing their way up the hill.

"It's your family!" Harry shouted.

Raymond glued his eyes to them.

"Carolyn! Jane! Sammy!" he called frantically. "Climb into the truck!"

The personnel carrier was falling further behind his family, and the distraction of the pair of tigers gnawing on their tires kept Harry from concentrating fully on climbing the hill.

"Can't you shoot the tigers?" Raymond yelled.

"I've wounded mine," Harry said, "But he won't stop. He's just getting angrier."

Raymond did recognize one advantage to Harry chasing his family up the hill. He was distracting the tigers, offering up the army truck as a more promising prey than the humans.

He scrambled backward in the rear compartment where Badger was trying to hold the flap shut. Tripping in the darkness and falling over several pairs of legs, he reached the canvas opening.

"What are you doing?" Badger shouted. "There's a pack of tigers following us."

Raymond fought to wrest the canvas from his hands. He would throw himself into the snow. Let them gnaw him to death. Just spare his family.

With a grinding lurch, the vehicle sent him flying off his feet once more. He came down hard on the corrugated metal floor as it came up to meet him. He scrambled to his feet only to have them skid out from under him as the vehicle rapidly gained speed.

It took him a few seconds of cold metal bashing against the back of his head to realize that they were moving again. In fact the truck must have breeched the top of the hill and was heading straight down the other side.

He scrambled to his hands and knees and faced the rear of the truck where Badger had lost his grip on the canvas. In the intermittent light, he caught sight of his family as the personnel carrier whizzed past them.

Raymond rose to his full height, his mouth agape.

Carolyn dashed through the deep snow, clutching her chest with one hand and clawing the air with the other. She ran at full tilt, with little Sammy clinging to the fabric of her sleeve. Then they passed his daughter Jane, who was running ahead of them. She always was a good runner.

He and the team were drawing too far ahead. They had to slow down!

Following closely in the snow kicked up by the rear wheels was a pack of a dozen tigers, streaking through the graying shadows after the vehicle.

"Hold on!" Harry cried through the opening to the cabin.

With both hands, Raymond clutched the metal rim that held the canvas roof in place.

A moment later his fingers were ripped from the metal and he fell backward under a jolting thud, followed by the clatter of a crashing fence. The collision had thrown him away from the canvas opening, but he scrambled to grab the rear gate and steady himself.

First the front wheels flattened the perimeter fence. Then the back wheels smashed what was left of the chain link fence into the snow.

And the tigers kept running.

Raymond pulled himself to his feet. His family slowed down, panting, to watch.

Harry was setting the tigers free!

The mass of orange and black and white fur and dark gums and gleaming fangs slowed as the beasts found themselves in unfamiliar territory.

Raymond was aware of the situation long before the tigers were. "You're free!" he shouted.

He threw his hands in the air to shoo them off.

"Run away. You're free!"

The personnel carrier was limping on several blown tires, but the furry predators didn't seem to care. Their attention had turned away from the chase, and toward their new horizon. One by one, they scampered off across the snowy fields that opened up before them, a land of farms and forests, where there were no fences to imprison them.

Raymond was the first to recognize that the personnel carrier's forward motion had stopped. He scrambled over the rear gate, jumped out, and landed on the flattened mesh that was embedded in the snow.

"It's me!" he shouted. "It's Daddy!"

He reached his family just as they stepped tentatively onto the broken fence. They looked at him without recognition.

"It's okay," he said. "It's all over. Daddy has come to get you."

Carolyn was leaning forward, coughing, and clutching a bundle within her coat. He grabbed her before she slumped to the snow.

"Raymond?" she asked, as if the name were coming back to her over a great distance.

"Yes, it's me!"

Her model-like, half-moon eyes with their light green irises could use a touch of makeup, her skin was worn with worry, her cheeks gaunt and sallow, and her hair had become streaked with gray. But her inner radiance seemed no worse for the wear. In fact, she seemed to have been invigorated by the romp in the snow. She was a survivor.

It was young Sammy who was in tears from the frightening events. He gasped for breath, and tried to rein in his racing heart.

With Carolyn holding onto him, Raymond raised Sammy into his arms and held him tight to his chest. The young lad was inconsolable.

"That's okay," Raymond said. "You may cry all you want."

He felt a tug from behind.

"Daddy?"

"Yes, honey," he said, turning to kneel beside Jane.

"You aren't wearing a coat."

"You're right! You're absolutely right! I am not wearing a coat, and I should be, shouldn't I?"

Carolyn let out an involuntary laugh.

"How silly of me not to be wearing a coat," Raymond said. "We'll have to do something about that won't we?"

Jane threw her arms around one of his legs, throwing him and Sammy slightly off balance. He had to lean against Carolyn for support.

Then a small whimper drifted out of the folds of her coat.

Carolyn smiled at him with a mischievous grin. "I think it's time you met Raymond, Junior," she said.

"Huh?"

She peeled back her collar and unfastened the top button. A small, bald head emerged, then a pair of hazel eyes blinking in the cold air.

"We have a new baby!" she announced.

Before Raymond could ask where Junior had come from, he knew the answer. He had last seen his family nine months before. Raymond Junior was his child!

He leaned down to touch the tiny round head with his lips. "Hi, fella," he said. "I'm your Daddy."

There was another whimper, this one of pleasure.

He stood back and looked at Carolyn. What a woman.

In the distance, he glimpsed a cluster of people scampering through the snow, dodging across open fields.

"Who are they?" he asked.

Tears rolled down Carolyn's cheeks. "That's the North Vietnamese," she said. "This man gave us all the keys to our freedom."

He found himself looking into the eyes of the man called Badger McGlade.

No amount of words could express his thanks.

He grabbed Harry Black by the lapels and drew him forward. "And this man gave me the keys to my freedom."

Carolyn stared at Harry, unable to comprehend the full story behind Raymond's harrowing journey to freedom.

"Shall we go home now?" Harry asked.

The term "home" seemed to have no particular meaning to Carolyn and the kids. Or to Raymond, for that matter.

Two more pairs of tigers bounded past them into the open field, mere streaks of color in the gathering dusk.

"I think we can find somewhere to take you," Harry said, a wisp of steam rising from his lips and disappearing into the vast Manchurian sky.

"We're not far from Russia," Boris piped up. "Anyone game for a ride on the Trans-Siberian Railway?"

Chapter 37

"Your Honor," Stanley Polk said, standing firmly before Federal Judge Henry R. Smith's desk. The two played golf every Wednesday during the summer, but that had no bearing on the formality with which he treated his judicial friend at the moment. The two were alone in the judge's chambers, yet Stanley treated it as a meeting on the record. "I would like you to convene a Federal Grand Jury in the Chinagate case."

"What sort of evidence do you have to present?" Smith asked in measured tones.

Even though a grand jury hearing, did not assert a defendant's guilt, it would look at all the evidence to be presented by the prosecution in order to determine if there were enough grounds to go to a full trial. Stanley believed that he had that evidence.

"Your Honor, I wish to present Raymond O. Flowers' testimony to the jury. This evidence will expose various crimes, all of which I am charging against the defendant."

"Such as?"

"I will accuse the President of taking a bribe, tax evasion, violation of laws limiting sources of income by federal employees, conflict of interest, financing terrorists, attempting to conceal a crime, fraud, misuse of government resources, and several other counts."

"Any other evidence?"

Stanley had to give him a sneak preview of whatever he wanted to see.

"Yes, a pathologist will assert that Flowers' family did not die of SARS, rather the State Department gave him an urn full of canine remains."

Judge Henry R. Smith rolled his eyes. "What witnesses do you wish to call?"

"I will move to subpoena various government employees, including the U.S. Trade Representative, the White House Chief of Staff, and the Director of Central Intelligence. Owing to the probability that many of said witnesses may plead the Fifth Amendment so as not to incriminate themselves, I will need to call on the President himself."

"Do you know that making the Chief Executive testify under oath in a court of law is unprecedented?"

"I am fully aware of that fact, your Honor. However, it does fall within your jurisdiction—"

"Thank you, counselor," Judge Smith cut him off. "I know my authority." He considered for a moment, and then made a pronouncement. "Due to the immediate and grave importance of this matter to our nation, I will convene a hearing at eight o'clock tomorrow morning."

"Thank you, your Honor."

On a snowy evening in Moscow, a bedraggled Raymond and his family appeared at the front gate of the monolithic American Embassy on Novinskiy Boulevard.

He held his arms protectively around his family as he urged them up to the guard booth that stood between them and the twelve-story half-glass, half-concrete chancery.

"Are you sure they'll let us in?" Carolyn asked, clutching their baby tighter. She was reluctant to move any closer to the forbidding window through which they could see nothing, only the reflection of their shivering, huddled family.

"Harry Black told me it would be okay," Raymond said. "I've trusted him so far, and I'm not about to stop."

"But don't they *want* you, dear?" Carolyn whispered to him, her moist, jade-colored eyes revealing the full extent of her fear.

"I have stopped running," Raymond said bravely. "Besides, Sandi DiMartino said I would get my charges dropped if I testify in court."

Carolyn looked beyond him, alarm registering further in her eyes.

"Come on, Daddy," Jane urged. "I see the American flag."

"Me, too," Sammy said.

Raymond looked around him. Strangers under umbrellas were

closing in on him.

His wife gave one final plea. "But will *the President* accept you back?"

Raymond shook his head slowly, words becoming stuck in his throat. He tried to take a decisive step forward toward the glass window, the Marines, the American Embassy, home.

But a hand held him back.

He turned around, and someone thrust a microphone in his face.

A television news correspondent posted to Moscow leaned into the heavy, driving snow. Wind howled against her microphone.

Sandi DiMartino stood nerve-wracked in Attorney General Caleb Perkins's office suite overlooking an oddly quiet Pennsylvania Avenue.

"A family finally returning to the United States a year after the SARS epidemic had swept through China would seem to have undergone a particularly harrowing experience."

The reporter paused to sweep snowflakes out of her hair.

"But just imagine that the American Government forced the family to remain there despite the enormous risk, confined to SARS wards and later a Chinese prison, all at the President's behest, merely for political expediency."

The woman set her script aside and spoke plainly to the camera.

"Is a President's political survival so essential to national security that he should be allowed to negotiate privately with terrorists and suppress the rights of American citizens? Is the President not only above the law, but above humanity?"

"Hey," Sandi said. "Isn't that Rob Reiner in the background? Probably taking down notes for his next Hollywood blockbuster."

Then, behind the reporter, a chant rose up from the throng of spectators. The words were in Russian, a foreign language to Sandi, but the impact was clear. It seemed to embolden the bespectacled Raymond, who prodded his wife and children toward the American Embassy. They took a few steps closer to the locked gate, but were met by imposing coldness.

Raymond leaned down to whisper to his family, or perhaps to shout in their ears as the cry from the crowd rose to a piercing level. Even veteran reporters set down their equipment to encourage the maverick American to step forward, for his homeland to take him back.

His small boy turned to look over his shoulder at the bank of cameras, a question mark written plainly across his face.

Then a tremendous roar rose from the assembled crowd. Sandi scoured the image to find out why. The cameraman was holding the camera high above his head, as the crowd buffeted him.

Snowflakes landed on the lens, but suddenly the cause for celebration became clear.

Slowly, as if the castle ogre had finally concluded his deliberations, the front gate of the Embassy began to swing open for Raymond.

Walking hesitantly toward it, he tried to reassure his family with pats on the back. Then, as an afterthought, he turned and waved at all the people who had gathered to give him encouragement.

Finally they disappeared from view on the Embassy grounds, and the gate gently swung back in place.

Sandi turned from the television with tears in her eyes. Caleb came up to her, offering his handkerchief.

"Thanks, Caleb," she said. "You're awfully nice."

"Nice? Isn't that a bit tame?" he asked. "I want to be gallant."

She smiled hopelessly at him.

The television anchor began to introduce another story. "Now, in related news, a New Jersey butcher named Hiram Klug was named today as the new President of Purang, a tiny island nation in the Pacific. Congratulations President Klug—"

Sandi leaned against Caleb Perkins' desk and was in the process of digesting that story when a blue seal with an American eagle flashed onto the television screen. It was the Presidential Seal. The news station was cutting to the White House for further breaking news.

She watched with fascination as the image dissolved to that of President Bernard White slumped behind his desk in the Oval Office.

She gripped the hard edge of Caleb's desk. She felt as if the entire world were tipped up on one edge, and ready to fall in either direction.

The President looked up from the white index cards that he held and appeared to want to speak candidly into the camera. But, then, losing nerve, he returned to his speech and began to read.

"My fellow Americans, due to recent events, many of which were beyond my control, it has become readily apparent that those who wish to obstruct me have put up insurmountable roadblocks to my

Presidency. So, as of twelve noon today, I will be stepping down as President of the United States."

He paused, his head still bowed as if he had even more painful news to impart.

He cleared his throat and then looked directly up at the television camera. "And I also wish to take this moment to announce that by mutual consent, Loretta Blythe Crawford and I have agreed to dissolve our engagement."

His own words seemed too hard to bear, and he remained staring at the camera, a painfully blank expression on his face.

Sandi caught a brief snatch of what sounded like Chuck Romer's disappointed voice in the background saying, "Cut. That's all."

She turned to face the Attorney General as the blue Presidential emblem returned to the screen.

Caleb Perkins was standing on the tips of his toes right before the television set, a smile frozen on his face. How could such a moment of triumph feel so awful?

Then the intercom crackled as if a normal business day was in progress. It was Caleb's secretary. "Mr. Perkins," she announced. "William Ford from Party headquarters is on the line."

Caleb shot Sandi a significant look. It was a look of a man with great fortitude, of one who could weather the trials of high office. Then he picked up the phone firmly and decisively.

"Hello, William," he said.

Sandi watched his expression as he listened attentively to his Party's kingmaker. Strangely, his features did not shed any light on the direction of the conversation. He merely listened, then thanked the Party chief, and hung up the phone.

She approached him cautiously. "What is it, Caleb?"

He leveled a look at her. "You're looking at our Party's next Presidential nominee."

She felt her jaw drop. "Caleb! They chose you!"

Smiling broadly, he enclosed her in his arms and planted a huge French kiss that took her by surprise.

But after several seconds, she realized that she was being French kissed by the next nominee for President. What a rush!

Behind her, beyond where Caleb was groping for her posterior, she heard a polite knock at the open door.

Caleb dropped his mitts and stepped away from her with a smile. He already had the calming Presidential smile down pat. He peered around her blonde hair to see who wanted to enter.

"Ah, Harry!" he said.

Sandi remained where she stood. Couldn't the visitor see they were kissing? She smacked her lips to even out her lipstick.

"Sandi, let me introduce Harry Black to you. He runs Piedmont Personnel down in Atlanta. He and his men were the ones who repatriated Raymond and his family."

"Repatriated?" she asked and turned around.

"Well," the stranger, a dark-haired, sparkly-eyed young man, said. "It took a little more than paperwork."

So the young stud was self-deprecating. That wouldn't get him very far in public life. She waited for him to continue, distracted by his virile charm and eyes that seemed to ooze intelligence.

"Er," he went on, "we had to sneak our way into China with a stealth bomber, locate his family, then shoot our way out."

"Oh," she said, tossing back her hair.

"Whatever," Caleb said, glossing over the young man's heroic deeds. "You do have Harry to thank for obtaining the testimony." He crossed to the wet bar to mix a few drinks.

"So that was you at Guantánamo Bay," she said, sizing him up somewhat differently. "I only saw the bald spot on the back of your head."

Harry felt the crown of his head with a troubled expression.

Sandi laughed. "No bald spot. I was just joking."

Harry seemed mildly relieved, but continued to regard her with caution. "So you work for Caleb?" he asked.

"No," she retorted, feeling slightly offended. "I work—rather, worked—as the principle investigator for Stanley Polk, the Special Prosecutor."

"Ah," Harry said, his eyes switching back and forth between her and Caleb as if certain puzzle pieces were fitting together in his mind. "So like me," he said, "you've been busy tracking Raymond down."

"All over the world."

He nodded, looking mildly impressed.

"Drinks, anybody?" Caleb offered. "Champagne?" He held up a pair of glasses fizzing with golden bubbles.

Sandi glanced at Harry, but he gestured for her to go first. The awkward moment passed quickly, and she stepped up to the bar.

"To us," she said, vaguely, and lifted her crystal glass.

Harry was standing opposite her, glass in hand. They clinked together, and an array of bubbles exploded in the air between them.

Was he looking into her eyes? She screwed up her lips and considered the moment. This Harry Black was making eyes at her!

"To the Presidency!" Caleb proposed to the room at large. It seemed like a hollow toast, shared with nobody but himself.

Harry recovered quickly. "Meaning what?"

Caleb explained. "The Party has just chosen me to run in the Presidential election."

Harry raised a thick, dark eyebrow. "Do you think you're really up to the job?" he asked.

To the handsome stranger's credit, he didn't seize the opportunity to suck up to Caleb.

"Well, that's not the point, is it," Caleb said. "Isn't winning the important thing?"

Caleb looked between the two who were stealing his thunder with every gesture, every thought they expressed.

"Well, let's get moving, everybody," he said, swallowing his drink in a single gulp. "I've got a lot of work to do."

"Work?" Sandi said, a thought striking her. "It suddenly hit me. With the Chinagate case slammed shut, I'm out of a job."

An amused, admiring look played in Harry's large brown eyes. "Congratulations!"

She took another swallow, courage welling up within her. "Atlanta, huh?" she said, shocked by her own audacity. "Say, you wouldn't need some expert legal advice down there in Georgia, would you?"

Harry gently took her glass from her fingers and set it on the bar. He tucked her fingers in the crook of his elbow as only a Southern gentleman could do. "Let me tell you about working in Georgia..." he said, leading her out the door.

As they passed the secretary's station, Sandi gave the kind lady a wave.

She returned the wave with a wink as she lay a finger on the intercom button. "Mr. Perkins, telephone call for you. It's Lori Crawford on the line."

ABOUT FRITZ GALT

Fritz Galt is an American novelist who has lived in the diplomatic community for over fifteen years and has experienced many world-changing events abroad. He has lived overseas in Cuba, Switzerland, Yugoslavia, Taiwan, India, and China. He is a world traveler and essayist, and his work has appeared in numerous publications. He is the author of the acclaimed Mick Pierce Spy Thriller novel series as well as other popular international thrillers including *The Trap* and *Water Torture*. He lives with his family in China. For an in-depth look at his work, visit his personal website at *spythrillers.com*.

Don't miss these other fine thrillers published by SIGMA BOOKS:

FRITZ GALT & STEVE DONALDSON

Water Torture

A pair of star-crossed lovers must save the world.

Only one force has the power to bring stability to the world during terrifying times. Meet Brad, a grad student with a crush on a female pilot...in the People's Liberation Army.

"EASILY THE FUNNIEST BOOK THIS YEAR"
Reader Review

∑ SIGMA BOOKS

FRITZ GALT

The Trap

Terrorists infiltrate America...with a nuclear bomb.

A CIA operative has teamed up with terrorists in Afghanistan, and only Army commando GEORGE FERRAR can stop them.

"THE BEST OF FRITZ GALT"
Amazon.com Review

∑ SIGMA BOOKS

**Available wherever books are sold or
to order call 1-866-462-6657 (Toll Free)**

Don't miss these other fine thrillers published by SIGMA BOOKS:

FRITZ GALT

Fatal Sting

Terrorists are back...with biological weapons.

Join all-American spy MICK PIERCE as he chases terrorists around the Indian Ocean in order to save the world, and his daughter's life.

"AUTHENTIC AND FASCINATING"
Barnes & Noble Review

ϟ SIGMA BOOKS

FRITZ GALT

The Geneva Seduction

A terrorist targets the President of the United States.

All-American spy MICK PIERCE combs the world for an elusive assassin who zeros in on his victims by preying on the human heart.

"MYSTERIOUS, INTRIGUING"
Reader Reviews

ϟ SIGMA BOOKS

Available wherever books are sold or
to order call 1-866-462-6657 (Toll Free)

375

Printed in the United States
81574LV00002B/256